LUCKY GIRL

§ A NOVEL §

Denise Gelberg

LUCKY GIRL: *A Novel*

Copy editing by Eileen Bach

Cover design by Nicholas LaVita

Interior design by Charles R. Wilson

Author photo by Charles R. Wilson

ISBN: 979-87-3978-3257

Also by Denise Gelberg

The "Business" of Reforming American Schools

Fertility

Engagement

"One must never forget that life is unfair. But sometimes, with a bit of luck, this works in your favour."

Peter Mayle

STOCKHOLM, 10 DECEMBER 2039

THE ESTEEMED GUESTS on the stage of the Stockholm Concert Hall looked on as the elderly woman rose from her chair. Wearing an elegant blue gown, she walked ramrod straight to the ultimate validation of her life's work, the Nobel Prize for Physiology or Medicine. To the flourish of trumpets, Sweden's Queen Victoria presented the Nobel Medal and Diploma to one of the few women ever to win the prize and only the second to win it outright. The new Nobel Laureate made a small bow to the queen, to the Nobel Assembly on the stage, to her family and the sixteen hundred well-wishers in the audience. She basked in the applause perhaps a moment longer than was warranted, savoring the recognition that was so long in coming. In that instant, Irene Adelson thought of the people she'd loved who had taken their leave before her day of triumph.

She knew that to the casual observer, little remained of the vital woman she'd been when she made the discovery that won her the Nobel. Time had surely exacted its price. But here she was in Stockholm, walking without assistance, thinking as clearly as she had when she did her trailblazing work. The dogged desire to find answers to perplexing questions defined her still, no matter how difficult the hunt or the derision it incurred. That yearning to unravel the mysteries of the natural world continued to govern her very being.

PART ONE

1956 - 1967

CHAPTER ONE

HER BEGINNINGS WERE HUMBLE. The first years of Irene Adelson's life were lived in the shadow of her sister Annie, whose antics and exuberance for life charmed all the adults in their orbit. Irene's features were plain, and her pale, straight hair hung limply around her face. She was shy, as likely as not to bury her head in the folds of her mother's skirt when someone stopped to chat as they walked to the butcher shop, the fruit store, or the A&P. The truth was, outside of the family's small apartment, few adults had heard her speak. Though her parents shared an unspoken understanding that Irene might be a bit slow, they loved her dearly.

Gladys and Meyer Adelson's assessment of their younger daughter was put in question when her kindergarten teacher, Mrs. Zuckerman, took Gladys aside during Open School Day.

"I'm having such a delightful time teaching your little girl. She is such a bright penny."

"Irene? The little girl drawing at the chalkboard? " Gladys asked with more than a hint of skepticism.

Mrs. Zuckerman smiled. "Yes, of course."

"You really think she's bright?" Gladys asked. "How can you tell?"

"I've taught long enough to know an exceptional mind when I see one. Irene thinks deeply and with extraordinary logic, particularly for so young a child."

"But she's so quiet," Gladys pointed out. "She hardly speaks."

"Very true, but when she does, her observations are remarkably astute. And her questions are sometimes breathtaking in their maturity. Just the other day she asked me who would be in charge of the country if President Eisenhower died from another heart attack. Most of my kindergarteners don't even know we have a president, no less that he's already suffered a heart attack, or would need to be succeeded if he passed away. You know what they say about still waters..."

As Gladys walked home hand-in-hand with her little girl, she began looking at Irene with new eyes. The teacher had said she had "an exceptional mind." Her silence may not have been, as Gladys feared, a sign of emptiness, but instead, of serious thought and reflection. "Imagine that!" she laughed to herself. "Wait until Meyer hears this."

§§§

Outwardly, Irene's home was no different from that of most working class families in 1950s Brooklyn. Her father worked two unfulfilling, poorly paid jobs so that she, her sister and mother had a roof over their heads and food to sustain them. On Thursday nights, Meyer would go straight from his job selling menswear in Manhattan to a shoe store near their apartment, where he peddled oxfords, sneakers, and Mary Janes. At closing time, he'd straighten the stock, tidy up the selling floor, and head home for a late dinner and the eleven o'clock news. On Saturdays, he'd awaken at six, have a lightly toasted bagel with lox and a schmeer of cream cheese, a cup of strong, black coffee, and read Friday's edition of The World Telegram and Sun. Then, just as the family started to stir, he'd leave for a day of fitting shoes. On his best day, he earned twelve dollars in commission. Days like that, coupled with his straight pay of a dollar an hour, made it possible for Meyer to put a little aside for a rainy day and an occasional indulgence for the family.

Meyer was nearing fifty, a late bloomer by his own admission. He didn't leave the family home until his mid-thirties and didn't marry for another four years. Three months after the carnage of WWII came to an end, he stood before a rabbi with Gladys Goldstein, the woman who had captured his heart two years before. More than a few of the wedding guests whispered that he was too old to be a first time groom. But Meyer certainly hadn't felt old the day he laid eyes on Gladys. It was August 14, 1943, in the waning days of his military leave. At his father's urging, he'd gone to his cousin's engagement party in Borough Park, Brooklyn, though he was unenthusiastic about wasting one of his few remaining days of leave chit-chatting with a bunch of civilians. As it turned out, it was the party that brought Gladys into his life.

Just as Meyer was grabbing a couple of pigs-in-a-blanket, Gladys caught his eye. He took a liking to her right off. Her petite figure was, to his mind, perfectly proportioned. And she had a smile that lit up the room. When they chatted over their glasses of ginger ale, he found her to be bright and funny. It turned out she, like him, loved movies and books. She'd just finished reading *A Tree Grows in Brooklyn*, and suggested he consider giving it a try. She asked about his work and seemed genuinely interested when he explained how he kept track of parts inventory and maintenance for B-25 bombers. She even laughed at his jokes. By the time his cousin's engagement party was winding down, he was smitten.

After a volley of correspondence and a dozen dates during his subsequent leave, he was certain of one thing: A girl who wrote him long letters twice each week, passed on books she thought he'd enjoy, and made his heart leap out of his chest every time she came into view, well, that was the girl for him. Long ago he'd given up hope on finding a woman to spend his life with, but Gladys Goldstein had reawakened that long-dormant dream. Now that he'd found her, he couldn't lose her. The next time he was home on leave, he had a plan to make sure he didn't.

It was a sunny July morning, his first full day back in Brooklyn, when he took the subway to the Diamond District on 47th Street in Manhattan. For over twenty years he'd worked in the family's stationery store, living upstairs with his parents and siblings. Though his father didn't pay him much, Meyer spent next to nothing, allowing him to squirrel away a tidy sum over the years. Now he would use some of that money to buy a ring for the only girl he'd ever loved. He took his time at the jewelry store, in the end choosing a sparkling round stone set in platinum. Meyer could hear the blood pulsing in his ears as he counted out nineteen one-hundred dollar bills and laid them on the counter. He left the store with a new spring in his step. Riding the subway to Gladys's apartment, his mind replayed the heartfelt and practical proposal he'd rehearsed in front of the bathroom mirror earlier that morning.

When Gladys opened the door in her floral sun dress, she nearly took his breath away. They walked hand in hand to a matinee of *Meet Me in St. Louis*, a movie Meyer's mother had raved about. Afterwards, they enjoyed ice cream cones on a stroll through Prospect Park, agreeing that the child star Margaret O'Brien was a wonderful talent. Meyer put his arm around

Gladys and led her to a bench off the beaten path where they'd enjoyed watching mother ducks and their ducklings many times. It was a perfect summer day. Gladys rested her head on his shoulder, and for a moment the two enjoyed the splendor of the scene before them. Then Meyer pulled the small, blue velvet box from his pocket and opened it. The facets of the diamond glistened in the sun.

Gladys gasped. "Oh, Meyer. Darling, what did you do?"

Meyer panicked when he realized she might turn him down, but he willed himself to remain calm. Mustering his courage, he replied, "I found a stunning ring for the girl that I love. I hope you like it."

"Meyer, how could any woman not like a ring like that? It's gorgeous."

"Please, sweetheart, say 'yes.' I promise you that after this stinkin' war is over, once we're married, you'll never again have to hold down a job. I'm a hard worker. I have savings. I can provide for you, Gladys. Say 'yes,'" he implored.

Gladys didn't hesitate for a moment. "Yes, yes, yes! I will marry you!" she cried. Meyer carefully slipped the ring on her finger, and they kissed. For Meyer, it was the happiest moment of his life.

It wasn't until they were married for more than a year that he realized that Gladys had a delicate constitution. Her stomach was touchy; the wrong food might cause multiple trips to the bathroom. But far more worrisome was the anxiety and nervousness that would, from time to time, consume her. During those spells darkness rained down on her. Those interruptions in their otherwise happy life scared Meyer silly. He had no sense what triggered them and even less of how to make them go away. He tried talking her through her fears. He tried comforting her, supporting her, holding her. Nothing worked. In his despair, he turned to God. Through every heart-wrenching episode, Meyer would go to synagogue and pray for Gladys to conquer the horrible forces that had her in their grip. And every time, after a little while, conquer them she did. Then he'd return to *shul* and give thanks to God for giving him back the woman he loved.

§§§

To an anxious person such as Gladys, Meyer Adelson was the perfect partner. She sensed from the first that he was gentle and kind. As they passed from courtship to marriage, they always discussed issues as they arose. Most often, Meyer put his desires second to hers. He was a good man who tried his best to provide for their family. Years later she would often smile when she remembered his proposal. He told her he had a small fortune — five thousand dollars in the bank — and that she'd never again have to be a straphanger in the subway. What he didn't say was that he'd left school at fourteen, had two peculiar siblings, never worked for anyone but his father and Uncle Sam, and had limited marketable skills. Try as he might, and Gladys gave him credit for being steady and reliable, he brought home very little money each week. She did her best to stretch it by walking from shop to shop to find good quality food, reasonably priced. She prided herself on serving fresh and healthy meals. For household goods and clothes, she shopped fund-raising "bazaars," where over-runs and damaged goods were donated by manufacturers looking for a tax write-off. It was often a motley assortment of merchandise, but when she was lucky, she'd find a bargain to bring home and enhance the family's life.

Gladys got satisfaction from managing the family's limited finances, but what she took the greatest pride in was keeping at bay the dread that had been her constant companion since she was a teenager. At times she could not quash it and it reared its ugly head; only once had it totally overwhelmed her. She was twenty-one then, and for months on end, every waking moment was an eternity. After she regained her footing she spent many hours in quiet reflection, puzzling out the reason for her descent into hell. Finally, she came up with a theory.

Two things had fed the terror that ran roughshod over her: her home life and her job. Living in the family's small apartment and sharing a bedroom with her four sisters was suffocating. And then there was her father, whose endless criticism kept her on edge. Try as she might, she couldn't forgive him for forcing her to drop out of City College. He called a girl's pursuit of a college degree "*meshugga*" — crazy — but then turned around and condemned her for not making anything of herself.

She had to admit he was right on that point. She worked for a penny-pinching boss who didn't even have the decency to supply toilet paper for the john. In exchange for keeping the company's books, he paid her nine dollars a week, far less than the thirty cents an hour federal minimum wage. When she pointed that out to him, he told her she could take the federal minimum wage and stick it up her ass. More than anything, she wanted to walk out and never come back to that dark, dank basement office. But the Great Depression still held the country in its grip. What if she couldn't find another job? What would her father say then? So she kept her head down and her mouth shut, returning day after day to an office where she had to pack toilet paper along with her lunch.

Years later, when Gladys thought about the time her life was commandeered by dread, she was sure that walking away from City College for that wretched job triggered her downward spiral. Instead of pursuing life's possibilities, she was trapped in a dead end. Without hope of deliverance, the dread flourished, soon occupying every corner of her mind. Nothing provided relief, not a trip to the movies or a good book. Her favorite foods held no appeal. Nights were the worst. Sleep eluded her. Her pain was so great she wished she had the courage to put an end to it all. Gladys cried on her way to work, at her desk, and on the way home. It didn't take long before her boss fired her. Her worried mother and mortified father sent her away to a poor man's version of a rest home in the Catskills. After two months of knitting scarves for everyone she knew and weeping as she walked along the quiet, country roads, Gladys began to get some respite from the dread. It was only fleeting at first, but that brief sense of calm gave her hope that there might come a time when the demons would take their leave.

Five years after coming undone and climbing her way back to an ordinary life she met Meyer Adelson. She often marveled at how lucky she was that Sylvia, with whom she wasn't particularly close, had invited her to her engagement party. Gladys had worn her best dress and fixed her hair with extra care. Luckiest of all, she was able to look like a girl who had never experienced the depths of major depression or crippling anxiety. Meyer was well-spoken and nice-looking in his khaki uniform. She could tell he was taken with her and she did her best to endear herself to him by being pleasant and attentive. Her heart sank when he told her he had only two more days of leave, but her hopes revived when he asked if he could take her out the next day.

He picked her up promptly at noon. They went for a walk in Prospect Park, took in a double feature at the Loew's Kings, and then had dinner at Garfield's Cafeteria on Flatbush Avenue. On Monday, when Gladys had to go back to work, Meyer came by her office and took her to lunch. Then he hung around Lower Manhattan until five and accompanied her home on the subway. When he walked her back to her parents' apartment, Gladys invited him in. Her mother asked him to stay for dinner.

At eight o'clock, Meyer thanked Bertha Goldstein and then added, "I have a 5 AM train tomorrow, so I'd better get going. But let me just say that all the way to South Carolina, I'm going to be thinking of that delicious brisket."

Gladys beamed hearing Meyer's flattery of her mother's cooking. By the time she walked him out to the brownstone's front stoop, she willingly accepted his goodnight kiss, and then kissed him back for good measure. Just as he was about to leave, she ran back into the house and brought out her copy of *A Tree Grows in Brooklyn*. "For your train ride tomorrow. I hope you like it as much as I did."

§§§

The US Army changed Meyer. He felt worldly for the first time in his life. Though stationed state-side, the men in his aircraft support unit hailed from all parts of the country. The lone Jew, he bunked with and worked alongside Gentiles of all stripes: Baptists, Methodists, Presbyterians, and Catholics. There were Italian boys and Irishmen. There was even an American Indian from Arizona who was a crackerjack engine mechanic. Meyer got recognized by several company commanders for his fastidious work in aircraft maintenance inventory control, eventually rising to the rank of staff sergeant. His work helped keep the boys in the air and their flying machines in good working order. In his own way, he knew he was helping to fight the Nazi bastards, and that made him proud.

Even before the war ended, Meyer decided he was never going back to work at his father's stationery store. Always a natty dresser, he planned to look for a job in menswear after the war. He wasted no time executing his plan after he was discharged. He put on his best suit, starched shirt and a paisley tie, and polished his shoes until he could see his own reflection. Then he took the subway to Macy's in Herald Square and applied for a sales position in the haberdashery department. With so many former servicemen looking for work, Meyer feared it might take time to land a job, but the manager in haberdashery hired him on the spot. The salary of thirty dollars a week seemed a windfall compared to the seventy-eight dollars a month he'd earned in the service.

It was on the subway ride home that Meyer remembered that in a matter of weeks he'd have the responsibilities of a married man. Thirty dollars would have to stretch for rent and the electric bill — things he'd never had to pay before — never mind food and clothing for two. He hated to renege on his promise to Gladys that she'd never have to work once they got married, but it would make things easier if she could stay at her bookkeeping job near Union Square until they started their family. He knew he would have to broach the subject carefully. The very last thing he wanted was for Gladys to think he wasn't a man of his word.

With a job in hand, Meyer and Gladys were ready to look for an apartment, but in the last months of 1945, vacant apartments in Brooklyn became as scarce as hen's teeth. They were competing with all the other returning servicemen and their wives or fiancées who were also eager to set up housekeeping. Despite looking for weeks, it soon became apparent that there was no apartment to be had in Meyer and Gladys's budget. The realization that they would have to live with his parents and siblings over the stationery store left them both deflated.

It was a long six months of biting their tongues and tiptoeing around Meyer's family. Every day on their subway ride to work, Meyer and Gladys scoured the classified ads for a place of their own. At last they found a two-room apartment above a kosher butcher shop, just a few blocks from the Goldsteins' apartment. Though a barebones affair, it offered the chance to begin building their life together. They dipped into their savings to buy the necessities: a double bed, an armchair, and a small kitchen table with two chairs. Gladys hand-sewed yellow curtains, which made the tiny flat look almost cheery. Their only indulgence was a Victrola that would play records from Meyer's collection. For their first dinner in their new home, Gladys prepared a roasted chicken, baked potatoes, and chocolate pudding for dessert. As they sat down to eat, the music from *Oklahoma* played in the background. "Our first meal in our little castle. It may not be fancy, but it's ours," Meyer said with pride. Then, reaching over to kiss Gladys, he added "And my queen is beyond compare."

Lucky for Meyer, Gladys decided she wanted to keep working at the job she'd landed after returning from her sojourn in the country. It paid three times what her previous job had and her boss treated her well. She liked the idea of being able to put away some money for herself and Meyer, and the family she hoped they would one day have. They were careful whenever they made love, checking to be sure the condom wasn't damaged and that Meyer had put it on securely. It turned out that vigilance was warranted. On their second anniversary, they had sex without using protection for the first time. That was the night Annie was conceived. And, three years later, when they tried for a sibling for their little girl, again Gladys got pregnant straightaway.

By the time Irene joined the family, the Adelsons were living in a small two-bedroom apartment, walking distance from Prospect Park. Gladys was a full-time homemaker and Meyer, now an assistant manager of haberdashery at Macy's Herald Square, was doing his level best to provide for his wife and children.

§§§

As a tot, Annie Adelson had been something of a handful, racing here and there, chattering nonstop, approaching strangers and striking up conversations anywhere and everywhere, including the restroom at the local Sears. It thrilled Gladys to know she had produced a fearless child who charmed people with the endearing things she said and did. Annie was blessed with Meyer's thick, curly hair and light eyes, so she was as pretty as she was spirited. If it had been up to Gladys, Annie would have been an only child. She feared they could not be so lucky twice, that the next child might be compromised in some way. Gladys also worried that she might not be able to handle another bundle of energy. This time Meyer was able to calm her fears. He listened carefully to her concerns, held her in his arms, and said, "The next one will be fine. You'll be fine. Let's give Annie a baby brother or sister."

Throughout her second pregnancy, Gladys sat with the other mothers in folding chairs in front of the apartment building as their little ones played on the sidewalk. The other women were emphatic that Gladys needn't worry that she'd have another Annie; her second baby would undoubtedly be nothing like her first. When Gladys thought about herself and her sisters, she saw they had a point. All five of the Goldstein girls were different. And Meyer was certainly nothing like his siblings, who remained unmarried, never having ventured from the nest. As her due date approached, Gladys felt ready – even a little excited — to be surprised by her new baby.

When their second daughter arrived, Gladys agreed to name her Irene, after Meyer's favorite aunt, Ida. Gladys was amazed at how tranquil her new baby was. Irene suckled well and slept through the night when she was all of three weeks old. She napped much of the day, as well. Gladys would tell the other mothers, "I hardly know I have a baby in the house." As challenging as Annie was, Irene was calm and agreeable. Gladys was glad Meyer had persuaded her not to give into her fears. Thanks to him, they'd brought this sweet, peaceful baby into the world.

§§§

Irene's quiet and unremarkable first five years of life were followed by indications that perhaps she was not as slow as her parents imagined. First, there was the comment from her kindergarten teacher. Then, a few months later, when the family visited Gladys's aunt and uncle in Canarsie, Irene sat down on the bench of their spinet piano, legs dangling above the floor, and played "The Itsy Bitsy Spider" with both hands. She was a bit abashed when her relatives applauded. When they asked if she would play another tune, she complied with a rendition of "Row, Row, Row Your Boat."

Meyer was stunned. "How do you know how to play those songs, *mein kleyne kind[1]*?"

In a small voice, Irene replied, "I just do."

"Can you play us another song, Reenie?" he asked.

Irene nodded, and then proceeded to play the Eddie Fisher hit, "Oh, My Pa-pa," something she'd heard many times on the family's Victrola. As her short fingers flew across the keyboard, the mouths of her relatives fell open, but no one was as surprised as Annie. When her little sister was done playing the final chords, Annie ran up to the piano and said, "Play it again, Reenie. This time I'll sing with you." Then Annie positioned herself next to the keyboard and sang with a clear soprano as her sister played the song again.

The applause began before they were even done. Annie relished the recognition, taking several bows, but Irene slid off the piano bench and hid her face in her mother's lap.

Towards the end of her kindergarten year, Irene surprised her family in yet another way. They were having dinner at the kitchen table. As usual, Meyer and Gladys were speaking to one another in Yiddish so the girls wouldn't understand the topic under discussion. This night Meyer was airing his complaints about a fellow assistant manager at Macy's. Jake made his life a misery, leaving the merchandise *ongepotchket[2]* every day,

---

[1] My little child
[2] Slapped together without rhyme or reason

and sometimes showing his true nature as *ein gonif*[1] by lifting merchandise when he thought no one was the wiser. In despair, Meyer concluded, "*A volf farlirt zayne hor, ober nit zayn natur*," something akin to the English saying about a leopard and its spots.

"Daddy," Irene asked, "will Jake have to go to jail?

Meyer was perplexed. "Why do you ask, Reenie?"

"Well, since Jake can't change the way he acts, I think they're gonna catch him stealing stuff. Don't robbers go to jail?"

"What are you talking about, Reenie?" Annie asked impatiently. "How do you know Jake steals stuff?"

"Because Daddy just said that he leaves all the shirts and ties mixed up and the suits in the wrong part of the rack. The worst part is he steals stuff when he thinks nobody is looking. And," she said with great expression, "Daddy doesn't think he will get better at it, either. I think he's going to get caught. Maybe they'll even send him to jail."

An astonished Meyer and Gladys looked at one another, and then at their little girl. They tried to respond as naturally as they could.

"Daddy didn't mean anything bad about Jake, honey," Gladys said. "He's just tired after a long day at work. Jake's not going to jail."

"That's good," Irene said. "It would be bad if he had to go to jail. But it would be good if he helped Daddy make things look nice in the store. And stealing, well, even I know that's a bad thing to do, and I'm just five and a half."

That was the last time Gladys and Meyer made the mistake of assuming their conversations in Yiddish were for adult ears only.

---

[1] A thief

CHAPTER TWO

B Y THE TIME IRENE WAS IN SECOND GRADE she'd figured out that the Goldsteins didn't think much of her family. She wasn't exactly sure why. Maybe it was because, unlike all of her cousins, she and Annie lived in a small apartment rather than a house, and they didn't own a car. On the other hand, Uncle Harvey and Aunt Phyllis's family was treated with great respect. Uncle Harvey's job of selling shampoo, hair dye, and permanents to beauty parlors allowed them to own a Cadillac and live in a big house on Long Island. They even had a Negro maid, who lived with her little boy in their basement. Irene didn't care for Uncle Harvey, though. He reminded her of a grown-up version of Alan Berkowitz, the bully in her class. Both of them were bossy and loud and acted as though they knew more than everybody else.

Despite the family's assessment, she liked her family just fine. Her mother always made sure everyone had what they needed. She bought delicious day-old bread and cakes from the corner bakery, cleaned their house until it shone, and washed, starched, and ironed the family's clothes. She even sewed dresses for Annie and Irene by hand. Irene sensed her parents worried about money. She figured that was why, every now and again, her dad would sit her and Annie down for a serious conversation.

"Annie, Reenie, I want you to know you don't have to be a boy to grow up to be a professional. You're both so intelligent, you can choose whatever profession you like – teacher, nurse, librarian, accountant. Both of you will go to college when you get older. Brooklyn College is a fine school, and it's close by. I can guarantee you that if you play your cards right, after you graduate you'll get a good job, make decent money, and have a pension to live on in your old age. That might not seem so important to you now; you're just kids. But listen to your papa. I know what I'm talking about."

"But, Daddy, I'm going to be a dancer," Annie protested.

"Nine to five, you'll be a professional. On nights, holidays, and weekends, you can kick your legs to your heart's content."

§§§

Irene adored her big sister, who was as charming and smart as she was pretty. Everyone liked her. When the phone rang in the living room, it was almost always someone calling to speak to Annie. She was not only popular; she also could dance as well as the teenagers on American Bandstand, which the Adelson girls watched faithfully after school. One of the things that fascinated Irene was how Annie could see a famous dancer do a routine on the Ed Sullivan Show and then mimic it in the living room. Of course, sometimes the downstairs neighbors protested by banging a broomstick on their ceiling. That generally put the kibosh on Annie's dancing for the night, but when they were lucky, Annie could do the whole routine without missing a beat.

As they got older, Irene was awed by something else her sister did. Wanting dance lessons and knowing there was no extra money in the family budget, Annie went on a mission to earn money. Too young to get working papers, her options were few, so she started babysitting for younger kids in the neighborhood. She saved every cent she earned so she could enroll at the neighborhood Arthur Murray Dance studio. The instructors always let her hang around after her class so she could watch the advanced dancers practice. Every time Annie would come home from the dance studio, she'd show off her new steps. Irene would make an effort to copy them, but no matter how hard she tried, she could not make her body move the way Annie's did. "Don't worry, Reenie," Annie would tell her. "I can't play anything but 'Heart and Soul' and 'Chopsticks' on the piano. We're all good at different things."

Irene figured her sister was probably right. She knew she excelled at school. When she was seven, her second grade teacher called home to tell Gladys that Irene would be skipping third grade. Fourth grade was still too simple for her, so her teacher, Mrs. Hudson, handed Irene a steady stream of interesting books to read. As soon as she'd finish one, Mrs. Hudson was ready with another. By December, Irene had devoured more than thirty books, her favorite being *Little Women*, with *The Secret Garden* and a biography of Marie Curie rounding out her top three. Every book she read transported her to another place and time. Her thirst for books soon became insatiable, leading her parents to remind her to, "Read by the lamp, Reenie. You'll ruin your eyes." Perhaps they were right. Halfway through fourth grade, she failed the vision test at school and had to be fitted for glasses. She chose blue cat's eyes frames, which she thought quite attractive. Her glasses brought the world into focus in a way she hadn't known was possible.

Other children routinely passed over Irene when choosing a friend, but adults tended to enjoy her, particularly when she spoke in Yiddish. Irene resorted to the *momma loshen*[1] when no English phrase could capture her meaning, like the time she opened a bag of hand-me-downs from Aunt Alice and pulled out a worn-out dress from her cousin. "Mommy, I need this like a *loch in kop!*[2]" Then she smacked her forehead, leading Gladys to laugh until she cried. Another time, when three-year old Susie from the next apartment pestered her to read the same story she'd already read her a dozen times, Irene said, "Susie, *hocht mir nit a tschainik*," the Yiddish equivalent of, "bug off." Susie's mother had to run next door and tell Gladys.

Like Annie, Irene loved music, but it was the piano rather than dance that called to her. Thanks to an arrangement Gladys negotiated with Mrs. Zuckerman, from the time Irene was five years old she was allowed to stay after school and play the kindergarten's piano under Gladys's watchful eye. That ancient upright grand allowed Irene to develop a vast repertoire of classical and pop standards over her elementary school career. A casual listener would never have guessed she read no music and had no formal training. Each day when she was done playing, the school custodian would call out, "Thanks for the concert, girlie. Someday you're going to give Liberace a run for his money. Mark my words!"

At one of the Goldstein family dinners, Gladys proudly announced that, despite being a year younger than her classmates, Irene was at the top of the fourth grade class at her school. Gladys's sister Iris, whose own children were notable for their repeated trips to the principal's office, asked

---

[1] Mother tongue
[2] A hole in the head

pointedly, "How the heck did you and Meyer get such smart girls? Who do they take after?"

Gladys held her sister's gaze for more than a moment and then replied with some satisfaction, "The girls take after Meyer and me, of course. Who else would they take after?" If Irene's chair hadn't been jammed between those of her cousins, she would have run over and covered her mother in kisses.

§§§

Irene's cousins had backyard swing sets, pet cats and dogs, and trees to view from their bedroom windows. Irene and Annie's bedroom window opened onto a brick airshaft. But despite their modest apartment, Irene felt cozy and safe in the family home. Everything from opera to show tunes played continually from the radio or the Victrola. The whole family watched news shows on the small black and white television in the living room. Over dinner each night they talked about what was going on in the world. Every week they paid a visit to the public library to borrow books. At least one Sunday a month, the family took the subway to museums in Manhattan. Irene appreciated all the things her parents did to make each day interesting. But of all the things they provided her, what Irene cherished most was the summer respite from Brooklyn.

For as long as she could remember, a "Woodie," a wood-sided station wagon, would pull up in front of their apartment house the Saturday after school ended in June. It would carry the family, their pots and pans, sheets and towels, clothes and a toy or two to a cabin in the Catskills. It was in that bungalow colony that Irene got to run free in the grass, swing on the swing set for as long as she wanted, and splash in the pool until her lips turned blue and her body shook from the cold. She loved every part of their summer in the country with the exception of missing her father. Meyer could only join Gladys and the girls on weekends. Once in a while, he would stay until early Monday morning, taking a bus back to the city in time for work, but most times he'd catch a ride on Sunday afternoon with another father from the bungalow colony. The moment the car would drive off, Irene would imagine her dad returning to their hot apartment, fighting off the mosquitos that came in through the open windows, and eating the only thing he could cook, boiled eggs and toast. Thinking of her father alone and miserable was her introduction to the feeling known as guilt.

The family's usual summer plans were upended during the spring of Irene's fifth grade year. Annie was offered a full-time summer job as a mother's helper for the neighborhood rabbi, whose wife had just given birth to their ninth child. At nearly thirteen, the fresh air and green grass of the Catskills did not impress Annie as much as the dance classes her earnings would buy. She wanted to stay in the city and she had an ally in Meyer.

Meyer put his best spin on the idea of staying in Brooklyn for the summer. "With the money we'll save, we can join Farragut Pool. It's only twenty minutes away by bus. Mommy and Reenie can go every day. Annie and I can go on the weekends. They have lounge chairs and cabanas to change in. There are places to barbecue hamburgers and hotdogs. They even have swim lessons. What do you say, girls?"

"It sounds okay," Annie said, "I'll probably be busy with my friends on the weekends, but it'll be nice for Reenie and Mom."

"Reenie, what do you think?" Meyer asked.

Irene knew the bungalow colony looked a bit sadder and shabbier each summer. She also knew her dad was weary of his long rides to and from the country every weekend. Still, she hungered for the place she'd spent every summer of her life. She nearly cried when she imagined another little girl living in the bungalow she'd thought of as her own. But thinking of all the lonely summers her father had endured helped her keep her tears in check.

"On the one hand," Irene said, "I really like going to the country, but on the other hand, it's about time I learn to swim properly. Doggy paddle is the only stroke I know, and I don't think that is even considered an actual stroke, so swim lessons would be fun as well as educational."

Gladys knew Irene was trying to please Meyer, just as she had the night before when he broached the subject of staying in the city. Like Irene, Gladys loved their summers in the country. The shade of the trees, the fresh cut grass underfoot, the water trickling over rocks at the brook behind their cabin, all soothed and fortified her soul. She was at peace in that rundown cabin, where she cooked on a two burner stove and the whole family slept in the same room. It was a simple, barebones life, but it was also a serene life. She never had to worry about the girls getting hit by a car while retrieving a wayward ball from the city streets. Gladys knew how lonely Meyer had been every summer. For more than ten years he'd acted selflessly for her and their children. It was her turn to sacrifice for him, so she'd agreed to his suggestion that this year they stay in Brooklyn.

Now, as they sat around the kitchen table, Annie and Irene looked to their mother for her judgment on the family's summer plans. "We'll have fun at the pool, Reenie. We can go every afternoon after I help Grandma out."

Irene knew Grandma Bertha needed a lot of help from her mom these days. It probably had something to do with Grandpa Herman staying in bed all the time. Her mother cleaned her grandparents' apartment, went to the laundromat, and ran errands for them. When Irene had a day off from school, she would bring a book and come along. One day, as she and Gladys walked back home, Irene asked why none of her aunts were helping out.

"Well, Reenie, that's because it's easiest for me. Phyllis, Alice and Iris live on Long Island. Doris just moved to New Jersey. They're all so far away now; it's too much for them to come every day. They do come on the weekends, though. You know that, don't you?"

"Don't they take turns coming? Last week was Aunt Doris's turn," Irene said. "No one else came to help."

"They do take turns. But you know I really like helping Grandma. I thought you liked helping her, too."

"I don't know if I help very much," Irene said. "Mostly we just talk and then I read my book."

"Well, talking with Grandma is good. It takes her mind off her troubles. So we're lucky, Reenie. Because we live so close by, we can make things easier for Grandma. Think of it as a gift we can give her that the rest of the family can't."

Irene was quiet for a moment. "I never thought of it that way."

"Just remember, *mein shaina maidela*[1], whenever you can be kind to someone else, don't think of it as a burden. Think of it as an opportunity."

§§§

The day after school was out, Irene and Gladys went to the library to borrow a stack of books while Annie went around the corner to start her summer job of being a mother's helper. Some mornings, Irene would accompany Gladys to her grandparents' house. She adored Grandma Bertha, who showered her with love and delicious homemade pastries. Her

---

[1] My beautiful little girl

feelings for her grandfather, though, were complicated. Irene could not remember a single time Grandpa Herman had ever given her a hug or mussed up her hair. It wasn't just her; he acted the same way to Annie and all of her cousins, too. The way he spoke to Grandma Bertha also troubled her. He expected her to wait on him, bringing him his newspaper or a drink, never once saying "please" or "thank you." Now that he was sick, she could hear him moaning from his bedroom. Sometimes he'd yell at Grandma if he didn't like the food she'd made for him. Every time he berated Grandma, Irene wanted to run and protect her.

On summer mornings when Irene didn't tag along to her grandparents' house, she would get things ready for the afternoon trip to the pool. She'd prepare tuna salad just the way her mom had taught her and then make sandwiches for their picnic lunch. She'd put on her swimsuit under her clothes, pack a bag with two towels, a pair of panties, the book she was reading, and the family's small transistor radio. By the time her mom got back at noon each day, Irene was ready to get to the pool. Though it wasn't the country, it offered delicious relief from their hot apartment. And, just as her father promised, every day at two o'clock Irene got to learn the basics of treading water, the breaststroke, and the crawl.

On the last Friday in July, Irene was impatient for her mom to return from her grandparents' house. The air was heavy and the sweat ran down her back. The night before, the mosquitoes had been especially bad. Since she and Annie couldn't bear to pull the covers over their heads in the heat, they both awoke covered in bites. The pool's cool water promised blessed relief.

§§§

As Gladys approached her parents' apartment on that hot, muggy day she had a bad feeling. Her father was growing progressively weaker; it seemed as though the life force that had sustained him for sixty-seven years was draining away before her eyes. The illness, which no one in the family would speak of, had transformed the tall, muscular family patriarch into an emaciated, frail old man. Caring for him was exhausting for her mother. Still, Bertha clung to habits that had served the Goldstein family well. Though it had been weeks since Herman could keep down anything but clear broth, she still prepared three complete meals a day. It was just the previous week that Gladys had finally convinced her that Herman needn't get fully dressed each morning. He could wear his pajamas as he lay in bed all day, saving her mother the chore of dressing and undressing the man who towered over her. Gladys savored her small victory.

Her father had never been an easy man to live with. He didn't believe in giving anyone a compliment for a job well done; neither did he take kindly to another person's point of view, unless it confirmed his own. But he'd worked hard all his life and never expected much in return, least of all, happiness. He was the sole survivor of his family of origin, having lost all of his siblings and their families in the Holocaust. Though he never spoke of them, Gladys knew their deaths affected him deeply. She wondered if that pain was the reason he'd never shown her any physical affection. She respected her father and she loved him, though he never gave her an opening to share her feelings with him on anything of importance. As debilitated as he was, his word remained law.

When she got inside her parents' apartment, Gladys gave her mother a hug. "Sorry, I'm so perspired, Mama. It's only nine in the morning and it's already a scorcher." As Gladys looked more closely at her mother, it was clear she'd been crying. Gladys feared the worst. "What's the matter, Mama? Is it Papa?"

"He wants to talk to you."

"But he's okay?

"The same."

"That's a relief. For a moment...I was afraid something had happened. Of course I'll talk to him, but didn't you want me to go first thing to the butcher and get you some baby lamb chops? I'd better get over there, before they're all gone."

Her mother shook her head. "You know your father. He wants to talk to you now."

Gladys studied her mother's face. Her look of defeat was co-mingled with exhaustion. "You're sure it can't wait until I get back?"

Her mother just turned her head in the direction of the bedroom she'd shared with her husband of forty-five years.

"Okay, Mama. I'll talk to Papa now, and then go to the butcher, unless you're willing to wait until next week for the lamb chops."

"Lamb chops. Chopped meat. What difference does it make?"

Gladys was mystified. Yesterday, her mother was emphatic about her getting those lamb chops first thing. Walking down the narrow hallway to her parents' room, Gladys figured the heat and fatigue had led to her mother's change of heart. She wondered what her father wanted to discuss. The last days he'd been so quiet, as though he were retreating from the world.

His eyes were closed when she came into the bedroom. He slept a good deal of the day now. She was turning to leave when she heard the raspy voice he'd developed.

"Come here, Gladys."

"I'm right here, Papa. How are you feeling? Mama said you wanted to talk to me."

"Sit."

Gladys pulled a chair over to her father's bedside. She almost reached over to take his hand in hers, but then thought better of it.

"I'm an *alta cocker*[1]."

"Sixty-seven isn't so old, Papa."

"I've lived long enough. I've seen things...terrible things." He closed his eyes and muttered something to himself in Yiddish. "This world is not for the weak. Only the *shtarkers*[2] survive. My mother, may she rest in peace, she was a *guteh neshomeh*[3]. So gentle...."

"I'm sorry I never got to meet her, Papa. She must have been a wonderful person." Gladys was moved when she saw her father tear up, something she'd never before witnessed. Now she reached for his hand. Despite the unbearable heat, it was ice cold.

"My mother was pure gold. But pure gold is weak. It's easy to bend, easy to break. That was my mother. If someone said a harsh word, her eyes would fill up. Thank God she died before her children and grandchildren were murdered. She would have gone *meshugga*[4]."

"I've thought of that, too; what a blessing it was that she and your father passed away before the nightmare of the Holocaust began," Gladys said. "I can think of nothing worse than seeing your children suffer."

Suddenly Herman became agitated. He started to cough as he struggled to sit up in bed, his face getting redder with each spasm. When

---

[1] Old man
[2] The strong
[3] Good soul
[4] Crazy

the hacking finally abated, he looked at Gladys with a strange expression, and then started bellowing. "This world is no place for the weak! You know why my brothers died before their hair turned grey but I lived to be an *alta cocka*? Because I got my ass out of Europe, that's why. I knew the *goyim*[1] hated us. I didn't have a chance in hell of a decent life there, so I got out. Whatever it took to get here, I did it." Then his face contorted into a look of disgust. "But you, Gladys, I can't believe you're my own flesh and blood. What a disappointment, and my first born, too. Your sisters…they know how to live in this *fahcokta*[2] world, but you," he spat out, "you're like my mother — and *your* mother. You have no backbone. You're weak. All of you, weak."

Gladys pulled her hand from his. "What a terrible thing to say, Papa."

"Everyone knows you had to be sent away. Such a *shanda*[3] you brought on the family!" he screamed, gaining strength from his tirade. "Your sisters, they're *shtarkers,* but you…you…you're a nothing, a *shvakh mensch*[4]."

Then Herman fell back into his pillow, gasping for air. Sitting there next to him, Gladys felt such a stabbing pain in her torso, she thought she might be having a heart attack. Grabbing her chest, she whispered, "Papa, I'm sorry to be such a disappointment." Then she got up from the chair and saw her mother standing in the hallway, tears coursing down her cheeks. She'd heard it all.

"Mama, doesn't he know I can't be like the others?" Gladys cried.

Bertha went to her eldest child, embraced her, and brought her into the hallway. "No, Gladys, your father doesn't understand why you're not like your sisters; he isn't *able* to understand. But I see you. I see all your beautiful qualities. I know who you are and I love you."

Every beat of her pounding heart reverberated throughout Gladys's body. Then suddenly she broke free from her mother and ran to the toilet, just in time to empty her bowels in a fit of diarrhea.

---

[1] The Gentiles
[2] Fucked up
[3] An embarrassment, scandal
[4] Pathetic person

CHAPTER THREE

IRENE OFTEN THOUGHT OF HER CHILDHOOD as divided into two separate and distinct periods. The first ended that July day when her mother went missing.

For many years thereafter, Irene looked on that day as the worst of her life. The heat was stifling. She was being driven mad by the mosquito bites that covered her body. When her mother didn't return at noon as usual, she waited thirty minutes before calling her grandmother. That's when she learned her mother had left her grandparents' apartment hours before, news that left Irene perplexed and worried. Her mother would have called her to say she was going to be late, that is unless something bad had happened. Irene's mind began to manufacture one dire scenario after another: her mother being hit by a car while crossing the street, or perhaps robbed and beaten, or kidnapped for ransom, as she had read about in more than a few of her books. As the hours passed and still, her mother didn't return, her thoughts ran to the cabin where she'd been so happy. She imagined sitting in the big oak tree, singing softly to herself with her mother below, reading in the old wooden chair. Oh, if only they'd gone to the country this year...

At three-thirty Irene was brought back to reality by the phone. It was her grandmother. "Hi, sweetheart. Can I talk to your mother?"

"She's still not home, Grandma."

"Still not home? *Gut in himmel[1]!* Come and stay with Grandma," Bertha implored. "I don't know where your mommy is and I don't like that you're all by yourself."

"But why is Mommy late? I am really, really worried. She's never, ever done this before."

"Mommy was upset when she left. Something Grandpa said made her sad. It's an unhappy time for all of us, Reenie. I'm so sorry."

"Me, too, Grandma."

"Come to Grandma's house. Please, Reenie."

"But if she comes home and I'm not here, she'll be wondering what happened. I'd better stay."

"Just promise me you'll have Mom call me as soon as she's back."

"I promise," Irene said.

At five, Annie came home from her day with the rabbi's children to find her little sister in a wretched state. An hour later, their dad walked through the door, bushed from his steamy ride in the crowded subway. He found his daughters on the couch, their hands entwined.

"There are my beautiful girls. My God, you two are a sight for sore eyes! A good day today?"

"It was okay for me," Annie said. "Rabbi Cohen attached the hose so we could spray ourselves to cool off, but Reenie's day didn't go so well." Then she turned to her sister. "Reenie, tell Daddy."

"Tell me what?" Meyer asked, the hairs on the back of his neck standing erect. He took a quick look around. "Where's Mommy?"

"That's the problem, Daddy," Irene cried. "I don't know where Mommy is."

The blood drained from Meyer's face. "All right sweetheart," Meyer said as calmly as he could. "Tell me exactly what happened."

The entire afternoon, Irene had held herself together, but now that her father was there, she crumbled. Meyer caressed and coaxed his little girl in an effort to soothe her. "*Mein shaina maidela[2]*, I can't help unless you tell me what happened."

---

[1] God in heaven!
[2] My beautiful little girl

Finally, between sobs, Irene told her story. "Mommy went to help Grandma. I got everything ready for the pool like I always do. But Mommy didn't come home at twelve o'clock. I waited for a while and then I called Grandma. She said Mommy wasn't at her house, either. I've been waiting and waiting and waiting all by myself the whole day. It's so hot, and I have so many mosquito bites," she wailed. "I'm so miserable, Daddy!"

The news filled Meyer with dread, but for the sake of the girls, he did his best to appear composed. "Of course you're miserable, Reenie. I would be too, if I'd had a day like yours."

"I wanted to go to Rabbi Cohen's house to find Annie, but Mommy has been very clear that I'm not to leave when I'm home alone. I've been asking myself since 12:30 where she might be."

"Reenie, I'm not sure where Mommy is, but I have an idea. Get your sneakers on, girls. We're going to look for your mom."

Meyer pulled off his tie, threw down his suitcoat and rolled up his long, moist sleeves. Not since Annie was a baby had Gladys gone off by herself. Years before, when she sought solitude, she'd go to the same bench in Prospect Park where they'd become engaged. It was a quiet spot, with little foot traffic. He prayed that she remained true to form.

Meyer and the girls left the apartment hand-in-hand. The air outside was as humid as the tropics, but the three of them ran to the park. When they came within thirty yards of the place Gladys had sought out in the past, they stopped short. There was a woman slumped over on a bench. Meyer let go of Irene and Annie's hands and dashed ahead. As he approached, he could see the woman resembled Gladys; her hair and clothes were right, but everything else was so wrong.

He slowed down as he approached, afraid of scaring her. Looking carefully, he knew it had to be Gladys, though her face and arms were beet red and her posture slack. He gently called her name. "Gladys, sweetie, it's me. I'm here to take you home."

She didn't look up. Reaching for Gladys's hand was all it took for her to topple from the bench to the ground. He knelt down, put his face close to hers, and felt her hot breath and skin. Her eyes were closed and, though he called her name and gently stroked her head, she remained unresponsive. Meyer could see she'd soiled herself, but that humiliation paled next to his terror at the state she was in.

The girls advanced with rising trepidation.

Annie's voice quivered as she asked, "What happened to Mommy?"

"Mommy's very sick. Run to the drugstore on the corner as fast as you can and tell them to call an ambulance. Hurry!"

§§§

When Gladys arrived in the emergency room at Kings County Hospital, her temperature was 105.3 degrees and the burns that covered her face, scalp, arms and legs were beginning to blister. The doctors diagnosed heatstroke, with her altered mental state being a symptom of the syndrome. They explained to Meyer that there was a risk the heatstroke could result in organ damage or even organ failure. There was no way they could give him a prognosis. Only time would tell.

Meyer gave the girls change and sent them to the cafeteria to get dinner. Then he went to a payphone and called Bertha. "Mom, I hate to add to your *tsoures*[1], but Gladys is in the hospital. She has heatstroke. I can't even describe the burns that cover her body. It looks as though she was sitting all day in the sun. I'm wracking my brain to figure out why in the world she did that instead of coming home and taking Reenie to the pool. Did she seem okay when she was with you?"

Bertha stifled a sob. "No, Meyer. She was upset, very upset. We both were."

"Why? What happened?"

"If I tell you, you'll blame me."

"Blame you for what?" Meyer asked.

"For not stopping him. I should have stopped him," Bertha cried.

"Stopped who? I'm confused, Bertha. Please. Just tell me what happened."

"It was Herman. First he mopped the floor with me. Then he started in on Gladys. I never should have let her near him this morning," she cried. "I'll regret that until the day I die."

Meyer tried to take in what Bertha was saying. Though Herman had prided himself on being a real "man's man," the cancer had reduced his father-in-law to a shell of the intimidating force of nature he'd once been.

---

[1] Troubles

"Mom, what in the world could Herman have done to Gladys? A newborn baby has more strength than he has these days."

"But unfortunately his mouth still works. This morning he started in on her. He called her weak, said she was like me and his mother; all of us weak. Then right to her face he said she was 'a disappointment.' I don't know where he got the strength, but then he began screaming that she was an embarrassment to the family, that she should have been more like her sisters. But the worst of all was how he said it, Meyer," she cried into the phone. "His own daughter! He's disgusted by her."

Meyer covered his eyes with his hand. The outcome of that tongue-lashing was almost more than he could bear.

"Are you still there, Meyer?"

"Yes, I'm here. Bertha. I am trying to figure out what kind of man says such things to his own child."

"*Ver veyst*[1]? He tore into me, too. I guess it wasn't enough that I bore him five children, raised them, took care of the house, took care of him for forty-five years. He thinks I'm weak, and to him, that's a crime. I ask you, could a weak woman live from such a man?"

"To be so cruel to you and to Gladys? He's her father, for God's sake."

"Let me tell you something, Meyer. Of all my girls, Gladys is the one who would give you the shirt off her back. Look what she's done for us since Herman got sick. She cleans, she shops, she washes and irons."

"She won't be able to help you now, Mom. She's very sick. The doctors mentioned something about the heat stroke causing organ damage. I didn't get everything they said, but I can tell they're worried." Meyer heard his mother-in-law whimpering. "I'm sorry, Mom" he said, "I know Herman's on death's door. I probably should be more charitable, but the truth is, he can go to hell."

"Meyer, you're a good man, a good husband to my beautiful daughter. Maybe one day you'll find it in your heart to forgive Herman. But I'll tell you one thing, I never will."

---

[1] Who knows?

§§§

Four days after Herman rebuked his wife and eldest daughter, the patriarch of the Goldstein family, took his last breath. The following day Bertha, four of her daughters and their families stood at the cemetery as the plain pine box containing his body was lowered into the ground. For the next seven days, the Goldstein women sat *shiva*[1] at Bertha's apartment, visiting with people who came to support them during their period of mourning. Notably absent from the events surrounding Herman's death, however, was his eldest, Gladys, and her family.

§§§

Early on in her hospitalization, the doctors succeeded in bringing Gladys's body temperature and electrolytes back into the normal range. They remained concerned, however, about her kidney function and her mental state. Though she could speak, she lay stock-still, staring into space from her bed. Even when Annie and Irene were given special permission to come up to her hospital room, she remained unresponsive. After the seven days of *shiva*, Bertha and her youngest daughter, Doris could not mask their shock at seeing Gladys so lifeless, so remote, so lost. It was very different from the time she'd been wracked with anxiety many years before; now she lay silent and withdrawn. Bertha was inconsolable.

That night, when she returned to an apartment filled with the remnants of seven days of company and condolences, Bertha wept as she thought of the damage Herman had wrought. His invective played over and over in her head. He might as well have taken a baseball bat to Gladys and beaten her from head to toe. She hated him for never appreciating their daughter, never seeing how hard she worked every day to keep herself on an even keel. From Gladys's earliest years, Bertha had always understood when her little girl would reason aloud with herself, trying to beat back her fears — be they of jumping rope or walking to the store to buy a loaf of bread. Though Bertha loved all of her girls, she was proudest of Gladys, who had to muster her courage to do what the others did so effortlessly. Why hadn't she protected her darling girl? If only she had stopped Herman, Gladys would not now be lying in a hospital bed.

---

[1] Week of mourning following a death

§§§

After thirteen days at Kings County, the doctors were guardedly optimistic about Gladys's recovery. Her kidneys were putting out more urine each day; her burns were healing. There appeared to be no lasting damage to her muscles. Her heartbeat was strong and regular. At this point, it was her mental state that concerned them most. Though she was able to answer simple questions, she remained quiet and distant. When Meyer explained that his wife had always been somewhat "delicate" emotionally, they suggested she be transferred to Brooklyn State Hospital, an asylum opened in the nineteenth century for lunatics and those suffering with nervous conditions. It was a terrible blow to Meyer. Picturing Gladys in an asylum dredged up images from *The Snake Pit*, a movie they'd seen when they were expecting Annie. It haunted them both for days, particularly the scene where the mental patient played by Olivia DeHavilland was put into a straitjacket. His jaw clenched remembering the horror of it. But what choice did he have? Gladys couldn't come home in the state she was in. The Brooklyn hospital was closer to home than Creedmoor State in Queens, the only alternative offered by the doctors. The bus that stopped near their apartment could get him to Brooklyn State in fifteen minutes. At least that was something.

§§§

The thing that kept Meyer from collapsing under the strain of Gladys's illness was the realization that his children were depending on him. Between work, household chores, and hospital visits, there weren't enough hours in the day. As he straightened the stock and rang up customers at work, he thought about his daughters, particularly Irene, alone in the airless apartment all day. His fear that Gladys would never come back to him and the girls made him lose sleep night after night. In the past, when she'd been anxious or blue, he'd gone to *shul* to pray for her and, in a couple of weeks, she'd always seemed better. Now, there was no time for *shul*. So he prayed when he got out of bed in the morning and again when he crawled under the sheets at night. The prayer was always the same: "Please, God, let Gladys get well."

A call from Gladys's sister Phyllis led to even more worry.

The conversation started out on a high note. "Meyer," Phyllis said. "I've talked it over with Harvey and we'd like to help out by bringing Irene to our house for a week. We'd take Annie, too, but Mama says she's busy with a summer job."

Hearing those words lifted an enormous weight from his shoulders. "Really? That would be so kind of you, Phyllis. Annie is holding up better than Reenie. She's older, she's busy, she goes out with her friends on weekends. I feel awful about leaving the little one alone all day. I can't tell you what a godsend your offer is."

"Well, I want to help out if I can. And, if things go the way they did the last time Gladys went off, she should come around in two or three months."

Meyer was brought up short. "What? What last time, Phyllis? When did Gladys go 'off' as you put it?"

"I thought maybe she'd told you. She had a breakdown once before — long before you two met. My parents sent her away for a while and she came back better than ever. I'm sure that's what will happen this time, too."

"Hold on. Gladys had to be sent away? Where? Where did she go?"

"I wasn't privy to the details. I was just a teenager at the time, but I think it was some sort of rest home up in the country. What I do know is that after she came back, she was a new girl. She pulled herself together and got a new job. She did it on her own. I can't tell you how relieved we all were. And then she met you, and had the girls. She's been good for such a long time. And she'll be good again, Meyer. Mark my words. You'll see I'm right."

§§§

Irene's week with Aunt Phyllis and Uncle Harvey stretched until school started up again in the fall. Never in her life had Irene been so sad; her longing for home was trumped only by her anguish over her mother. She tried her best to fit in with her cousins and make conversation with her aunt and uncle, but her heart wasn't in any of it. She found some solace in playing with Anthony, the maid's little boy, who lived with his mother in the studio apartment carved out of one corner of the basement. Though he was younger than Irene by three years, she saw him as a kindred spirit, another child who didn't belong, making the best of an awkward, lonely, uncomfortable situation.

When her Aunt Phyllis drove her back to Brooklyn on the Saturday before school was about to begin, Irene promised herself never, ever, to complain about anything again. All she wanted was to be home with her family. It didn't matter that there were no screens on the windows or that they had to walk five blocks to the laundromat or ate in a restaurant only once a year, in celebration of her parents' anniversary. But the moment she entered her apartment, it was clear things had changed in her absence. It looked as though a great wind had blown through, moving all that was familiar to unfamiliar places. And it was dirty. Dishes were piled in the sink. Irene could write her name in the dust and grit on the windowsill. But what alarmed her most was her father. He looked so old, more like a grandfather than her dad.

"Come here, *mein kind*[1]," he said, holding out his arms. "Do you know how much I've missed you?" Irene ran to him and hugged him so hard, he laughed. "It's good to see you, too, sweetheart, but I need the blood to circulate in my body!"

"Sorry, Daddy. I'm just so happy to be home. Where's Mommy? And Annie?"

"Annie first. She's at her favorite place — Arthur Murray's — taking a dance lesson."

"And Mommy?"

"Well, Mommy isn't quite ready to come home yet, but she is feeling better than she was. Maybe another few weeks or so. Then we'll have her back where she belongs."

What Meyer didn't go into was that the psychiatrists at the hospital had diagnosed Gladys with Major Depressive Disorder. They chose to treat her with electroconvulsive therapy (ECT) — medically induced, seconds-long seizures — three times a week for the last month. Meyer was heartened after the first treatment; Gladys spoke to him at length for the first time since falling ill. She also regained her appetite and took some interest in her surroundings. But with each successive treatment, she seemed to grow more confused.

After the last treatment, she looked at the menu for dinner and asked, "What's pot roast?"

"I may be mistaken, but I think it's something like brisket. Sweetheart, you make brisket for us almost every Sunday."

---

[1] My child

"I do? How do I make it?" Gladys asked.

"Well, you know I'm not much of a cook. Annie has actually been making most of our dinners since you got sick. But I think you put the meat in a pot and cover it. It cooks for a long time. Your brisket is delicious. Very tender."

"Really? I guess I'll try the pot roast for dinner tonight."

Meyer didn't go into any of that with Irene. He concocted a story about how her mother missed her very much and talked about her and Annie all the time. In fact, Gladys seemed to be entirely in the moment, something the doctors said would pass in time. Meanwhile, they would start her on a new type of drug called an antidepressant, in the hopes it would help her recovery. When she could come home, however, remained an open question.

§§§

Life without Gladys was hard for the Adelsons. Each suffered in their own way. Annie felt she had somehow been catapulted into adulthood. While she enjoyed the freedom to come and go as she pleased, she had many more responsibilities. She packed lunches for the family every morning and put dinner of one sort or another on the table each night. Annie made weekly treks to the laundromat to make sure they didn't run out of clean clothes. She also kept a list of things her dad had to buy at the grocery store every Saturday. Annie played the role of enforcer when it came to Irene's bedtime on school nights. At nine, she would tell Irene to stop reading whatever book she had her nose in; then she would turn off the bedroom light. Through it all, Annie hid her mother's hospitalization from her friends, embarrassed that Gladys was in a mental hospital, ashamed that she and Irene had been left to fend for themselves.

As for Meyer, on top of being exhausted from his work and home responsibilities and bereft that Gladys was so sick, he also felt abandoned. With the exception of Gladys's sister Phyllis, neither the Goldsteins nor the Adelsons stepped forward to come to his aid. To be fair, Bertha's world had been turned on its head by the painful prelude to Herman's death. The best she could do was to call Meyer every night at ten to check on Gladys's progress. His parents and siblings didn't even do that, nor did they invite them over for a meal or offer to take the girls for the day. Worse yet, Meyer's mother informed him that she'd been suspicious of Gladys from the start. "She never seemed quite right to me," Naomi Adelson proclaimed one night when Meyer called in hopes of wrangling an invitation to Sunday dinner. "And it wasn't just me, either," she continued. "We could all tell something was wrong with her. You went and bought that big diamond ring for the girl without so much as a word to anyone. If you'd asked, I would have told you to run for the hills."

Meyer became so indignant he nearly spat into the phone. "Well, imagine that. Of all the people to call Gladys 'not quite right.' You, who never leaves the neighborhood or reads a book, or thinks intelligently on any subject. You're a grandmother who's never shown one act of kindness or love or generosity to the only grandchildren you will ever have. You know what, Mom? First you can go to hell, and then you can go fuck yourself." He slammed the phone down and turned to see Irene standing by the door.

"What happened, Daddy? I never heard you say the F word before. You must be pretty mad."

Meyer got on his knees and hugged her. "I'm so sorry you had to hear that, Reenie. I never use that word, but you're right. Someone made me very angry."

"Was it Grandma Adelson?"

Meyer shook his head. "There's no hiding anything from you, *mein kind.* Yes, I was talking to your grandmother. She and I had a disagreement."

"About Mommy?"

"Oh, about a lot of things that haven't been right for a long time. But I don't want you to worry about it, sweetheart. You, me and Annie – and I hope soon, Mommy, too – we're going to be just fine."

Despite her father's assurances, Irene knew deep in her bones that all was not well. The absence of the mother who brought sweetness to life made her heart ache. She tried her best not to think about how much she missed her, waiting until she was under the covers in bed and Annie had switched off the light before she cried. Then she would weep and weep until finally sleep came, bringing a temporary respite from her grief.

§§§

Irene had an appreciation for the way holidays could enrich life. Around Christmas time Gentile families and the neighborhood stores put up pretty decorations. Her father always brought home a special box of chocolates on Valentines' Day for the family to enjoy. On Easter Sunday the girls attending the neighborhood Catholic school came out of their apartments in lovely pastel dresses, looking pretty and festive. Irene enjoyed the story of Passover on Seder nights, and the Purim tale of Haman's defeat by Queen Esther. But one holiday she never warmed to was Halloween. She couldn't understand the thrill other kids' got from trying to scare one another with gruesome masks and costumes.

After her mother got sick, she knew real fear, and it had nothing to do with goblins and ghosts. The fact that illness could turn a person into someone else, or even take them away forever, scared Irene silly. Her mother's long hospitalization also triggered two questions in her mind: How could sickness overcome a healthy person? And, once it grabbed hold of someone, how could illness be conquered and health restored? She turned those questions over and over in her mind as she waited for the day that her mother would come home.

In November the doctors told Meyer they felt Gladys was well enough to leave the hospital. Though she lacked a sense of vigor, both in body and mind, they felt that being home with people she loved would help her recovery. Physically, the muscle atrophy caused by being hospitalized for months would abate as Gladys returned to her normal activities. The only lasting effect from the heat stroke might be what the doctors referred to as "weak kidneys," the result of the compromised blood supply during the hours she baked in the sun. As for her memory, though her recollection of words for foods and everyday objects was returning, she was unclear as to why she'd ended up in the hospital.

The day Meyer brought Gladys home, the girls had cleaned the apartment as best they could and made a big "WELCOME HOME, MOM" sign for the kitchen. When their parents walked through the apartment door, Irene and Annie took turns hugging and kissing her. Gladys seemed pleased, if a little surprised. Though she remembered her girls, she seemed confused as to why they were so happy to see her.

In anticipation of Gladys's return, Meyer, Annie and Irene had come up with a plan: Everyone would be extra good, extra kind, extra gentle. No one would argue or complain or do anything to upset Gladys during her recuperation. And the plan seemed to work. Week by week, Gladys seemed better. By New Year's, Meyer was certain God had answered his prayers. The Gladys he'd fallen in love with so many years before was back. She had to remember to drink lots of water to support her kidneys, but other than that, she returned to her previous routines and way of life. Their tiny home resumed its immaculate state. Freshly washed and ironed clothes filled the family's drawers and closets. Dinner was prepared and the kitchen cleaned each night. But best of all, the mother Annie and Irene needed, and the wife Meyer longed for, was with them once again.

As for Gladys, each day brought greater awareness of what had befallen not only her, but Meyer and their girls. Just as they were careful not to upset her, she was careful to appear calm and happy. The latter was not too much of a stretch. When she looked at the calendar and realized she'd been gone for one hundred twenty two days, she was grateful beyond words for the chance to return to the people who meant more to her than life itself. It was something of a wonderful honeymoon for the family, a time when every normal thing was appreciated and celebrated. As time passed and her memories came into sharper focus, Gladys remembered the last time she'd seen her father. The words of his venomous rebuke still smarted, but now she was certain he'd been wrong. She was no pathetic, feeble creature. Twice now, she'd climbed out of the depths of the abyss and reclaimed her life. Only a *shtarker*[1] could do that.

---

[1] Strong person

CHAPTER FOUR

A T THE END OF SIXTH GRADE, Irene was selected to be part of a special program that would allow her to finish junior high school in two, rather than three years. Unlike her prior experience at leapfrogging a grade, this time she was "skipped" with an entire cohort of academically able kids. The best part of the program from Irene's point of view was that it offered formal instrumental music lessons. She chose the oboe for practical reasons — it was light enough to carry to school and small enough to fit in her apartment — but also because she was drawn to its clear, haunting sound.

Through the music lessons offered in school, she was introduced to musical notation: the staff, scales, time signatures, whole, half, quarter, eighth and sixteenth notes. For Irene it was nothing short of a revelation. She could see how the music she'd played by ear fit into the ingenious framework. As for the oboe, she worked diligently to master the fingering and breathing. In a matter of months she was nearly as proficient on her new instrument as she was on the piano. In short order, she was a prime candidate for oboe solos in small ensembles as well as in the school orchestra. For the first time in her life she experienced the pleasure of making music with others.

Just before turning thirteen, Irene began tenth grade at Erasmus Hall High School. Less than five feet tall and with the body of a little girl, the sheer size of her new school — eight thousand students — was daunting. But she soon realized she was seeing many of the same faces over and over again in her AP and honors classes. She admired many of her classmates, particularly those who reasoned clearly and expressed themselves with confidence — and occasionally wit — while addressing the class. She wondered if one day she might develop that kind of presence in speaking before her peers.

Her favorite subject turned out to be biology, which promised to unlock the secrets of how organisms function. Her curiosity about sickness and health grew stronger in the years following her mother's illness and recovery. Even before arriving at Erasmus, she'd decided to pursue a career in medicine. Any class that could help her achieve that goal was a class she wanted to take. Advanced Placement biology fell into that category, and the fact that it was taught by Mr. Thomas Lawrence, chairman of the department and something of a faculty celebrity, only made the prospect more appealing. A former poet, Mr. Lawrence not only had a reputation for presenting science as a great adventure, but also had a track record of successfully shepherding students through the annual Westinghouse Science Talent Search (STS). By the time Irene arrived in his class in her junior year, he'd taught more than thirty finalists of the lauded competition. One year his students represented five of the forty finalists selected from all across the nation.

Unlike Annie, who loved the thrill of dance competitions, Irene generally retreated from situations that sorted people into winners and losers. But Mr. Lawrence talked about the Westinghouse STS as less of a competition and as more of an opportunity to explore a specific research topic that interested a student. He didn't sugarcoat the process; it would take stamina, ingenuity, and intelligence to complete a project for the STS. No one in the class was required to participate, but for those who had the interest and the determination to stick with their research for up to a year, he would support them. By midyear, seven students had accepted the challenge. Irene was the only girl among them.

She decided to focus her research on ethology, or in layman's terms, animal behavior. Irene knew it was an odd choice for a person raised on a busy Brooklyn street, where the only animals she ran across for the first years of her life were the neighborhood alley cats, squirrels, pigeons and the occasional stray dog, all which seemed to coexist with humans in a "live and let live" sort of way. Then of course there were the mice, rats, and roaches within her apartment, which were met with revulsion and mostly futile attempts at eradication. As for domesticated animals, few families in Irene's building had any pets, and those who did favored a lone, caged parakeet. There was, however, one exception: Joe Sansiveri, the building super. It was Joe who was responsible for Irene's fascination with animal behavior.

Though most of the building's tenants knew nothing of it, Joe's hobby was racing homing pigeons. Irene never would have become privy to Joe's passion for pigeons had it not been for one particularly oppressive evening years before when she, her mother, and sister were away in the Catskills. That night Meyer took a folding chair and sat outside the entrance to their building, trying his best to escape the stultifying heat in the apartment. Joe, who lived alone and mostly kept to himself, came out to have a cigarette. The two men commiserated.

"Miserable night. Even my place in the basement is hot as blazes," Joe said.

"No matter how long I live, I don't think I'll ever get used to the city in the summer," Meyer replied. "The heat is worse than South Carolina."

"You've been down south?"

"During the war."

"Army, Navy, or Marines?" Joe asked.

"Aircraft support at the Army base in Columbia. How about you?"

"I did basic training at Fort Dix," Joe said. "Then I had some more training in Jersey before being shipped overseas."

"No kidding," Meyer said. "I did basic at Fort Dix, too. Where were you stationed overseas?"

"Italy."

"Whoa, Italy was rough."

"I had it relatively easy. I don't know if you've heard of it, but I was part of the Signal Pigeon Corps," Joe said. "We worked with carrier pigeons to get information across enemy lines."

"I'll be damned!"

"Oh, yeah, we used tens of thousands of pigeons during the war. And there were three thousand of us pigeoneers. My buddy trained G.I. Joe, a rock star in the pigeon world. During the Italian Campaign he delivered a message that prevented us from bombing a village the Brits had just taken from the fascist SOBs. G.I. Joe flew twenty miles in twenty minutes with the message in a tiny capsule strapped to his leg. He arrived just as our bombers were about to take off. They figure he saved a thousand lives. He was even given a medal for the most outstanding flight made during the war."

"Geez, I didn't have any idea," Meyer said. "My work in aircraft support was pretty interesting, but what you did is in a whole different category. Do you miss it?"

"No way I miss the war. I'll never forget it, much as I'd like to. As for the pigeons, I would miss them, except that I have my own loft."

"Really? Do you keep it in the city or someplace up in the country?"

Joe laughed. "Mr. Adelson, my loft is right here on the roof of the building."

"You've got pigeons on the roof?" Meyer asked incredulously. "Oh, and forget that Mr. Adelson crap. It's Meyer."

"Well, Meyer, if you're interested, sometime I'll introduce you to my brood. They're the geniuses of the pigeon world. They can fly hundreds of miles in a single day and then zero in on a destination. They're phenomenal racers. Thanks to them, I'm the envy of pigeon lovers all across the five boroughs."

Meyer could hardly believe that he'd lived for years in the building without realizing he was sharing it with racing pigeons. He felt honored that Joe was willing to introduce him to his brood. "I would really enjoy seeing your pigeons, Joe. Thanks for the invitation."

And so Meyer – and by extension, the rest of the Adelsons — were welcomed into Joe's world of pigeon racing. When Irene was in ninth grade Joe's prized pigeon, Velocita, placed first in a race from the Catskill Mountains to Brooklyn. Like a proud papa, he asked Meyer if he and the family would like to come up and have a little celebration with the golden girl herself. They made a date to meet after dinner. As usual, Annie was off at dance class, but Meyer, Gladys and Irene took the elevator to the sixth floor before climbing the stairs and knocking on the locked door to the roof. Joe greeted them with Velocita in his hands. Irene took a careful look at the ordinary-looking bird that, the day before, had flown one hundred miles from the Catskill Mountains to Flatbush. A question took root inside her mind: How could such a small and apparently simple creature find its way home? That question rattled around in her head for a couple of years, but it wasn't until Mr. Lawrence pitched the idea of entering the Westinghouse competition that she decided to see if she could find the answer.

Once she made the decision to develop a research project for the STS, Irene jumped in with both feet. She began by reading everything on pigeon navigation she could get her hands on. After exhausting the school and local libraries' resources, she put in a request for books from the main branch of the public library on Fifth Avenue in Manhattan. Everything she read complemented what she was learning from Joe, who was only too happy to find someone as excited about his birds as he. Before long, Irene was working alongside him each day, helping to feed and exercise the pigeons. But it turned out that despite her firsthand experience with Joe's pigeons and all of her reading, the other Erasmus students in the Westinghouse competition had a leg up.

Each of the boys working on a project for the STS came from homes where the parents had attended college and did professional work of one sort or another. If any of the boys' parents couldn't help their son with the nuances of their research project, they knew someone who could. But Irene came from a different world. In her parents' small circle of friends and their entire extended family, not a single person had graduated from college or had any inkling about the scientific method. Mr. Laurence helped Irene where he could, but finally he suggested she try to find a mentor who could offer guidance in the design of her experiment in animal behavior.

He could have just as well asked her to find someone to help her design a rocket to the moon. The adults in her life could teach her many things, but designing a project for a national science competition was not among them. She walked into her music ensemble's practice wearing a long face. As a rule, making music lifted her spirits. But that day, even the prospect of playing *Vivaldi's Concerto for Violin and Oboe in B Flat Major*, a piece she loved, didn't help her shake her sense of defeat. After her first lackluster solo, the music teacher, Mrs. Feldman, asked Irene to try it again. The second effort was only marginally better. When the period was over and everyone was packing up their instruments, Mrs. Feldman asked to have a word with Irene.

"I know I messed up today. I promise to do better tomorrow, but I can't stay and talk, Mrs. Feldman. I've got to get to math," Irene explained.

"I won't keep you long. I just want to know if everything's all right. You seemed a little preoccupied as you were playing. That's not at all like you, Irene."

"It's just this science project I'm trying to get off the ground. Mr. Lawrence told me I need to find a mentor. If I can't, I guess I'll have to drop out of the Talent Search. It's not like I'm expecting to win or anything like that. I just want to figure out how pigeons navigate. It's more or less driving me crazy."

Mrs. Feldman studied Irene's face. Though she was nearly a head shorter than most of the other students in the orchestra, she was light years ahead of them in terms of her musicality. "Tell you what. After your last period today, drop by my classroom and we'll talk."

"Mrs. Feldman, I promise I'll be better tomorrow," Irene insisted.

"I am not worried about your solo, Irene. I'm sure tomorrow will be a better day. But I may be able to offer some help with your science project."

"Really? Are you an ethologist as well as a musician?" Irene asked.

"I'm not sure I know what an ethologist is, but I'm married to a scientist who is very smart and also quite amiable. We'll talk more later. Now get to math. I don't want to be responsible for your being marked late!"

§§§

The following Saturday, Irene and her mother took two buses to Mrs. Feldman's house in the Midwood section of Brooklyn, a tree-lined residential neighborhood that was also home to Brooklyn College. The moment Mrs. Feldman welcomed them into her Tudor-style house, Irene and Gladys were taken with the large, airy living room. One entire wall was lined from floor to ceiling with books. Irene couldn't imagine what it would be like to have a library in her house, to have a question arise and then to search for the answer in one of her own books. When she peered out the window onto the backyard, Irene was amazed that her teacher had her own slice of the country right in the middle of Brooklyn. There were no signs that children had ever lived in the house, but the Feldmans had Peaches, a very friendly miniature poodle. The stray dogs that occasionally made an appearance on her street frightened Irene, but when Peaches sidled up next to her, she found her to be gentle and affectionate.

"Arthur, our guests have arrived," Mrs. Feldman called from the living room.

In a moment a tall man with a shiny bald head hurried in from another part of the house. "My goodness," he laughed. "It looks as though Peaches has found a new best friend! You know, she's an excellent judge of character. It appears she's given you her seal of approval, Irene." Arthur Feldman extended his hand to Gladys and then to Irene. "Welcome to our home Mrs. Adelson, Irene. Sit, sit," he encouraged. "Make yourselves comfortable."

Gladys and Irene found a seat on the sofa directly across from Arthur Feldman's well-worn leather chair. Gladys spoke first. "My husband and I are so grateful Irene has this opportunity to discuss her project with you. Much as we would like to, we are really at a loss as to how to help her."

"Well, the truth is, after my wife came home and told me about Irene's project, I couldn't wait to hear about the work she's doing."

Irene saw this as an invitation to launch into the speech she'd rehearsed several times in front of the bathroom mirror. "Thank you so much, Mr. Feldman. I don't know how much Mrs. Feldman has told you, but I am hoping to enter the Westinghouse Science Talent Search with my study of pigeon navigation. I'm fascinated by the question of how pigeons find their way back to their loft over hundreds of miles of unknown terrain. It seems quite likely that they don't navigate solely by the sun," Irene explained. "For example, my friend Joe, who is a pigeon fancier, can release his birds from Queens on a cloudy day and they make it back to their loft before he can drive home in his truck. It's really quite extraordinary when you think of it. But the question is, if the pigeons aren't using the sun, what *are* they using to navigate? My hypothesis is they use the earth's magnetic field. There's a professor at Cornell, William Keeton, who has just started investigating this. I would like to do my project testing this hypothesis."

She was just a small slip of girl, but her earnestness and enthusiasm delighted the middle-aged professor. Her hypothesis also intrigued him. "I guess the first question is, do you have access to pigeons?"

"Oh, yes, I do. Joe is our super. He lives right in our building and keeps his pigeons in a loft on the roof. The best part is that Joe is eager to help with my project. He has already taught me so much about the pigeons' behavior and the care and training they need to perform well. He's agreed to allow the pigeons to participate, provided I do nothing to put his birds in jeopardy, which of course I would never do. I've grown quite fond of them."

"You've got access to pigeons, so the most important hurdle is cleared. As a physicist, I'm fascinated by your notion of the role the earth's magnetic field plays in bird navigation. About ten years ago I read a study by a German scientist. I think his name was Fromme. As I remember, he theorized the robins he worked with relied on the earth's magnetic field to guide their migration to Spain each winter. You may be onto something important. I certainly can help you with the physics of the magnetic field. I admit, though, that my entire knowledge of animal neurobiology and behavior comes down to what I've learned from Peaches," he said, petting the dog that had moved to her master's side. "I do have a good friend and colleague, though, who knows quite a bit more than I do about ethology. His special interest is the navigation system of crustaceans, which perhaps could have some carry-over to your project."

"I certainly would appreciate any help you could offer in understanding the workings of the magnetic field. I haven't taken physics yet, so my knowledge is limited to what I learned in general science and the articles on pigeon navigation that I've read."

"Well, that's a start. Let me talk to my friend and see if he has the time or the inclination to meet with you. I can't promise anything, but I'll ask."

"Really? That would be fantastic," Irene said, her spirits soaring. "To tell you the truth, before I spoke with Mrs. Feldman, I was rather pessimistic about my project, but now I feel I may, in fact, be able to bring it to life." Just then, Mrs. Feldman appeared with a tray of tea and pastries, including Irene's favorite, chocolate rugelach. Irene smiled and gave her mother a look as if to say, "Can you believe this is really happening?" Then she gave herself a tiny pinch just to make sure she wasn't in the middle of a wonderful dream.

§§§

Irene couldn't believe her good fortune. Arthur Feldman introduced her to his friend, Professor Bertrand Goldfarb, an expert on crustacean navigation. He, in turn, wrote her a letter of introduction to Professor Keeton at Cornell, who sent encouraging words and sage advice about what pitfalls to avoid as she designed her experiment. Thanks to the guidance provided by the triumvirate of college professors, Irene was able to construct an experiment to test her hypothesis about the role played by the earth's magnetic field as pigeons navigate unfamiliar terrain. She would have some of Joe's pigeons fly while wearing small magnets — which would confuse the birds' orientation relative to the Earth's magnetic field — while others would fly under identical conditions except that the magnets would be replaced by an inert material of equal size and weight.

Her budget for the experiment was limited, her only income coming from babysitting her neighbor's little boy after school each afternoon. But it was enough for the slim, inch-long steel magnets she needed to buy and the "dummies" created from stainless steel by the hardware store down the street. Joe designed a small harness for the pigeons that would hold either a magnet or a dummy. Following his design Gladys hand-sewed six harnesses from old nylon stockings. Each had stitches so small she had to use a magnifier as she worked. Once the harnesses were done, Irene and Joe began experimenting with different weather conditions — sunny, cloudy, windy, calm — to see if those variables had an effect on the speed or ability of the pigeons to return to their loft. They also varied the experiment by whether the pigeons were familiar or unfamiliar with the terrain. Most times Gladys, now personally invested in the experiment, would ride along in Joe's old pickup truck to the place where the pigeons were released. For the rest of Irene's junior year, the three conducted test flights nearly every weekend, with Irene fastidiously recording her observations before, during, and after each trial.

She spent the summer before her senior year analyzing the massive amount of data she'd collected during the months-long experiment. It soon became clear that the pigeons wearing magnets were markedly slower in returning to their loft, particularly when the terrain was unfamiliar and the cloud cover was great. By summer's end, she had reached her conclusions: Pigeons likely use a variety of cues to navigate – terrain, the sun, magnetic force, perhaps even smell – but during cloudy weather and while flying over unfamiliar terrain, the earth's magnetic field lends critical navigational assistance to pigeons in search of their loft. That September, two days before she turned fifteen, Irene went to the post office to mail off her project to the Westinghouse Science Talent Search. It was also the day she got her period for the very first time.

§§§

Irene's deep dive into pigeon navigation taught her that forces undetectable to the five senses could affect and even control animal behavior. Surely the earth's magnetic field wasn't the only unseen force in the universe that influenced living things, forces she had yet to learn about or had not even been discovered. Might they affect not only animal behavior, but human behavior, as well? That question intrigued her.

Years had passed since her mother had fallen ill, but that terrible time was tattooed on her soul. Every so often, she and Annie would whisper about it, always careful to be sure Gladys was out of earshot. They'd recall how shocked they were to see their mother lying in the hospital, so lifeless, so remote. Annie long ago explained that their mother had suffered a "nervous breakdown." Lately, Irene had begun to wonder about the factors that might "break" a functioning human being, landing them in a mental hospital for months or even years. For the sake of her mother and all the other broken people and their families, Irene hoped there were scientists around the world trying to figure out that enigma.

For Irene, her study of Joe's pigeons ignited a love affair with science. With near religious fervor, she looked to it as the holy grail, the path to truth and understanding. She doubled down on her decision to go into medicine. She thought of the doctors who had treated her mother. It was their scientific knowledge that had given her family another chance at happiness. Irene couldn't imagine a job more important or gratifying than being a physician.

§§§

At sunset on the last day of Chanukah, Irene began reciting the Hebrew blessing and lighting the candles of the family menorah. There was a delicious aroma wafting through the apartment as her mother fried potato *latkes*[1] on the stove. Annie and Meyer would be home soon and the family would have a special dinner to mark the end of the holiday. Irene hoped her parents would like the gift she'd gotten them: an LP of the new Broadway musical, *Man of LaMancha*. Just as she lit the eighth candle, there was a knock on the door.

"Reenie, can you get it? My hands are full."

Irene quickly replaced the *shamash*[2] in the menorah and ran to the door. Peering into the peephole she saw a uniformed courier. She opened the door. "Yes? Can I help you?"

"Western Union telegram for Irene Adelson."

---

[1] Pancakes
[2] The "servant" candle used to light the other candles of the menorah

"Mom," Irene yelled. "There's a man at the door with a telegram. He says it's for *me!*"

Gladys quickly wiped her hands and grabbed a quarter from her purse. "Thank you very much," she said, tipping the courier as she took the telegram. "You have a good night."

Gladys closed the door and handed the telegram to Irene. "Here it is, sweetheart."

"Do you think this could be from the Westinghouse Science Talent Search?"

"Well, there's only one way to find out," Gladys said, putting her arm around her daughter.

Irene was trembling. She'd never received a telegram before. She wondered if the STS notified both the winners and losers by telegram. She stared at it for at least a minute.

"For God's sake, Irene, open it already," Gladys urged. "The suspense is killing me."

"I don't know why I'm hesitating, Mom. I've enjoyed the process of learning from Joe's pigeons irrespective of the competition."

"Yes, I know, sweetheart. Open your telegram."

Very gingerly, Irene tore open the envelope.

To: Irene Adelson

Congratulations! You have been selected as a finalist in the Westinghouse Science Talent Search. More information to follow by U.S. mail.

It was with both joy and pride that the Adelson family celebrated Irene's achievement that night. After dinner, Irene shared her astonishing news with Joe who, like a proud papa, called the *New York Daily News* to let them know that Irene had been chosen as a finalist in the nationwide competition. In short order the tabloid sent a photographer to snap a picture of Irene and Joe's prized racing pigeon, Velocita. The photo and accompanying story graced page thirteen of all three million copies of the Sunday edition.

§§§

In March of her senior year, Irene and the other thirty-nine Westinghouse finalists were invited to an all-expenses paid week in Washington, D.C. Never having gone further than Manhattan by herself, her parents tutored her on the needed skills for her trip: How to hail a cab, pay the driver, and ask for a receipt so she could be reimbursed by the STS. They also explained the role of the hotel bellhop, and how a twenty-five cent tip would be sufficient when he carried her bags to her room. Both Meyer and Gladys accompanied her to Penn Station, helping her with her luggage and making sure she was on the right train. Irene wasn't positive, but she thought her father might have teared up when they hugged goodbye. Then the doors closed, the train pulled out of the station, and she was off on her solo adventure, a bit nervous about remembering everything her parents had coached her on, but mostly filled with joyful anticipation.

Hours later, when she arrived at DC's Union Station, Irene knew her first job was to get a cab to the hotel designated in the STS packet. There was only one problem: Her bags were heavier and more cumbersome than she'd imagined; one packed to the brim with clothing, the other filled with photographs, charts, and written materials for the project exhibition. Though she'd grown nearly six inches in the past year, now standing almost five foot eight inches tall, she tipped the scales at just one hundred ten pounds. As she hauled her luggage through the station to the street, she thought she might *plotz*[1], to use an oft-heard phrase from Grandma Bertha. Irene must have started and stopped at least a dozen times, massaging her hands during every break. It was during one of those time-outs that she noticed someone else struggling with two large suitcases. It was a teenaged boy with a head of unruly curls. Seeing him wrestle with his bags made her realize the problem she was having was not hers alone.

When she finally emerged from the station, what her eyes beheld nearly took her breath away. In the distance stood the Capitol Building, something she'd only seen as a backdrop on the evening news. There was no doubt about it; she was really, truly on her own in Washington, DC! As per her parents' instructions, she got into a waiting cab, promising herself that as soon as she got her belongings unpacked, she would explore the nation's capital.

---

[1] Fall down in exhaustion

The taxi ride to the hotel lasted only a few minutes. A bellman dressed in a smart, red uniform took her suitcases and showed her to the check-in desk. This was another first. Irene had never before stayed in a hotel of any type, no less one so splendid. Despite the busy staff and numerous patrons, there seemed to be a hush inside the luxuriously furnished lobby. Irene got the sense that something important, perhaps even sacred, might take place within its walls.

Irene made no effort to hide her wonder. The desk clerk had to clear his throat to get her attention.

"May I help you, Madame?

Irene turned around to see if there was a woman standing behind her, but there was no one else in line. "I hope so. In the packet of materials I received I was told to come to this hotel, that you'd have a room for me."

"Your name?"

"Irene Adelson," she said, her voice turning up as though she was asking a question rather than stating a fact.

"Yes, Miss Adelson. We have you staying for six nights. Your hotel charges are covered so I need no billing information. You will be on the third floor. Would you like one key or two?

"What do people usually take?"

"I should say it all depends on their circumstances," the desk clerk replied. "I think one should do," he said, handing her a single room key. "I see on your reservation that you're part of the Westinghouse group. I have a welcome gift for you." The clerk reached beneath the counter and brought up a small bag.

"This is certainly unexpected. Thank you very much," Irene said earnestly.

"Perhaps you should direct your gratitude to the Westinghouse staff," the bemused clerk suggested.

"Yes, of course. I definitely will."

"Is there anything else I can help you with today?"

"I'm not sure if you know the answer to this question, but have any of the other Westinghouse students arrived?"

"Oh, yes. A number have already checked in. Some have left to see the sights."

"Really? That's just what I plan on doing as soon as I unpack."

"You know what they say about great minds, don't you?"

"No, I don't," Irene said.

"They think alike."

Irene mulled this over for a moment. "Not to be disagreeable, but I believe great minds often think differently, for example Galileo and Isaac Newton."

The clerk studied the tall slip of a girl for a moment before responding. "Touché, Madame, touché."

§§§

Irene had never had a room to herself, no less one in a well-appointed hotel. She carefully unpacked her suitcases, taking extra care to see that her formal dress for the evening gala, hand sewn by Gladys over the past months, was hanging free of wrinkles. On the mahogany dresser she laid several eight by ten inch photographs of the pigeons, their loft, the harnesses outfitted with magnets, as well as the charts and graphs she'd painstakingly created to illustrate her observations and findings. When Irene finished unpacking, she gave herself a moment to take it all in. Here she was in one of the handsomest rooms she'd ever seen, about to spend a week in the nation's capital with some of the most talented science students in the country. She never could have conjured up a moment like this.

But if she wanted to explore the city, time for taking stock of her good fortune had to be cut short. Quickly Irene grabbed the map from her gift bag, got on her coat, and headed out. When the elevator doors opened into the lobby, there stood the curly-haired boy from Union Station. In his teeth were the handles to the same gift bag Irene had received. Each of his hands gripped a large suitcase. Irene held the doors open for him as he maneuvered himself and his bags into the elevator. Due to his clenched jaw, his attempt to say "thanks" was muffled, but she could tell he was happy for the help. Irene wondered why he hadn't given his bags to the bellhop. Perhaps he didn't have the twenty-five cents for the tip.

With the help of her map, Irene navigated down Connecticut Avenue towards the White House. She hoped there'd be time to see the Capitol Building, too. It was a mild day for early March, perfect weather for sightseeing. She walked wide-eyed and with a spring in her step as she munched on the cookies her mother had placed in the inner pocket of her coat. She'd never felt so grown-up.

§§§

Irene found the White House impressive. She studied the mansion's design and its manicured grounds for quite a while, paying particular attention to the windows of what she thought might be the Oval Office. She imagined President Lyndon Johnson and Vice-President Hubert Humphrey sitting together in the Oval Office at that very moment, discussing what Mr. Humphrey might include in his keynote address for the STS gala later in the week. The President could suggest the Vice-President concentrate on the thrilling breakthroughs scientists, doctors, and engineers had made in just the last years: the invention of the laser, astronauts orbiting the earth, satellites transmitting images across the ocean in real time, the first kidney transplant, a calculator so small you could put it in your pocket. But then she thought about the difficulties facing the President and Vice-President. Lots of people were angry about the war in Vietnam. Annie, now a sophomore at NYU, had participated in a number of demonstrations against it. Her parents thought the war was a terrible waste of life. Every week hundreds of American servicemen were being killed, to say nothing of the mounting Vietnamese casualties. All the more reason, Irene thought, for Mr. Humphrey to take the opportunity to celebrate the power of science to improve the lives of people around the world.

In her reverie, Irene lost track of time. When she checked her watch, she realized a visit to the Capitol would have to wait for another day. She had to get back to the hotel and change for the first STS dinner. She already knew what she would wear that night: her grey pleated mini-skirt, the white blouse her mother had ironed that morning, and her favorite sweater, a royal blue cardigan Grandma Bertha had knit for her. The weekend before, she'd gone with Annie to shop for the black fishnet stockings and new Mary Jane shoes. Irene walked back to the hotel at a steady pace, filled with great expectations for the evening ahead.

Once back in her room, she stood in front of the mirror, trying to remember Annie's detailed instructions for applying black liquid eyeliner: not too thick, hold your hand steady, go across the lid with one steady, continuous motion. Her first effort was an abject failure. Irene quickly washed the wayward black lines from her eyes. Her second try, though not as handsome as the thin, graceful lines that adorned Annie's lids, achieved a better result. Relieved, Irene decided not to test fate. Her effort would do. She put on her outfit, parted her hair down the center and brushed out the snarls, grateful that her stick-straight hair had finally come into fashion. The last thing Irene did before leaving the room was to pin her STS name tag to her cardigan. A look in the full length mirror on the way out the door left Irene satisfied by what she saw.

In the elevator there were two boys wearing ties, sport jackets and STS name tags. They smiled awkwardly and nodded. All three of the young scientists then fixed their eyes on the elevator floor display rather than try to engage in conversation. When they arrived at the lobby, an STS staffer guided them toward the other waiting finalists. Irene carefully positioned herself next to three girls standing beside an enormous potted plant.

"Hello. I'm Irene," she said, extending her hand to each of the girls. "I'm glad to meet you." The girls, in turn, introduced themselves. Small talk ensued about where they came from and how they'd gotten to Washington. Mary from Iowa commented on the "fine looking guys" milling about in the lobby. Irene's thoughts immediately went to the curly haired boy, whom she had yet to spot among those waiting to go to dinner. As she checked her watch, she was startled to hear someone say, "Thanks, Irene. You saved my life."

She looked up and saw the curly haired boy. "Oh, hello," she said, staring into his clear blue eyes. "How exactly did I do that?"

"Speaking figuratively, of course. You held the doors open when I was trying to haul my bags into the elevator."

"Oh, that. Well, I know how hard it is when you're carrying so much. But how do you know my name?"

The boy laughed. "That name tag was a dead giveaway."

Irene felt her cheeks grow hot. "Oh, I forgot all about it. In any case, I was happy to help."

"As you can see here," the boy said pointing to his nametag, "I'm Albert, but only my parents call me that. Everyone else calls me Al."

"Hello, Al. Everyone but my family calls me Irene."

"What does your family call you?

"I'm Reenie to them, a term of endearment I guess."

"Endearment or nickname, it's nice. I like it."

Just then there was an announcement that all the STS students should move into the dining room. "Shall we go in?" Al asked. She didn't know why, but suddenly Irene felt her cheeks grow hot again. She nodded at the three girls standing beside the potted plant and said, "Sounds like a great idea."

§§§

The week flew by. Jam-packed with one memorable event after another – the meeting with the Nobel Prize winning chemist, the visits to laboratories, the lectures given by researchers in the forefront of their fields, the sightseeing, the lunch in the famous Cosmos Club – Irene was walking on air. Her high spirits were on full display during her presentation to the STS judges. After listening to her explanation of the pigeon navigation experiment, they lingered at her exhibit for quite a while asking a series of probing questions, all of which Irene handled with ease. Her curiosity about the pigeons' uncanny ability to find their way home, the passion she felt for her investigation, and the in-depth description of her findings combined to make a positive impression on the judges.

The culmination of the STS week was the black-tie gala. Irene felt beautiful in the emerald green satin dress her mother had made. She put her long hair up in a chignon, following Annie's written instructions, then took extra care with her eye make-up. When she arrived at the gala and got her place card, she saw both she and Albert Jaffe had been seated at Table Three. Over the past days they'd become friends, so much so he agreed to let her call him Albert – as she said, like Einstein and Schweitzer — if he could call her Reenie. Just as Irene entered the ballroom, Albert came up behind her.

"What table are you at?" he asked.

"Three, just like you."

"So, my bribe to the event planner paid off!"

Irene was aghast. "You bribed someone so we could sit at the same table?"

"Reenie, I ask you, do I look like the kind of guy who has money to pay bribes?"

"Well, no, not really. I see no evidence of wealth."

"Hah! I have so much wealth that I borrowed this suit, tie, and shoes from my friend Josh, who wore them to a Bar Mitzvah last month. Has anyone ever told you that you're a bit gullible?" Albert asked.

"Am I?" Irene asked, chagrined.

"You definitely are one of the most sincere, trusting people I have ever met."

"Is that the same as being gullible?" Irene pressed.

"Well, maybe just a little. But I like you that way. I never have to guess what you're thinking. When I'm with you, there's no hidden agenda. You say what you mean."

"Of course," Irene said. "What else would I say?"

"Exactly. And that's why I am so happy to be sitting at Table Three with you."

Irene chose a seat that gave a good view of the lectern and then Albert took the chair beside hers. Sitting there together, Albert reached for her hand. It felt so perfectly natural to Irene, as though they'd known each other all their lives. Together they listened as Vice-President Humphrey gave an inspirational talk about the power of the individual to affect the course of scientific discovery. He told them not to fear offending orthodoxy, to ignore "any and all advice to move with the herd." Only then, he said, was discovery of truth possible. He warned that their path ahead would be arduous, that science was a demanding discipline. But, quoting Louis Pasteur, he said, "Chance favors only the prepared mind." The preparation that lay before them would make it possible for them to venture forth from the "safe harbors of the known" into the "oceans of truth."

Both Irene and Albert applauded enthusiastically when the vice-president concluded his remarks.

And then, it was time for the announcement of the top five projects in the competition. Irene had been awestruck by her peers' projects, which ranged from the earthly — how fiddler crabs' shells harden — to the astrophysical, the aging process in a binary star, which was Albert's project. Had she been in the judges' shoes, she would have been hard pressed to choose the top five. Of one thing she was certain: There was no chance she would be singled out for one of the prizes. Perhaps that's why, when her name was announced as the third place winner, she shook her head in disbelief. Her eyes filled with tears as she heard the applause from her fellow finalists. Not only had the judges singled her out from so stellar a field, the third place award brought with it a scholarship of six thousand dollars, just a hair less than her father earned in an entire year. Albert reached over and hugged her, then whispered, "You'd better get up there,

Reenie. Go get your prize." As she walked to the lectern, she glanced back at Albert. He was applauding with his hands over his head.

The acknowledgment of her work and the generous scholarship would have been more than enough to leave Irene euphoric, but the week had also given her the chance to mingle with people who shared her love of inquiry and discovery. The STS finalists were not only whip-smart, but many also knew how to have fun. They spoke of foods and sports and places Irene had only read about. Just talking with them brightened her world. But of all the people she enjoyed, it was Albert Jaffe, the tall, lanky boy from Cleveland, who affected her most. Just being in his presence made her happy. More thrilling still, it appeared he felt the same way about her. When the week drew to a close, they shared a cab to Union Station. As the time came for them to go off to their trains, Albert came in close and kissed Irene on the lips. They stood locked in an embrace until Albert broke the mood by saying, "Now go *schlep* your suitcases, Madame Curie. You have a train to catch."

"Promise you'll write," Irene implored.

"You're gonna get tired of all the letters I'm going to send you," Albert said.

"No, I won't," Irene protested.

Then the two parted, each struggling to carry their luggage to their respective trains, with destinations five hundred miles apart.

§§§

A month after Irene's glorious week in Washington, four fat letters of college acceptance arrived in the Adelsons' mailbox. At fifteen, the decision of which offer to accept was a daunting one. Cornell University, Vassar and Barnard had offered her full tuition scholarships, which put them at the same cost footing as Brooklyn College, a tuition-free school for students who met its exacting entrance requirements. She examined the colleges on their merits, weighing the pros and cons of each. She knew she would get a good education at any of the four, but her thoughts kept returning to Barnard. Like Vassar, it was a relatively small liberal arts college for women, but its students could take classes from Columbia University's vast offerings, putting it on the same academic plane as Cornell. More factors in Barnard's favor included its location in Manhattan and the fact that it had dorms for its students. She could live away from home, but her family would be only a subway ride away. She was sure she'd made the right decision when she put her commitment letter to Barnard in the mail.

That spring was a good time for all of the Adelsons. Annie finished her second year at NYU on the Dean's List, ensuring the continuation of her scholarship to study psychology and dance. Shortly before his sixtieth birthday, Meyer was promoted to manager of the haberdashery department at Macy's Herald Square. As for Gladys, with her last child about to leave the nest, she mustered the courage to sit for the school secretary civil service exam. When she earned the top score, she was offered the position of secretary to the principal at the neighborhood elementary school. Having spent nineteen years as a housewife, the prospect of going back to work gave her pause, but after weighing the pros and cons she decided to accept the job.

Later, Irene would remember that spring as halcyon days, when everyone in the family was well and there was extra cash on hand to make life easier. Meyer got his driver's license and bought a used, four-door Chevy Biscayne. He and Gladys found a three-bedroom apartment on a nearby quiet, tree-lined street that had room enough for Grandma Bertha. They gave Bertha the largest bedroom, allowing her to bring her favorite pieces of furniture from her household of more than fifty years. For Irene, the only sad part of moving was giving up her daily visits to Joe's pigeon loft. But, she reasoned, soon she'd be a college student, living in a dormitory on the Upper West Side of Manhattan, taking classes that would stretch her knowledge of the world. It was time for her to leave the nest.

PART TWO

1967 - 1978

CHAPTER FIVE

GLADYS AND MEYER FOUGHT OFF TEARS as they carried Irene's two suitcases, oboe, music stand, and portable typewriter into her dorm room in Brooks Hall. The record player that Grandma Bertha had given Irene as an early present for her upcoming sixteenth birthday was also moved into the double room, as were the Gershwin, Barber, and Copeland LPs Irene loved so much. The clock radio was a gift from Annie, who said it would help her get to her 8 AM classes on time. In short order, all of Irene's belongings were neatly lined up on her half of the long, narrow room.

"We'd better go now, sweetheart," Meyer said. The meter is just about up and I don't want to get a ticket."

"That's okay, Daddy. I have lots of unpacking to keep me busy. Don't worry about me."

"I wish there was time for me to make up the bed for you," Gladys fretted. "Promise me you'll remember to eat, Reenie. I know how you get when you get involved in things. You're such a skinny malink."

"I promise I will eat," Irene assured her mother. "I have my meal plan book right in my pocketbook."

"Okay then, I guess we'll be on our way," Meyer said. "Take good care of yourself and call if you need anything. Anything at all. It's a local call. You can use any phone booth or the dormitory phone."

"I know, Daddy. And I'll do what Annie does. I'll call at least once a week."

"But if you need something, you can call in between the weekly call," Gladys urged.

"And don't forget to look both ways when you cross the street," Meyer warned. "People drive like maniacs here. I mean it, Reenie."

"I promise to be careful crossing the street and to call at least once a week. Thanks so much for moving me in," Irene said, hugging her parents a final time before they disappeared down the long corridor.

The small pang of sadness provoked by her parents' leave-taking was almost immediately succeeded by the thrill of liberation. Now that she was a bona fide college student, she was looking forward to the kind of personal freedom she'd enjoyed in Washington. Just thinking of Washington made her thoughts go to Albert, with whom she'd shared an epistolary relationship over the last months. They'd written faithfully each week, sharing their deepest thoughts and greatest hopes. She'd kept every one of his letters. Alone in her dorm room, she opened her suitcase, reached for the manila envelope with his missives, and reread his last letter.

September 3, 1967

Dear Reenie,

I'm packing now, sorting through my dresser and closet for the right clothes to bring to Stanford. One thing's for sure — the winter will be a helluva lot warmer in Palo Alto than in Cleveland. A high school buddy who's a sophomore at Stanford told me that people don't even have winter coats. Can you imagine? That's just one of the advantages Stanford has over MIT. Their financial aid package, their work in optics and lasers — particularly Professor Schawlow's — the chance to study in sunny California, all influenced my decision last spring. The only downside to Stanford is that it's so far away. I mean that. When I was choosing between the two schools, distance to New York was the one big advantage MIT had over Stanford. Now I don't know when you and I will have the chance to see one another again.

I feel so lucky we connected in Washington. After spending a week together I feel closer to you than to friends I've known all my life. I can't explain it. It's just a fact. There's something so honest about you. You never play games. You don't even know how beautiful you are.

I hope you have a terrific time at Barnard. (Is it selfish that I'm glad you're going to an all-girls school?) You're going to do great there. I just know it. Make sure to save some time each week to write (dorm address below). Even though we'll be on separate sides of the continent, through our letters we'll be able to see what the other is seeing, learn what the other is learning, feel what the other is feeling.

Love, Albert

Irene refolded the letter and put it with the others. She wondered how he could think her beautiful. She'd always known she was an ordinary girl, nothing like Annie, with her bright eyes and thick wavy hair. Irene wasn't dissatisfied with her looks; she just recognized and accepted the truth. She was plain. One of the many things she'd learned from Annie was the need to take care in the way she presented herself to the world. As Annie pointed out, the reason movie stars looked so good was they worked at looking good. Hair, clothes, and make-up all give the world an impression of a person. So Irene did her best, working with what she saw as pedestrian features, to enhance her appearance. Still, there was no way she believed she met the threshold of beauty. All the more astonishing that Albert thought otherwise. He seemed so pleased that she'd chosen a women's college. Was he really concerned that someone else would compete for her affections?

Stanford was decidedly not a single-sex institution. What would happen if Albert met another girl whom he found beautiful? Would his letter-writing continue? Of course, she could meet a boy from Columbia who might endear himself to her. Just thinking about it caused a knot to form in her stomach. But Irene decided not to worry about what was to come. Soon enough, time would provide answers to all her uncertainties.

§§§

Because she'd spent nearly all of her life in small spaces, the room she had to share with the not-yet-arrived Nancy Morse from Bloomfield Hills, Michigan, which was only nine feet wide and less than double that in length, appeared perfectly adequate to Irene. The beds took up most of one wall, and the desks, dressers, and bookcases did the same on the other. Irene felt sure her clothes would easily fit in half of the closet and the dresser drawers. But Irene wondered about the girls who were arriving at the dorm with multiple trunks, stereos, fans, and luggage-style portable hairdryers. One girl even brought a bicycle. Irene had no idea how those girls would fit all of their belongings into the confines of their room.

Hours after Irene had unpacked her things, made her bed, found the dining hall for lunch, and took her foreign language placement exam, her roommate arrived. It seemed to Irene that Nancy Morse had brought clothes enough for three girls. Mrs. Morse immediately went to work stowing the many color-coordinated outfits. Incredibly, she found a place for all the skirts, sweaters, and oxford shirts. Her secret was filling one suitcase with earth-toned outfits and another with casual wear. Both could fit under Nancy's bed. By the time Mrs. Morse left for her flight back to Michigan, new matching bedspreads were on Nancy and Irene's beds, photos of the Morse family and their large Dutch colonial home were neatly arranged on Nancy's dresser, and a list of important phone numbers was placed in her top desk drawer.

The moment her mother left, Nancy began peppering Irene with questions. "When did you get here?" "What's your major?" "Do you have a boyfriend?" "Adelson, that's Jewish, isn't it?" The rapid-fire inquiries felt like an interrogation. Irene thought Nancy's behavior odd, but she chalked it up to nervousness. After all, her mother had just left her alone in a place very far from home. Irene didn't mind the questions. They seemed harmless enough, with the exception of the last one; that one gave her pause.

Nancy went on to explain that she and her mother had opened a checking account at a nearby bank before coming to the dorm. That was something Irene could relate to.

"We did, as well, though we opened the account last week at a branch near my house in Brooklyn. I'd never even written a check before. I had to practice before we left home to make sure I was doing it right," Irene confessed.

"I've never written a check, either. Is it hard? Maybe you can show me how."

"I'd be glad to," Irene said.

"My mom opened the account with two-hundred and fifty dollars. She said she'd transfer another two-fifty on the fifteenth of each month. I'm not sure that will be enough," Nancy fretted. "I love shopping, and New York is *the* place to shop. Do you think I'll run short? I guess if I do, my mom can always wire more money."

Irene couldn't believe her ears. Thinking of her expenses for the entire freshman year, she and her parents had withdrawn four hundred dollars from her STS scholarship account and deposited it into her checking account. "I should think you'll have more than enough money. After all, our meals, our room, our tuition are all taken care of. I plan on using my checks for incidentals and books. I know books can be expensive."

"Oh, yeah," Nancy said. "My sister's at Mount Holyoke. She warned me about that."

"So did my sister."

"Where does she go to school?" Nancy asked.

"She's a junior at NYU," Irene explained. "Part of the reason I chose Barnard was because she's just a subway ride away. I know we'll both be busy, but maybe I'll get to spend some time with her on weekends."

"My sister is the last person I'd want to spend a weekend with. Talk about being a total drag. All she does is study."

"I'm sure we'll have our share of studying to do, too," Irene said. "After all, we're college students now."

"I'll do what I have to, but I'll tell you right now, I am no grind. We're young, our parents are nowhere to be seen, and there are thousands of guys right across the street. We can do whatever the hell we want. As for me, I plan on partying hard for the next four years and leaving this place with my MRS. degree."

§§§

It soon became clear that getting along with Nancy required strategizing. Having always shared a room with Annie, it wasn't as though Irene was used to having much privacy. But Nancy turned out to be what Grandma Bertha would call a *yenta*, a busybody who lived to gossip. Never before had Irene had to fend off the prying inquiries of someone like Nancy. She decided the safest bet was to say as little as possible and listen quietly as Nancy reported who was dating whom and which girl came from what she called, "real money." Sometimes Irene would feign sleep just to avoid another installment of Nancy's investigative reporting.

Though they marched to different drummers, somehow the girls co-existed. As the term progressed and the workload increased, Irene's classes and labs filled her days, and study sessions at the library filled her nights. During class, she hung on every word her professors uttered. She was an eager disciple, believing they had the power to reveal objective truth. She saw every task they assigned as an opportunity to learn something new. Annie had forewarned her about how bright Barnard students were; getting an A was not a foregone conclusion, even for a top student. But what separated Irene from most of her peers was her insatiable appetite for learning. When she overheard one girl say she was going to skip class, Irene couldn't imagine why anyone would choose to miss an opportunity to acquire new knowledge. Even before midterms, her inquiring mind and meticulous, insightful work caught the attention of her professors.

Outside the classroom though, Irene was less sure-footed. She couldn't put her finger on the exact cause, but she knew she was having a hard time connecting with the girls in the dorm. She'd never had a wide circle of friends or even a single best friend. In that sense, her sojourn in Washington was as unique as it was revelatory. She'd met peers with whom she'd felt completely at ease. She wasn't sure why, but she couldn't recreate that with the girls on her dorm floor. She had the sense they saw her as an outsider, "less than," inferior. When they referenced their summer homes on Nantucket or "the Vineyard," equestrian trials, and tennis competitions, Irene had nothing to contribute. They spoke of their travels halfway around the world the way Irene might talk about going to her Aunt Phyllis's house on Long Island. Many of their fathers were doctors, lawyers, and bankers; their mothers kept an active social calendar. A couple of the girls talked nonstop about how the preparations were going for their December debut to society at the Waldorf-Astoria. At least a third had gone to private school, Nancy included, some even to boarding school. For most of the girls, the highlight of the week was the next invitation to one of Columbia's fraternity parties, something that held no appeal to Irene.

One morning, when Irene went to brush her teeth after breakfast, she put her toiletry bag next to the sink being used by Evangeline Preston, one of the debutantes-to-be. Irene always admired how artfully Evangeline applied her make-up and was thinking she might pick up some pointers as she brushed her teeth, but Evangeline suddenly threw her cosmetics into her bag and moved to the other battery of sinks across the bathroom. Irene thought it odd, but said nothing. She brushed her teeth and then hurried off to English class.

That night, when Irene came back to her room after an evening in the library, Nancy was chomping at the bit to engage in a gossip fest. First she listed the girls who'd apparently snagged some "cute guys" from a Columbia fraternity. She moved on to the subject of Rosario Lopez, the quiet girl at the end of the hall who'd packed her bags and left for home the day before. Nancy questioned whether she'd left voluntarily or was asked to leave because of poor grades. Then she mentioned Evangeline.

"Evangeline and I always have lunch together after French class. You wouldn't believe what she told me at lunch today. She thought you had horns. No kidding. She said she saw the horns on Michelangelo's statue of Moses in Rome and figured all Jews had them. I had to tell her that I would have seen them if you had them since your hair is so thin. Isn't that hysterical?"

Irene was stunned. It took her a moment to think of what to say in response. "I'm astonished that a Barnard student could be so ignorant. Thank you for correcting her."

"Just between you and me, Evangeline is no fan of the Jews. She was talking at lunch about how it gives her the creeps that there are so many Jewish girls at Barnard and how mad her father would be if he knew the big donations he made were going to scholarship students like you. I never knew any Jewish kids until I came here, but I told Evangeline you're a good egg and that I have absolutely no problem rooming with you."

Irene felt herself trembling. She'd never encountered bald-faced anti-Semitism before, but she was determined not to reveal how it rattled her. She spoke slowly, using every ounce of resolve to keep her voice from quavering. "Thank you, Nancy. It's good to know I've helped broaden your horizons. We can only hope Evangeline's experience at Barnard will eventually have the same effect on her."

After Irene crawled into bed that night, sleep eluded her. How many more Barnard girls, she wondered, harbored the feelings Evangeline felt so free to express?

§§§

Her conversation with Nancy led to Irene feeling even more isolated. Though she'd kept to herself before, she'd never imagined girls might dislike her because she was Jewish. She continued to go to class, do her work, and eat alone in the dining hall, using an open textbook for company. It was only in her letters to Albert that she poured out her heart, telling him about her courses, her response to Nancy's recitation of Evangeline's vile sentiments, and how lonely she felt among the other girls. She freely admitted to him that she had to fight the urge to take the subway back to Flatbush every Friday afternoon. The lure of being enveloped in love was strong. But rather than turn tail and go home, she was trying hard to adhere to Barnard's motto, "Following the way of reason." She shared her analysis of her problem with Albert.

October 27, 1967

Dear Albert,

I can't tell you how much I enjoy your letters. Your descriptions of your life at Stanford jump off the page. You're not only a thoughtful science student, but also a wonderful writer. Your letters provide me with such lively entertainment!

In this letter I am going to explain a problem I am dealing with. Please think about it and, if you can, offer some advice.

As I've already told you, I am exceedingly happy in class, in my labs, in the library. My grades have exceeded my greatest expectations, with my lowest so far an A- on an inorganic chemistry test. I have not made any progress in making a friend, though. I still spend mealtimes alone. On Friday and Saturday nights, when the library is closed, I sometimes play my oboe in my room or go to movies on campus by myself. I have absolutely no interest in joining the others in getting drunk at parties at Columbia. I guess that makes me a grind. I imagine the other girls probably think that also makes me a dud.

I have tried to analyze the cause of my failure to connect with any of the girls. I refuse to believe it's due to anti-Semitism. Until I see further evidence beyond the hateful Evangeline, I have chosen to focus on other possible causes. For example, I've lived a very different life from most of the girls on my dorm floor. Another issue I've been thinking about is my age: I just turned sixteen. Nancy will be nineteen in a couple of months. Most other freshmen are at least a couple of years older than I. We are likely at different developmental stages. Couple that with the fact that we come from very different worlds (rich vs. working-class, Christian vs. Jewish, and well-traveled vs. local) and our differences are magnified. I know from studying Joe's pigeons that maturation for an individual member of the species cannot be rushed. Perhaps my relative youth is contributing to my isolation. What do you think of my analysis, Albert? I really value your opinion.

I hope you are continuing to make friends and enjoy your classes. It sounds as though you've landed in the perfect dorm at a great university. I am so happy for you.

Love,

Reenie

It took almost a week for one of Irene's letters to get to California and another week to receive a reply. If Albert was busy with exams or a particularly vexing problem set, it could be even longer. It was hard for Irene to be patient as she waited for Albert's view of her conundrum. But much to her surprise, only ten days after mailing her letter she received an envelope from Albert with extra postage marked "Air Mail."

November 2, 1967

Dear Reenie,

You? A dud? A grind? You've got to be kidding! Reading your letter made me wish Star Trek's transporter could beam me to Barnard so I could tell you in person how wrong you are. I don't know what those other girls are doing, but I know that you are taking full advantage of everything your professors, classes, and labs have to offer. That makes you a winner in my book. I am doing much the same as you. As daunting as my courses are, I've jumped into the deep end of the pool, and as hard as I swim, I'm just managing to keep my head above water. Who knows? Maybe one day it will get easier, but I'm not counting on it. Suffice it to say, my lowest grade is quite a bit lower than A-! But the point is, I am making the most of this opportunity to study and learn, just like you.

You may be onto something about being sixteen. Some things can't be rushed. I am not the same person I was two years ago. But I wouldn't let your relative youth worry you. Instead, I think you should seek out people who are as excited about your classes as you. Didn't you write me that half of the freshmen at Barnard graduated first or second in their high school class? That should add up to lots of possibilities for friendships. The truth is, all you need is one local friend (unfortunately I am your long-distance friend). You need someone to eat with, go to the movies with, have bull sessions with (some guys and I have one every night at nine during coffee break). I suggest you seek out a girl in one of your classes or labs who

seems as engaged as you. Step right up and introduce yourself. Strike up a
conversation. Make the first move. Ask her to go see a movie this weekend.
Your BOY friend slot is filled. Now go fill that GIRL friend slot.

Love,

Albert

   P.S. I just thought of something else, Reenie. Given your streak of A's,
is it possible that some of your classmates view you as the person who
ruins the curve? Ridiculous as it seems, that could be cause for resentment
— or even jealousy — among some.

   Albert's letter brought Irene to tears. He was her champion, much as
her parents were, and she and Albert weren't even related. What did he see
in her that she couldn't see? More than seven months had passed since
they'd been together in Washington. But instead of their connection fading,
it had grown stronger. Her heart quickened whenever she held one of his
letters; the memory of their kiss and embrace in Union Station burned
brightly still. Writing to him and reading the thoughts he put to paper were
the closest things to intimacy she'd ever known.

§§§

   Albert's friendship not only delighted Irene, it stiffened her spine. It
had never occurred to her to go on a mission to find a friend. When she
was a child, she had no interest in going roller skating or hanging out at the
playground with the neighborhood kids. She was always pleasant to the
other children, but she had trouble making small talk. Living on the
periphery of their world was enough for her. It was her books, her music,
and her family that brought her happiness. It was only after leaving home
that she realized how inexperienced she was in forging connections. Unless
she learned how, strangers would remain strangers, never progressing to
companions. Now, in keeping with Albert's instructions, she would keep a
sharp eye out for someone who had the potential to become a friend.

   A few days after receiving Albert's letter, she noticed a petite blond
girl in her biology lab working across the room. Even at a distance, Irene
could tell how absorbed she was in her experiment. They were among the

last ones out of the lab. As the girl reached for her pea jacket, Irene introduced herself. "Hi. I'm Irene Adelson. I noticed you were quite engrossed in the catalase experiment. What were your findings?"

"It was a neat experiment, though I already did a variant of it last year in AP biology," the girl said. She spoke with a slight accent that Irene couldn't place. "As I expected, the catalase enzyme broke down the peroxide. But what amazed me was how increasing the temperature or the pH increased the rate, but only up to a point. After that, it was like diminishing returns in economics. Oh, by the way, I'm Raisa, Raisa Sokolov," she said, extending her hand.

Some students at Barnard bonded over the hunt for a boyfriend, others over movies or politics or sports. Some made friends writing for the school newspaper, *The Bulletin*. But for Irene and Raisa, it was science that brought them together. The two continued their talk about the experiment over lunch. By the time they had to go to their next class, Irene asked Raisa if she was interested in seeing *Georgy Girl* the following night.

"*The Bulletin* had something about that. It's showing on campus this weekend, isn't it?"

Irene nodded.

"I meant to see it when it was in the movies last year. I like the Redgraves so much – all of them, the father Michael, and the kids Vanessa, Corin and Lynn. They're becoming something of an acting dynasty in the U.K. Sure. I'd love to go. "

Irene couldn't believe her ears. "That's great! Maybe you can tell me all about the Redgraves tomorrow night. Should we have dinner before we go?"

"Sounds good. Would it be okay if I brought along my roommate, Fredi? She might like to take in a flick."

"Sure," Irene said.

"Shall we say six, right here in the dining hall?"

"Six is perfect," Irene said. "See you and Fredi tomorrow."

Irene couldn't wait to write to Albert. His advice had worked like a charm.

§§§

Raisa Sokolov arrived at the dining hall the next night with three girls in tow. Although Irene was a bit uncertain when she saw the four of them walk toward her, she soon discovered what an affable group they were. Like the people she'd met in Washington, they were clever, curious, and approachable. Raisa's roommate Frederica (Fredi) Garcia was, like Irene, aiming for medical school. Meryl Paolongoli and Maxine (Max) O'Connor, roommates and neighbors from Raisa's dorm, were, like Raisa, planning on careers in research. It didn't take long for Irene to learn the girls played just as hard as they worked. A Friday and Saturday night did not pass without a plan. They took turns scouring *The Bulletin* for ideas: cheap rush tickets to performances at Lincoln Center, movies on campus or off, and even an occasional sports event were all fair game. Almost immediately and with no perceptible effort, the girls widened their circle to include Irene.

If being part of a group of friends was a new experience for Irene, getting to know each of the girls was like discovering a hidden treasure. Raisa was born in Israel to Jewish refugees from the Soviet Union, which explained why she was fluent in Russian, Hebrew, and English. She'd spent the last five years in Philadelphia, where her parents worked at the University of Pennsylvania. Fredi, one of the numerous valedictorians in the freshman class, was a product of a public high school in Queens. She was the social crusader of the group, fighting for parity in treatment between the Columbia men and the Barnard women. The issue that she was currently focused on was Barnard's curfew, which Fredi felt was patronizing and ridiculous.

One night at dinner Fredi was particularly miffed as she relayed a conversation she'd had with the Dean of Students about the effectiveness of curfew. "They think they're preserving my purity by making me come back to the dorm by eleven. But you know what I told the Dean? I can screw someone at one in the afternoon just as easily as at one in the morning."

Irene was aghast. "You used the word screw in speaking to the Dean?"

"Well, I used intercourse instead of screw, but yeah, that's just what I said. Not only that, I asked her why Columbia wasn't worried about preserving the boys' purity? She didn't have a response to that!" Fredi said, quite satisfied with herself.

Meryl, a native Floridian, was hands down the most socially adept person Irene had ever met. Meryl could interact just as effortlessly with the cook behind the grill as with the lecturer on DNA research. She also had enormous upper body strength from her high school varsity swimming career. Then there was Maxine, who hailed from Worcester, Massachusetts. Max, as everyone called her, was the only one of the group who was religious. By the time they met for breakfast every Sunday, she'd already been to mass at Corpus Christi Church on 121st Street. Although Irene had never felt the call of religion, she admired the spirituality that permeated Max's very being. She was one of the kindest and most thoughtful people Irene had ever encountered.

Of all the girls, Irene felt closest to Raisa, whose seriousness and focus on work felt so familiar. One night, as they were studying for a biology exam in the living room of Raisa's dorm, Irene discovered they had something else in common. When she got up to stretch, she walked over to the grand piano in the corner, pulled out the bench, and started to play "To Sir, With Love," a song that had been lodged in her head since seeing the movie the weekend before. It didn't take long before girls started wandering into the living room, drawn in by the music. Shyly at first, they began to sing along, and soon Raisa added her rich alto. Irene finished with a flourish just as her friend joined her on the bench.

"You've been holding out on me," Raisa teased. "I had no idea you could play."

Irene blushed. "Actually, I've been playing most of my life."

"Well, you're not the only one." Then, addressing the girls gathered around the piano, she asked, "What do you say to a little concert? How about the Beatles?"

There wasn't a naysayer in the group.

Raisa began playing and singing "All You Need is Love," with a voice richer and more powerful than Irene would have imagined possible from so small a person.

"Your turn, Irene. What else have you got?"

Irene didn't hesitate, immediately going into her rendition of "Penny Lane." Before long, more girls joined the impromptu singalong as Raisa and Irene took turns at the keyboard. Raisa was lead vocalist for "Good Day, Sunshine," "Yesterday," "Eleanor Rigby," and "Yellow Submarine." After finishing "Day Tripper," Irene checked the clock. Curfew was fast approaching. She reluctantly packed up her books, bid Raisa and the others goodnight, and headed back to her dorm.

She was on such a high from her adventure in music making that she skipped all the way to Brooks Hall. Maybe people like Evangeline despised her because she was a Jew. Perhaps others viewed her as the girl who ruined the curve on exams. But there was Raisa, and all those girls standing around the piano tonight. She never knew acceptance could feel so good.

CHAPTER SIX

GLADYS, MEYER AND GRANDMA BERTHA were delighted to have the girls back home for the Thanksgiving holiday. The house was livelier with the young ones around, even with Annie out dancing or reconnecting with high school friends much of the time. As for Irene, with the exception of a short reunion with Joe, Velocita, and the rest of the pigeons, she spent Wednesday to Sunday with the family. They walked together to the park, visited the library, saw *Wait Until Dark* at the Loew's Kings, and went grocery shopping. For Gladys and Meyer, it was almost as though the girls had never left for college.

That was precisely the problem for Irene. Though she'd looked forward to going home to the family she loved, what she hadn't factored in was how college had changed her; not until she was back in her family's embrace did she realize how much. Without any parental help or supervision she'd remembered to eat, done her own laundry, reconciled her checkbook, balanced a heavy academic load, and looked anti-Semitism in the eye. She even found time to make music on occasion. Now a home and community that had felt warm and secure seemed somehow small and confining. Worse, her parents' efforts to be attentive to her every need struck Irene as suffocating.

On the Saturday after Thanksgiving it came to a head when Gladys asked Irene if she could do her laundry.

"No, it's okay, Mom. They have washers and dryers on campus," Irene said.

"I know they do, but why should you struggle with doing laundry? Let me take that off your shoulders this one time. It will free you up to do something more fun," Gladys said.

"Mom, I said I was okay. You don't have to do my laundry. I'm a big girl now and can handle that and all sorts of far more difficult responsibilities on my own. You have to realize that after three months of living without your help, I've learned quite a lot about managing things."

Gladys's face fell. Her look of dejection sent shock waves through Irene, dredging up memories of her mother lying catatonic in the hospital bed.

Shoulders slumped, Gladys shook her head. Her voice was just above a whisper. "I'm sorry, Reenie. I'm very sorry. I was just trying to help. I can see I've made a mistake."

But Irene knew it was she who'd erred. She put down her book and went to embrace her mother. "You have nothing to apologize for. I'm the one who owes *you* an apology. What an ungrateful, selfish response to a kind and generous offer. You're the best mother anyone could ever have. Even now that we're older, you're always thinking of ways to make things easier for me and Annie."

Like a wilted flower that was given a much-needed watering, Gladys perked up. "Oh, sweetheart, I do try. One day I hope you'll know that feeling of wanting to make life easier or sweeter for your child."

"Annie and I hit the jackpot when we got you as our mom. I hope that if I ever have a child, I can be half as good a mother as you."

"When the time comes, you'll be terrific," Gladys said. "I know that, sure as I'm standing here."

"Well I'm certainly not ready to take care of anyone else, but I am starting to take care of a lot of things for myself, Mom. I'm growing up."

"I know, sweetheart. It's just that it's happening a little too fast for my liking. First Annie, and now you. I am going to have to try to remember that you're not my little girl anymore."

"I will always be your girl, Mom, just a grown-up version."

"So what do you think about the laundry?" Gladys said, trying again.

"It isn't necessary, but it would be very nice of you to help me out," Irene said.

"I know you can take care of it yourself, sweetie. Thanks for humoring me."

Grandma Bertha had listened quietly to the entire exchange. "Gladys, while you're making life easier and sweeter for Reenie, I wouldn't mind having my sheets and towels done."

"Thank God for you, Mama," Gladys said. "At least someone still needs me."

§§§

Annie's anti-war activism began during her freshman year at NYU. She thought the war was unjust and unnecessary, an aggressive, colonial incursion on the internal affairs of a sovereign nation halfway around the world. She felt compelled to work against it, not only to save the innocent people of Vietnam, but also the young Americans drawn into the war machine. She was a regular at anti-war demonstrations, both in New York and Washington, something that caused her parents great consternation.

Over bagels and lox on the Sunday before Annie and Irene were to return to school, the anti-war movement became the topic of conversation. "I'm really psyched about an upcoming protest. 'Stop the Draft' demonstrations are going to take place at induction centers all across the country during the first week of December," Annie explained. "We expect this one to be big, really big. I'll be going to the draft office in downtown Manhattan. Did you know that particular induction center 'processes' two hundred fifty guys every single day? It's disgusting. But we're going to do our best to put a stop to it."

Meyer and Gladys looked at one another. Senator Joseph McCarthy's relentless hunt for communists during the Red Scare of the 1950s was still fresh in their minds. They feared their daughter's political activism could endanger her future, particularly if she ran into trouble with the law. They'd seen countless images of protestors being hauled off to jail.

"Sweetie, do you really think you need to go?" Meyer asked. "What good will it do? You've been protesting for quite a while, and the war keeps getting bigger and bloodier. Every night on the news they report how many poor souls lost their lives in that horrible mess over there. It's awful; truly a national disgrace. Mom and I agree with you one hundred percent. We have no business being there. But you have to be careful. I'm sure there are powerful people in the government who don't take kindly to these demonstrations. It wasn't that long ago that the government rounded people up for not being 'patriotic' enough. Careers were ended. Lives were ruined. Mom and I don't want anything bad to happen to you."

"Dad, I am not crusading alone. The government is going to have to round up tens of thousands of people, because that's how many will be demonstrating during Stop the Draft week. Every one of my friends will be there. I wish Reenie would come, too. It's time she got her head out of her books and did something to put an end to the atrocities being committed by our government."

The censure caught Irene by surprise. Annie had always been a solicitous big sister and her criticism stung. "For your information, Annie, I know quite a bit about the war. I do read the paper, you know. As Dad says, we all agree with you. The point is, will your protests lead to a change in President Johnson's foreign policy?"

"Well, who says Johnson will be president after next year?" Annie countered. "We're hoping Eugene McCarthy will challenge him for the Democratic nomination. The protests going on all across the country make it abundantly clear that the people are ready for a radical change in our foreign policy. And besides, I am not someone who can just sit by and do nothing while innocent people are caught up in a nightmare. How will I be able to live with myself if I don't try to stop the war?"

After listening to both sides of the debate, Grandma Bertha weighed in. "I think Annie's right," she said. "Of course, I don't want her to get arrested, but I think a person has to stand up for what they believe. What if more people had stood up against the Nazis? Most people kept their heads down and did nothing. I'm not talking just about Germany, but right here in America, too. What if more people around the world had welcomed Jews who tried to get out of Europe, instead of slamming the door in their faces? What if people had stuck their necks out and said 'No, we're not allowing millions of people to be transported to their deaths?' So much suffering and loss of life could have been prevented. But people didn't have the courage to act on their convictions."

"Thank you, Grandma!" Annie said, getting up to give Bertha a hug and kiss. "I guess I get my social activism from you."

"No, *bubbelah[1]*. I had a big yellow stripe down my back until late in life. It's only since your grandfather died that I found my courage. It's the biggest regret of my life that it took so long," Bertha said, looking directly

---

[1] Sweetie or darling one

at Gladys. "But I'm glad you have the guts to stand up for your beliefs. It makes me very proud of you."

"Yes, we're proud," Gladys said, "we are, but promise me you'll be careful, Annie."

"You're my family, so you worry about me. But what about the boys who are getting drafted into this hellacious war? Their parents love them, too. We've got to do something to end the loss of life of so many innocents, Mom. And yes, I'll do my best to be careful, but putting it in perspective, my risks are nothing next to the eighteen year-old boy who, as we speak, is sitting on a transport plane headed to Saigon."

§§§

As Irene rode the subway back to Barnard, she re-lived the conversation that took place around the breakfast table that morning. Irene's admiration for her sister made her disapproval sting all the more. Irene could see that Annie had a point; she'd lived in a tightly circumscribed world. Annie's argument for protesting the war also seemed spot on. Even Grandma Bertha agreed that Annie was right to stand up for her beliefs. Irene could see it was time she did the same. By the time she'd gotten back to her dorm room, she'd decided to join Annie on December fifth at the demonstration in front of the Whitehall Street Selective Service office. It would start at 5 AM. She figured she could protest the war and be back in time for chemistry class at nine.

The night before the demonstration, Irene caught a few hours of sleep at her sister's Lower East Side apartment. In the dead of night, Annie, her roommates, and Irene crept down the apartment building's stairwell, and then took the subway to Whitehall Station. The moment the doors opened, they could hear the protestors on the street above them chanting repeatedly, "Hell, no, we won't go!" The instant they emerged from the station, they were caught up in the crush of the crowd. Street lights illuminated the thousands of protestors, many carrying signs above their heads. One in particular resonated with Irene: "*My Son Died in Vietnam. For What?*"

The protestors were met by hundreds of uniformed NYPD officers lining the barricades in front of the nine-story red brick induction center. Officers were escorting people who'd crossed the barricades to paddy wagons lined up in the street. Irene clung to her sister's hand in the sea of protestors. Then Annie started yelling, "Hey, hey, LBJ, how many kids have you killed TODAY!!" Her voice was one of many, alternating between that chant and, "One, two, three, four, we don't want your fuckin' WAR!!" At first Irene felt shy about joining in, but soon she was shouting at the top of her lungs along with the rest of the demonstrators. Within an hour of their arrival, Irene had witnessed hundreds of anti-draft protestors being taken into custody. Among them were pediatrician Benjamin Spock, writer Susan Sontag, and poet Allen Ginsberg,

On her subway ride uptown, she couldn't shake the images of the police arresting people exercising their rights of assembly and speech. It seemed unreasonable and unjust that they could be taken into custody for their peaceful protest. Thinking about it only reinforced her newly-energized opposition to the war. And then there was the sign, *"My Son Died in Vietnam. What For?"* She thought of Albert, who was free to live the life of his choosing because of his student deferment; those eighteen year-old males without it were being sent to the jungles of Vietnam to kill or be killed. The realization brought home the fear that boys just a couple of years older than she had to live with every day.

She got to chemistry class minutes before it started. Her first foray into political protest had left her hoarse and exhausted. As the professor began his lecture on coordination compounds, Irene realized her attention was now divided. There were her studies, which she loved, and there was the anti-war movement, which deserved her support. Somehow she had to do right by them both.

§§§

Irene was headed for bed when the phone in the dorm corridor rang a few minutes after eleven. She picked up and was pleasantly surprised to hear Annie's voice. "Hey, Reenie, there's going to be a strategy meeting on Saturday morning at Columbia. It's sponsored by SDS, you know, Students for a Democratic Society. The point is to take stock of the demonstrations at the induction center. I'm going and I thought you might like to come along."

"Saturday? How long do you think it will run? I have a fifteen-page paper on George Eliot due for English Lit on Monday, a calculus exam on Tuesday, and a chemistry lab to write up."

"Okay, then. I just thought I'd let you know," Annie said. "I'd better go."

"Don't hang up, Annie. I'm not saying no."

"Hey, it's okay if you don't want to go, Reenie. We each have our priorities."

"The meeting *is* a priority for me. I'm committed to working against the war. It's just a matter of how to fit it in."

"Welcome to the world of the student protestor. We get creative in fitting our work in with our anti-war activism."

"Okay, I'll figure something out. Tell me when and where," Irene said, "and I'll be there."

§§§

Irene asked Raisa and the other girls if they wanted to join her in going to the meeting. Though sympathetic to the cause, they begged off, saying they were buried in work. Irene knew the feeling, but she also knew she wanted to hear what Columbia students against the war had to say. She got up before sunrise that Saturday so she could get some work done before meeting Annie at the 116th Street subway station at 10:30. Irene arrived first, and was surprised when Annie emerged from the station with a young man.

"Reenie, this is Spence," Annie said, introducing the tall, good-looking guy. "I guess now's as good a time as any to tell you that Spence is my old man."

Irene's puzzlement must have shown on her face.

Annie clarified. "Reenie, Spence is my *boyfriend*. We've been together for over a year."

"Nice to finally meet you," the bearded young man said. "Annie's told me a lot about you. I hear you're generally the smartest person in any room, and also really cool. Glad you've joined forces with us in the movement."

Taken aback, Irene cleared her throat and extended her hand. "Nice to meet you, too, Spence; though I don't see how I can be as smart as you say if I didn't figure out for over a year that my sister had a boyfriend."

He smiled. "Chalk it up to Annie's amazing skill at covert action."

"I guess I'll have to sharpen my observation skills," Irene said, trying to mask how hurt she was that her sister had kept something so important from her.

Irene remained quiet as the three walked the few blocks to the meeting. When they got inside the basement level lecture hall, the air was warm and stale. About fifty people were milling about, mostly male, nearly all with long, unkempt locks and at least a few days' growth of facial hair. Spence seemed to be acquainted with many of them. Annie pointed out members of Columbia's SDS steering committee. One of them, Steve Shapiro, called the meeting to order. Irene thought the big, burly fellow dressed in a plaid shirt, jeans, and boots, looked more like a lumberjack than an Ivy League college student.

Irene had read in the *New York Times* that despite the daily demonstrations at Whitehall, over a thousand young men had been inducted there that week. She came to this meeting hoping the SDS leaders would lay out steps to prevent thousands more boys from being sucked into the seemingly unstoppable war machine. Instead of sharing a strategic plan though, they focused their rhetoric on condemning President Johnson, J. Edgar Hoover and the FBI, as well as the Columbia University administration. The NYPD was lambasted as pigs who hauled off peaceful protestors to jail. There were repeated denunciations of blood-sucking capitalism, which was cited as the cause of subjugation of working people, minorities and women. But as to actions aimed at stopping thousands of eighteen year-olds from being inducted, the only idea discussed was the possibility of occupying Whitehall. Given the huge police presence and the mass arrests of the protestors over the last week, Irene thought the idea unrealistic at best.

As they walked out, Annie put her arm around Irene. "Thanks for coming, little sister. Glad to see you're widening your horizons."

"Thanks for suggesting I go to the protest," Irene said. "I feel it was one of the most important things I've ever done. As for this meeting, though, I didn't really get the point."

"I admit I was expecting more planning. But I give them credit for keeping the energy levels high," Annie said. "Plus, you can meet some really interesting people at these gatherings."

"No kidding, Irene. That's how your sister and I met. I will be forever grateful to the movement for that," Spence said, embracing Annie in the middle of West 121st Street. She leaned into what turned out to be a very deep and lengthy kiss.

Irene had little to do but watch. When they were done, she said, "I think you should bring Spence home to meet Mom, Dad, and Grandma."

Annie spun her around so fast Irene didn't know what hit her. "You can stop right there, Reenie. Spence is going nowhere near Mom, Dad, or Grandma. Got it?"

Irene was so startled she could hardly speak. "But…but why? Why are you keeping him a secret? Are you ashamed of our family?"

"That's ridiculous. Why would you even suggest something like that? I'm proud of what Mom and Dad have accomplished, despite the hardships they've endured as working people in a capitalist society."

"I frankly can't imagine any other reason you would keep your boyfriend from them."

"Well maybe you're not as smart as I thought," Annie said.

Spence felt the need to step in. "Annie, play nice. Your sister just learned about us. Give her some time."

But Irene persisted. "I admit I don't have a lot of experience in this area, but isn't it customary to introduce a long-time boyfriend to your family?"

"Not this boyfriend," Annie said.

Irene was baffled. She turned to Spence. "Wouldn't you like to meet them? Our parents are really lovely and our grandmother thinks we're right to protest the war. Mind you, she's seventy-four years old!"

"I don't doubt your family's great, but the relationship your sister and I have is complicated. It's definitely not for parents — not yours, not mine. Annie, what do Jews call men like me?"

"Spencer Robertson, you're nothing but a *schagetz*[1]," Annie cackled, castigating him with her pointed index finger.

"That's right. I'm a *schagetz*," Spence agreed. "That's one strike against me, but your sister has three strikes against her, at least as far as my parents are concerned."

Irene objected. "But how can that be? Everyone likes Annie, and I do mean everyone."

"Did I fail to mention my rich, privileged WASP parents are closeted anti-Semites? I don't think they'd take too well to a Jewish scholarship student who advocates for the redistribution of wealth."

---

[1] Gentile male

"And don't forget the part about you being next in line to run your family's large and highly profitable business," Annie added. "My father sells shirts in Macy's."

"So you *are* embarrassed by what Daddy does for a living," Irene said.

"Absolutely not true," Annie protested. "But I do understand our society's class stratification. Spence's parents are expecting him to pair off with a girl from the upper class, and there's no fuckin' way that's me. And don't forget, our parents have expectations, too. Not only is Spence a *schagetz*, he's a politically radical *schagetz*. I don't think he'd meet with their approval."

"I think you're selling them short," Irene said. "It is possible Mom, Dad and Grandma might like Spence even though he's not Jewish. And they've voiced their opposition to the war many times."

"Let's just get something straight." Annie said, looking Irene directly in the eye. "That kumbaya moment is never going to happen. Here's the bottom line: I've brought you into my confidence and I'm swearing you to secrecy. Say nothing about Spence to the family."

§§§

Despite her disappointment with the SDS meeting, Irene felt it had been an important morning. She'd discovered that Annie had been living something of a secret life. She wondered why her sister had decided to finally share her secret with her. Could it be that she'd proven herself worthy in Annie's eyes by joining the anti-war movement? She'd looked up to Annie for as long as she could remember, but now Irene worried there were other things her sister might be keeping from her.

She spent the rest of that Saturday writing her paper in the library. It was actually a relief to concentrate on Eliot's portrayal of poverty in *Middlemarch* rather than the morning's revelations. Afterwards Irene returned to the dorm, stopping as she did on most days to see if there might be a letter from Albert. She smiled when she saw his familiar stationery in her mailbox. She ran up the stairs, curled up on her bed, and opened the envelope with care.

December 3, 1967

Dear Reenie,

Given Stanford's quarter system, I am in the throes of the crazy last weeks of this round of courses. I have so much work to do and exams to study for that I'm barely sleeping four hours a night. Some people can do that without a problem. I, unfortunately, am not one of them. I am dragging all the time. Being sleep deprived doesn't help me do my best work, but I also can't imagine how I'd get things done if I slept more than a few hours a night.

Just so you don't worry, I am not alone in this madness. All my buddies are in the same predicament. I guess there's no way out of this but to just plow through.

Speaking of which, I am looking forward to the Christmas break. Not only will this all be over soon, but my parents wrote that my aunt and uncle have invited us to their house in New Jersey. It's about four hundred fifty miles from Cleveland, so we don't go very often, but my uncle is making a surprise party on Christmas Day for my aunt's fiftieth birthday. We'll be staying for about a week.

Which leads me to the question I have been dying to ask you since I heard the news: Will you be in Brooklyn over Christmas? If so, I would like nothing better than to spend time with you. We can have fun making plans. I am up for anything, from hanging out at your house to exploring the streets of Manhattan. You name it, and I'm on board. We'll make it into a fun adventure.

I'd better get my nose back to the grindstone.

Love,

Albert

PS Sorry to be so negative about school, but I think it's just the exhaustion talking.

§§§

In a rapid-fire volley of airmail letters, Irene and Albert laid out possibilities for their five days together in New York City. Albert was emphatic that he wanted to come to Irene's house and introduce himself to her family, something she found bittersweet in light of Annie and Spence's situation. She and Albert decided he would meet her family on their first day together. It would take him two hours on an assortment of trains to get from New Jersey to Brooklyn. To let her know he'd arrived in Penn Station, he'd call Irene's number and let it ring twice. An hour after getting the signal, she would meet him at the subway station near her apartment.

Irene woke up on the day after Christmas so excited she could hardly eat breakfast. Once she heard the phone ring twice, she counted down the minutes until she would see Albert again. She got to the station early, just in case he arrived ahead of schedule. As she waited, she wondered if their long separation would make them shy with one another. They'd shared a single kiss nine months ago, but since then they'd revealed so much of themselves in their letters. As she waited she thought she saw him many times, but when he finally emerged from the train, there was no mistaking the tall, slender boy with the head full of curls. Their eyes locked and it was as though no time at all had passed since they'd been together. She opened her arms wide and they embraced. "Just so you know," Albert whispered in her ear, "this is the moment that kept me going through those last, terrible weeks of the quarter."

Irene studied his face. "I have to say you look no worse for wear. Maybe just a bit taller?"

"It's funny how my jeans shrank since arriving at Stanford. Who knew you could grow in college?"

"You wear your enhanced height very well, Albert. I really have to look up to see your eyes now."

As she tilted her head, Albert kissed her gently on the lips. Scores of passengers hurried by, but the couple was oblivious to them all. "I can't believe you're really here," Irene said. "Thank you for traveling all this way. Come, it's time to meet the women in my family."

"Just the women?"

"My dad sends his regrets and his regards. He works in retail and the day after Christmas is his busiest day of the year."

They walked the five blocks hand in hand and arrived to a warm welcome from Gladys and Bertha, who were anxious to meet the first young man in Reenie's life. Even Annie seemed happy for her sister. They were all impressed that Alfred had traveled from Cleveland — by way of New Jersey — to see Reenie. Gladys and Bertha felt it only right to provide him with a meal fit for a kosher king: matzo ball soup, sandwiches piled high with homemade pastrami, potato and kasha knishes, and dill pickles. Annie provided the dessert. The aroma of her homemade chocolate chip cookies greeted Irene and Albert the moment they walked through the door.

At lunch Albert and the family sat around the table and talked as though they'd known each other forever. Everyone enjoyed the meal, and Albert had seconds of everything. Gladys and Bertha got a kick out of watching the tall, skinny boy eat with such gusto.

"Mrs. Adelson, Mrs. Goldstein, I don't know how you knew I'd be so hungry, but this meal really hit the spot," Albert said. "I can tell you one thing, if you opened a restaurant near Stanford, there would be lines out the door."

"Are there a lot of students at Stanford who would appreciate a kosher deli?" Bertha asked.

Albert's light-hearted demeanor changed. "Let's just say Stanford hasn't covered itself in glory in terms of admitting students from all religious and ethnic backgrounds. Although theoretically non-denominational, it only recently dropped its quota for Jews. I have met other Jewish kids, though. We have a small Hillel office in the basement of an old building called the Clubhouse."

"I'm happy you've met some *lantsmen* at college," Bertha said. "Can we offer you a cup of tea or coffee? Annie made a batch of her scrumptious homemade cookies. She's turned out to be the best baker in the entire family."

"Coffee please. It's become my beverage of choice since going to college. And the aroma of Annie's cookies baking in the oven won me over the minute I arrived."

After helping with the dishes, Irene and Albert headed out for a visit to the Brooklyn Museum to see its Egyptian collection. As soon as they left, Bertha didn't hold back on her assessment of Reenie's young man. "That Albert has beautiful manners. The poor kid was starving but he always asked if he could serve anyone else before taking another portion. And did you see how he treats Reenie? I was watching very carefully because small things can tell you a lot about a person. He helped her with her coat and opened the door for her. It's obvious that he's crazy for her. He sat on trains for two hours to get here and then he'll have to sit for another two hours to get back to his aunt's house. A boy doesn't do that for just anyone. I think he may be serious."

"Mama!" Gladys scoffed. "They're just kids. How can he be serious? I can't argue about Albert's manners, though. I couldn't believe he helped wash and dry the dishes. And the truth is, he and Irene are awfully cute together. It'll be nice for them, for as long as it lasts."

Annie took this all in, unable to quash the envy rising within her. No matter how polite or thoughtful Spence was, she could never imagine him being welcomed into her family home. Though her parents weren't religious, they would see her relationship with Spence as a betrayal — of their roots, of their traditions, of their people. But Albert Jaffe, in addition to being nice-looking, smart, and well-mannered, was a member of the tribe, something Spence could never be.

§§§

The week with Albert was filled with more happy moments than Irene could count. He'd done his homework, suggesting sights they might see and things they might do so that each day was filled with adventure from morning to night. They had lunch in Chinatown, took the Staten Island ferry, visited the Statue of Liberty, and went to the Observation Deck of the Empire State Building, all new experiences for them both. Irene told Albert about Lincoln Center's rush tickets for students, which made it possible for them to enjoy a concert by the New York Philharmonic. They saw *The Graduate*, which they both loved. Though Irene protested each and every time, Albert insisted on paying for everything. They also spent lots of time walking, one day from the Battery to Central Park, and the Cloisters to Columbia's campus on another. They never ran out of things to talk about, with topics running the gamut from their new college friends to politics. Albert was in complete agreement with Irene's views on the war. They both believed in ending the draft and bringing the troops home. Irene saw it as further evidence that they were two people entirely in sync.

On their last afternoon together, Irene brought Albert up to her dorm at Barnard, which was open for the students who couldn't go home for the holidays. When they arrived at Brooks Hall, the door was open and there was no one at the reception desk. Rather than having to sneak Albert in, as girls normally did when they wanted to bring a boy to their room, Irene took him by the hand and led him up the stairs. Though they had shared many kisses over the last days, finally they could be alone together. They made out without restraint, stopping now and again to talk. They even dozed off, their arms wrapped around one another. Of all the time they'd spent together, these moments were the sweetest. When their time was coming to a close, Albert cupped his hands around Irene's face and said, "You are the best thing that's ever happened to me."

"You probably say that to all the girls you date."

"I swear to you that those words have never passed my lips until this moment."

"You've changed my life, too, Albert. I've never known anyone like you."

"I know being so far apart makes it hard. I could see how you might want a boyfriend closer by, like across the street, for example. But I am hereby applying for the job of Reenie Adelson's boyfriend. If I get it, I promise to make the most of every chance to see you — that means vacations and summer break. I mean it."

Irene smiled. "Well, let me see. Hmm. After a quick but thorough consideration of your application, I have decided to accept your offer. You are not only my boyfriend, you're my best friend."

"You wouldn't kid about a thing like that, would you?" Albert asked.

"No, I wouldn't. Meeting you has changed me in all good ways. I wish we were geographically closer, but we've done pretty well these last nine months."

"It won't be another nine months, Reenie, I promise. I'll figure something out."

"Letters. Lots and lots of letters. And I've been pretty stingy with my scholarship money. I think I could afford a long distance call to California every now and then."

"That sounds great."

Through Irene's window, they could see the sun low in the sky; it was time to get Albert to Penn Station. His family was planning on driving through the night to Cleveland. Their precious interlude was coming to an end; when it might be repeated was anyone's guess.

CHAPTER SEVEN

A T THE START OF THE SECOND TERM of her freshman year, Irene felt like an old hand at college. The GPA she'd earned during her first term was even higher than she'd expected, putting her at the top of Barnard's freshman class. She'd been singled out for a cash prize for her performance in inorganic chemistry, something that made her parents extremely proud. The recognition of her hard work pleased Irene, but she was just as proud of the friendships she'd formed with Raisa, Meryl, Fredi, and Max. Most of all, she prized the relationship she had with Albert. Despite two phone calls since he'd left for home, she missed him terribly. Their faithful letter-writing continued, each pouring their hearts out to the other in long, weekly missives. As the new term began, Irene took stock of her life, declaring it richer and more satisfying than she ever imagined possible.

Once classes started up, she was as meticulous as ever in her studies, but she made sure to carve out time to remain active in the anti-war movement. Her motives were mixed; not only did she believe in the cause, it was the cause that connected her to Annie and Spence. At their urging she read *Vietnam: An Anti-War Comic Book*, by the civil rights activist Julian Bond. When she finished that they gave her the *Autobiography of Malcolm X, Soul on Ice*, by Eldridge Cleaver, and the *Souls of Black Folks* by W.E.B. DuBois. Every couple of weeks, she would spend a weekend afternoon with them. Sometimes they'd take in a movie; other times they'd engage in high-spirited discussions about something in the news or the nature of civil society. Irene was in awe of the knowledge they'd gleaned from their studies, their readings, their activism. But, as Spence pointed out, they'd been reading, thinking, and learning about those issues far longer than she. His advice: "Give yourself time, Reenie. Be patient. You'll get there, too." Soon she was looking at Spence as not only her sister's boyfriend, but as her friend. She was so pleased that he and Annie had decided to let her into their world.

§§§

Perhaps it was because she was so busy that the term seemed to fly by. Albert was true to his word about doing whatever it took to be with Irene. He made another odyssey to New York at the end of his winter semester in March. This time, he stayed with a college friend whose family lived on the Upper East Side of Manhattan, which simplified the logistics of being together. However, Irene was not on her spring break, so Albert found himself sitting in on her classes, generally the lone male in a sea of females. His presence in the common areas of the dorm also caused a stir. Many were surprised that the studious Irene Adelson had such a handsome and agreeable boyfriend, perhaps none so much as Evangeline Preston.

They had a wonderful few days together, albeit very different from Christmas break. Albert got to meet Irene's friends, whom he immediately took a liking to, and they to him. The girls took turns having him as a guest in the dining halls, sparing him the need to buy meals. When he sat in on a jam session with Irene, Raisa, and Meryl — who turned out could play a mean tambourine — he learned of Irene's prodigious musical talent. Every day he spent with her seemed to unearth another delightful quality. It made him all the more taken with her.

As much as Albert enjoyed getting to know Irene's friends, he hungered for time alone with her. Thanks to Nancy's busy social life, she was often out and about, which opened up the possibility of some private time. The dorm rule was that if a male visitor was in a room, the door had to be kept open a book's width. The standing joke at Barnard was that a matchbook was also a book, and that's precisely what Irene and Albert employed to have some privacy. This time, their make-out session proceeded beyond French kissing to "second base," with Albert exploring beneath Irene's blouse. It was the most erotic experience either had known, awakening something new in each of them. Irene felt her underwear grow wet as Albert's penis became hard.

On Albert's last night in New York, they celebrated by going to a fondue restaurant on the Upper West Side. They both enjoyed spearing a toasted bread cube with a long fork before immersing it in the hot, melted cheese. It was a messy and delicious affair. When they'd nearly finished all the cheese in the fondue pot, Albert said, "Here's a riddle, Reenie. Where do you think I'll be working this summer?"

"Riddles generally offer a clue or two," Irene pointed out. "After all, the possibilities for your summer employment are endless."

"You want a clue? Here's one: It's a famous institution that studies astronomical phenomena."

"Are you going to work for NASA?"

"Well, I would, if NASA were in Manhattan," Albert said, unable to wipe the smile from his face.

"You're going to work on astronomy in Manhattan?"

"You're getting warmer," Albert said with glee.

"That narrows things down quite a bit. I don't know much about where astronomy is studied in the city. Actually, all I can think of is the Hayden Planetarium. Are you going to work at the Hayden Planetarium?" Irene asked.

"You are correct! I think that deserves a reward," Albert said, reaching across the table to deliver a kiss.

"Holy cow! I can't believe you're going to be here all summer long. How did you arrange that?" Irene asked. "And from so far away? I'm in awe of your ingenuity."

"I had some help. My professor put in a good word for me. He went to school with the assistant director."

"And you're a brilliant, Stanford-trained young scientist. That didn't hurt either," Irene said, her face glowing in the candlelight. "Where will you live?"

"That's something I haven't worked out yet. But I have a few months to figure it out."

"To think we'll have the whole summer together. I haven't even thought about getting a summer job yet and you're all set. It's only March. You're incredible, Albert!"

"I promised you I would take every opportunity to be with you and I am a man of my word."

"Yes you are. And I love you for it," Irene said.

"Did I hear the four-letter word I've been waiting for?" Albert asked, grinning like the cat who swallowed the canary.

Irene blushed. "It's a figure of speech, Albert."

"Oh, so you don't love me?" he teased.

"Well, I wouldn't say that."

"So you do love me, which is fine, because I love you and I am not afraid to say it. Here, watch." Albert stopped the waitress who was balancing a heavy tray on her shoulder. "Excuse me, ma'am, I just want you to know that I love this girl."

The waitress looked at Albert and then at Irene. "Well, enjoy it while it lasts," she said, before continuing on her way.

"That's not exactly the reaction I was hoping for, but I hope I made my point."

"Yes, you did. But don't expect me to be stopping strangers to tell them I love you," Irene said, "even though...well...I do love you."

"You do?" Albert asked.

"Yes, I do," Irene replied.

"As long as you tell me, Reenie, I don't care if you don't tell another living soul."

§§§

The spring of 1968 saw the Columbia and Barnard campuses rocked by protest as a critical mass of hot-button issues came to the fore. Students raised a hue and cry after an SDS activist discovered Columbia's ties to the Institute for Defense Analysis, a think tank conducting weapons research in support of the Vietnam War. A long-simmering conflict between Columbia and the Harlem community erupted over Columbia's appropriation of public land in Morningside Park for the construction of a university gym. Across Broadway on the Barnard campus, a student co-habiting with her boyfriend faced expulsion after violating the rule prohibiting off-campus residence unless the student was working as domestic household help. Fredi started a petition calling for Barnard to shed the *in loco parentis* doctrine, as Columbia already had done for its male students. The petition garnered the signatures of more than half the Barnard student body. Then on April 4th, Martin Luther King was assassinated.

Things came to a head on April 23rd when SAS, Students' Afro-American Society, occupied Columbia's Hamilton Hall in protest of the planned gymnasium. Then white students from SDS occupied Columbia President Grayson Kirk's office suite in Low Library. Soon, three more buildings were occupied by Barnard and Columbia students. Activists mobilized a strike, paralyzing both colleges. In a show of solidarity, protesters from across the country flocked to Morningside Heights, joining journalists and photographers covering the student revolt for the national media.

Annie and Spence, in full support of the protestors, were among the first to arrive. Irene, too, felt great sympathy with the occupiers' grievances, but, unlike many other students, she had misgivings about their tactics. When she heard the Mathematics building had been taken over, she couldn't imagine how canceling her calculus class would remedy any of the issues at hand. Making education a victim of political protest seemed counterproductive. Irene did cheer up a bit, though, when her calculus professor pulled a chalkboard from the occupied Mathematics building and set up his class outside. She was one of the few students who attended.

Annie and Spence shared none of Irene's ambivalence. They were working to put an end to the misuse and abuse of power by the government, military-industrial complex, police, and college administrators. They saw the takeover of buildings by Columbia's SDS as the start to a revolution that would toss out the privileged white men who used the levers of power to maintain a status quo rife with bigotry, sexism, and economic inequality. That so many of Columbia's SDS members sprang from that very same powerful, patrician class was something they chose to overlook. After all, that was Spence's pedigree, as well.

A number of communal apartments rented by activists bordered the Columbia campus. Annie and Spence used one in particular — nominally belonging to SDS leader Steve Shapiro — as a place to crash, to shower, and to make food for those occupying the buildings. It was there they created signs out of oak tag and markers expressing their grievances: *Power to the People, Law and Order = Racism, Self-determination for Vietnam and Black America,* and *Let the People of Harlem Decide Columbia's Fate.* As for Irene and her friends, since most of their classes were no longer meeting, they had time to work on signs in the communal apartment, too. Irene's favorites were *In Loco Parentis is a Relic of*

Patriarchy and, in reference to the proposed gym that would have a separate basement entrance for Harlem residents, *Gym Crow*.

Together with her friends, each day Irene stood outside Low Library proudly holding her signs aloft and singing "Solidarity Forever." Sometimes they would go with Annie to the apartment to make food for the occupiers. Irene found it odd that the women in the anti-war movement were doing the same type of work women traditionally did: buying food, cooking, serving. Still, she enjoyed the atmosphere at the apartment, which was a mixture of celebration and resolve.

On Saturday night, four days after the start of the occupation, about thirty protestors congregated in the apartment; Irene, Raisa, Fredi, Annie, and Spence were among them. The ostensible reason for the gathering was to plan for the next day's protests, but people were ready to take a break after four days of shouting, chanting, and sleep-deprivation. Irene noticed guys and girls alike walking through the door with brown bags filled with tall, narrow-necked bottles. The lights were dimmed in favor of candles and Joni Mitchell's "Chelsea Morning" blared from the stereo's speakers. A few dog-tired protestors slept gape-mouthed on worn-out armchairs. Others were drinking sangria and passing around reefers which, as Fredi explained to Irene, were hand-rolled marijuana cigarettes. Someone in the corner pronounced the hashish being shared as "outta sight." Irene was surprised when she saw Annie accept the pipe, inhale deeply and hold her breath. It occurred to her that drugs might be yet another of her sister's secrets. It gave her a moment's pause. Though she had no interest in experimenting with either the marijuana or hashish, she gave the sangria a try. She thought it tasted like a delicious variant of fruit juice. She liked her first cup so much, she had another. Soon, she had to use the toilet.

The hundred-watt bulb in the bathroom was a bit startling. She looked around and thought someone ought to give the room a good scrubbing. Afterwards, she stepped out into the dimly lit hallway, hoping Fredi and Raisa were ready to call it a night. They'd been warned *ad infinitum* by the Barnard staff not to walk alone after dark in the area surrounding the campus. If her friends were amenable, they could head back to campus together. But before Irene made it back to the living room, she felt a hand on her arm. In the blink of an eye she was pulled into a pitch black room. A giant of a man pinned her against the wall and pressed his body against hers.

Irene struggled to get free. "What's going on? What are you doing? Let go of me," she demanded. "I need to get back to my friends."

"This is about what *I* need. You don't have your sister's rack, but you're fine in that school girl kind of way." Then he put his big hands all over her chest. Irene was horrified. No one but Albert had ever touched her there. And now this stranger was kneading her breasts. She tried to place the voice. She'd heard it before. If she could call her captor by name, perhaps he'd release her, but no name came to mind. She decided to appeal to his better angels.

"I know you're a good person because you're here, working to end the war, to better the lives of the working class," she said as she felt his hand grab her rear end. "As an activist for equality, I'm sure you recognize a woman's right to free movement and self-determination."

"That bullshit? Every man with a cock knows a woman needs to be managed. Stop being so uptight. I'll take care of everything. You're gonna love it."

When he turned the lock in the door, Irene panicked. But just then her captor began to cough, and his grip loosened. She seized the moment, unlocking the door, but the instant she did, he gripped her by her hair. Her head lurched back hard; she thought something in her neck must have broken. He locked the door again with his free hand and then pushed her onto the bed. Irene began to scream for help. That's when he got on top of her and covered her mouth and nose with his mitt-like hand.

"Shut up, bitch, or I'll shut you up."

Like a trapped animal, she struggled to breathe, flailing under the weight of her attacker's massive body. Frantic, she dug her nails into his face. Now it was his turn to bellow as he hauled off and punched her in the face. Her skull snapped backwards and she saw stars.

"You wanna play rough? I'll show you rough. He ripped open her blouse, pulled on her bra until her breasts were exposed, then bit her on the nipple.

Irene cried out in pain. "Oh, God. Please. I'm begging you to stop!"

"You're ruining the mood, bitch. Shut the fuck up!" He slapped her hard across the face.

She whimpered as he put his hands all over her bare breasts. Then she felt him fumbling for something. A moment later he thrust his hardened penis into her mouth.

"There bitch, suck my dick."

She choked as he drove his penis into the back of her throat. And then, when she was sure she was going to die, a warm, sticky liquid began spurting into her mouth. That's when she started to gag and retch. Realizing what was about to happen, her attacker leapt off her just as she vomited on the bed.

"You fuckin' cunt! Get the hell outta here before I make you lap it up."

He shoved Irene off the bed with such force she crashed onto the floor. She lay sprawled, her head and neck throbbing, the taste of semen and vomit mixed in her mouth. She got on all fours and crawled to the door, reaching for the knob to pull herself up. Instinctively, she pushed her breasts back into what was left of her bra and pulled the ripped ends of her blouse together before unlocking the door. Then she went in search of Annie. Annie would make things all right.

Holding onto the wall to steady herself, she made her way to the living room. It was so poorly lit it took a moment to make out Annie on the sofa. She went to her, wanting to scream, but when she opened her mouth, nothing came out. Annie was too high to notice her little sister's distress, but Spence realized immediately that something was terribly wrong. He led Irene into the kitchen where the light was somewhat brighter. That's when he saw the tattered, vomit stained blouse, the blood oozing from a cut under her swelling eye, the wild hair and the bloodied fingernails.

"Oh my God. Who did this to you?"

Barely audible, she mouthed, "I don't know."

"Let me see your eye. It's swelling up fast. Who the hell did this to you?" he asked again.

That's when Steve Shapiro walked into the kitchen, the blood fresh on his cheeks from where Irene had dug in her nails. "Hey, has anyone seen the fuckin' ice bucket?"

Spence took one look at Irene's bloodied fingernails and then, he hauled off and slugged Shapiro, first in the nose and then in the gut. Normally he would have been no match for the brute of a man, but unlike Shapiro, Spence was sober. When Shapiro crashed to the kitchen floor Spence kicked him as hard as he could.

"You sonofabitch. You fuckin' asshole. How could you? And to Irene, of all people? "

By now, a crowd had assembled in the kitchen, Raisa and Fredi among them. Raisa took one look at Irene and, tiny though she was, she pushed her way through the mass of people. "Oh God. I'm so sorry, Irene. Let me take care of you. I've got to get you to a doctor."

Irene stood glassy-eyed and expressionless.

"Everyone move!" Raisa yelled. "This girl has been assaulted, I'm assuming by that disgusting piece of shit on the floor. She needs medical attention. Move! Everybody! Now!"

It was as though the seas parted. Everyone stepped aside as Raisa guided Irene out of the kitchen. Spence shook Annie out of her torpor and Fredi grabbed all of their coats. Together they hailed a Checker cab and asked the driver to take them to the nearest hospital.

§§§

The emergency room at Harlem Hospital might have been a source of succor as well as medical treatment that night, but the doctor who treated Irene worked silently, stitching up the cut under her eye, rotating her head and neck, and cleaning out the bite mark on her breast. When he was done, he remarked, "I see your boyfriend got a little rough tonight. Maybe you like it rough. Have a little too much to drink, did you?" Without waiting for an answer, he added, "You probably both did."

Raisa couldn't contain herself. "Don't you get it? She was attacked by someone she hardly knew. "

He stared at Raisa. "Then she needs to be more careful about where she goes and who she hangs with. Only a fool doesn't know boys will be boys."

Annie rose from her cannabinoid daze to her sister's defense. "So you think it was my sister's fault that she was attacked by that bastard? What kind of a doctor are you?"

Spence and Fredi were waiting on the other side of the curtain. "Annie, just let it go," Spence called out. "We can discuss this with his supervisor later."

The doctor was unyielding. "You privileged white kids can't touch me. Go right ahead and talk to my supervisor. He'll back me up one hundred per cent. Your friend is stitched up. Her wound has been irrigated. Nobody is going to question the care I delivered. Take her home." The doctor pulled off his gloves and tossed them in the waste bin. Then he opened the curtain and walked off to his next patient.

As they got Irene into a cab, they sat in silence, stunned by what the doctor had said and all that he'd implied. Fredi vowed to herself that if she were lucky enough to get into medical school, she would never treat a patient the way that doctor had treated Irene. For Annie, the seeds of guilt were sown. That she'd been too stoned to take care of her little sister when she'd needed her most was almost more than she could bear. Spence, too, felt culpable for bringing Irene into Steve Shapiro's path. He'd make sure the SDS leadership knew it had a predator in its ranks, a predator that needed to be excised from the movement.

Raisa alone was thinking of how she might help bring Irene's attacker to justice. When they got back to Barnard, she raced to her room and got her camera. Then she went to Irene and took pictures of her face and her breast. "If you want to press charges," Raisa said gently, "these pictures will provide evidence of what that monster did to you."

§§§

In the early morning of April 30th police were called in by Columbia's administration to break up the student occupation. They stormed the campus, employing different tactics for black and white protestors. The black students in Hamilton Hall were peacefully removed by a tactical squad of all-black police officers, with black attorneys standing outside the building ready to represent them. As for the white protestors in and around Low Library, police relied on tear gas and nightsticks, dragging protestors — sometimes by the hair — to waiting paddy wagons. One of them was Steve Shapiro. It took three cops to drag him away. In all, over seven hundred were arrested; more than one hundred suffered injuries. The following day, the brutality continued. Students armed with sticks and tree limbs fought police. Others threw a wide variety of projectiles out of their windows at the police. One officer, a father of three, was permanently disabled after his back was broken by a student who leapt from a second story window and landed atop him.

Under normal conditions, a Barnard freshman with a black eye and facial stitches would garner a lot of attention from the watchful eyes of the dormitory staff. But in the midst of the worst college revolt to rock the country, no one took much note of Irene's injuries. Nancy, who had joined the counter-demonstrators opposing SDS, was surprised but not shocked when she saw Irene's battered face. Neither she nor anyone else complained as her sister and friends stayed with her day and night.

Following the attack, Annie left her sister only to use the bathroom or to call Meyer and Gladys. They were worried sick after watching footage of the campus revolt on the evening news. They wanted Irene to come home, to be safe, but Annie said it wasn't necessary. She was staying with Irene, right in her room. Her bottom lip quivered as she promised, "Mom. I'll keep her safe." Meyer made Annie swear to protect Reenie from all the chaos outside the building. That was easy enough to do. Of course, the damage had already been done.

As the days passed and Irene showed no improvement, Annie worried more. Her sister lay on the bed in the fetal position, sometimes crying, other times staring into space. Once in a while she would doze off only to awaken with a start. She refused all food and wanted nothing to do with the tea Annie repeatedly made for her. Finally, Annie put her foot down. "I'm not asking you, Reenie, I'm telling you. You know how important fluids are to the human body. You must drink this tea!"

On the fifth day, Annie persuaded Irene to get in the shower. She wept when she saw how thin her sister's battered body had become. She gently washed her, taking care to avoid the bruises and cuts with the washcloth. When she was done, she wrapped her in the thick terry robe she'd given her for her birthday. Then she combed out her snarled hair and helped her put on clean clothes. When Raisa came by with food, Annie fed her soup and held the cup as she drank hot tea.

"Reenie. I am so sorry. I didn't protect you."

Irene looked up. Almost inaudibly, she whispered, "I didn't know I needed protection."

"You shouldn't have needed protection. I thought Shapiro was one of the good guys. I was so wrong. I'm sorry!"

"But he didn't rape me. He may have stuck his penis in my mouth and beaten me, but he didn't rape me. I guess I'm lucky."

Raisa and Annie cringed as they exchanged glances. Raisa couldn't let her comment stand. "Irene, there is nothing lucky about being sexually assaulted."

"It was partly my fault. Like the doctor said, I drank alcohol. It was my first time, too. I had two cups. If I hadn't, maybe I could have gotten away."

"No part of this is your fault. It's all on him," Annie said.

"If you want to press charges, we'll go to the police with you," Raisa said. "What he did was a felony. You have four witnesses to corroborate your story."

"No. I could never, never do that. I'm so ashamed."

"You have nothing to be ashamed of. You did nothing wrong," Raisa said.

Irene closed her eyes and shook her head. "Please, don't tell anyone. Especially not Mom and Dad, or Grandma Bertha," Irene begged.

"Shapiro is the one who ought to be ashamed. You are entirely blameless," Raisa said.

"I don't feel blameless. And more than anything, I don't want people to know."

"If that's how you feel, I'll keep your confidence," Raisa said.

"That's how I feel."

"All right then. I'll talk with the other girls and tell them you want this to stay within our little circle."

"And I won't say a word to the family. I promise," Annie said.

Now the sisters were even. Each had a secret to be kept.

§§§

In the madness of the following days, Irene's convalescence barely registered a blip on anyone's radar. Students were allowed to get grades based on their work prior to the building occupations or opt for a pass/fail option. Since Irene couldn't concentrate on anything, she considered herself lucky that she could finish the term with the good grades she'd earned prior to the assault. She thought about her long-running experiment in biology lab, now surely lying in ruins due to inattention. Just for a moment, her sadness at the loss of the experiment superseded the eddy of emotions swirling inside her.

Given how many students had been beaten by the police, Irene was just another person on campus with a black eye and stitches. When the chaos died down, most students, including her roommate, Nancy, left for home, but Irene knew she couldn't. Her parents would take one look at her and immediately know that something terrible had happened. She couldn't do that to them. Despite being in turmoil, of one thing she was certain: She would not allow her mother to become collateral damage of the assault.

After a couple of weeks, she began creating a replica of normal life. At her urging, Annie went back to her apartment. Irene set the alarm for seven and got out of bed each morning. She even took a walk around campus with her friends. But she knew that soon they, too, would be returning home for the summer. Irene had no idea what she would do once the term officially ended. Where could she go? She thought about Albert. Although she hadn't gone down to her mailbox since the attack, she imagined he'd been writing her with plans for the summer. She recoiled at the thought.

Alone in her dorm room, she did a lot of crying over what the attack had cost her. Her innocence was gone, of course, but also gone was her belief that being touched by a boy could be pleasurable. After Albert left in March, she'd made the decision to "go all the way" with him when he returned to New York for the summer. They were in love and she thought it right that they consummate that love. But that was before she'd been attacked. She looked at herself now as damaged and dirty; certainly not fit to be with someone as fine as Albert Jaffe.

Three weeks after the assault, Irene found a note taped to her dorm room door stating that the contents of her mailbox would be discarded if she didn't pick it up within the next day. She dutifully went to the box and removed the accumulated mail. There were assorted ads and several letters from Albert. She tossed the ads in the trash and put Albert's unopened letters in the manila envelope with the others.

§§§

After the dust settled from the building takeovers, the protestors declared victory. The plans for a gym were scrapped. Columbia severed ties with the IDA think tank. The demonstrators were granted amnesty, and both the university president and provost resigned. Columbia's reputation took a major hit. Irene caught a break when so many anxious parents whisked their students away from the troubled campus. Summer jobs that had previously been filled were suddenly vacant. She saw a posting for a resident advisor position in her dorm. That, and any menial job on campus she could find, would buy her room, board, and the time she needed to face her parents and grandmother.

§§§

Irene got through her trauma the way she approached everything in life. Though distraught, she willed herself to rationally examine the problems she faced. Had she suffered only physical injuries, the path would have been clearer: a combination of medical treatment and the body's natural healing powers would, in time, return her to a state of health. How to heal from her emotional wounds was less clear. And then, there was the nagging question of how it was that she'd become vulnerable to a sexual assault in the first place.

It didn't take long for Irene to decide that the root of her problem was the mistaken belief that she could be like Annie, that she could do it all — academic studies, artistic expression, a boyfriend, political activism. For a brief moment in time, she'd embraced them all. But venturing out into the wider world had exposed her to a threat she didn't know existed. Yes, the college had warned the girls not to walk at night on the streets bordering campus. But she'd been attacked in the apartment of someone who was admired by people she trusted. She had never known that evil could be so artfully masked. It was a lesson she was unlikely to forget. Another lesson was that two cups of sangria had made her more vulnerable to Shapiro's treachery. Giving a scoundrel an advantage was a mistake she would try never to make again.

So there were two lessons learned. But now she had to find a way to deal with the fallout from the attack. Trying to behave normally, as though nothing had happened, was excruciating and exhausting. She had a brand-new fear of people, a fear that made her hesitant and jumpy around those she didn't know well. The thought of any male touching her, even someone she trusted, made her blood run cold. She had terrible nightmares and woke up in a cold sweat almost every night. As she ticked off the changes since the assault, she was reminded of what she'd learned about trauma in her psych class. Obviously, she wasn't the first person who'd survived an ordeal. Experts had studied trauma victims since the nineteenth century. She felt sure psychologists had developed methods to help them rebuild their lives. Perhaps if she researched their latest discoveries, it could help her emerge from her nightmare. It was her "aha!" moment. That very day she went to the library and took out a book on psychological trauma.

She read that book the way other sixteen-year old girls might devour *Glamour* magazine. She learned that trauma was an emotional response to a negative incident that made it difficult for the victim to live normally in its aftermath. Psychologists made many discoveries through their work with war veterans. Anxiety and depression often followed on the heels of a traumatic event. The symptoms of anxiety — feeling restless or tense, having trouble concentrating and sleeping, being fearful — entirely jibed with her experience. Now she had a word for what was tormenting her: Anxiety. Giving a name to what haunted her was a help, but she found the treatments recommended for trauma victims less helpful. Irene couldn't imagine discussing the events of that night with a therapist. It was bad enough that Annie kept asking her if she was all right, if there was anything she wanted to talk about. Divulging the sordid details of her attack with a total stranger was unthinkable. As for the other recommended therapy, anti-anxiety medication, the list of side effects scared her off: Drowsiness, fatigue, and weakness, the possibility of addiction. No, she would address her anxiety differently. She decided she would learn how to defend herself.

Irene found a beginner's karate class that met three times a week during daylight hours just two blocks from campus. She threw herself into every session, so hopeful that her effort would bring rapid results. But it became obvious that, despite listening to every word the *sensei* said and trying her best, her performance was terrible. Her problem was a lack of physical strength and coordination. Years of reading, studying, and playing music had done nothing to enhance her stamina or develop her large muscle groups. She'd never valued physical toughness before, but now she was single-minded about making gains on that front. Not only would she persevere in karate, she would also take up running.

Irene's first attempt at jogging around the campus lasted all of two minutes, leaving her doubled over from the stitch in her side. She was shocked by how weak she was, but she was determined not to remain weak. Each day she ran around the six block-long campus until she could run no more. Slowly, her endurance grew. When she could run for thirty minutes without stopping, she celebrated by buying herself a copy of *The Double Helix* by James Watson. As her physical stamina grew, she noticed a flicker of her former optimism returning. Perhaps there was some hope for her, after all.

§§§

After deeming her attempt to follow Annie into the wider world a failure, Irene retreated to her old loves — academics and music – with the added focus on physical prowess. She decided it was good that she'd learned her limitations early. Now she could proceed with her life, disabused of the notion that she was someone who could venture forth fearlessly into all manner of new endeavors. Accepting her new truth brought her a degree of calm. She decided she was ready to see her parents and grandmother again.

When Irene told Annie of her plans to spend the weekend in Brooklyn, Annie asked if she wanted her to come along. "I can be there for you, Reenie. It might be easier if you had someone there to support you. I'll be a distraction if nothing else. You know how Mom and Dad worry about my activism."

But Irene said she could manage on her own. The long subway ride home was soothing in a way; so familiar, so mundane. No one on the train knew what had happened to her. She sat between two women who rode the train all the way to lower Manhattan. When they left and the train thinned out, she sat by herself, looking at her reflection in the window. The bruises on her face and body were gone now and the stitches had healed. She looked like an ordinary person again, not the victim of an assault. That gave her the courage she needed for her visit with the family.

It didn't take Gladys more than a moment to see the scar on her daughter's face. Irene had planned her story with care: She'd been reading a book while walking on campus and walked right into a tree branch. Yes, she'd needed stitches. No, she was fine. Maybe there would be a small scar. Irene was happy to absorb her mother's reprimand. "Reenie, you are going to have to take your nose out of your books long enough to walk safely between your classes." Then, satisfied she'd offered up a sufficient admonishment, Gladys turned her attention to making Irene's favorite dinner, stuffed cabbage. As for Meyer, he was so happy to have his little girl home he was blind to any changes in her. He took no notice of Irene trying hard not to shrink from his touch when he wrapped his arms around her and gave her a big hug.

It was Grandma Bertha who sensed that perhaps something more than a collision with a tree limb had injured Irene. Despite the smiles and the idle chatter about her summer typing job and new hobby of jogging, Bertha felt that something was different about her granddaughter. She also knew that sometimes an old grandma could be easier to talk to than a parent. The next morning, when it came time for her daily walk to the bakery, Bertha asked Irene to join her.

"Come, *bubbelah[1]*, keep me company. I have to get some rolls and half a seeded rye for lunch. It's a beautiful day. You can tell me about how you decided to take up jogging."

Irene was actually relieved to have an excuse to leave the apartment. It was taking a lot of effort to appear relaxed. She put on her sandals and was waiting at the door before Bertha could get her purse.

"So, what's new? Before you tell me why you've decided it's a good idea to get all perspired running around your college every day, tell me about your job at the dormitory."

"I was quite lucky to get a resident advisor position. It looks like it could go beyond the summer and into the fall, too. The job is easy enough. I just have to be around to answer questions for students living in the dorm during summer school, and there aren't too many of them... students, that is. I get a free room, all to myself. I've never had my own room before. I like it very much."

"And you're in summer school, too?"

"No, I'm just typing in the library, working on the card catalog. It requires great precision. I'm pretty good at it; at least I don't get a lot of cards returned for corrections. Plus, I'm earning enough money for my food. Maybe even a little extra for concerts and a movie or book now and then. I also like the women in my office. They're so friendly and helpful."

"And what about Albert? Didn't you say something when you were home for Passover about him working in the city this summer?"

Hearing his name made her throat tighten. She swallowed hard and told herself that no matter what, she could not betray her distress. "Yes, I believe he's still coming to the city, but I don't imagine I'll be seeing much of him.'

"And why is that? You two seemed very nice together. He's a lovely young man."

Her grandmother was not making this easy.

"You're right, Grandma. He is lovely, very lovely, but I think we took things too quickly," she said hurriedly. "I think I need a break."

"Oh. I'm sorry to hear that. Have you told him how you feel?"

"Actually, I've been avoiding that."

---

[1] Sweetie, darling one

"As a person who found my nerve late in life, I can tell you that it's no good to be afraid to speak the truth. Most of my life I was a big chicken, Reenie. Don't follow in your grandma's footsteps. Tell Albert the truth. He deserves that much."

§§§

It was a beautiful June day. Irene was returning from eight hours behind an IBM Selectric typewriter when she spotted Albert sitting on the steps of her dorm. The moment he caught sight of her, he stood up and pressed his hands on the creases of his pants. Irene would never forget his look of uncertainty. She stopped in her tracks, that is until Albert started approaching her. Then she did an about-face and starting walking in the opposite direction. "Reenie," he called after her. "Why didn't you answer my letters?"

Irene picked up her pace as she heard Albert's steps closing in behind her. When he put his hand on her shoulder, she spun around. "Don't touch me!"

Albert couldn't have pulled his hand away faster had he made contact with hot coals. He closed his eyes and stifled a sob. Irene, too, started to cry. "Please Albert, whatever you do, don't touch me," she said, more gently. Her mind flashed on what Grandma Bertha had said about him deserving an explanation, about having the courage to speak the truth. "I'm sorry. I didn't mean to shout. I just…please…don't touch me."

"I must have done something pretty awful for you to find me so revolting."

"No, no, no. You're the antithesis of revolting, and you've done nothing wrong. You've always been kind and loving."

"Then why? It didn't seem to bother you when I touched you before. Why can't I now?"

Irene couldn't respond.

"And why didn't you answer my letters?"

Again, Irene was helpless to provide the explanation Albert was desperate to hear.

"Is it that you've met someone else? I need to know, Reenie. I've been going crazy trying to figure out what happened."

"I can tell you this much: You're the only boy I've ever loved. Promise me you'll always remember that."

"This doesn't make any sense. If you love me, then why can't I touch you?"

His anguish made it plain that Grandma Bertha was right; she owed Albert an explanation and it had to be the truth, or as much of the truth as she could bear to utter. "I know you deserve a reason. It has nothing to do with you. You are not at fault in any way. It's about me, about what happened to me. I'll do my best to explain, but I may not be able…" Her eyes burned as the tears rolled down her face.

"Come, Reenie. I won't touch you, I promise, but come. Let's sit down somewhere and talk."

Irene nodded and they began their silent walk to Riverside Park. When Albert saw a bench, he motioned to Irene to sit, careful not to let his arm touch hers. "Here. This is a quiet place. We can talk. You can tell me what's going on. I knew something had to have happened. This isn't like you."

"That's just it. I'm not me anymore, Albert."

"That doesn't make any sense. How can that be?"

"Something happened that broke the person you knew. That person was hopeful, trusting, and so happy. I *was* a happy person, wasn't I?" Irene asked.

"Yes, of course. That's one of the things I love about you, Reenie. You're so positive, so optimistic. It's rubbed off on me. Because of you, my whole outlook on life has been brighter — that is until you stopped answering my letters. At first I thought it was because of the demonstrations. I imagined you were protesting and too involved to write. But after the protests died down and there was still no word from you, I finally had to face the possibility that your feelings for me had changed."

"You're right about one thing. I was involved in the demonstrations. But you're wrong about me changing my mind about you. I don't think I'll ever change my mind about you. I will always think of you as a brilliant, wonderful person, a kind and thoughtful human being I was so lucky to have known."

"I still don't get it. If I'm so wonderful, why speak about me in the past tense? Why not answer my letters? Why did you turn your back on me just now? What's happened, Reenie?"

"I was…attacked. Can we leave it at that?"

It took Albert a minute to process what she'd said. "Attacked? Sexually attacked?"

Irene looked down and nodded. She began to weep again. Instinctively, Albert wanted to put his arms around her, to soothe and comfort her, but he didn't dare.

"I'm so sorry, Reenie. Here I was thinking it was all about me. I couldn't imagine — can't imagine — anyone wanting to hurt you. You're one of the purest souls I've ever met."

"Not anymore."

"Reenie, please, let me help you get over this terrible thing that's happened. I promise I won't touch you or ask anything of you. Just let me spend time with you. I came all this way for us to be together. If we can't be the way we were, we'll find a new way to be. Don't shut the door on me. I love you. Please let me help."

"You deserve someone who hasn't been tainted by depravity. I'm not worthy of you, not anymore."

"I refuse to accept your premise or your conclusion. You are the same beautiful person I fell in love with. I don't want to…I *can't* give you up. The creep who did this to you can't be allowed to ruin what we have together."

"I'm sorry, Albert, but don't you see? It's too late. He already has."

§§§

The summer was so different from what she'd imagined when Albert shared his news about his job at the planetarium. She'd closed the door on their relationship, and with her friends gone for the summer, she was alone. That was fine with her. She felt calmer when she was by herself. She kept working on her running. Her performance in karate improved. She earned her yellow belt in August. The months of typing, running, and learning self-defense were so entirely new — almost alien — to the life she'd led before the attack. She saw that summer as marking a new beginning. Never again would she be weak in the face of a physical threat. Never again would she allow alcohol to leave her open to unknown perils. And she was determined to follow her grandmother's advice about living with courage. To that end, as August came to a close, she wrote to Albert, using the last address she had for him at Stanford.

August 29, 1968

Dear Albert,

I am so sorry that I hurt you. You did nothing whatever to deserve it. I owe you more of an explanation than I was able to provide when we met in June. I'll do my best in this letter.

It was during the week of demonstrations on campus that a Columbia anti-war activist brutalized and sexually assaulted me... and I was unable to stop him. I will likely bear scars on my body for the rest of my life as reminders of what he did to me. After all, scars are the way the body heals when wounded. I can only hope there'll be some way for my spirit to be repaired, as well.

Over the summer I made it a goal to improve my physical strength. That has bolstered my confidence somewhat. I am not as sad as I was. I am angry, though. The man took away my identity as a person of virtue and worth. I'm no longer fit to be with anyone, particularly someone as fine as you. The man who attacked me stole many things from me that night, but that loss was far and away the most painful.

I don't quite recognize myself. While I refuse to surrender to fear, I am cautious of people in a way I never was. I hope as time passes I will come to terms with what happened and to the person I've become. Maybe one day I will know what it feels like to be optimistic, happy or trusting again.

I have so many regrets when I think of you. High on the list is that you came all the way to New York so we could spend the summer together. If I could have, I would have told you not to come, but I was in a bad way. I am so sorry.

You brought me more happiness than I can say. I wish you only the best of everything. You will do great things, Albert. That much I know is true.

Irene

PS I beg you not to share this with anyone. I've kept the attack from my parents, who would suffer greatly if they knew.

Unbeknownst to anyone, at the end of the summer Annie, too, composed a letter of her own. The typed missive was sent to the parents of Steve Shapiro, whose Short Hills, New Jersey address was easy enough to find in the Columbia student directory. Enclosed in the envelope were copies of the photos Raisa had taken after the attack.

To the Parents of Steve Shapiro:

I am writing to inform you that your son Steve beat and sexually assaulted a minor, a virgin, an innocent on the night of April 27, 1968. There were several witnesses. The underage girl is too traumatized to go to the authorities so your boy will get off easy. Perhaps this is not the first time the son you raised has brutally attacked a girl. Odds are it won't be the last. As they say, a leopard can't change its spots.

How does it feel to have a sexual predator for a son? More to the point, what do you plan to do about it?

A Concerned Bystander

CHAPTER EIGHT

I RENE'S SUBSEQUENT YEARS at Barnard took place within the boundaries she drew in the aftermath of the sexual assault. She made good on the promise she made to herself about concentrating on her courses, her music, and her pursuit of physical strength. As for her studies, she excelled beyond her wildest imaginings, winning several academic prizes over the rest of her college career. Irene also had the opportunity to do original research in physical chemistry with Professor Bernice Segal, a mentor for Barnard students aiming high for a career in science. Segal was a formidable woman with a commanding voice and high expectations for her students. At first she intimidated Irene, but Segal's bountiful comments in Irene's lab book were akin to a personal tutorial in chemistry. And when the professor agreed to mentor her independent research project, Irene felt like jumping for joy — and might have — had it not been so clear that Professor Segal was all business.

It wasn't only her studies that helped Irene reestablish a sense of normalcy in her life. The autumn after the attack, her friends Max and Meryl, both certified lifeguards, took her under their wing in the Barnard pool. They taught her the basic strokes, guiding her to a level of proficiency that allowed her to increase her strength and endurance. Soon, she became a regular, hooked on the meditative tranquility she found in lap swimming. And then there was her music. As first oboist in the Columbia concert band, she found joy collaborating with other musicians to bring a composer's work to life. She continued her study of karate, attending classes several times a week through the year. Her dedication helped her slowly rise through the ten "kyu" levels signified by different colored belts. Each time she qualified for a new level, she marked it as a private victory over Steve Shapiro.

§§§

There were lasting remnants from the attack. One was Irene's hesitancy to venture off alone to new places. She tried mightily to master her fear, remembering what Grandma Bertha said about not being a chicken. In time, she found a degree of success on that front. One thing that didn't change with time was her steering clear of situations that might lead to romantic involvement. Anytime a Columbia student in one of her advanced labs or math classes showed an interest in her, Irene immediately pulled away. As for politics, she gave it, and all its associated activities, a wide berth. Though she remained steadfast in her opposition to the war in Vietnam, Irene never again went to a demonstration or made a picket sign.

The sexual assault had a ripple effect, changing the lives of Annie and Spence, as well. They withdrew in protest from SDS after the steering committee turned a blind eye to what Shapiro had done. Discovering the leaders of a movement for equity and justice had feet of clay was a terrible blow, and they struggled to come to terms with their disillusionment. Spence decided he would become an attorney and work for people most often left out of the American dream: the poor, minorities, and women. Annie elected to train as a clinical psychologist focusing on major depression and the fall-out from sexual assault. When, in the spring of 1969, they announced they had both gained admission to graduate school at Columbia, Irene could not have been happier.

§§§

As had been true throughout her life, her family remained Irene's lodestar. The more time she spent with Annie and Spence, the more she began to see Spence as being part of her family. She trusted him implicitly. Never would she forget the way he defended and cared for her on the worst night of her life. It troubled her that his existence remained a secret that had to be kept from the rest of the family. From time to time, she'd gingerly broach the subject of introducing him to Gladys and Meyer — and by extension, Grandma Bertha — but it always came to nothing.

One bitterly cold Sunday during her senior year at Barnard, she sat across from Annie and Spence at a diner on Broadway discussing a cousin's upcoming marriage. It likely was the excitement of being invited to her first wedding that loosened Irene's tongue. "I wish you could join us, Spence. I can guarantee our Aunt Phyllis will spare no expense for Alana's big day," she said. "It'll be quite the *simcha*[1]."

"Translation: Over-the-top catered event," Annie added. "We'll give you a blow by blow account of the big affair after the bride and groom leave for their equally over-the-top honeymoon at the Fontainebleau Hotel in Miami."

But Irene couldn't let it go. "I still think Spence ought to be able to be with us. He's more like family than a lot of our family. I see you as a brother, Spence. I love how you love Annie, how you care for her and look out for her – and she for you. You two are so good together. I will concede that there are some obstacles created by your differing backgrounds. But obstacles can be overcome. You love each other. That's not something that comes along every day. I think it's worth fighting for."

Annie turned crimson and Spence shifted nervously in his seat. Irene immediately sensed she'd said too much.

After a moment Spence said, "You know what? Reenie's right. I'm tired of hiding you, Annie, and frankly, I don't want to be hidden anymore."

"I don't like it either, but I refuse to be reckless," Annie countered. "I don't want to be the cause of you losing your family and your inheritance. Who will pay for law school if your family cuts you off? And if you became estranged from your parents because of me, what do you think that would do to our relationship? All the opportunities they can offer you — gone — because of me."

"I don't know how many times I've told you: I'm willing to take that chance. If my parents make me choose, I'll choose you. But maybe I won't have to choose."

Irene felt like an intruder eavesdropping on an intimate conversation. She excused herself, saying she had to use the bathroom. She made sure to linger in the restroom a bit longer than was needed. When she returned to the booth, she found Annie and Spence embracing. On Annie's left hand was a ring made out of a paper straw's wrapper.

---

[1] Joyous celebration

"Reenie, you can be the first to know," Spence said, smiling more broadly than Irene had ever seen. "I've proposed to your extremely stubborn sister and much to my surprise, she's accepted. Hang on. We may be in for a rough ride, but it's thanks to the little nudge you gave us that we're going to come clean to both our families."

Annie laughed. "I'd call that more of a shove than a little nudge."

Spence agreed. "Okay, it was definitely a shove, but one that we clearly needed. Thank you, Reenie." Spence reached across the table and planted a kiss on Irene's check. Much to her surprise, it didn't make her wince.

"Now that you've helped us take the plunge, don't go running for the hills," Annie said. "I expect you to be right with us when we tell the folks. If we're going down, we're all going down together."

§§§

Neither the Robertsons nor the Adelsons were pleased when they were introduced to their child's choice of life partner.

Meyer and Gladys were not only surprised and dismayed; they were wounded. Since Annie left for college, they'd wondered if she dated. She mentioned no boyfriends, so they assumed it was her strident politics at work. Perhaps the crusade for women's equality precluded the possibility of having a boyfriend. When Annie and Irene asked if they could bring along a friend for Sunday dinner, it never occurred to them it would be someone Annie had agreed to marry. They were deeply hurt that their daughter hadn't even introduced the young man before making so enormous a decision. And if that wasn't bad enough, he was not a Jew. They both felt stricken.

As they spent their first afternoon with Spence, they could see why Annie found him attractive. There was no doubt he was intelligent and well-educated. Though a bit scrawny for his tall frame, he was nice looking. He shared Annie's sense of social justice. A law student at Columbia, he'd likely become a good provider. Irene seemed to like him and feel comfortable with him, which led both Meyer and Gladys to wonder how long she'd known about Annie's young man. Had she, too, kept the relationship a secret? To think their girls might have conspired to deceive them stung them both. They had always been so proud of their children, but clearly they'd failed somewhere along the line. What would the family think when they revealed that Annie had gotten engaged to a *goy¹*?

It was an awkward dinner, with the young people doing their best to keep the conversation light. Afterwards, Annie and Spence volunteered to clear the table and wash the dishes. The rest of the family went into the living room, where the morose mood followed close on their heels. Irene decided music might brighten things up a bit, so she went to the hi-fi and put on a Benny Goodman LP. Then something happened that caught everyone in the living room by surprise. All of a sudden Annie's Gentile fiancé took her into his arms and danced her into the living room, the two of them moving in perfect sync to "Don't Be That Way." Gladys and Meyer were affected in ways they would have struggled to articulate. The way the two lovers looked at one another, how effortlessly each anticipated the other's movements, the joy they radiated, all reminded Gladys and Meyer of another time, so many years before, when they met. Their own love had provided them such delight and succor through good times and bad. In their heart of hearts, they each sensed this match Annie had made without any help from them was a good one. Their beautiful girl had fallen in love with a man who adored her. Spence made her happy and she, him. Perhaps that was more important than his being a Jew.

Over dessert of Bertha's chocolate *babka²*, the mood was a bit less tense. Annie told tales of how Spence, a self-proclaimed "two-left-footer," had become the fine dancer he was. First he asked her to teach him something simple and she complied by coaching him in the foxtrot. Once that was mastered he pressed her to show him another, and yet another dance until he developed a repertoire that included East and West Coast swing, rhumba, samba, cha-cha, and tango.

"Dance is such a big part of Annie's life," Spence explained. "I wanted to be able to share that with her. She's a wonderful teacher, really patient. I'm a hack next to her — she's really a gifted dancer — but she makes me look good."

Meyer couldn't resist. "That's what I always say about Gladys. She makes me look good."

"I don't know about that," Gladys said. "I think it's more like we help one another do our best and be our best. After all, that's what a good marriage is all about."

---

¹ Gentile
² A yeast based loaf coffee cake

Annie couldn't believe her ears. Things were going better than she had dared to hope.

If Meyer and Gladys were giving signals that they were persuadable, Grandma Bertha was another story. Throughout dinner and dessert she'd said not a word. Though she was liberal on many matters, intermarriage was not among them. As she stood to clear the dessert dishes from the table, she finally spoke her peace. "It's lovely you two can dance together. It really is. I enjoyed watching you. But marriage brings with it many issues, many decisions. If there are children, what religion will they be with a Jewish mother and a Gentile father? They'll be all mixed up, neither fish nor fowl."

"Bertha, what you say is true," Spence said. "That's why I am planning to convert to Judaism."

You could have heard a pin drop. Everyone was stunned, Annie included.

Bertha put the dishes back down on the table. "Really," she said, with more than a hint of skepticism.

"Yes. I've studied what it entails, given it a lot of thought, and I've decided to do it."

"That's a big step," Bertha said. "It's a long process. You have to find a rabbi to study with. You can't do it to make yourself more appealing to Annie's family."

"I couldn't agree more. It's serious business; I have an appointment with Rabbi Levine at Columbia on Wednesday."

Annie couldn't hide her shock. "How...when did you decide all this?"

"Actually, I've been thinking about it for a long time. Remember that rabbi during the Columbia demonstrations? Rabbi Goldman? They called him Rabbi Bruce. He was a vocal supporter of the student occupation. He was and remains a fierce opponent of the war. He impressed me then and he got me thinking about Judaism. Let's just say it's been a process."

Annie blinked back tears. "You would do that for me? Give up your religion and become a Jew? I would never ask you to do that."

"You didn't need to ask me. I decided it's what I want to do for us, for the family we're going to create."

"Good answer, and I hope it's sincere," Bertha said. "You certainly can't go through the *mutshen*[1] of conversion to impress someone else or to make them happy. It has to be what *you* want."

Spence took Bertha's words with the gravity they conveyed. "It is. I promise you."

"I can tell you from experience that a husband and wife have plenty to disagree about. Religion shouldn't add to the list."

"I appreciate the wisdom in what you say," Spence said. "I know there'll be plenty of things that will come up, things we'll have to hash out over our lifetimes, but what religion our children will be raised in won't be one of them."

Bertha was starting to think that this well-spoken *shagetz* had potential. Perhaps he could grow into a good husband to Annie and a father to her children. "Tell you what. If you're sincere, if you study hard and take Judaism as your own faith, I will bless your marriage and dance at your wedding." Then, almost as an afterthought, she added, "But you know, I'm not getting any younger, so I suggest you get a move on with that Rabbi Levine."

§§§

Spence and Annie knew they were not entirely out of the woods, but they were heartened by the response of her family. It exceeded Annie's best hope for what they would accomplish over that first Sunday dinner together. Over the next few months, they made sure to give her parents and grandmother many opportunities to get to know and appreciate Spence. With each visit, Annie could see the beginnings of real affection taking root between the people she loved most in the world.

Neither she nor Spence expected the Robinsons to take the news of their engagement as well. They waited until fall, preparing themselves for their meeting as best they could, thinking of a wide variety of responses that might dilute the criticisms the Robinsons would undoubtedly level at their decision to marry. Spence paid a visit to a barber, something he hadn't done in years. The Sunday morning they were to meet the Robinsons for brunch, Annie put on her best dress. They both were nervous, but determined.

---

[1] Torture

Spence introduced his parents to Annie when they arrived at the upscale restaurant the Robinsons had chosen. "Mom, Dad, I'd like you to meet someone who is very special in my life, Annie Adelson." The Robinsons shook hands with her and were cordial. It was when Annie handed her coat to the girl at the coat check that Althea Robinson caught a glimpse of the Star of David around her neck and the diamond ring on her left hand. Althea could feel her cheeks flush as she realized her only son had gotten himself tangled up with a Jew.

After they'd ordered, Althea asked Annie about her ring.

"Isn't it beautiful? I'll let Spence tell you about it," Annie replied.

"I've asked Annie to marry me and she's accepted," Spence said, reaching for Annie's hand. "She even said yes when all I had for a ring was a wrapper from a paper straw. We chose this ring together just last week. I feel like the luckiest man on earth that someone as beautiful and talented as Annie has agreed to be my wife."

His parents remained calm. Dexter's only response was, "Oh, I see." If he and Althea were angry, they hid their ire well, conversing politely, never once raising their voices. They listened to Annie answer their questions about where she was raised, her career plans, and "her people." Dexter saved religion for last, prefacing his question with an explanation of the Robinson family's strong ties to the Episcopal Church. After listening politely over Eggs Benedict, they leveled no recriminations as they explained that despite Annie's many charms, they could not — would not — support a marriage between her and their son.

"It's simply out of the question," Althea stated.

Despite his irritation, Spence matched his parents' cool resolve. "Mom, Dad, you'll always be my parents, but I'm a grown man now. I'm going to follow my heart. You are just going to have to accept that."

"Ah, but that's where you're wrong, Spencer," Althea responded. "You hold the mistaken belief that you're at liberty to follow your heart. You are not. You have obligations to this family and to our business. You probably think you're in love, and perhaps you are. But that's entirely irrelevant. Your duty to this family trumps any personal desires you may have."

Spence shook his head in disbelief. "Love is irrelevant? All I can say in response to that is I couldn't disagree more."

Dexter Robinson turned to Annie. "I'm sure your parents would like you to marry someone from your own background. It's my understanding that the Jews are rather insular."

The way he said "the Jews" made a chill run up Annie's spine. She took a minute to compose herself before answering. "Actually, my parents had some misgivings when they met Spence. But the more time they spent with him, with us, the more clearly they could see that we're right for one another, despite growing up with different traditions."

"Well, I'm sure it didn't hurt when they found out Spence came from people of means," Althea said under her breath.

"Funny you should mention that. My parents know nothing about what 'means' Spence comes from," Annie said. "They overcame their reservations about him after getting a sense of his character, his kindness, his intelligence." Then, turning to Spence, she added, "Actually, I think swing dancing into the living room was the thing that turned the tide that first time you came for dinner."

"Don't be ridiculous," Dexter scoffed. "What does dancing have to do with creating a workable partnership?"

"In my book it's more relevant than how rich a girl's parents are or what faith they follow," Spence said.

"Well, Spencer, I admit I'm disappointed in your inability to recognize the seriousness of your misstep. I shouldn't be surprised," Dexter said. "The fact that you were hoodwinked by all that socialist nonsense, demonstrating in the streets, letting your hair grow like some primitive tribal warrior, dressing like a beggar…it all should have prepared me for this moment. Frankly, I thought you'd turned the corner when you decided to go to law school, but I see now I was mistaken.

"Your mother and I will have to consider how to proceed," Dexter continued, "but I must warn you that our economic support does not come without conditions. We've groomed you since you were a little boy to one day take over the reins of the family business. The finest schools and camps, the skiing, sailing, and tennis lessons…they were all selected purposefully."

"Oh, and I thought you did all that to give me opportunities to learn about the world and myself, not to mention to have fun."

"Nothing was chosen at random. It was with great care and deliberation that we provided what you refer to as 'opportunities' to our only son. The point was to help you grow into a man who would be able to assume the responsibilities awaiting him in adulthood. And to meet those responsibilities, you'll require a suitable partner. Annie, you seem nice enough, but Spence will require someone with qualifications that differ markedly from your own."

Though seething, Spence responded in measured tones. "You so casually dismiss the woman with whom I've chosen to spend the rest of my life. You know nothing of Annie, or what we've created together. You speak out of pure ignorance. You have every right to cut me off financially," he said, holding Annie's hand in his. "And if you decide to go that route, I'll respect your decision. All I ask is that you extend the same respect to mine. Just so you know, having to support myself will not change my decision to marry Annie."

Dexter cleared his throat and straightened his tie. "I'm sorry you feel that way, Spencer. I guess there's no time like the present for you to begin paying your own bills. Shall we split the check?"

Spence colored when he took out his wallet and realized he didn't have much more than carfare for the subway. Annie opened her purse and found eleven dollars and seventy five cents. They pooled their money and laid it on the table. Standing up, they said a cursory goodbye to Dexter and Althea. Then, the young lovers got into position and tangoed out of the dining room. The spectacle caused heads to turn and prompted more than a few diners to break into applause.

§§§

The passage of eighteen months, Spence's graduation from Columbia Law School, and one thinly-veiled, unsuccessful attempt to "buy" Annie out of her engagement to Spence did nothing to heal the rift between the Robinsons and their son. Althea and Dexter did not respond to the wedding invitation, nor did two of their three daughters. Spence's youngest sister, Deidre, defied her parents and RSVP'd her intention to attend. Spence was nearly overcome when he read the response card. "I'm looking forward to meeting my future sister-in-law and seeing my big brother tie the knot." Deidre's courage buoyed him. He knew the hell she would catch for going to the wedding and cavorting with what his parents surely thought of as "working-class kikes." Even so, she'd decided to come. For Annie, it meant the world to know at least one Robinson would be celebrating with them on their wedding day.

It was a small wedding, for which the Adelson's local temple in Flatbush was perfectly suited. There were the several absences from the Goldstein and Adelson families. They cited calendar conflicts but, in truth, they wanted no part of Annie's marriage. As far as they were concerned, Jews were born, not made. No amount of Talmudic study on the part of her *goyisha* fiancé would turn him into a Jew. Her relatives' rebuff smarted, but Annie's admiration for Spence only grew. In choosing her, he'd lost so much. And yet, he seemed not only at peace with his decision, but exhilarated by the prospect of becoming a Jew and spending his life with her.

Their marriage exposed their families' small-minded bigotry, but those who cherished Annie and Spence showered them with love and good wishes on their wedding day. Friends outnumbered relatives three to one. The ceremony was performed by two rabbis, Rabbi Greenberg, who had known the Adelsons for decades, and Rabbi Levine, who'd guided Spence through his conversion to Judaism. The two men of the cloth worked in tandem, blessing the new couple the required seven times as they spoke their vows and sipped from the wine glass.

Following the traditional breaking of the glass by the groom, there was a great celebration, with more food than any sixty people could possibly eat. Raisa took a break from her graduate studies in Boston to sing at the wedding. With Irene on the piano, they got just about everyone to their feet. So many of the guests were talented dancers that the wedding party could have been mistaken for a dance competition, with couple after couple defying gravity as they executed the most intricate and elegant moves.

True to her word, even Grandma Bertha cut the rug with her granddaughter's new husband. She and Spence danced a waltz as Raisa sang a poignant rendition of the *Music Man's*, "Till There Was You." After their dance, the new husband and elderly grandma took a bow, causing more than a few guests to stop applauding long enough to wipe away a tear or two.

CHAPTER NINE

THROUGHOUT HER TIME AT COLLEGE, Irene mulled over possible career options. She was torn between the desire to go into medicine so she could heal the sick, and her love of doing research. Just weeks after graduating *summa cum laude* from Barnard, Irene began a program at Columbia that merged those two passions: the Medical Science Training Program (MSTP). The course of study would be intense, but it would allow her to earn MD and PhD degrees by the time she was twenty-six. Only a handful of students were admitted to the program, and the National Institutes of Health (NIH) covered their tuition while providing them with a stipend. The goal was to create physician-scientists who would go on to make scientific discoveries that advanced clinical practice. Of the six in Irene's cohort, she was the lone female. Four of the students had been out of school for a while; all had significant research experience. At nineteen, Irene was, by far, the youngest of her group.

From the start, her fellow MSTP students struck her as aloof, or perhaps even dismissive of her. She wondered if she was imagining things, but two weeks into the program, she overheard a conversation between two of her classmates which gave her some idea about the cause of their frosty behavior. As she sat studying in the library, she heard Billy Connelly's whispered Texas drawl coming from the other side of a bookcase. "That Adelson girl is easy on the eyes so you know she's just gonna get married. What's *she* gonna do with her high-class education while you and I are working on a cure for cancer or eradicating heart disease? Figuring out how to cure her brat's diaper rash, that's what. It ticks me off that instead of giving that seat to a guy, who'll work his tail off for the next fifty years, the head honchos went and wasted it on a future housewife. I tell you one thing for sure, by kowtowing to the feminists, the med school is throwing a shitload of time and money down the crapper."

His study partner, who Irene had more trouble identifying, agreed. "Precisely my thoughts. What a waste."

Listening to Billy Connelly and his friend raised Irene's hackles. Their dim assessment of her future prospects may have spurred her to work a little harder and a little longer every day. As the weeks and months passed, it became clear that one student's performance surpassed that of the other highly talented physician-scientists in training. Much to the dismay of Billy Connelly and his comrade, that student was Irene Adelson.

§§§

After Annie and Spence's wedding in the summer of 1972, Irene joined her sister and new brother-in-law in renting a modest two bedroom walkup apartment on West 116th Street. For her, it was a welcome change from years of dormitory life. She found the arrangement economical, convenient, and *haimish* — cozy and homey, as did the newlyweds. Annie, who was in the last stages of her clinical psychology PhD, could walk to Columbia's campus. Spence, a clerk for a federal appeals court judge, could get to the courthouse in lower Manhattan in less than thirty minutes. As for Irene, who took classes on Columbia's main campus, as well as at the medical school on 168th Street, the location was ideal. All three worked such long hours; most days they were like ships passing in the night. But Sunday mornings they established a routine they all enjoyed: lingering around the kitchen table for hours, sharing sections of the *New York Times*, and savoring fresh bagels, and strong coffee.

Money was tight for them all. The tuition aid and stipends Annie and Irene had been granted by Columbia and the NIH were godsends, but living expenses in New York were not cheap. Now that Spence was earning a paycheck, he'd begun chipping away at the debt he'd incurred for law school after his parents cut him off. For Spence, Annie, and Irene, an unanticipated benefit of working such long hours was that no one had the time to buy anything but the bare necessities, which most often translated into stocking the fridge and making sure the bathroom didn't run out of toilet paper. All of them regularly patronized the neighborhood cobbler, who repaired their shoes, sometimes repeatedly.

§§§

While her girls were off working hard at making their way in the world, Gladys was doing her best to manage the inner tumult that had hounded her since her sisters' vilification of Annie. Before telling them of Annie's decision to marry Spence, she'd had no illusions that they would approve. She'd tried to steel herself against their criticism, but she was unprepared for their cruelty. They seemed to take pleasure in rubbing Gladys's nose in what Doris deemed, "Annie's fall from grace." Iris, whose children had advanced from trips to the principal's office to skirmishes with the local police, was worst of all. "So your high-and-mighty daughter with all her fancy education can't even get a Jewish man to marry her. And you're paying for her wedding to the *goy*! Have you lost your mind *again*?" After that phone call, Gladys hung up and sobbed. Despite repeated efforts on the part of Meyer and Bertha, she refused to divulge the hateful things her sister had said. But the damage had been done. Her sisters' ridicule awakened old demons from their slumber.

Meyer could tell Gladys wasn't herself in the lead-up to the wedding. She'd been good for so long that he'd almost convinced himself that her spells of melancholy were a thing of the past. But the signs were unmistakable: the crying, the trouble sleeping, the loss of appetite and bouts of diarrhea. He tried to encourage and support her – as did Bertha – attributing her nervousness to the wedding preparations. It was a testament to Gladys's strength that she was able to hold things together until after Annie and Spence left for their camping honeymoon in the Adirondacks. Then she surrendered, and despair ran roughshod over her. Soon, getting out of bed was an insurmountable challenge. Bertha had to call the principal to tell him Gladys was too sick to come to work. When weeks passed and there was no change, Meyer knew what had to be done. He took Gladys back to the place he hoped never again to enter — Brooklyn State Hospital. He wept the whole way home.

Once again Meyer wore the yoke of caring for his wife while shielding the children from their mother's breakdown. He was impossibly proud of his girls; he couldn't abide the thought of Gladys's illness derailing their pursuit of a professional education. He swore Bertha to secrecy and together, they kept Gladys's condition from Annie and Irene. When they called on the weekends, he or Bertha made excuses: Gladys was out shopping, she was getting her hair cut, she was laid low with a stomach bug.

After three weeks in the hospital and seven ECT treatments, Gladys returned home, quiet and subdued, but no longer in distress. A few days later, when the phone rang she picked up before Meyer or Bertha could grab it. When Irene heard her voice — so tentative and lifeless — her blood ran cold. She asked her mother to put her father on the phone. When she asked him to tell her what had been going on, he denied any problem. "You're imagining things, Reenie. Mom is fine. Just a little tired."

When Annie got on the phone she would have none of her father's evasions. "Listen, Dad. By the end of the year I'll be a licensed clinical psychologist. Tell me what's happening with Mom."

"All right, all right. I didn't want to bother you kids. Mom hit a little bump in the road, that's all. She had to go into the hospital but this time it was very short, just a few weeks, not months like last time. Many fewer treatments. She's coming around much faster than before. You can pay us a visit and see for yourselves."

In an instant Annie grasped what had happened. Her beautiful wedding — that had been boycotted by Robinsons, Goldsteins, and Adelsons alike — had exacted a hefty price from her mother. Althea and Dexter hadn't even had the courtesy to RSVP to the invitation Gladys had so carefully addressed. In the run-up to the wedding, Annie had spent so much time worrying about Spence's frayed ties to his family that she blinded herself to the strain her mother was under. She ought to have known better, to have taken precautions, to have helped her mother cope with the inevitable censure her marriage to Spence provoked. She'd failed, not only as a daughter, but also as a therapist.

For Irene, the news of her mother's illness dredged up memories of that horrible summer day when her mother went missing. The panic she felt back when she was nine years old washed over her; it was as though she were a little girl again, alone and terrified in that stifling apartment. Irene willed herself to remember she was no longer that frightened child; she was a grown woman who'd survived trauma, earned a black belt in karate and, more to the point, would one day be a physician-scientist. She would not — could not — shrink in the face of her mother's illness.

Annie and Spence visited Gladys that very day; Irene stayed behind so as not to overwhelm her. The next morning Irene awoke before dawn and was holding hands with her mother on the living room sofa before breakfast. Irene was gentle, speaking calmly about mundane things: the weather, what Grandma Bertha was cooking in the kitchen, how long she had to wait for the subway. She thought back to the time so many years before, when everyone tiptoed around her mother as she recovered. This time, too, it would take a while for her mother to regain her footing in ordinary life and routines. Irene knew that anti-depressant medications had advanced since her mother's last bout with depression. This time the doctors wanted Gladys to stay on the tricyclic anti-depressant *imipramine* as a prophylactic measure against another recurrence. From what she'd learned in her psychiatry class, that was a viable treatment option.

As thankful as she was for the ECT treatments and the psychotropic medication, Irene questioned what biological mechanism would permit major depression to hijack her mother's life. As she sat on the sofa that morning with a docile and somewhat forgetful Gladys, she vowed to search for an answer.

§§§

Irene and the other MSTP students in her cohort took their pre-clinical courses along with Columbia's med school class of 1975. She found great comfort in the company of Fredi, who was one of twenty-five women in the class of one hundred and forty med students. Being with Fredi was effortless; there were no explanations needed or given. Fredi knew what Irene had endured and survived. And Fredi made her laugh. When they shared a class, the two were inseparable. They dissected their human cadaver together in anatomy lab, ate their bag lunches in the cafeteria, and studied before exams. Once it became clear how exceptional a student Irene was, other med students — including a couple from the MSTP — sought to join their informal study group. Fredi played gatekeeper, and when she gave someone the nod, she made it clear they were on probation. "We'll give it a try," she'd always say. If she sensed a new entrant made Irene uncomfortable, she would take them aside and tell them it wasn't working out, always putting the blame on herself. "I've got anxiety issues. I'm really sorry." Irene knew exactly what she was up to. The quiet protection she provided gave Irene the comfort of knowing that with Fredi around, someone always had her back.

But sometimes Fredi wasn't around. When Irene took graduate courses on the Morningside Heights campus, she often was the sole female in the room. She understood it was irrational to worry that one of her fellow students or the professor might attack her, yet she made sure never to be alone with any of them. She was highly adept at self-defense now, something she thought of whenever she got a bad feeling from a man walking behind her in a stairwell or a corridor. She would think about how she'd fend off an attack, which moves to execute first, second, and third to subdue the aggressor. And each time the man exited the stairwell or ducked into an office, she'd breathe a sigh of relief.

Her isolation in her graduate school classes reminded her of her first months at Barnard. Involuntarily, her mind flashed on the advice Albert had written her years before: *Step right up and introduce yourself. Strike up a conversation. Make the first move.* By following that advice she'd discovered Raisa, and Raisa had led her to Fredi, Max, and Meryl. She knew how the world worked. Isolation produced loneliness; putting oneself out there allowed for the possibility of new relationships. Still, when she closed her eyes and tried to imagine approaching a male student and introducing herself, her throat tightened and her palms would sweat.

Irene decided that when it came to the doctoral portion of her program, she would be single-minded in her study of the mysteries of the human body and the workings of the mind. She would relent only long enough to maintain her physical strength or pay the occasional visit to her family. Of one thing she was sure: she had no desire to be viewed as a sexual being. To that end, she made herself plainer than plain, pulling her hair into a braid and eschewing the makeup that added definition to her pale features. On the days she had graduate classes, she switched to glasses rather than the contact lenses she'd started using in college. As for clothes, she wore shapeless pants and an oversized shirt or sweater that hid her hips and bust. Sexless, she felt invisible in a sea of fellow students.

Irene began studying exclusively for her doctorate in the third year of the MSTP. Just as Fredi was immersing herself in the clinical portion of her training, Irene was zeroing in on the original neuroscience research that would occupy her for the coming years. As exhilarating as that prospect was, she missed Fredi's ready laugh and quick wit. Without them, there was no counterweight to the intensity of her classes, labs, and research.

One Sunday Irene stared into the mirror in her bathroom and saw a drab, asexual creature staring back at her. True, she'd chosen to abandon the trappings of the female gender. The only time she put her hair into an attractive topknot, put on makeup and a pretty dress was when she went to visit her parents. But concealing herself behind dreary clothes, trying to be inconspicuous among her classmates day after day was wearing. She hadn't realized how much energy it took to hide in plain sight. The thought of the remaining years in the MSTP suddenly seemed overwhelming. She knew she wanted to do more than help individual patients; it was the origins of disease that most intrigued her. But she wondered if she had it in her to complete the long and lonely marathon that lay ahead.

Each year a student or students would drop out of their MSTP cohort, opting for either a medical or a doctoral degree. At her lowest point, Irene understood their decision to abandon the quest for an MD/PhD, but as had happened throughout her school career, gifted teachers shone a spotlight on the path forward. The new chairman of the Department of Neurology, Dr. Lewis Rowland, was ahead of his time in terms of championing careers in medicine for women. Long before it became illegal to discriminate against women in education, he and his wife Esther, who counseled Barnard students, actively promoted women's full participation in the sciences. For Irene, the atmosphere Dr. Rowland created was a breath of fresh air. And the department he led was alive with explorations into the effects of psychopharmacological agents, something that dovetailed neatly with Irene's interest in the biological underpinnings of depression. She was drawn to the work of Eric Kandel, who had recently moved up from NYU to lead the new Center for Neurobiology and Behavior. Kandel believed the brain's biology — rather than Freudian psychology — was critical to explaining mental processes. When he established a partnership between the Center and Columbia's Department of Psychiatry, a pathway opened for Irene to conduct her research.

Just by chance, as she read the bios of some of the luminaries in her departments, Irene discovered Drs. Rowland and Kandel had both graduated from her high school, Erasmus Hall, albeit more than two decades earlier. At a small post-symposium reception, she gathered up her courage and introduced herself to each of them. She asked if they, too, had studied with Mr. Lawrence, explaining how important he'd been to her decision to enter the Westinghouse Science Talent Search. Although each said their time at Erasmus had pre-dated Mr. Lawrence, both were happy to make her acquaintance. They were impressed that she'd done so well in the competition and asked quite a few questions about her pigeon navigation project.

Afterwards she very nearly skipped all the way to the subway station. It tickled her to know that such eminent leaders in her field had walked the same halls, perhaps even sat in the same seats she did at Erasmus. Though she would be the first to admit it was illogical, she viewed it as a sign that she'd landed in the perfect place for her doctoral research.

§§§

In 1970, the Nobel Committee awarded the prize in Medicine or Physiology to Julius Axelrod, a researcher at the National Institute for Mental Health. His research focused on epinephrine and norepinephrine, the neurotransmitters that function as part of the body's stress response. Working on MAO inhibitors, the type of anti-depressant medication given Gladys when Irene was a child, Dr. Axelrod showed that neurotransmitters such as norepinephrine continue to work after they are released in the synapse, taken up again by the pre-synaptic nerve ending, held in an inactive form, and used by the sympathetic nervous system when needed. Being recaptured or "reuptaken" allows the neurotransmitters to be utilized later for subsequent transmissions.

Irene was fascinated by Axelrod's discovery. For the first time she understood the workings of the anti-depressant her mother had been prescribed. It prevented the brain enzyme MAO-A from meddling with the reuptake of neurotransmitters, allowing the nervous system to work as it should. The more she read about Axelrod's work on how anti-depressants affected neurotransmitters, either blocking or stimulating their action, the more certain she became that this was the area of research she would pursue.

Irene chose her doctoral advisor with care. She wanted someone on the cutting edge of research into the efficacy of psychotropic medications for mental illness. Beyond that, she hoped he — and it would almost certainly be a he — would be someone driven by the desire to unlock the mysterious linkage between the brain and the mind. After great consideration, she chose Dr. Alexander Glassman, a clinical researcher who was among the first to demonstrate that calibrating the blood concentration of antidepressant medication led to increased treatment success. Not only was he devoted to his research, he was an extraordinary clinician, known for caring for his patients with warmth, wisdom, and kindness. After conferring with him and reviewing the literature of what was known about the biological basis for major depressive episodes (MDE), Irene decided to study the relationship between the regulation of monoamine levels and MDE.

It was known that the three major monoamines — serotonin, norepinephrine, and dopamine — affect mood, behavior, sleep, digestion, pleasure, movement, and motivation. As Dr. Axelrod had already demonstrated, monoamine oxidase A (MAO-A) was the enzyme which metabolizes monoamines. Irene's hypothesis was that MAO-A is overly active in some people, leading to lower levels of the critical neurotransmitters, which in turn lead to major depressive episodes. After hearing her lay out her theory and research plan, Dr. Glassman was on board. Irene was on her way.

As she worked on her experiments, she honed her research skills, developing a matchless technique for observation, preparation of slides, and painstaking data collection and analysis. In short order she was recognized by others in her lab as an up-and-coming investigator. From time to time, when she was lying in bed after a long day, she wondered about the role the assault played in her growth as a scientist. Before the attack she'd opened herself up to the world, to the possibility of personal happiness with Albert, to taking on the responsibility of citizen protest. The attack drove her to retreat back into herself, her family, her work. In her college English classes the concept of irony was something she'd never fully grasped. Now she thought it was likely ironic that the assault had caused her to become a better, more dedicated scientist.

CHAPTER TEN

THE THREE YEARS IRENE SPENT on her doctoral research were among the most intellectually engaging and personally barren of her life. Her only break from work came from time spent with her family and the occasional outing with Fredi. Once a year she'd give herself permission to take a weekend off and travel by train to Boston to see Raisa, who was similarly immersed in the last stages of her doctoral work in the pathogenesis of atherosclerosis. With the exception of the Sunday *New York Times*, Irene read nothing that was not related to work. Although she missed playing music, there was just no way to fit it in. The only non-work related activities she engaged in were tied to remaining physically strong and capable: her twice a week karate classes and her five-mile weekend runs along the Hudson River. Occasionally, she'd give herself the gift of a mile-long swim in Columbia's pool. With those exceptions, Irene concentrated on her research with laser focus. Each day she awoke eager to get back to the lab.

She loved working with doctors and scientists from the Center for Neurobiology and Behavior and the departments of Neurology and Psychiatry. They had so much to teach her; she sometimes wished they all had the capacity to go without sleep so she'd have more time to learn from them. Weekly seminars in neurobiology explored cutting-edge research into the ways neurological processes affect mental health. The more she learned, the more riveted she was to her quest to understand how the disease process intercepted the normal, elegant functioning of the human brain. But attendance at rounds at Columbia's Psychiatric Institute provided a stark reminder of the human cost of that disease process, how schizophrenia, depression, and manic depression robbed patients of their chance to live a full and happy life.

As an MSTP student, Irene could move seamlessly between the departments of neurology, psychiatry, and physiology with little bureaucratic difficulty. With an exception or two, her professors were male. A few discounted her out of hand because of her gender, but other faculty members made up for that ignorance in spades, willingly shepherding Irene into their area of expertise. Dr. Kandel and his wife inspired her. Denise Kandel, PhD, an epidemiologist in the psychiatry department, conducted longitudinal studies on the first-time use of legal and illegal drugs. Eric Kandel's lab was investigating the physiological basis for memory in neurons, studying the lowly sea slug and analyzing the synaptic changes that occur during learning and memory storage. Kandel felt certain the sea slug's process of learning and memory would ultimately translate to humans. His latest breakthrough – the discovery that the neurotransmitter serotonin was involved in the gill-withdrawal reflex – was causing quite a stir in the field of neurobiology.

The Kandels were not the only lodestars for Irene. Dr. Ronald Fieve, a believer in the role of brain chemistry in mental illness, was doing pioneering work with lithium carbonate as a treatment for manic depression. In one seminar, he stressed how many of society's most gifted people suffer from the malady. Be it scientists, writers, politicians or artists, he postulated that it was their manic energy that enabled them to achieve at a lofty level. But, while few sufferers complained of the dynamism provided by their highs, their depressive lows often brought them to the brink of suicide. To Irene, the knowledge that lithium – a naturally occurring mineral – could treat this life-threatening disorder was incredible. She felt so lucky to be studying at an institution where the frontiers of the unknown in psychiatric illness were being pushed back each and every day.

Her own research was going well. She was making steady progress in demonstrating the role of monoamine oxidase A in the monoamine imbalance found in patients with MDE. She was on time to complete and defend her dissertation by the end of the school year, after which she would start her clinical work back at the medical school. One thing that made Irene a bit glum was the realization that Fredi wouldn't be there when she returned. Although Fredi had ranked Columbia as her top choice for her internship and residency, the national residency matching program matched her to Mount Sinai, her second choice. So, at the very time Irene would join Columbia's medical school class of 1978 for its third year and the start of clinical rotations, Fredi would be across town, an actual physician in the thick of her obstetrical training.

The thought of becoming part of a new cohort gave Irene pause, but she reminded herself how she'd faced down the fears she'd had at the start of her doctoral work. Nearly eight years had passed since Steve Shapiro had unleashed his depravity on her. Since then she'd fortified her body, mind, and soul. She was proud of the quiet confidence that had slowly taken root within her. At this point she was, first and foremost, a scientist; the gender or amiability of the people with whom she associated mattered not to her. The work was all that mattered. Whatever the third year medical students at Columbia might send her way would not derail her from her mission of becoming the best physician-scientist she could be.

As she approached the completion of her PhD, the family got some happy news: Annie and Spence were expecting their first child in the summer. Everyone was elated at the prospect of a new baby joining the family. Preparations immediately got underway. Despite her arthritic fingers, Grandma Bertha began a knitting frenzy, making sweaters from newborn to size one in gender-neutral hues. Meyer and Gladys went crib and carriage shopping with the expectant parents. Annie, now on staff at Bellevue, and Spence, an attorney with the American Civil Liberties Union (ACLU), found a three-bedroom apartment closer to their jobs in lower Manhattan. Their new home was in Stuyvesant Town, a huge complex of over one hundred apartment buildings. They begged Irene to move downtown with them, enticing her with the promise of time each day with her new niece or nephew, but Irene declined, believing it was best that Annie and Spence have time alone with their first child. She'd lived with them for four years. In her heart of hearts she knew it was time for her to strike out on her own. She felt ready. She was, after all, twenty-four years old.

§§§

The arrival of a healthy newborn has some similarities to an artillery shell landing in the family living room; everything that existed prior to its appearance is tossed into the air. Some things are destroyed, never to be seen again; others continue to exist, albeit in an altered state. Both the tangible and intangible are reordered. And so it was when little Peter Adelson arrived in June of 1976. Gladys and Bertha — and sometimes Meyer, when he wasn't working — came often that summer to help Annie with the infant who didn't require much sleep. Peter was an alert baby who liked nothing better than to be held and talked to, walked around and allowed to see what was going on. During her maternity leave, Annie found her family's support nothing short of a godsend. Thanks to them she could grab catnaps between daytime feedings, which fortified her for Peter's frequent awakenings during the night. Some Saturdays Irene or Spence's sister Deidre would come over and spend time with Peter, giving Annie and Spence the chance to zip out for a quick dinner. On a rare evening, Irene would sleep over and Annie and Spence would go dancing, something that should have tired them out but somehow always left them feeling energized. The next morning they and Irene would reprise their Sunday morning ritual of bagels and coffee, with the *New York Times* now taking a backseat to Peter as the focus of their attention.

Before Peter was born, what his surname would be was up for discussion. Annie hadn't changed her name when she and Spence married. Their address labels referred to their household as the Adelson/Robinson Family. They agreed early on that hyphenating their names for their children would be too cumbersome. It was over Sunday dinner at Gladys and Meyer's house that Spence suggested they give their first born child Adelson as a surname, and then he added, "and for the sake of family unity, maybe I'll take Adelson, too. If I take the ADEL from Adelson and SON from Robinson, we'll all share the same last name."

Though the family thought Spence was joking, he was deadly serious. He legally changed his surname to Adelson a month before the baby was born. Erasing the Robinson lineage from his and his child's moniker gave Spence a bittersweet sense of satisfaction. His parents had made no contact since before he and Annie married. Despite leaving a message on their answering machine that they were expecting the first grandchild in the family, Althea and Dexter made no effort to respond. Had it not been for Deidre, Spence wouldn't have known their father had anointed their cousin Archie to be heir-apparent of the family firm. And, after Peter was born there was no call, no visit, not even a card, and certainly no gift. Apparently, his parents had cut him out of the warp and woof of their lives. Spence viewed his new family name as a symbol of the life he had chosen to lead.

§§§

When Peter was three months old, Annie returned to work. Although she choked back sobs after dropping him off on her first morning back, she knew he was in good hands with her neighbor, Judy Pasternack, who ran a home daycare out of her apartment. Pained as Annie was to be separated from her baby, she was anxious to get back to treating patients who had experienced sexual violence. She was also eager to return to the nascent campaign aimed at changing the way the nation dealt with sexual assault. The movement was beginning to make some headway. Rape crisis centers were being established in metropolitan areas on both coasts. The legal and medical systems were beginning to change the way they treated sexual assault victims. Protocols in medicine were being examined so that no woman or girl would experience the heartless treatment Irene faced in the emergency room after her assault. Annie was energized by the crusade against sexual violence. What it lacked in size, it made up for in tenacity and determination.

Annie's own research studied the mental health effects of sexual assault on victims and their loved ones, as well as the efficacy of psychological treatments for the aftermath of sexual violence. Thanks to her growing reputation, in the spring of 1977 she was invited by Columbia's School of Public Health to participate in a panel discussion on adolescent sexual assault. When Annie arrived in the auditorium on the day of the symposium, she was encouraged by the size and makeup of the audience. She frankly didn't expect so many people to attend an open public forum on so taboo a subject. Though the vast majority of sex crimes went unreported, Annie knew at least one in six women and girls would experience sexual assault in their lifetime. Perhaps some in the audience knew a victim of sexual assault. Perhaps others were themselves victims. Though most of the hundred or so in attendance were women, a few men stood out. Two had been Annie's professors during her doctoral work.

The discussion was as animated as it was wide-ranging. Many in the audience were surprised and dismayed when Annie cited a study by the sociologist Eugene Kanin, done nearly two decades earlier, "Male Sex Aggression on a University Campus," which found sexual aggression widespread. Kanin posited a model where men used secrecy and stigma to pressure and exploit women. Annie's own research found that one in twelve college males anonymously volunteered that they had engaged in or tried to engage in forced sexual contact with a woman. Almost none of the young men in her study thought they had committed a crime and none faced punishment for their actions. The panel was unanimous in declaring that unless the silence was broken, the shame for victims removed, and consequences for predators became the norm rather than the exception, large swaths of the population would continue to fall victim to sexual assault.

The panel discussion and the comments from the audience lifted Annie's spirits. The movement was catching on; sexual violence was being taken more seriously. Peter would come of age in a different world from that of his parents and his Aunt Reenie. As the meeting broke up, she packed her briefcase feeling more optimistic than she could remember. Change was in the air. She walked a little taller as she made her way up the aisle of the auditorium. When she got to the lobby a nice-looking, bearded young man approached her.

"Pardon me. I wanted to thank you for your contributions to the panel. I found your comments very helpful. It's the first time I actually heard people talk about the trauma young girls experience when they're victims of a sexual attack."

Annie extended her hand, immediately curious about what drew this man to the topic. "Annie Adelson. Thanks for that. It's not often young men express interest in our work."

"I admit there was a time I wouldn't have given it a second thought," the fellow said, "but it's something I've wondered about for several years now. I don't imagine you remember me, but we've met once before. It was actually at your parents' house. I'm Al Jaffe."

Suddenly everything came into focus. "Reenie's Albert?" Annie asked.

He frowned. "Maybe once upon a time. Perhaps there's a shred of truth to that even now."

"I never knew exactly how things ended up between you and Reenie. She wouldn't discuss it with me, but she told our grandmother that she just wanted to move on. I've always suspected there was likely much more to it than that."

Albert's penetrating blue eyes stared unblinkingly at Annie. "It's true that she did want to move on. She told me it had nothing to do with me, which at the time I didn't believe. Even though I knew she'd experienced an assault, it wasn't until I listened to the discussion just now that I understood she was telling me the truth. It wasn't me. Things had changed for Reenie and those changes made our relationship impossible for her."

Annie searched the face of the young man before her. She found no trace of the happy and hopeful boy she'd met so many years before. The man before her was nothing if not serious, perhaps even glum. She looked at her watch. She had ninety minutes before having to pick up Peter from Judy's.

"Do you have time to grab a cup of coffee?"

Albert looked at his watch and nodded. "I can make the time."

The two found a booth in the diner on Broadway where Annie and Spence got engaged. They ordered, and then Annie initiated the conversation. "It may have been long ago, but I'll never forget how jealous I was of you and Reenie that day you came to visit us during Christmas break."

"Jealous of us? I had no idea. I guess I was too busy trying to impress you, your mom and grandma, while taking pleasure in every moment I had with Reenie. May I ask why we made you jealous?"

"My boyfriend at the time was not Jewish. I felt my family would never welcome him the way they were welcoming you. It's funny how things work, though. Now that boyfriend is my husband and he is Jewish, and my family loves him, but that's a story for another time. Suffice it to say that back then, I had no hope of ever being able to bring him home. My grandmother was so enamored of you. She was sure you were serious about Reenie."

"Your grandmother was right; I was a goner for Reenie. I think there's a part of me that still is. I know how ridiculous that must sound. It was so long ago and we were just kids at the time. A lot of water has gone over the dam in the intervening years."

"It doesn't sound ridiculous at all. Kids can love deeply, too. So what have you been up to in those intervening years?"

"After finishing up at Stanford I went to Cal Tech for my doctorate. I'm doing a post-doc in astrophysics here at Columbia. That's how I found out about the symposium. I saw the posters for it in Pupin Hall. That's my home base on campus."

"Isn't life funny? By chance you saw a poster and now, after all of these years, we're having a cup of coffee together. May I ask what drew you to the symposium?"

"The summer after freshman year, Reenie told me she'd been attacked. That was her reason for breaking things off with me. A couple of months later she wrote me a letter that filled in some of the blanks. She said that she'd been 'brutalized,' her word, left with physical scars. That letter has haunted me, left me wondering what something like that does to a person. I mean it was obvious that she'd changed. The last time I saw her, which must have been soon after the attack, the way she looked at me...it was awful. She seemed to find me offensive, maybe even scary. I don't mind telling you that hurt. I was completely undone by the way her feelings did a one-eighty. Her letter helped a bit. She apologized, saying she wasn't fit to be in a relationship with me. To think such a terrific girl could think that way...well, it was just staggering," Albert said, staring into his coffee cup.

"The assault certainly left its mark on her," Annie said, "but it also left its mark on me. I know my guilt for not protecting Reenie led to my decision to focus on sexual assault for my doctoral research. As you saw today, it remains the field I work in. The attack on Reenie changed my husband, too. At the time we were both active in Students for a Democratic Society. It turned out the assailant was one of Columbia's SDS bigshots, but even after my husband informed the SDS leaders of the attack – which they already had heard about from the rumor mill — they did nothing. The only consequence the assailant suffered was the scratches to his face Reenie managed to pull off during the attack and the bloody nose my husband gave him afterwards. The *coup de grace* was when SDS, which was all about espousing equality between the sexes, promoted the sonofabitch to "chief spokesman." We both ran for the door after that. Now my husband is an attorney for the ACLU, working with the Women's Rights Project. I know his strong commitment to equal rights for women stems, at least in part, from that awful night.

"Of course, Reenie was changed most by the assault. For her, it's been a long path of recovery. I'm proud of her. She's done what she's had to do in order to live every day. She didn't barricade herself in her room and curl up into a ball, which would have been completely understandable. But even though she continued to function out in the world, part of her was lost in the attack, certainly her innocence. She's had to overcome a fear of strangers. Today she's well and using her extraordinary mind to become a physician-scientist, researching the biological underpinnings of mental illness. It pretty much consumes all of her waking hours. She's actually right here at Columbia."

Albert froze. "She's here? At Columbia?"

"Well, at the medical school. In a little more than a year she'll graduate with her MD and a PhD in neuroscience."

Albert could hear the blood rushing in his ears. Knowing that Reenie was so close opened the floodgates to the memories of the time they spent together and the agony of their breakup. He closed his eyes and shook his head trying to subdue the flood of emotions.

Annie sensed she'd touched a tender spot. "I'm sorry. I didn't mean to upset you."

Albert cleared his throat. "It's…it's all right. I'm just surprised that she's so near. For some reason I'd always imagined her up at Cornell because of that professor she thought so much of, the one who studied pigeon navigation. Of course, I wish her the very best. She has an amazing mind. I've worked with some very bright people at Stanford and Cal Tech, but she's a match for any of them."

"I don't doubt it. She's been extraordinary since she was a little kid. I do worry about her being so single-minded about her work, even though it brings her great satisfaction. We all know there is more to life than work."

Albert cracked a smile. "Really? Like what?"

"Well, relationships, for example."

"In my experience relationships often produce the opposite of great satisfaction. Maybe Reenie's smart to just focus on her work."

"It's certainly been a very productive coping mechanism," Annie said. "I think she's content with her life. But some part of me always hopes that someday, if she meets the right person, she'll be open to the possibility of a relationship. Her positive experience with you provides proof that not all men are predators. She also has a great relationship with my husband. He's like her big brother. He was so protective, so kind after the attack. It made me love him even more."

"It sounds as though you married a really good guy."

"I got very lucky."

"You know, when I met Reenie that's exactly what I thought: I got lucky. I really thought she was the one. You know how it is, the power of first love."

"But you intimated that you've had other relationships. You must have gotten past that first love."

"I've had other girlfriends, including some long-term ones. So far, no one has worked out too well. I realize I bear some responsibility for those failures. It may sound crazy, but somehow I always end up comparing whomever I'm with to Reenie. They all fall short in one way or another. Maybe I'm just protecting myself against being hurt again. At least that's what my last girlfriend told me before she handed me back my key and walked out the door."

It was now obvious to Annie that, like her sister, Albert, carried scars from the attack. "You know, the research shows that loved ones of sexual assault victims have issues of their own," she explained gently. "A person dear to them has suffered and changed; their relationship is altered and sometimes comes apart. Think of it as a ripple effect, a 'secondary trauma' tied to the assault. Many loved ones feel guilty, blaming themselves for not protecting the victim. I had to deal with that. I was just in the next room from where Reenie was assaulted. The stereo was blasting and I was too wrecked to hear Reenie's screams. I don't imagine I'll ever forgive myself for that."

"It's odd that you bring up guilt. Once I realized what had happened, I berated myself for not going to MIT. I figured if I had, I would've been able to see Reenie more often and maybe the assault wouldn't have happened. I know it's foolish because proximity doesn't always translate to being able to protect someone you love."

Annie grimaced. "I'm living proof."

The two of them sat quietly for a moment before Annie continued. "Boyfriends and husbands of female victims respond in different ways. Some thirst for revenge. Others get very angry about what's been lost. A lot of men feel the need to hover over their girlfriend or wife to make sure something awful doesn't happen again. Believe it or not, some men even feel a sense of jealousy. All of those are normal reactions."

"I think I experienced every one of those at one time or another, with the exception of hovering over Reenie. I never got the chance, but I would have, had she let me. Knowing that something so terrible had happened to her really freaked me out."

Annie suddenly felt very close to Al. "You and me both."

"I had no idea people were studying the boyfriends of assault victims. How did anyone think to take their research in that direction?"

"It became obvious that it's not just the victim who is affected by sexual violence. Since the assault victim is traumatized, her interactions with the people who love her are affected. That has an emotional impact on each of them. Researchers like me are examining the nature and dimensions of that impact. "

"Funny how all these years later, this is still so raw for me. Sometimes it really bugs me that I haven't been able to throw it off."

"That's the insidious power of trauma."

"I was egoistical enough to think it was only me. I guess it's a relief to know I'm not a nutcase."

"No, you're certainly not crazy; just a caring person who suffered a loss."

"Thank you. I think I needed to hear that." He stood up and extended his hand to Annie.

"I'm so glad you sought me out, Al. Before you go I want you to understand that I'll be telling Reenie that we met over coffee. I have no idea how she'll take it. But I don't keep secrets from her. Being able to trust people again has been a long journey for her. I won't do anything to undermine that."

"I don't want to cause her any distress. Just seeing me made her so upset the last time we met."

"But that was a long time ago. These last couple of years she's been good, really good. She's living on her own now. She's a black belt in karate. She even teaches classes. You should see the punches, chops, and kicks she lands in *kumite* sparring. I have to remind myself that I am watching my bookish little sister rather than some Japanese master. Then, of course, she loves her work. I'd say she's in a good place. That's a roundabout way of explaining why I think she'll be okay with the news that we've spoken."

Albert put his hands together and bowed. "The astrophysicist happily defers to the wisdom of the eminent psychologist."

§§§

The Saturday after the symposium Annie accepted Irene's offer to watch Peter, which would allow her and Spence to see Woody Allen's newest movie, *Annie Hall*, something they'd been itching to do since reading the review in the *New York Times*. But the first thing on Annie and Spence's agenda for the day was to finally baby-proof the apartment. Now that Peter had started walking, it could be put off no longer. They got an early start and were making steady progress. But just as Spence installed the first childproof lock on the cabinet under the kitchen sink, he got a panicked call from his office. The case headed to the Supreme Court had run into a snag. They needed him ASAP.

Left to her own devices with an active and curious ten-month old who didn't nap, Annie got almost nothing accomplished that day — neither in terms of babyproofing nor preparing the stuffed cabbage and roasted potatoes she planned to serve for dinner. She had wanted to surprise Irene with her favorite dish, but minutes before she was due to arrive, Annie threw up her hands in surrender. Tonight would be yet another pizza night. Spence could pick it up on his way home.

At four o'clock, Irene walked through the door and immediately noticed her sister was still wearing her pajamas. A quick scan of the living room told Irene all she needed to know. She hugged Annie and then bent down to pick up Peter. "How would you like to take a stroller ride to the playground with Aunt Reenie?" she asked. Though Peter didn't yet speak, he understood a lot. The moment he heard "stroller" and "playground," he started clapping his hands.

"Really?" Annie asked. "Would you do that for me? I know I sound like a terrible mother, but I could really use a few minutes to myself. I feel like I've been attached to a whirling dervish all day. I'd give my finest china for a chance to jump in the shower and wash my hair."

Irene was perplexed. "Annie, to the best of my knowledge, you have no fine china."

"Right, but if I did, I'd give it away in a heartbeat."

"I did it again," Irene lamented.

It was Annie's turn to be perplexed. "Did what?"

"I have to learn not to take things so literally."

"Are you kidding? Then you wouldn't be you, and I think you're perfect just as you are."

Irene laughed. "I know that as my sister, your options are somewhat limited, but thank you all the same."

§§§

In the hour and a half Irene and Peter were out of the house, Annie showered, restored order to the living room, baby-proofed a number of electrical outlets, made a salad to accompany the pizza and some chocolate pudding for dessert. By the time Spence came home with the pizzas in hand, Annie felt on top of her game again. Over dinner, while Peter persisted in his attempt to feed himself with a spoon, the three adults caught up with what the week had brought. As her psychiatry rotation was winding down, Irene listed the pros and cons of doing a residency in psych, as opposed to neurology. Spence talked about Ruth Bader Ginsburg's ingenious theory of the case for *Califano v. Goldfarb,* the lawsuit going to the Supreme Court. Ginsburg, head of the ACLU's Women's Project, was challenging the regulation that allowed the Social Security Administration to refuse survivor benefits to a widower based on his deceased wife's work record. Such discrimination, Ginsburg argued, was based on gender stereotypes. It not only devalued the work record of wives, it resulted in harm to husbands. A lively conversation ensued about how clever she was to bring a case on gender discrimination based on harm to *men.*

When it was Annie's turn, she shared her excitement about the panel discussion at Columbia, how well attended it had been and how on point the comments and questions were. Then she casually added that Al Jaffe had been in the audience.

Irene was sure she must have misheard. "Who did you say was in the audience?" she asked.

"Your old boyfriend, Albert."

Irene could feel her face grow hot. "How could you be certain it was him? You said there were a lot of people there."

"You're right about that. I never could have picked him out in the crowd, but he came up to me afterwards and introduced himself. Even then I never would have recognized him. He's got a beard now. He's grown into quite a handsome man."

Irene wished she could will her pounding heart back into normal sinus rhythm. "Well, what did you say to him?" she asked with an urgency that surprised them all.

Annie met Irene's agitation with calm. "We spoke a bit and then I asked him if he had time to grab a coffee so we could catch up," she explained.

"What? You wanted to catch up with Albert? Why?" Irene inquired. "Why would you want to do that?"

"Truthfully?"

"Yes, of course."

"Because he looked a bit forlorn. And also because he said the subject of sexual assault was something he'd been mulling over for many years. Plus, I really was in the mood for a cup of coffee."

"And?" Irene asked impatiently.

"He agreed."

"Do you plan on telling me what happened?"

Annie stepped carefully now. "I'll tell you as much as you want to know."

"I would have preferred you asked me before you met with him, but since you didn't, of course I want to know the details of what the two of you discussed."

"All right. As we talked, it became clear that the lovely young man you liked so much has changed quite a bit. I guess that's not surprising, given all the time that's passed. But what did surprise me was that I saw no trace of that happy, eager boy you brought home back in the day. He's quite solemn now, very accomplished, and I would say a bit sad. He did his PhD in astrophysics at Cal Tech. Now he's doing a post-doc in the city."

"Where in the city?" Irene asked.

"At Columbia. That's how he saw the signs for the symposium."

Irene didn't say anything more. She focused her eyes on her plate and moved the remnants of the salad around with her fork.

"Don't be angry, Reenie," Annie said. "I told Albert I don't keep secrets from you, so I would be telling you that we'd spoken."

"And I imagine I was a topic of discussion, as well," Irene said, her resentment rising.

"Yes. That's true. Albert more or less said that he never got over you."

Irene felt her eyes begin to smart. "You had no right, Annie, no right at all to talk about me like that. The poor, victimized Reenie. I can see it all now."

"Yes, we spoke about you, about the hard fight you fought, and about how well you're doing now."

Irene sat stone faced, her eyes still locked on her plate.

"But we spoke mostly about Albert and also about me and about sexual violence generally," Annie continued. "He said you'd told him about the assault and that you'd elaborated more about it in a letter, explaining the break-up wasn't his fault. Apparently he took the news that you'd been hurt pretty hard. Reading between the lines, I think he took losing you even harder. From what he said, I think he's struggled to understand what happened between the two of you. I explained to Al that his reaction is quite common in the aftermath of an assault."

As the tears streamed down her face, Irene stood up and threw her napkin on the table. "You had no right, Annie. I've worked so hard to put that brutal time behind me. I can't believe you just went ahead and dredged up the whole bloody mess again, and with Albert, of all people."

Just as she turned to leave, Peter started to wail. Spence picked up the crying baby and followed Irene to the door.

"Reenie. I can only imagine how hard that was to hear," Spence said. "Annie meant no harm. You know your sister, if there's someone in distress, she's there to help. That's who she is. It sounds as though the attack left its mark on Albert, too. It probably was good for him to talk to someone who understands the ripple effects of something so traumatic."

Spence searched Irene's face, but she refused to meet his gaze. "It's a lot to digest. Take whatever time you need to process what Annie told you, but please...don't be a stranger. We love you, Reenie. Even Peter is crazy about you." Spence put his free arm around Irene and hugged her. Peter, now merely whimpering, planted a wet kiss on his aunt's cheek. For a moment, Irene didn't resist, but then she broke free, grabbed her coat, and rushed out the door.

§§§

She walked for miles along First Avenue. Long after sunset, Irene continued to picture Albert and Annie casually discussing the most painful time in her life. Awash in anger and shame, her verdict on her sister's decision to have a tête-a-tête with Albert was as swift as it was harsh: Indefensible. What gave her the right? Just thinking about it brought Irene to tears again. As she passed the tram to Roosevelt Island, her thoughts drifted to what Annie had said about Albert, how the breakup had been difficult for him to come to terms with. Annie called him "a bit sad." Why would that be, Irene wondered? And why would Albert go out of his way to attend a symposium on sexual assault? It was hardly something the average twenty-seven year old male would be drawn to.

Years before, when Annie told her that she'd chosen sexual violence as the focus of her doctoral research, Irene squirmed; it distressed her to think of her sister plumbing the depths of the evil that had changed her life. Still, she understood Annie's decision. But that Albert would seek out a lecture on sexual assault was curious. Nearly nine years had passed since they broke up. Could he still be probing the reasons she pulled away? And what of the sadness Annie spoke of? Try as she might, Irene could not imagine Albert as anything other than the ebullient, hopeful boy he'd been. What had caused the change?

When she got to Ninety-Sixth Street her fury at Annie continued at a low boil. Still, Irene knew only she could answer the questions ricocheting around in her head. She found a payphone and dialed the number. When Annie picked up, she launched into the question that seemed most pressing. "In your professional opinion, why is Albert, as you put it, forlorn?"

Annie formulated her response with care. "We only spoke for a little while, but I think Albert was entirely frank with me. Losing you hurt, but his inability to get over the relationship after all this time worries him. He thinks of it as a character flaw. He also is deeply troubled by the knowledge that you were harmed. He wishes he could have protected you; barring that, that he could have at least helped you in some way in the aftermath of the attack. He used the word 'haunted' to describe how the assault has affected him. In my professional opinion, I think he suffered a secondary trauma."

"Thank you, Annie."

"That's the least I can do. I'm sorry I upset you."

"Spence was correct when he said it's a lot to digest. I have to sort this all out. Sorry about not staying and watching Peter."

"You have nothing to be sorry for. I probably would have fallen asleep as soon as they darkened the theater. And Reenie?"

"Yes?"

"Thanks for taking Peter today. You were a lifesaver. And if I overstepped my bounds, I'm sorry."

"You did, but I know it wasn't your intention to hurt me."

"I would never do that. You know that, don't you, Reenie?"

"Yes."

"Please remember what Spence told you. We all love you."

"I have to go now." Irene placed the receiver on the phone and thought about all that Annie had said as she walked the remaining miles home.

§§§

In the days that followed, questions about Albert intruded into Irene's normal, comforting routines. She kept wondering about his decision to attend a symposium on sexual trauma. It stunned her to think that he might still be troubled by the knowledge of what had happened so long ago. It also infuriated her to think that Steve Shapiro's poison had infected not only her, but Albert, too. She'd never imagined Albert as anything but happy, carrying on with his life and work in the years following the break-up. It was hard to accept that she'd caused him lasting distress. She mulled that over and over again in her mind, and always came to the same conclusion: She had to try to make amends.

Irene went to the Columbia directory and found that Albert Jaffe was residing just a block from where she, Annie and Spence had lived for so long. It was strange to know that Albert lived on a street she'd walked countless times. Realizing he was so close frightened and excited her. She'd worked so hard to achieve a sense of balance in her life, but since Annie's revelation, everything was out of kilter. More than anything, she wanted to get a handle on the feelings that were washing over her. The only way to do that was to confront her fear of seeing Albert again.

She reached out to him in the way that had once been so comfortable and familiar.

Dear Albert,

You can imagine my surprise when Annie told me you and she had spoken. I had no idea you were in New York, or that you were doing research at Columbia.

If you're amenable, I would like the chance for us to meet. There are some things that were left unsettled and unsaid all those years ago. Perhaps we can put them to rest now.

I will understand if you'd rather not, of course. I was not at all kind to you the last time we were together. I'm afraid I was incapable of being kind then.

I am free this Sunday morning. I'll be on the steps of the Museum of Natural History at ten. Perhaps I'll see you then.

Either way, I send you my very best, Albert.

Reenie

Once the letter was in the mail, Irene felt better. She prepared for the possibility that Albert might ignore her invitation, but she also prepared for an acceptance. That Sunday morning she got up early, ran five miles, showered and dressed. She put her hair up in a top knot, put in her contacts, and resurrected her make-up skills, aiming to strike a balance between looking well but not alluring. Should Albert decide to meet her, she wanted to appear calm and confident, not someone looking for something, be it pity, protection, or something more. And, if Annie was right and Albert was in need of comfort, she hoped she would be able to provide him some relief from his unhappiness.

She got to the museum a few minutes before ten. She thought it lucky that the weather was cooperating, particularly because she'd said to meet outside. She found a good spot on the base of the flagpole, out of the way of people ascending the stairs. The museum would open soon. She brought a book to prepare herself for the possibility that Albert might be late, or might not come at all. At ten on the dot she looked up from her reading and saw some young men approaching the stairs. Three seemed to be in a group and one appeared to be on his own. It's a good thing Annie mentioned the beard, because Irene might have looked right past Albert as he walked up the steps in her direction. He had filled out since he was a teenager, the gangly boy replaced by a well-proportioned, attractive man. But his curly hair was still wild in the wind. As he came near, Irene felt sure she saw the hint of a smile on his face. What surprised her most was the stirrings of feelings she hadn't experienced for so long. It was as though she were sixteen again and meeting Albert at the subway station in Brooklyn. Everything between that moment and the present fell away.

She stood up to meet him. Their eyes met and held one another's gaze for what seemed a long time. As much as he wanted to, Albert didn't dare touch her. The image of her recoiling from him in front of her college dorm was burned into his memory. It was Irene who stood on tiptoes and kissed him gently on the cheek, then took his hand and guided him to sit beside her under the flagpole.

"Thank you for coming," Irene said. "I wasn't sure you would."

"Truthfully, I wrestled with the wisdom of meeting again. It seemed like it would be pulling the scab off an old wound. Maybe not such a great idea."

Irene winced. "I am so sorry that you were hurt. If I'd had it in my power, you would have never been, at least not because of me. I hope you know that. When I think back, the months we were together were the happiest of my life. But the last time we met —there's no sugarcoating it — I was in a bad way. I imagine Annie would have more clinical terms for the state I was in."

Albert couldn't help but stare at the graceful neck and expressive eyes of the lovely woman sitting beside him. Like Irene, he was transported back to the time when they shared their deepest emotions and an easy laugh. He realized Irene was awaiting his response. "Pardon me. What were you saying?"

"Just that I apologize for being in such a state when we met last. I never meant to hurt you."

"Please," he said, shaking his head, "no apology is needed. Annie's panel discussion taught me a lot about what people go through afterwards...as they try to heal and resume their lives. I admit I had no idea. I'm sorry I wasn't able to be a help to you then. I'm sure you could have used a good friend."

Irene smiled. "It was thanks to *you* that I had good friends. You remember your advice about meeting people during my freshman year?"

Albert smiled. "Actually, I do."

"Fredi, Raisa, Max, and Meryl — maybe you remember them from one of your visits — they did their best to help me regain my footing. I can't say enough about Annie and her husband. She didn't leave my side for days. Thinking back on it now, I can see I was very lucky. I had a bounty of love and support to help me through that awful time."

"But none from me. I was no help at all. In fact, from the way our last meeting went down, I'd say I was the antithesis of help."

"You're being too harsh on yourself. You visited a happy, hopeful girl on spring break, a girl who was in love with life and with you, and when you returned three months later you found a damaged and lost girl. There was no way for you to know what was wrong or how to help. When I think of it now from your point of view...you had to be mystified by my behavior."

"That about sums it up."

"As wrapped up as I was in my own pain, I could see from the expression on your face how nothing added up. It must have seemed like a bad dream or a terrible prank."

"You've got that right," Albert admitted, "the only difference being that dreams and pranks end. I never quite managed to get on top of my confusion — or my disappointment. I started to doubt everything that had happened between us."

"You wandered into my nightmare and suffered because of it. I regret that very much. You should never have had to doubt how happy we'd been."

"So it was real."

"Yes," Irene said. "Very real, and very wonderful."

Albert studied her face and then reached for her hand. He was heartened when Irene didn't pull away. "I didn't understand any of it. I just knew the girl I loved rejected me."

"It doesn't seem fair that kids of sixteen and eighteen should have to experience so much pain."

"I'm not ashamed to admit that it nearly did me in," Albert said. "The summer of '68 was the worst time of my life."

"And for me, as well."

They sat quietly for a while watching the pedestrians walk along Central Park West.

"Do you think people can get used to being hurt?" Irene asked. "Maybe being wounded confers some sort of immunity from a future insult."

"Wouldn't that be nice?" Albert asked dubiously. "I don't think it works that way, at least not from my experience. I may be a sample size of one, but I can say that subsequent relationship disasters were no easier to weather."

Irene looked at him and smiled. "So you tried again?

Albert nodded.

"I'm glad you did."

"Tried and failed. Many times."

"I admire your courage. I never did try again. At first I was terrified of almost everyone, thinking they could turn on me at any time. I admit that

I'm still pretty suspicious of men I don't know well. Karate, which has become such an important part of my life, helped me overcome my fears."

"Your sister told me you took up karate. I'll try to remember to keep your considerable self-defense ability in mind," Albert said, a hint of his boyish smile making a reappearance.

"I'm happy to report I've never needed my karate sparring anywhere but in the studio."

"That's a relief for us both," Albert said, marveling at how the girl he'd loved and mourned had found a way to rebuild her life. "You're right about it taking courage to put yourself out there again, to be open to love, knowing it could end badly…probably *will* end badly."

"Though I haven't yet found the nerve to try again, I do take comfort from Annie and her husband," Irene said. "They found each other when they were sophomores in college. If anything, they're closer now than they ever were. I think if you keep trying Albert, you'll get lucky."

"I was already lucky. I found you. The thought has crossed my mind that maybe I used up my luck."

Irene had to fight to keep her composure. "I refuse to believe that's true."

"Well, I'm sitting here next to you and my heart is racing in my chest like I'm sprinting around a track, so maybe you're right. Maybe luck hasn't abandoned me completely."

It seemed like the most natural thing in the world when Irene put her hands on Albert's face and gently kissed him. "You'll get lucky again, Albert. You'll see."

§§§

Although the years had marked and altered them both, some things remained constant for Irene and Albert. That beautiful April day in 1977, when they met on the steps of the museum, something verging on the magical happened; the foundation for a bridge that would span the years and reconnect their lives began to be laid. They took it slow. Albert was loath to do anything that would remind Irene of the last time she had sexual contact with a man, so he held back and followed her lead. They met for dinner, caught a movie on a rare night both had free, took walks along the Hudson River. They held hands. Irene would nuzzle her head in his neck.

They kissed upon meeting and leaving one another. It was difficult for Albert. He'd lived with two women over the years, and sex had become part of his life. But he swore off all others as he took the time to see what would come of this new beginning with Irene.

They both had some time off coming up in June. It was Irene who suggested they take a trip to the Hudson Valley. "I don't know if I ever told you how much I love the country. There's a sculpture park I read about in Mountainville: Storm King. We can get to it from Grand Central. We could take the train up and if we're having a good time, we could stay over."

Irene's last words hung in the air.

"Together?" Albert asked.

"Yes, I think so, Albert. Would you like that?"

Albert embraced her. "Oh, yeah, I'd like that very much. I've been ready for a while, but I want you to be ready, too. I want this to be everything we hoped for all those years ago."

"I'm not certain it's possible, but I am willing to try, and for that I'm grateful."

§§§

What struck Irene after she and Albert made love was that there could be any connection between the wonder and ecstasy they'd experienced and the violence of sexual abuse. That they were both categorized as "sex," seemed illogical to her. Where one was gentle, the other was vicious; where one was reciprocal, the other controlling. Besides the genitalia involved, there seemed to be no common ground. While the assault set her apart from the world, she was at one with Albert as they made love, two parts of a whole finally brought together in the act of physical congress. For Irene, the joy of the moment was followed by the realization that she had, at last, cleansed herself of the toxin Steve Shapiro had injected into her life. His savagery, which had defined her for so long, was replaced by the tenderness and pleasure she and Albert had created together.

§§§

Though overjoyed with the way their weekend had turned out, Albert reminded himself more than once not to hope for too much. Though it seemed that Reenie had come back into his life — the same earnest, smart, gorgeous girl he'd fallen for as a boy — he knew much more about the pitfalls of relationships than he did when he was a teenager. He decided to deem his time with Reenie as a gift, but one that might be taken away at any time. As much as he loved being with her again, he refused to make assumptions about its staying power. As he knew all too well, things could turn to dust between them. Still, it took all his self-control not to engage in the "what ifs." He loved Reenie as much – maybe more – than when he was a boy. Now she was a fully grown woman, someone who'd overcome so much and achieved so brilliantly in the intervening years. There was much more to love, to long for, and admire.

It was good that he had his research on neutrino oscillation to keep him busy.

Astrophysicists discussed and endlessly speculated on neutrino oscillation, but for Albert the field had the additional advantage of being a steadying force in his personal life. All those years ago, as he was trying to get over Reenie's rejection, he became intrigued by the large discrepancy between the theoretical prediction of solar neutrino flux and what was directly measured by neutrino detectors, something referred to in physics as "the solar neutrino problem." It put in question the assumption that the neutrino had zero mass, which in turn, led to doubts about the accuracy of the bedrock of modern science, the Standard Model of Particle Physics. The solar neutrino problem fueled his doctoral research, while seeing him through a number of unsuccessful relationships. It never failed to intrigue him, and remained at the core of his post-doctoral work. Now it also provided refuge from the storm of emotions his new affair with Reenie had let loose.

One beautiful Sunday morning in August, Irene suggested they have a picnic brunch in Central Park before going to work that afternoon. They picked up some bagels and coffee and headed for the North Meadow. Lying on their blanket, they watched bicyclists whiz by and streams of young families and older couples out for a stroll.

"Albert. I've been thinking. This is the last year of my program. I have to submit my residency application very soon. I've been wondering how to put this to you. I don't want to seem as though I'm making assumptions, but the truth is I am."

Albert was ready. This was it. Irene had discovered she could be in a sexual relationship and feel safe. Now she could strike out on her own.

He'd been good for her, he'd helped her, that much he knew, but as he sat up on their blanket, he braced himself for the worst.

"I have to make plans for the future. Maybe I won't be matched to a residency program in the city. I know of someone who matched to Birmingham, Alabama, so I have to be ready for anything. But the more thought I've given to this, the more I know I can't imagine my life without you. I want to experience the future *with you*. I was wondering, would you consider marrying me? I am entirely in love with you, Albert. I don't know if you feel quite the same way, but..." She was interrupted mid-sentence when Albert scooped her up in his arms and kissed her so many times she started to giggle.

"Oh, yeah, Reenie. I feel quite the same way," he whispered into her ear. "As a matter of fact, I think your proposal is first-rate." Then he kissed Irene again before putting her down and snuggling beside her.

"I'm aware that traditionally it's the man in the relationship who does the asking, but I thought that was a vestige from another time that we could dispense with. I hope you don't mind."

"I couldn't agree more. But here's the thing, Reenie," Albert said, sitting up and looking at her earnestly. "Did you get me a ring?"

Irene was taken aback. "Oh, I didn't think of that. I wasn't aware of engagement rings for men. It must be a new trend. I've been so busy these last several years I probably missed it. If you'd like a ring, perhaps we can get matching ones. Actually, I'd like that."

"One of the things I will never stop loving about you is how guileless you are, though it's just one of the many reasons I'm mad for you. I second the motion for matching rings. What do you say we save them for the day we get married?"

§§§

Neither Irene nor Albert had much interest in a wedding party. As far as they were concerned City Hall would accomplish the goal of joining their lives together just as well and far more easily than a big, expensive wedding. But neither set of parents would hear of their children being married without guests, formal clothes, bountiful food, and joyous music. Although they hadn't met in person, Gladys Adelson and Irma Jaffe bonded over the phone and through letters as they planned a June 1978 celebration befitting their children's marriage. The mothers were ecstatic that Albert and Reenie had found one another again after so many years. It was as though the buoyancy and hopefulness their children had misplaced on their way to adulthood had been reclaimed.

The families met for the first time at Irene's medical school graduation. Just a week later, the proud parents walked their children down the aisle. In the end, Irma and Gladys's thoughtful planning gave rise to a beautiful day for the bride, the groom, their families, and guests. Irene and Albert were beaming throughout the ceremony and the festivities that followed. Annie, Irene's sole attendant, wore an attractive gown that artfully concealed the early signs of her second pregnancy. Albert's brother Robert, a newly-minted doctor himself, did the honors of best man. Even two-year old Peter got into the act. He moseyed down the aisle at his own pace, stopping to say "hi" to the guests. Eventually, he arrived at the *chuppah*, the wedding canopy, and handed the box with the wedding rings to Albert, just as his father had instructed him to do.

Once again, as she'd done for Annie and Spence, Raisa ensured the wedding party would be one filled with music and dancing. This time she brought along her beau Theo, who helped fund his MIT education by playing saxophone at upscale events around Boston. Two of his bandmates — also MIT-trained scientists — tagged along. Together the brain-trust of an ensemble welcomed the guests into the reception hall to "The Things We Do for Love."

As people sat down to dinner and the champagne was being served, Irma and Burton Jaffe and Meyer and Gladys Adelson toasted their children, wishing them every possible happiness under the sun. Annie was up next. She struggled to keep her voice from cracking as she spoke of her sister as her inspiration, a quiet little girl from Flatbush who had, throughout her life, exceeded everyone's expectations. In Albert, Reenie had found her equal, a partner with whom she could share her life. She closed with her toast. "To Reenie and Albert, who prove to me every day that truth and love are the most potent forces for good in the world. *L'Chaim!*[1]"

When Annie handed the mike to Robert, he told the guests how Reenie had transformed his brother from the serious egghead he'd become over the years back to the cheerful brother with whom he'd grown up. "He hasn't been this much fun since I was in junior high. He even short-sheeted my bed last night...I kid you not. You should have seen this brilliant

---

[1] To life!

astrophysicist with degrees from Stanford and Cal Tech rolling around on the floor laughing as I struggled to get into bed. What can I say? He's a new man. Levity and joy have returned to his life. I don't know your secret, Reenie, but if you bottle it, I think you could make a bundle."

Just as Robert was finishing up, Albert and Irene took the microphone to make a toast of their own. Irene was up first. "To the best sister in the world, Annie Adelson, who brought us together again." Albert picked up seamlessly from his bride. "For the rest of our lives we will give thanks to her wisdom and her kindness, her generosity of spirit and her great, good sense. Though we *think* it was unintentional, we give thanks for her incomparable matchmaking ability. It's because of her that we stand here before you as husband and wife."

Then, they raised their glasses, "To Annie!" Every guest in the room joined in. "To Annie!" they cheered.

PART THREE

1978- 2000

CHAPTER ELEVEN

MARRIED LIFE CAME EASILY to Irene and Albert. It was as though they were custom-made for one another, so naturally did they find a rhythm and routine for their life together. It quickly became apparent that Albert was the more accomplished of the two in the kitchen, so he took over all food-related duties: shopping, cooking, washing the dishes. Irene was the neater and more orderly of the pair, so she tidied up their one bedroom apartment on East 95th Street and took on the vacuuming, dusting, cleaning and laundry responsibilities. They rarely disagreed on mundane issues such as whether to cap the toothpaste or to have the shades drawn when they turned in for the night. When a difference of opinion arose, each explained his or her point of view. Albert learned early on that Irene found a logical argument hard to resist. As for Irene, what she wanted most was for Albert to be happy. It was a formula for marital harmony.

Irene and Albert shared an egalitarian view of their marriage. They agreed that each would keep their surname; when children came along, Adelson Jaffe would be their middle and last names. In terms of their future goals, they decided early on that neither career would take precedence over the other. They aimed to find work in a location where they'd both have the opportunity to thrive. That likely meant settling in a city — neither's first choice — where Albert could do his research, probably at a university, and Irene could find an academic position at a medical school. As for starting a family, something they both looked forward to, they decided to hold off until Irene completed her four-year residency.

During the early years of their marriage, their demanding schedules limited their time together. As a psychiatry resident at Cornell Medical's Payne Whitney Psychiatric Hospital, Irene's workweek routinely surpassed eighty hours. At first she found it difficult — sometimes even painful — to spend her days and nights with people who, like her mother, suffered from mental illness. Most of the in-patients had a diagnosis of schizophrenia or bipolar disorder; others were coping with major depression. The lucky among them had friends and family who stood by them, despite how difficult that often was to do. It was sometimes loved ones who gave Irene a window into the lives her patients led when not tormented by their disease. Knowing that the young man beset with delusional thinking had been a class valedictorian, or the woman in the midst of a bout of mania was an up-and-coming attorney when she remained on her medication, heightened Irene's drive to find treatment options that could free them from the clutches of disease. Her commitment, which she thought of at the start of each day, was to give her patients another chance to live the life they were meant to live — and likely would — had they not been stricken by a mental illness.

Albert's schedule, though less punishing, was demanding in its own right. After completing his post-doc, he'd been appointed assistant professor in Columbia's physics department. When crafting his lectures, he thought back on his favorite professors at Stanford and attempted to make his as engaging as theirs had been. He was surprised — and more than a little chagrined — at how many hours each week he needed to devote to his teaching. Even with all his preparation, he always felt just one step ahead of his students in terms of the curriculum. Then there was what he referred to as his "real job," his research. What time remained after teaching never seemed to be sufficient for that. Perhaps if Irene had been curled up on the sofa back at their apartment, he would have tried to bring work home rather than stay late at the university, but most often Irene got back after he did, sometimes after he'd been asleep for hours. He found that being home without Reenie made him sad, so he generally grabbed something for dinner from a bodega near campus and worked until nine each night.

The free time they shared was a precious commodity. They rarely passed up an opportunity to have sex, and Albert never tired of hearing Irene say how much she enjoyed making love with him. Family was important to them both. Once a month, they took the subway to Brooklyn for Sunday dinner at Gladys and Meyer's. It gave them the opportunity to see Grandma Bertha, whose mind remained sharp despite her growing frailty. They also got to spend time with Peter, now school-aged, and his little sister Rachel, who was born five months after her Aunt Reenie and Uncle Albert's wedding.

Though they lived at a distance, Albert's parents were woven into their married life, as well. Irma and Burt trekked to New York three or four times a year, always coupling their visit with a cultural marathon of museums, concerts, and Broadway plays. When they were back in Cleveland, Albert and Irene made sure to call every week. They also carved out time each year to travel to Ohio, always coordinating with Robert, a cardiology resident at the University of Rochester, so all the Jaffes could be under one roof for a little while, at least. As for vacation getaways, Albert's love of the ocean — something he developed during his years in California — tipped the balance in favor of a long weekend or two at the shore each summer. One visit to Cape May, New Jersey — with all its charming Victorian architecture and beautiful beaches — was all it took for it to become their favorite seaside destination.

In his third year as a professor Albert began to hit his stride. He was astonished when his students nominated him for a teaching award, citing his ability to make difficult concepts in physics accessible and even entertaining. Now that he'd developed a comprehensive set of lecture notes, he viewed the time with his students as a welcome respite from the growing intensity of his research. He found his fellow faculty members bright and collegial. When Leon Lederman left Columbia for Fermilab, Albert took it hard. He sorely missed his comrade's brilliance, his mentorship, and his wicked sense of humor.

As happy as Albert was at Columbia, the chances were only fifty-fifty that he would stay on long-term. First, there was the hurdle of tenure, which was not easily cleared no matter how hard or smart a young assistant professor worked. Second, once Irene finished her residency, she would need to do a post-doc somewhere to bring her back up to speed in terms of research. Only then would she be qualified to land a position as a professor at a medical school, her ultimate goal. Where Albert would ultimately end up working was an open question, and one he tried his best not to dwell on.

In early spring of Irene's third year of residency, they decided to start trying to conceive a child. After studying infertility in her obstetrics rotation, she understood that it might take several months — or even a year — to conceive. But the morning after they had unprotected sex for the first time, she awoke feeling a bit queasy. A groggy, unsettled feeling soon became her constant companion. One Saturday morning, two weeks after Irene had missed her period, she and Albert availed themselves of a new product, the home pregnancy test. It took two hours for the results to appear, so they decided to go out for breakfast and then take a walk in Central Park. At the coffee shop down the street from their apartment, Albert ordered a three-egg omelet, home fries, an English muffin and coffee. The only thing on the menu that looked vaguely appealing to Irene was an order of buttered white toast.

As the food was delivered to their table, the aroma of Albert's omelet was almost more than Irene could abide. Her stomach did somersaults as she watched him pour ketchup on his home-fries. "I bet you dollars to donuts you're pregnant," he said in between bites. You are so pregnant that you aren't even tempted by this delicious, cheesy omelet filled with mushrooms, onions, and peppers," he said, taunting his wife. "Or these cooked to perfection home-fried potatoes."

"Albert, you're going to be sorry if you continue to tease me this way," Irene warned, looking away from the food as a wave of nausea hit. "Obviously my appetite is altered, but women have been known to experience all the symptoms of pregnancy while not being pregnant. I diagnosed a patient with *pseudocyesis* last year. Sometimes it's caused by psychological factors, but in my patient's case, she had an ovarian tumor that mimicked the signs of pregnancy."

"Let's look at the probabilities, Reenie. You never felt like this before, and you only started to feel this way after we tried to get pregnant," Albert reasoned.

"Of course, it's probable that the test will show a positive result, but it's not a certainty. I'm explaining other possibilities because I don't want us to be disappointed."

Albert reached for her hand and kissed it. "If it's not positive this time, we'll have more fun trying for that positive result another time. But, if I were a betting man, I'd bet the farm that we're not going to be disappointed."

They got back to the apartment precisely two hours after they started the test. There, at the bottom of the test tube, was a distinct dark circle indicating Albert had been right: They were expecting. The two of them held hands and jumped around their living room like little children. If things went as hoped, a tiny boy or girl would join their little family in late

December. The enormity of what awaited them — the miracle of the new life, as well as the responsibility — filled them with awe and anticipation.

§§§

They made a concerted effort to make the most of the months leading up to the arrival of what Albert jokingly referred to as "the little physicist." Irene fit in a karate class every week. As her belly swelled, Albert sometimes shook his head and laughed as she was preparing to leave for class. "My wife, the mother of our unborn child, a physician-scientist, off to deliver karate chops and kicks!"

"Laugh all you want. One day you may need my protection, and since I love you, I'll provide it, even though you make fun of me," Irene said as she kissed him goodbye and rushed off.

As for Albert's recreation, he combined his love of the water with family bonding by organizing a males-only fishing trip to Lake Ontario the July before the baby was due. Meyer, a man who'd never laid hands on a fishing rod, gracefully declined, but Spence, Robert and Burt signed onto the plan. Irene was happy that Albert would have the opportunity to be on the water, something he longed for. It would also give her some time to spend with her parents, Annie and the kids, and Grandma Bertha, whose health seemed more delicate with each passing month.

§§§

The moment Irene entered her parents' apartment, she knew something was wrong. For starters, there was no music playing on the living room hi-fi. Now that Meyer was retired, he spent most afternoons listening to classical music or opera. But there was only silence. Irene walked through the foyer to the living room to find her mother and father embracing on the sofa. Not wanting to disturb their private moment, Irene pivoted to the kitchen. That's when her father called to her.

"Come, sweet girl. Come sit with us. We have something we have to tell you."

Irene sat down and braced herself. "What's happened?"

"We just got a call from Grandma's doctor. He ran some tests this week. The results are not good. She has leukemia," Meyer said, stifling a sob.

Irene leaned her head against Meyer's shoulder. She guessed it was AML, acute myeloid leukemia, which was more common in the elderly. The prognosis for a woman in her late eighties was poor. She, too, started to weep.

"*Mein kind*, don't be sad," Meyer said. "We've been so lucky to have had her for so long. I think she's been happy with us all these years."

Gladys objected. "I'm not ready to part with her. I don't care how old she is or how old I am. She's *my mother*, and the only one in my whole damned family who really got me from the start. I can't imagine life without her in it."

"Mommy, it's not just Grandma who gets you. Daddy, Annie, and I get you, too. And we love you, more than words can express. You're such a good mother. I'm sure Grandma showed you the way. I hope I can do half as well with this little one," Irene said, as she put her hand on her stomach.

"I know you all love me. But my mother was there from the time I took my first breath. You'll see, sweetheart, when you have your baby. That bond is like no other. And it's hard to let go of it," Gladys said, bringing a tissue to her eyes.

Irene nodded. "Have you told Grandma?"

Meyer smiled wryly. "Grandma told *us*. She didn't know what it was called, but last week she told us she was dying. That's why Mom insisted on taking her to the doctor before her scheduled checkup next month."

"Does she know the diagnosis?" Irene asked.

"We told her just before you came. She said she wanted to take a little nap before you, Annie and the kids arrived," Meyer said.

"If it's okay with you, I'd like to just sit with her for a while."

"Sure, sure," Meyer said. "Go be with Grandma."

§§§

Irene had seen death's approach many times during her training. She knew the signs: coolness of the hands and feet, restlessness, inability to eat or drink. But when Irene looked at her grandmother resting peacefully and felt the warmth of her hand, a sense of relief flooded over her. She noticed the glass of juice — mostly finished — at her bedside. There was still some time. Irene sat back in the chair and took the opportunity to close her eyes and drift off.

She wasn't sure how long she'd been asleep when she heard her grandmother's familiar voice. "Reenie, your belly is growing fast."

She leaned over and gave Bertha a kiss on the cheek. "Yes, the doctor says I'm large-for-date, which means the belly is unusually prominent for being only eighteen weeks along."

"Some women show early, that's all," Bertha said knowingly.

"You're probably right. You certainly had a lot of personal experience," Irene said.

"Five live births and two miscarriages."

"I didn't know you'd suffered miscarriages," Irene said. "I'm sorry."

"Five was enough. Some might say *more* than enough," Bertha laughed weakly.

"Is there something I can get for you or do for you? I am a doctor, you know, Grandma. Feel free to ask for anything," Irene said.

"You may be a doctor now, but you were my sweet little granddaughter first. All I want is to look at you and talk to you while I still can."

"Whatever you want, Grandma. You're the captain of this ship. We will all do whatever you want."

"I want you to know how much I love you, how proud I am of you. And I love Albert, too. I knew he was the one for you back when you two were just kids. You're a wonderful couple. And you'll be wonderful parents. I'm pretty sure I won't be around to see that, but I know you'll be a good mother and Albert will be terrific, too."

Irene tried her best to hold back the tears. "Grandma, no one knows how long any of us will live. I say that because being a doctor has humbled me. We *think* we know what's coming, but sometimes even doctors get surprised."

"I don't need to be a doctor to know my time is near. I accept that. I've lived a full life. I have only a few regrets. Mostly, I've been blessed. Look at me, living with my children who love me, visited by my busy, successful, grandchildren, living to be a great-grandmother. You know, a person can't be greedy." Bertha chuckled a bit at her own joke.

"No, we can't be greedy," Irene agreed. "I would selfishly like you to meet whoever is in here," she said, tapping her belly. "Promise me you'll tell me if you're in pain. We can help you with that."

"A heroine I'm not, so I'll tell you if it gets too difficult," Bertha said. "I accept that my life is coming to a close, but I am a little worried about what happens before the end. Knowing you can help if things get rough gives me peace of mind. Thank you, *bubbelah*[1]."

"I'll talk with your doctor. We'll keep you comfortable. I promise." That broke the dam and Irene started to sob.

"Don't be sad, sweetheart. I lived a long life. We've had so many wonderful times. And you'll have a lot more good times."

"It won't be the same if you're not with us, though," Irene cried.

"It's okay to miss me after I'm gone. To be honest, I like knowing that you'll miss me. But mostly, I want you to live your life. Be good to yourself, Reenie. You work too hard sometimes. Soon you'll have someone who needs you for everything. Take the time you need to enjoy your baby and give the little one what he needs. Work is important, especially your work. I know that. But being a parent is also important. Always remember that you'll be the only mother your baby will ever have."

§§§

Over the next two months Bertha had a parade of visitors. Women from the building she and Herman lived in for decades had their children or grandchildren bring them by to spend time with their old friend. Her daughters Iris, Doris, Phyllis, and Alice took turns coming over, one each day. Gladys had never forgotten their repudiation of Annie and Spence, their shunning of the wedding, and the nervous breakdown that came in its wake. Their visits were daily reminders of a grim time in her life and the gulf that separated her from her own flesh and blood. Still, they were Bertha's children, too. She accepted whatever help they offered in that spirit, and for the respite it provided from the round-the-clock care Bertha required.

---

[1] Sweetie, darling one

In August, Albert and Irene came to share some news. "Grandma," Irene said, unable to wipe the smile from her face. "Remember how I told you the doctor said my belly was large-for-date?"

Bertha was sitting in the medical recliner Irene had suggested her parents rent. "Yes, of course. And you're so much bigger now."

"Well, it appears there's a reason for this large belly," Albert said with an equally irrepressible grin. "You're not going to believe this Bertha, but Reenie and I are having twins!"

"*Gut in himmel!*[1]" Bertha exclaimed with all the energy she could muster. "What news! The first twins in the family. *Oiy vey!* Boy oh boy, are you two going to be busy!"

"I know, Grandma. I'm a little nervous about it, to tell you the truth. I'm not sure how we're going to juggle taking care of them with my finishing the last months of my residency and all of Albert's work."

"God gave you two those big brains for a reason. If any two people can figure it out, it's you. Just remember what I told you when I thought you were having one baby. Your work is important, but you will be the only parents these babies will have. And…they're babies for just a very little while. You'll see. You'll find a way to manage."

§§§

Bertha died after the High Holy Day of Yom Kippur. By the time she passed, the entire family – even Gladys – was relieved her trials were over. Throughout the last weeks of her life, Irene was true to her word, making certain her grandma was not in pain. But Bertha didn't like needing others to help her bathe and dress, things she'd done independently since she was a little girl. On Rosh Hashanah Eve, she soiled herself for the third time in as many days as Gladys helped her to the bathroom. Gladys was gentle with her as she suggested that they get adult diapers at the neighborhood pharmacy. Bertha knew she had no choice but to submit to the indignity, but it was the final straw. She wanted no part of a life that reduced her to helplessness. She stopped eating and drinking the day after Rosh Hashanah. Ten days later, she was gone.

---

[1] God in heaven!

§§§

Given Gladys's breakdown around the time of her father's death, Irene and Annie feared how Gladys would face life without Bertha. The two sisters made a pact to ensure their mother felt wanted, needed and valued. Many babysitting requests were made by Annie, and Irene called nearly every day to ask Gladys's advice on things she should buy in preparation for the twins' arrival. It was during one of those phone calls that Gladys — with Meyer on the extension — made a surprising offer.

"Now that Grandma's gone, we have a lot more time on our hands," Gladys said. "What do you think about us taking care of the babies through the end of your residency? We'd love being with them; they're tiny for such a short time. Plus, we'd like to help you and Albert out."

Irene was incredulous "Really? Are you sure? I imagine it will be a lot of work."

"It will be, but it will be good for me, and for Dad, too. We'll do it together."

"I looked into hiring someone who did infant care, someone recommended by one of the attending doctors at the hospital. But her fee was nearly as much as I take home every paycheck. Plus, I've been trying to quell my misgivings about leaving the babies with a total stranger."

"Well, we won't be able to do it forever. But while they're small, the two of us will be able to manage," Gladys said.

"As long they stay where we put them, it'll be fine," Meyer agreed. "But once they start crawling around, I'm telling you now: I'll be handing in my letter of resignation."

"Yes, absolutely yes," Irene rejoiced. "On behalf of Albert, myself, and the twins, I accept."

§§§

With the money they'd be saving on daycare, Albert and Irene started hunting for a bigger apartment. Eight weeks before the babies' were due, they moved into a spacious if pricey two-bedroom sublet on York Avenue. Though the rent would eat up nearly all of Irene's salary, they felt lucky to have an apartment two blocks from the hospital, with room enough for Gladys and Meyer to stay over on nights when she was on call or a winter storm hit the city. Albert's commute would be quite a bit longer, but he viewed it as a reasonable price to pay for the convenience the new apartment would provide the rest of the family.

They hired a moving company that transported all their things to York Avenue and then stacked their labeled boxes in the appropriate rooms. Irene and Albert immediately unpacked some essentials and left the rest for another day. When Gladys and Meyer stopped by to see their new place two weeks later, the apartment was still filled with boxes piled high. Without consulting his wife, Meyer floated an idea. "Albert, Reenie, what would you think of Mom and me unpacking for you? I hear rich people actually pay the movers to do it. We'll do it for you — no charge."

The thought of setting up the new apartment appealed to Gladys. She'd just given away the last of her mother's belongings, leaving her with a terrible sense of emptiness. It would be good to have something hopeful and happy to do. But...she feared Meyer had overstepped. "Honey, we can't foist ourselves on our children. They're capable of taking care of it themselves."

"Actually, we're not," Irene admitted. "Packing everything up for the move set both of us back at work. The truth is, we don't have the time to unpack."

"Well, if that's the case, we'll be happy to help out," Gladys said.

And so it was settled. Irene knew that at her best, her mother was a marvel of organization, and Gladys did not disappoint. For the better part of two weeks, she and Meyer took the subway to 68th Street every morning after rush hour. She devised a system of keeping track of everything they unpacked and where it was put. One morning when Albert was searching for the peanut butter to make his lunch, he put Gladys's method to the test. The spiral notebook with her hand-written guide led him to the exact shelf in the correct cabinet in less than a minute. Although he'd been something of a doubting Thomas on the issue of having his in-laws set up their household, after experiencing Gladys's organizational skills first hand, he joked that she and Meyer should start a new business: *Organizers, Inc. — We'll Set Your Household Straight.*

Having her parents in the apartment every day gave Irene the chance to keep an eye on Gladys as she processed the grief of losing Bertha. Irene watched carefully, trying to detect any possible early warning signs of depression. She wasn't alone. Her father and sister were also on the look-out for indications that Gladys might be struggling. Though she'd been rock solid since recovering from her last episode nine years prior, they all worried the loss of her mother could put her on shaky ground.

One morning as Gladys and Meyer were unpacking the china the Jaffes had given Albert and Irene as a wedding present, Meyer asked as casually as he could, "How are you feeling, sweetheart?"

Gladys stopped in her tracks with four dinner plates in her hands and gave him a penetrating look, "You know, Meyer, I wasn't born yesterday, and I'm not as fragile as you think. I know what you're all doing, watching me like a hawk, keeping me busy so I won't feel so bad about my mother."

"Sweetheart, it's just that we know difficult times can trigger things for you, things that make life hard and painful. We love you so much — *I* love you so much — I just want that you should be well. That's all. Plus, the kids really do need our help. Who would unpack all of this if not for us? They both work so hard and with such long hours, they need all the help we can give them."

"I'm more than happy to help, but it makes me feel small to know you're all so nervous about me. I felt small for most of my life, worrying what people thought of me, that I didn't measure up, that I was less able, less well-off than my sisters. Well, I refuse to feel small anymore. You can stop worrying. I miss my mother every minute of every day. That doesn't make me crazy. She and I were close. Of course I miss her."

"You're right, sweetheart. I'll tell the girls not to worry, that you're just grieving as any good child grieves a loving parent."

"You can tell them that I'm like this bone china," she said looking at the dinner plates, "delicate-looking but strong. That's the new me. Now, let's finish unpacking these dishes so Reenie and Albert can have a bite to eat when they get home from work."

§§§

Early in her pregnancy, Irene and Albert had decided jointly to forego pain medication during labor and delivery. They viewed birth as a natural process women had experienced without analgesics or anesthetics from the beginning of time. Surely Irene could, as well. Albert and Irene studied the Lamaze method of natural childbirth in the months before the babies were due. Her contractions started ten days before her due date, something her doctor said was common with twins. At the hospital, she and Albert breathed and puffed through contraction after contraction, but as the intensity mounted, the searing pain was almost more than Irene could bear. Switching to transition breathing, she wondered if the breathing exercises were anything more than an attempt to distract her from feeling she was being split in two. When the contractions reached a crescendo, she grabbed onto Albert's wrist and squeezed so hard he thought she might break a bone. The power of her grip, the contortions of her face, scared him, but no one on the medical staff seemed the least bit concerned by the level of Irene's pain. Perhaps this was what women had endured for the ages. It gave a whole new meaning to the term, "natural" childbirth. The longer Irene suffered, the more upset he grew.

"Reenie, it's okay if you want pain relief. This may be more than we bargained for," Albert said when a contraction eased.

"No," Irene said emphatically. "I want to keep trying."

"Just know that you can change your mind anytime. I don't want you to hurt so badly."

"I'm doing what's best for the babies," Irene said breathlessly, just as another contraction hit.

After twelve hours of hard labor and another hour of pushing, the first of the twins, a boy, emerged. The nurse wrapped him in a blanket and brought him to Irene. The miracle of his perfect face and body brought her to tears. That respite lasted but a few minutes before she was gripped by another contraction. "I can see the next baby's head crowning," the obstetrician said. "Give me a good push, Irene." That's all it took for their daughter to enter the world with a lusty cry. She was swaddled and given to Albert, who brought her to Irene. The two exhausted, relieved, ecstatic new parents shared a kiss before relinquishing their hard-won babies to the nurses. Their newest adventure had begun.

CHAPTER TWELVE

IT WAS NO WONDER Irene's belly had been mountainous in the weeks leading up to the birth of the twins. Each of her babies tipped the scales at over six pounds, with a length of twenty-one inches. Her son came into the world with a shock of wet, dark hair that would soon show signs of his father's mane: thick and wavy. He was quiet and seemingly attentive from birth. He latched onto his mother's breast while still in the delivery room, and continued to suckle well whenever offered the opportunity. Irene and Albert named him Ian, Isaac in Hebrew, after Albert's paternal grandfather Izzy. Ian's twin sister, seven minutes his junior, was given the name of Brin, Breina in Hebrew, after Irene's beloved Grandma Bertha. Unlike Ian, Brin had no hair to speak of, but was the hands-down winner in terms of letting everyone know her needs and wants. Every time she cried, they thought about what the delivery room nurse had said: "This one has a great set of lungs." She matched her brother in terms of suckling skills, but unlike him, she did not wait calmly when she was ready for another go at her mother's breast.

During the first weeks of their lives, Irene nursed the twins seemingly all day and night. Soon she'd lost all the weight she'd gained over the nine months of her pregnancy and more. No matter how much she ate — and Gladys made sure she had several nourishing meals each day — she grew thinner and thinner. As she dressed to take the babies to their two-week appointment, she had no trouble zipping up the jeans she'd worn before becoming pregnant. While the babies were filling out, she was growing skinny.

It didn't help that Irene was getting almost no sleep. No sooner would she get one baby to nod off than the other would awaken and need to be nursed. Someone from the La Leche League, who had successfully nursed twins, came to the apartment to help Irene learn how to position the babies in a way that would allow both to suckle at the same time. Almost immediately Albert advocated for getting the babies on a feeding schedule, pointing out it was less a question of childrearing philosophy and more one of survival. It was agreed that everyone in the family — including Irma and Burt, who'd come in from Cleveland — would do whatever they could to keep the babies occupied for the two to three hours between their feedings. Ian was relatively easy to keep happy between naps and feedings, but Brin was a tougher nut to crack. When she wanted her mother's breast, no amount of walking or singing would placate her. She tested the endurance of her father and her four grandparents, who took countless walks around the apartment building's lobby trying to soothe her. It was thanks to their efforts that Irene was able to get snatches of sleep throughout the day and night. As a medical resident, she'd learned to get by on less sleep than most people, but now she ached for four or five hours of uninterrupted, deep and restorative sleep. It was not to be.

By the time Irene went for her post-partum appointment with the obstetrician, he told her in no uncertain terms that she had to seriously consider supplementing her nursing with formula. "You're growing painfully thin, Irene. One hundred five pounds at five foot eight isn't healthy, and it's twenty pounds below where you were before you got pregnant. Exclusive nursing of two babies is taking its toll."

Irene was not convinced. "The evidence is incontrovertible that breast milk is best for them. I want to do what's right for my children," she insisted.

"What's right for them is having a healthy mother. And I don't have to remind you that you'll be back at work in a couple of weeks. You've got to start transitioning the twins to bottle feedings anyway. There are several very good formulas on the market now."

The thought of feeding her babies formula and handing over their care made her heart ache. How could she leave her tiny infants? It was against nature. A mother and her newborns belonged together. Ian and Brin deserved to have a mother who would nurture and sustain them. She was exhausted, famished, and gloomy as she walked home from the doctor's office.

Gladys read the signs as soon as her daughter walked through the door. Irene collapsed in a chair and unbuttoned her shirt so she could feed the babies. She wore a look of defeat. Though that feeling had nipped at Gladys's heels throughout her own life, never once had she seen either of her girls wear the mask of hopelessness. Until that moment Irene had seemed tired but in good spirits as she continued the endless loop of feeding, diapering, and cat naps. Gladys helped position the twins for nursing. Then she asked, "Did everything go as you'd hoped at the doctor's?"

Irene laid her head back and closed her eyes. "The uterus has just about returned to its pre-partum size. The episiotomy has healed. But the doctor feels my continued weight loss is a concern. He wants me to give the babies formula." Her tone was bleak.

"To stop nursing entirely, or just to supplement your feedings?" Gladys asked gently.

"He presented it as a supplement, but some babies give up nursing once they're given formula. And the less they nurse, the less my milk supply will be. It's just a matter of time until they refuse the breast. It's not what I envisioned. I wanted to nurse them for at least six months, if not until their first birthday."

"Oh honey, there's only so much you can do. There are two of them and one of you. Being kind to yourself now will help you be a better mother. Look at what you've already done. You have two beautiful babies, each one growing into their own personality. Pat yourself on the back, sweetheart. And soon — just two weeks from now — you'll be across the street at work, and we know how important your work is. *I* know how important your work is. You have the ability to ease your patients' suffering. That's a gift. So it won't be just the babies depending on you. Sweetheart, don't be so hard on yourself. Believe me, I had to learn that the hard way."

Irene teared up as she thought of her mother's travails, the anguish she endured during her bouts of major depression. "I just want to do the right thing by everyone. Apparently, that's impossible to accomplish. Just taking care of Ian and Brin seems to be more than my body can achieve. Look at me. I'm wasting away. And when I think of the patients I work with, people who have lives and families waiting for them if we can help them regain their footing, I am overwhelmed. I just don't see how I'll be able to do it all."

"That's where Albert, Dad, and I come in. And Irma and Burt, too. This is more than you can do by yourself. We all love these little ones more than you know. And we love you. We're so happy to be in a position to take care of the babies when you go back to your residency. You're their mother, and you'll nurse them for as long as you want, as often as you can. That connection you have with them, the nourishment you provide them will continue. We'll give them bottles while you're at the hospital. Before you know it they'll be eating solids. Everything will change then. The burden on your body will be so much less. You'll see. "

"Mom, I'm not sure I can do it; surely not without you," Irene said, as her tears fell on her baby boy. "What would I do without you and Dad?"

"You'd find some way to manage. You're my plucky girl, sweetheart."

"I don't feel so plucky right now."

"You're exactly who you've always been, just a lot more tired. You will continue to excel in everything you do, just as you always have. I am so proud of you and Albert, at what you've already accomplished, at what you're working towards in your professions. And the crown jewels are Ian and Brin, these beautiful twins. Dad and I, and Burt and Irma will do whatever we can to make things manageable for you and Albert. Believe me when I say it's our joy to help."

§§§

Irene was scheduled to return to work six weeks and three days after the twins were born. Ian, now over eleven pounds, had started sleeping midnight to six each night, but his sister continued to wake up for a 3 AM feeding. The night before Irene's first day back, Albert begged her to let him give Brin a bottle, but Irene wouldn't hear of it. She said she didn't want to miss a chance to share some cuddle time with her. The problem was, after Irene nursed her, Brin refused to go back down until half past four. Irene slept through her 6 AM alarm. Albert had to gently shake her to wake her up. Then he handed her the babies so she could nurse them one last time before her workday began.

"I'll go make the coffee," he said as the babies settled in.

Irene called after him, "Make it strong, really strong."

§§§

The fourth year of a psychiatry residency provides the doctor-in-training with far more latitude than the previous three. Electives are the name of the game, allowing a resident to follow her interests, including participation in research. For many fourth year residents, the finish line of their medical training marathon is in sight. Just one, relatively relaxed year to go before the newly-minted physicians can go off and practice on their own. But for Irene, her fourth year of residency provided no respite from the long hours or high intensity that marked the previous three.

At the end of her third year, Irene was honored to have been chosen by the faculty as Chief Resident for Payne Whitney's Emergency Department. She took on the challenge of supervising her fellow residents just as she entered the second trimester of her pregnancy. The list of her responsibilities was long: creation of the call schedule, the teaching and supervision of junior residents, management of daily problems as they arose, working with med students, and attendance at meetings with hospital and department administrators. She embraced the position with an eye to improving processes in the ER.

Irene also sought out an opportunity to do research during her final year of residency. She chose to do an elective with Dr. Allen Frances, a young professor studying how patients are matched to treatment options. On more than one occasion, Irene had been troubled by diagnoses that seemed to have been taken "off the shelf" rather than arrived at after careful analysis. Dr. Frances's research was driven by the hypothesis that many patients are given incorrect or even unnecessary treatment. He was part of the team preparing the DSM III, the *Diagnostic Manual of Mental Illness*. Irene felt she learned something new and essential in diagnosis and treatment of patients each and every time she got to work with him. As tired as she was, particularly as she grew heavy with the twins, she considered it time very well spent.

In addition to her work in the ER, her research, her weekly seminar with the other residents, she continued her own psychotherapy, a requirement of all psychiatrists-in-training. Over the years she'd come to enjoy her sessions, deriving insights into her family of origin and her relationship with Albert. Eventually, she also waded into the trauma of her sexual assault. The therapist's gentle probing of how she'd coped in the aftermath of the attack did not, as she'd feared, re-traumatize her. On the contrary, she felt stronger once she recognized the survival mechanisms she worked so hard to cultivate were now woven into her very being. It gave her a newfound confidence about her ability to face down adversity.

The only thing Irene had backed away from in the months preceding the birth of the twins was her work in the outpatient clinic at Payne Whitney. As much as she'd wanted to pursue a continued relationship with patients she'd met during their hospitalization, she'd sensed it would likely be one commitment too many, particularly after the babies' arrival. Grandma Bertha's words rang in her ears, "Your work is important, but you will be the only parents these babies will have." As it turned out, it was a wise decision.

§§§

Irene had expected re-immersion into work would be hard, but she was unprepared for how hard. On her first day back she cried all the way to the hospital, leading a few passersby to view her with genuine concern. When she got to her desk she found stacks of paperwork, some more than a foot high, awaiting her attention. When, she wondered, would she ever find the time to go through all of them? Once back in the ER, as her patients told their stories of pain and struggle, she had to continually redirect her attention to them rather than her imaginings about what Ian and Brin were doing back home. The *coup de grâce* was the icy reception she got from Ben Scibelli, the fellow who'd filled in as chief resident during her leave. He wasn't the only one to meet Irene with a frosty, "hello" or a perfunctory nod. Irene knew firsthand how hard it was to be down a person for even a day or two, no less six weeks. All of the residents had picked up the slack during her leave, Ben Scibelli in particular. There were some who forgave her absence and were truly happy for the safe arrival of her twins, but even they had no inkling of how she was still recovering from labor and delivery, or how her whole being was attuned to the needs of her babies. Everyone expected her to jump in and resume the hectic pace, the quick analysis, the juggling of all that needed to be done: patient care, charts, pharmacy orders, scheduling, teaching, keeping the peace between the nursing staff and the residents. Irene felt outmatched by everything she faced.

By noon on that first day back, milk leaked through her nursing pads, her bra, her blouse, and even her white coat. She went to the bathroom, tossed out the soaked nursing pads, and replaced them with folded up paper towels. As she was cleaning herself up her eyes focused on the scar on her breast, a permanent reminder of the assault. It was the first time she really looked at it since the babies were born. Now she couldn't take her eyes off it. If she could have, she would have curled up into the corner of that bathroom and cried herself to sleep.

§§§

Work became a trial of endurance. Her therapist reminded her that she'd survived other challenges by dint of her determination, persistence, and courage. This time, Irene wasn't sure she had the energy to access any of those noble traits. She worked non-stop, and having used up all of her sick leave and vacation time for her maternity leave, there was no possibility of any time off. It became immediately apparent that her plan to come home during the day to nurse the twins was unworkable. Hers was not a job with normal hours and mandated breaks; she worked as long as needed to get done what had to be done. By the end of her first month back at the hospital, the only time she reliably nursed the babies was first thing in the morning and before she went to bed. Sometimes if she got home very late, she'd lift them from their cribs and nurse them as they slept. Many nights she crawled into bed so defeated and exhausted, she didn't care whether or not she woke up the next morning.

Albert suffered, too. As hectic as the household had become, he would have managed better had he not missed his wife. When Irene was pregnant, he'd loved seeing her body change shape as the twins grew. He found her alluring throughout. They even managed to have a delightful, albeit cautious, sexual encounter the day before Irene went into labor. But since their birth, the babies seemed to have stolen his lover and best friend. His rational mind rebuked him for being jealous of two helpless infants — *his* infants. Obviously, Irene had done a wonderful job of caring for Ian and Brin when she was on leave. Even now that she was back at work, her devotion as a mother was beyond question. The problem was, he wasn't sure where he fit in. Irene had grown the twins within her body; she nourished them from her breast. She and the twins formed a tight bond, an exclusive triad. The babies responded best to her and she wanted to spend the little time she had at home with them. He felt like a bystander in his own family. Between work and caring for the babies, Irene had nothing left for him. Sex between them became infrequent, more of a duty than a joy. The closeness they'd known since coming together again seemed to be slipping away.

After he wallowed in self-pity, he was overwhelmed with guilt.

The one bright spot in his situation was the introduction of bottle feeding for Brin and Ian. Being able to offer nourishment to his children helped him bond with them in a way that diaper changes had not. He was also their sole caretaker in the hours before grandparents arrived. It was during those frenetic mornings that Albert slowly began to fall in love with his children. By the time they were four months old, he would have laid down his life for theirs. He was thrilled by every new "trick" they mastered. One spring morning, when they started rolling around the living room floor in opposite directions, he laughed until he cried. He couldn't believe these comical, endearing, ever-changing little beings were his. The wedge their arrival had created between him and Irene remained, but the pain and resentment in his heart had to move over to make room for the growing love he felt for his children.

§§§

One Saturday, when Irene had a rare afternoon off, Albert suggested they put the babies in their carriers and take a walk to Central Park. He thought it a marvelous idea. Irene looked at him as though he'd lost his mind.

"Albert, I can't remember the last time I slept more than three hours in a row. Having this time at home is so precious. I want nothing more than to play with Ian and Brin and then sleep when they do. Right now, the thought of a nap is the most appealing thing in the world."

"Right. Of course. It's what you want. It's what you need."

Albert's tone surprised her. "Is it unreasonable to want to rest when I can?"

"No, but what about what I need, Reenie? Does that count at all in our family calculus?"

Irene looked at him curiously. "What you need? What it is that you need, Albert? Would you like me to do something I'm not already doing?" Her voice was calm, her tone inquiring, but Albert thought she was mocking him.

"Don't look at me like that, like I'm pushing you past your limits. I'm here, too. I have needs, too. Everything's changed between us. I hardly recognize us anymore."

As exhausted as she was, his words not only brought her to full attention but stoked fear in her heart. Despite doing her best, apparently she was failing Albert. Her mind raced as he stood glumly awaiting her response. "I'm not sure what to say except that I hardly recognize myself. I feel like a lab rat running endlessly on a wheel. If I stop, I'm afraid of what will happen. What awful mistake will I make with one of my patients or with the babies? So I just keep going. But even so, I see I've made you unhappy. I'm so sorry, Albert."

Something primal — the fight to reclaim his mate, his woman, his love — wouldn't let him back down. "Look, since the babies arrived, it's been tough on you *and* on me. A whole new world has been thrust on us both. The guys at work say that even one baby changes everything, and we've got two."

Irene pursed her lips as she imagined Albert detailing their personal circumstances to his colleagues. Had he complained to them that he was unhappy? She was embarrassed just thinking of the possibility. It also struck her as disloyal. "You've been telling your colleagues about how miserable you've been since the babies' arrival?"

"It's just a bunch of us guys shooting the breeze over lunch. The ones who are fathers seem to have sensed what I'm going through."

"What you're going through?" Irene asked. Now her words were tinged with bitterness. "Tell me, what exactly are you telling people at work?"

"Look, don't fault me for talking to friends. It's been a help. To tell you the truth, I've been pretty lonely these last months. These babies, as wonderful as they are, have brought chaos into our lives. I can endure the chaos. Really, I can. But what I'm having trouble with is not knowing whether you and I are okay. We came first. Though it's hard to imagine now, someday Brin and Ian will grow up and leave us. We need to protect *us* so when that day comes we'll still be here together. Please, Reenie." Albert came over and put his arms around her. "I need my best friend back. I miss you."

That's when Irene felt the tears falling on her cheek. She pulled away and saw Albert weeping.

"What can I do? Please tell me, Albert," she begged. "It's painful for me to see you so sad." She took him by the hand and led him to the sofa. "Let's try to work this out together."

"I know it's stupid," he admitted, averting his eyes, "but it feels as though you've thrown me over like you did back in the day. I didn't understand then why you were suddenly pulling away. The only thing I was certain of was that you hurt me and I was miserable. It feels something like that now. I know you're just holding on, trying to finish your residency while caring for the twins. But in my heart of hearts, I feel abandoned. Believe me when I say it's not something I'm proud of…"

"Abandon you? I would never abandon you, Albert. I can't believe you feel that way."

"You have to understand, Reenie. You're everything to me. You bring light and grace and love into my life. I get my energy and my purpose from you. Sure, I know how to go through the motions without you; I proved that pretty convincingly when we were apart for all those years. But I can tell you there was no joy in living that way. Once we found each other again, I knew what it meant to embrace life together, to have you in my corner. There was something so reassuring, so heartening about knowing you always had my back."

"You're using the past tense, Albert. Do you believe all of that is now lost?"

"Maybe not lost, just misplaced," Albert said, seeing how stricken Irene was to hear him voice his grievances. "Don't get me wrong; the day Ian and Brin were born was probably the happiest day of my life."

"For me, as well," she said, brightening a bit.

"And then things changed for us in a gargantuan way."

"The reality of caring for them did hit home rather fast," Irene agreed. "What I wouldn't have given for a more gentle immersion into parenthood."

"Exactly! We were instantly thrust into the deep end of the pool, whether or not we were ready or even knew how to swim."

"But we're in it now, and the instinct to protect and care for them is so powerful, it sometimes frightens me. I think I would do anything for them."

Albert bit his lip. "I know that feeling, too. I'd stop a bullet with my body if it meant saving them. But I also want to protect what we've had. Does that make me a terrible person?"

"No. It's good that you're telling me how you feel. Seeing our situation through your lens is helpful. Before now, I was just trying to make it through one day at a time. But now I see we have a problem to solve. Somehow we have to carve out some space just for us. We're both intelligent people. We love each other and our babies. Somehow we'll find a way. I promise."

They shared a kiss and an embrace. In that instant, everything felt right in the world, but their sweet moment of reconciliation was soon interrupted by Brin, who began wailing in her infant seat. Albert went to her, picked her up, and brought her to Irene. "I think that was our longest, most heartfelt conversation since the little interlopers were born," he said.

"What happened to the 'little physicists'?" Irene asked, as she put the baby to her breast.

"Maybe one day, but for now, they're still something of gatecrashers to our party."

"They're here now. We just have to learn how to include them in our merrymaking. You'll see. We will," Irene assured him, as she watched Brin happily nursing.

"Yeah, until they're teenagers and then they'll see *us* as the ones ruining their fun," Albert mused. "I guess we'd better make the most of our advantage while we have it."

§§§

Just after the babies were born, Irene was accepted by Columbia's Psychiatric Institute for a two-year postdoc starting in September of 1982. As much as she valued her clinical work in the hospital, she was hungry to return to researching the biological underpinnings of the devastating illnesses that derailed her patients' lives. Nothing excited her as much as working with colleagues to formulate an interesting question and then designing a series of experiments to explore possible answers. Columbia was in the forefront of research into the neuroscience of psychiatric disease. Now that molecular neuroscience — the biology of the nervous system examined through molecular genetics and protein chemistry — was allowing researchers to examine the brain's functioning at the molecular level, Irene was optimistic that answers to age-old questions about mental illness were on the horizon.

Not only was the prospect of doing research full time inviting, Irene felt sure her schedule as a post-doc would be more forgiving. She'd arranged to have a ten-week break between the end of her residency and the start of the post-doc. Albert thought he could get some time away from work, as well. They were excited at the prospect of a much-needed respite. Perhaps they'd take the babies and leave town for a while. Now she just had to hold on until the summer. Then she would have the chance to find her footing again and perhaps even experience the joy of a full night's sleep. It was the promise of summer that gave Irene the courage she needed to soldier on until June.

§§§

Ten days after Irene finished her residency, she and Albert rented a fifteen-passenger van and drove Meyer and Gladys, Annie and Spence, and the four little ones to Cape May. For Meyer and Gladys it would be a two-week, all-expenses paid vacation from Irene and Albert; a token of gratitude for the months of wonderful care they provided their family. The plan was for Annie, Spence, and the kids to stay for the first week, and then Irma, Burt and Robert to join them at the beach house for the second week.

The time with Annie's family was a rare treat for Irene. Since the twins' birth she could barely fit in a haircut, no less a visit with her sister and her family. She enjoyed spending time with Peter and Rachel, now six and three-and-a-half respectively. She also appreciated the chance to compare notes with Annie on being a working mother. Her sister offered encouragement, telling Irene that parenthood got better and better as the children grew beyond infancy. Still, she was honest: "A working mother's juggling act never ends." Her advice was simple: "Don't beat yourself up for not meeting some ideal of perfection. It doesn't exist."

Since her earliest memories, Irene had seen her big sister as the embodiment of confidence and mastery, so it was with surprise that she learned that Annie, too, had moments of self-doubt and recrimination. Annie freely admitted that since becoming a parent there were times she'd failed to meet someone's needs at work or at home. "There's only so much a person can do," she explained. "Your child is sick, your husband is out of town, and you're on call. Guess what? Something is not going to get done." As for the house, Annie was simple and to the point, "Hire someone to help clean as soon as you and Albert can see your way clear to afford that luxury." For Irene, it was something of an epiphany: Luxury for a woman determined to couple a family with a career is having the money to pay someone to wash the kitchen floor.

§§§

The two weeks at the shore gave Irene her first taste of relaxation since Ian and Brin's birth. The sliding glass door in their bedroom opened right to the beach. She awoke to the sound of water lapping on the shore and seagulls wailing. The only responsibilities she had were to play with her babies, who were just beginning to crawl. Brin started sleeping through the night while the family vacationed at Cape May. For the first time in months, Irene enjoyed seven hours of uninterrupted sleep each night. Being stress-free and refreshed likely contributed to the return of her libido, something that made Albert a very happy man.

Every morning after breakfast Gladys and Meyer parked themselves on beach chairs under the large, multi-colored umbrella. Sometimes they'd watch Peter and Rachel play in the sand. Other times they would read their books or simply recline in their chaise and take a nap. One afternoon, as Irene watched her parents asleep on the beach, she thought how time had left its mark on them both. Meyer, especially, had the bearing of an old man. It gave her pause to realize that medically speaking, as a man in his mid-seventies, he was geriatric. But when Irma and Burt arrived and they, too, spent their days lazing on the beach, Irene felt better. Mere "youngsters" at sixty-two, they enjoyed relaxing on their chaises as much as Meyer and Gladys.

As their two-week idyll was coming to a close, Albert and Robert headed to the kitchen to whip up a special meal for their last dinner together. Meyer and Burt made a grocery run for the needed ingredients, leaving Irma, Gladys, and Irene in the living room with the twins.

"When they were tiny, Brin and Ian kept me busy feeding them. Now they keep me busy preventing them from self-harm," Irene said, as she monitored the babies' explorations into every nook and cranny of the nautical-themed living room. "I have such admiration for moms who do this full-time. It's demanding work."

Irma, who'd worked outside the home from the time Robert was a toddler, nodded. "You bet it's demanding. Demanding and *nudgy*[1], too. Some days feel as though they last forever. There were times when the boys were small that I would have given anything to have a conversation with another adult. I say, 'Hats off' to the women who can stay home with

---

[1] Boring, annoying

their kids all day. But there's really no right or wrong on the issue of staying home or going to work. I think the defining factor is whether the mom is happy, since a happy mother is the best mother for her children."

Gladys agreed. "Well said, Irma. Every woman has to decide what's best for herself and her family. Sometimes finances force a woman's hand, making her go out to work even when she'd rather stay home. I know that's not true for you, Reenie. I know your work isn't about putting food on the table."

"No, we're lucky in that way. We could probably manage on Albert's salary alone. But I couldn't imagine walking away from my work," Irene said.

"It's obvious to anyone who knows you that your work sustains you," Irma said. "And it's such important work, too. I hope you know how proud Burt and I are of what you do."

Irene went over and gave her mother-in-law a hug. "Thank you so much, Irma. Your support means so much to me."

"You and Albert are like two peas in a pod, so bright and so committed to your science. It makes us happy to see you both working to achieve your dreams," Irma said.

"What you said about work sustaining me, that was certainly true before the twins arrived. I hope it's true again once we get them into some sort of manageable routine," Irene said. "To be completely honest, the last months of my residency were grueling. There were days I didn't think I'd make it. If it hadn't been for Albert, and for all of your help, I never could have done it."

Gladys, not sure whether she was overstepping her bounds, waded in cautiously. "Reenie, all of us were more than happy to help you finish up your residency. But now you're starting fresh with your post-doc. You know I never interfere with how you conduct your life; you're far smarter than I ever was. But you may need to change the way you think about your work. Before the twins, you fit your life into your work. Now that they're here, that's not possible. Raising children takes a lot of time and energy. Something's gotta give. You've been a perfectionist since you were not much bigger than Ian and Brin, but sometimes 'good enough' may have to do."

Irma listened intently and then added, "Your mom is right. And it's not just you who's going to need to rethink things, Reenie. I'm going to have a talk with Albert, too. He's going to have to make adjustments to his work schedule. But I won't lie. Even when you have a terrific, hands-on partner, a greater burden often falls on the mom. I hope Albert is the exception that proves the rule."

As Irene listened to her mother and Irma, Annie's words came to mind: "A working mother's juggling act never ends." She thought about the science that drew her to it like a moth to a flame. She wanted it, just as she wanted to share her life with Albert and nurture her twins. If juggling would allow her to have it all, she planned on becoming a master.

CHAPTER THIRTEEN

IT WAS WITH A MIXTURE of enthusiasm and trepidation that Irene approached the start of her post-doctoral fellowship at Columbia. The prospect of conducting research with the group led by Dr. Ronald Fieve, perhaps the most influential American psychiatrist in the treatment for bipolar affective disorder, was nothing short of thrilling. Dr. Fieve had pioneered the use of the naturally occurring mineral lithium for patients struggling with the debilitating mood disorder. The National Institutes of Mental Health (NIMH) was funding his research on the biogenetics of affective disorders. The hope was that the lab could pinpoint enzyme and genetic marker data on depressed and bi-polar patients and their relatives.

Though attracted to the project, Irene felt more than a tinge of sadness as the days of summer ticked by. With nothing more pressing than taking the twins for their daily stroller ride along the river, she settled into a calm and lovely routine, a routine that provided a healing balm from the tumultuous, exhausting months after their birth. Many days, Albert would leave work early, allowing them to have some much needed time together. Irene knew this summer respite was an opportunity that might not come again for quite a while; she cherished it.

Ian and Brin were changing daily. Both Irene and Albert were tickled when one or the other of the twins reached a new milestone. Although it appeared that Brin was the more agile of the two, by August both babies could crawl with amazing speed and pull themselves up into a stand. If they were awake, they wanted to explore their world and its wonders. Brin discovered one particular wonder under the bathroom sink: a bottle with a shiny metal cap. Catastrophe was averted when her attempt to take a swig of rubbing alcohol was foiled by her father. That episode motivated Albert and Irene to commence a joint, emergency baby-proofing session that very night.

As comfortable as they were in the York Avenue apartment, it was inconveniently located not only for Albert, but soon for Irene, as well. They decided working parents of infant twins needed convenience on their side so, as exhausting as a move to the West Side would be, it would be worth the effort to dramatically cut their commute times. They settled on the neighborhood near the Psychiatric Institute for its location and affordability. They targeted the vicinity near Wright Park, which had the benefit of having a playground and some green space, as well as being only a few subway stops away from Columbia's Morningside Heights campus.

One Saturday in August, Irene and Albert began their hunt for their new apartment in earnest. As they wheeled the twins around Washington Heights in their stroller, the ethnic restaurants, traditional dress of the passersby, and the Spanish, French, and Russian spoken by pedestrians made it clear they were moving to an area awash in cultural diversity. Albert turned to Irene and joked, "Forget pizza and fries. Living here the kids will develop a taste for *Habichuelas Guisadas* and *Pirozhkis*."

"I know. Think of the interesting take-out we can get on busy nights, which actually will be most nights, come to think of it," Irene said.

"Not only that. I'll be 'papi' instead of 'dada' once they start to talk."

Irene stopped walking and took a hard look at Albert. "Actually, now that you mention it, you look more like a papi than a dada," she said, in one of her rare attempts at jest.

"Really," Albert deadpanned.

"Yes, really," Irene replied. "In fact, I may start calling you Papi myself."

"Not if I have anything to say about it," Albert said, scooping Irene up into his arms. "I'm Albert to you, my dear Reenie. Anyone who calls me Papi has to be under four feet tall. That's my last word on the subject. Deal?"

"It's a deal," Irene laughed in agreement. "Can I be put down now? The children are looking at us with funny expressions."

It was true. Ian, especially, looked perplexed.

"All right, as long we have that straightened out."

When Irene's feet hit the ground they picked up the pace, closing in on the next apartment on their list. "You know what Grandma Bertha would call this neighborhood?" Irene asked.

"What?"

"The 'League of Nations.' So many countries and cultures represented. No need for books to teach Ian and Brin about ethnic differences. It will be as natural for them as breathing," Irene said. "I think we've found the right place for them and for us."

As happy as they were thinking about living amidst so many cultures, after looking at several dismal places, one dirtier and shabbier than the next, Albert and Irene's mood turned somber. The reason the apartments they'd seen were "affordable" was their state of disrepair. By the time they got to the last apartment on their list they were both ready for another disappointment, but when they arrived at the building on West 171st Street, they found no trash in front of the entry. Flowers filled window boxes in a couple of the first floor apartments. The glass on the front door was smudge-free and the buzzer system worked when they rang the landlord's bell.

Instantaneously it seemed, the landlord buzzed them in and met them in the lobby.

"How do you do?" the forty-something Latino man said, extending his hand. "We just finished painting the apartment yesterday. We still have a little more maintenance to do on the unit before it will be ready, but I think you'll be able to get a sense of things." Then he led them to a spacious three-bedroom apartment with a new gas stove and refrigerator in the kitchen. "We still have some work to do in the bathroom; repairing the grout around the tub, that sort of thing. I want to get another coat of varnish on the living room floor. We have a couple of cracked windows to replace. Nothing major, but the time between tenants is the time we like to take care of it. I think it should be ready for occupancy by the end of the month. Rent is two-twenty-five, due the first of the month, heat included. Electric is on you."

A meaningful look passed between Irene and Albert. Though the rent was higher than the other apartments they'd seen, it was still hundreds less than they were paying for their two-bedroom on York Avenue. It was close to Wright Park and had expansive views of the river and the George

Washington Bridge, plus it had a third bedroom that could accommodate visiting grandparents.

"We'll take it," Irene said quickly.

Just as they were leaving the apartment, a middle-aged man came out of his apartment carrying a bag of trash. The landlord introduced them. "Natan, these people are going to be your new neighbors. We're off to sign the lease."

"Welcome," Natan said, pronouncing the "w" as a "v." "Very nice to meet you. You'll see. Hector is the best landlord in the Heights. He keeps this place beautiful."

The conversation in the hallway drew a middle-aged woman to Natan's side.

"Yelena, this young couple will soon be our neighbors."

"Welcome. I'm Yelena, Yelena Smirnow," she said, extending her hand. Her English, too, was heavily accented. "What Natan says about Hector is one hundred percent the truth. We are so lucky to have him."

"Well, it's a two-way street, Yelena. You and Natan are good tenants."

"Why wouldn't we be?" Yelena asked. "We're so happy here! And now it will be even nicer with two little babies next door! I miss my girls, but they flew away."

"Flew the nest," Natan corrected.

"Oh yes, flew the nest. We have our niece with us, though. Very exciting! She just arrived from the Soviet Union. Tatiana," Yelena called out. "Come here and meet our new neighbors."

A short, stocky girl soon appeared in the doorway. "Hello," she said, smiling broadly. "I'm Tatiana. So nice to meet you. What lovely children! Are they twins?"

"Yes," Albert replied, bowled over by the girl's fluent, nearly accent-free English. "Your English is flawless."

"Thank you very much," Tatiana said, her cheeks turning pink. "I studied linguistics at the university before I was granted an exit visa to join my aunt and uncle in America."

There was something so bright and appealing about their new neighbors, Albert and Irene could have stood there talking with them longer had it not been clear that Hector was anxious to get their signatures on the lease and the security deposit in hand. When the Smirnows invited them to come up for tea after finalizing the rental agreement, Albert and Irene, who'd walked miles that day, happily accepted.

By the time they returned, Yelena Smirnow had set a beautiful table with an assortment of pastries, tea, and coffee. Someone listening in to the conversation that followed would have noted an easy-going camaraderie. Albert talked about his work. Irene mentioned her upcoming post-doctoral fellowship, but mostly spoke about Brin and Ian, how their dispositions had been different since birth, although they now showed signs of joining forces to have fun at their parents' expense. Then it was the Smirnows' turn. Yelena and her husband Natan described how they'd emigrated to America in 1973. A pharmacist back home, Natan now worked as a taxi driver. Yelena kept the books for a bakery on the West Side. Their two daughters had learned English much faster than they, and both graduated from the City University of New York. Now their elder girl taught Russian in a high school near Coney Island, and the younger daughter was getting a graduate degree in chemistry at the University of Michigan. Then it was their niece's turn to share.

Irene and Albert were spellbound as they listened to Tatiana Kramarov's story. An only child who'd lost both parents by the time she was seventeen — her mother to illness and her father to the harsh conditions of a labor camp — she realized the pervasive anti-Semitism in the Soviet Union would sharply limit the possibilities for her future. When the opportunity to come to America presented itself, she leapt at it. Although she planned on ultimately returning to university, she first wanted to earn some money to repay her aunt and uncle for buying her plane ticket and welcoming her into their home.

Just as Tatiana started describing her plan to start taking classes at Lehman College in the winter, Brin began to fuss. The young woman got off her chair and squatted down to Brin's level, speaking to her in a sweet, lilting voice. Immediately Brin put her hands up, a sign she wanted to be picked up by her new friend. She settled quickly onto Tatiana's lap. That gave Irene an idea. Perhaps the twenty-year old émigré would consider working as a nanny for the twins, at least until she was ready to return to college. Daycare for Ian and Brin was the only outstanding question Irene had to answer before starting her post-doc. Perhaps the answer was right before her eyes.

§§§

As Albert and Irene rode the bus home from Washington Heights, each holding fast to one of the babies, Irene brought up the possibility of hiring the intelligent and amiable Tatiana.

"That crossed my mind, too," Albert said. "Ever since we toured those daycare centers, I've had to fight the urge to dismiss each and every one of them out of hand. Though there was nothing obviously wrong or dangerous, there was also nothing particularly right or inviting about any of them."

"I wasn't comfortable with them either. To think of the twins being there all day, in such an institutional setting, two among so many babies…it seems far from ideal. I think Tatiana would certainly be a better alternative — if she's interested and would consider it."

"We'd be very lucky to have someone of her caliber — not to mention warmth — taking care of Ian and Brin. She seemed to have a natural affinity for our little guys. And they'd be in their own home, around their own things. That would be my preference. We have nothing to lose by asking. Let's go for it."

The moment they got back to their apartment Albert looked up the Smirnows' in the phone book, and dialed their number.

"Hello, Natan. This is Al Jaffe. I wonder if I could speak to Tatiana. Irene and I have a question for her."

"Sure, sure, here she is."

"Hello. This is Tatiana."

"I hope you don't think us too presumptuous, but Irene and I were so impressed with you. We know you're looking for a job before you return to the university. Would you consider working for us? Caring for our babies?"

"Well, I don't know," she replied. "Could you please tell me more about what you had in mind?"

"It would be four, ten-hour days each week of caring for the twins. Irene's parents, and sometimes my parents, will come to watch Ian and Brin for one day a week, probably Wednesdays. We can pay one hundred sixty dollars a week, cash if you prefer. And I might add, it would be a very easy commute!"

"As I told you, I am hoping to resume my studies this winter. I would only be available to work for you until then."

"We understand and we support your return to school."

"Would it be all right if I gave it some thought?" Tatiana asked.

"Of course. Think about it and let us know what you decide."

That night, after Irene and Albert had gotten the babies to sleep, they cuddled on the sofa reviewing all the things they had to do to get ready for their move uptown. When the phone rang they both tried to tamp down their hope that it was Tatiana. Irene took the call.

"Yes, yes. Oh, that's wonderful," she said smiling as she nodded to Albert. "Hector is allowing us to move in a day early, August 31st. I start at Columbia on September 13th, but I am sure we'll need your help as we get the apartment set up. So, shall we say September 1st will be your first day?"

Irene hung up and ran to give Albert a hug. "Oh, what a day we've had! A new apartment and our daycare problem solved, at least for the moment."

"You know, if I believed in astrology, which of course no respectable astrophysicist would admit to, I would say today our planets aligned."

"I can't believe how relieved I feel. I didn't even realize how tense I was about finding good care for Brin and Ian."

"Me, too, and I know a great way to celebrate." Albert stood up, popped an Al Green tape in the stereo, and pulled Irene from the couch. "Right this way," he said, leading Irene by the hand to their bedroom.

§§§

Returning to the place where she'd studied during her MD/PhD program would have been a bit like coming home, except for the chaos and disruption wrought by the construction of the Psychiatric Institute's new, fourteen-story research annex. Irene had no doubt the upheaval would ultimately be worth it, with ninety new, state-of-the-art research laboratories promised for Columbia's department of psychiatry. However, stepping into the building left Irene feeling disoriented. She even had trouble finding the women's restroom, which she needed rather desperately since, on her walk to the hospital, her period had returned for the first time since she'd gotten pregnant with the twins. One thing took the edge off her sense of being hopelessly lost, and that was seeing the familiar faces of the security guard at the relocated main desk and the custodian pushing a broom down the hall. Both had worked at the Institute when Irene was there years before, and though they'd never exchanged more than "hello," or "good morning," she was surprised by how comforting it was to see them again.

After stopping to ask directions twice more, she made her way to the incoming post-docs' orientation, where she picked up her nametag, forms to be completed, and the glossy publication describing the work of the Psychiatric Institute. As she filled out the requisite forms, Irene looked up and counted the new post-docs in the room. Of the forty present, six were women. As had been the case since leaving Barnard, Irene would be in a distinct minority among her cohort. She wondered how many of the post-docs were married or had children. She thought it was likely she was the only one who had delivered twins in the last year.

As she waited for the meeting to start, Irene mulled over what her mother had said about rethinking how work fit into her life. Early in her career, she'd kept her distance from male colleagues out of a lingering anxiety and generalized fear of men. The passage of time, the confidence she gained from karate and psychotherapy, and the joy of being with Albert had all helped her overcome those vestiges of the assault. Now, rather than fear, it was the desire to maximize her time with Albert and the children that would keep her from getting chummy with her associates. She aimed to be pleasant at work. She would certainly bring her very best to the research efforts in the lab from eight in the morning until five in the afternoon. But at five o'clock she planned to switch gears, leaving the lab behind and going home. Her plan for her new *modus operandi* was to be business-like, efficient, and pleasant.

§§§

Everyone at the Fieve Lab, from the primary investigator (PI) to the post-doctoral and doctoral students, had knowledge and curiosity in spades, essential assets for people working to discover the etiology of mental illness. The work was arduous, which didn't faze Irene in the least. In fact, the more difficult the work, the greater the challenge, the more she was drawn to it. Running the experiments in the lab required meticulous technique, and over the years, she'd grown into a virtuoso of technique. She loved the experimental work, but found herself equally drawn to the outreach efforts to patients and their first order relatives. The people skills she'd acquired and honed during her psychiatry residency made her particularly valuable for that aspect of the research. In short order, her empathy and ability to listen made her the "go to" person whenever a new subject was brought into the study. As intriguing as were the biogenetics at the heart of the lab's investigation, working with the people who either suffered from depression or bipolar disease — or suffered watching their loved one held captive by their mental illness — offered Irene a different kind of satisfaction.

A couple of months into the post-doc Irene almost pinched herself because things were going better than she'd dare hope, both in the lab and at home. The twins were thriving under Tatiana's patient, loving care. The young nanny had even found and enrolled in an advanced course in linguistics that met on Wednesdays at Lehman College, allowing her to kick-start the resumption of her university education. On the nights that Irene knew in advance that she had to stay late at the lab, Albert was able to come home early and relieve Tatiana. For the first time since becoming a mother, Irene felt the juggling act Annie described was possible. Looking in the mirror one day as she was getting ready to go to the lab, she noticed her clothes fit again; she'd finally regained all the weight she'd lost after the twins' birth. She took it as a sign that she'd reached a new, post-baby equilibrium.

§§§

In late November the lab had a very bad day. The power company, Consolidated Edison, experienced a failure in one of its substations. Normally the building's generator would kick in and take over, but that day the generator was unable to start despite the maintenance engineers' best efforts. The cryogenic refrigerators and the on-going biological experiments required strict temperature control, which could not be maintained without continuous power. One of the post-docs, a former engineer, went so far as to run to a nearby hardware store and buy a portable generator in order to keep all the temperature sensitive equipment running. Despite all her ministrations, she couldn't get it hooked up and working. Nearly five hours passed before Con Edison restored power to the lab.

The researchers were apoplectic. For some, months of work had been jeopardized by the power failure. At four-thirty that afternoon Amelia Moody, the lab manager, called an emergency meeting of all investigators to try to salvage what they could of their work. Irene made a quick call to

Tatiana to see if she could stay late, since Albert was in Boston giving a talk. But Tatiana had already committed to caring for the children of another family that night.

"I'm sorry Amelia, I can stay until five," Irene explained, "but then I have to go home to my kids. The nanny has to leave by five-thirty."

Amelia Moody, a fifty-ish single woman who had never been responsible for the care of anyone other than herself, was not sympathetic. She held nothing back when she lit into Irene. "This is precisely why people don't want women in labs! The work is not on a clock and it's not a hobby that you can do when you feel like it. What has to be done must be done or we'll lose the blood, sweat, and tears we've put into the experiment to date. You've made your choice. You wanted to be a mother. Now go home and be a mother. Do us all a favor and leave the bench research to the rest of us."

Blind-sided by Amelia's naked hostility, Irene tried her best to mount a defense. "I believe you're drawing a false dichotomy," she protested. "Being a mother doesn't preclude being a bench researcher, and I assure you, this is no hobby for me. I'm committed to the research. Any other day, my husband would step in during an emergency such as this, but he's at M.I.T. at the moment, and won't return until late tonight. Amelia, I'll do what I can to salvage what's salvageable for the next half hour and I will come back to the lab as soon as my husband walks through the door. But I will have to leave at five."

"I have no time for this. Your priorities are clear as day," Amelia said. Then she turned on her heels and went to assist three beleaguered med students attempting to save what was left of their temperature-sensitive specimens.

§§§

That November day was a harbinger of things to come. Amelia Moody was never in any danger of being thought of as warm and fuzzy, but she was damned good at her job and had the discretion to dole out the lab's resources. Once she made up her mind that Irene was not fully committed to the lab's work, whenever Irene put in an order for a particular piece of equipment or materials to further her study, the response time was long and the answer was most often, "I'll see. There are a lot of requests ahead of yours."

No matter how hard Irene tried to demonstrate she was all-in on the project — including coming in after midnight the night after the power failure — Amelia was unyielding. But Irene remained sanguine. If Amelia was a lost cause, she'd work around her, proving herself to everyone else, including the lead investigators. After the power failure debacle, she made sure to arrange backup care for the twins when Albert was out of town. She modified her original plan to keep a strict separation from work and family time. Weekends, nights, and holidays were not off-limits if there was pressing work to be done. As it turned out, her research on the autosomal blood markers and the enzymes cholinesterase, ATPase, and the dopamine-metabolizing enzyme catechol-O-methyl transferase (COMT) was beyond reproach. She was the lead author on one of the papers coming out of the lab. Beyond that, the videotaped interviews she continued to conduct with nearly two hundred families participating in the study were received with universal acclaim. Irene was pleased that her efforts in the lab and in the lithium clinic were being recognized.

When Albert was granted tenure at Columbia, they were both over the moon with delight. During the second year of her post-doc, Irene attempted to make her own position at Columbia more permanent by applying for a faculty opening. If she landed the job, she'd have a joint appointment at Columbia and the Psychiatric Institute. Being part of the world class departments of psychiatry and neurobiology, having the opportunity to collaborate with the likes of Eric Kandel, Donald Klein, and a host of other top notch researchers, would be nothing short of a dream come true. Given how well her post-doctoral research was being received, Irene was optimistic about her chances. That made learning that the job went to an outside candidate — a male post-doc from Penn — all the harder to accept.

For the first time in her life, Irene knew the disappointment of failing to attain a longed for goal. She'd gained entry to every program she'd ever applied to, won kudos from all the professors and mentors she worked with. She'd always believed success was within reach if she did her best. But now, despite work that had won her acclaim, the job she'd coveted had gone to someone else. Irene wanted to believe that the selection committee had chosen the fellow from Penn because he was the best candidate, but a small voice inside her head raised the possibility that Amelia had poisoned the well.

When her animus erupted on the day of the power failure, it struck Irene as being so irrational as to border on the absurd. But Amelia's hostility persisted, manifesting in unexpected ways. When Albert and the twins occasionally came by to pick her up at the end of the day, her lab mates would always engage with the toddlers for a moment. They seemed to enjoy how Brin and Ian, just turned two, could name most of the people in the lab as well as the test tubes, pipettes, and centrifuge. Amelia, however, would go out of her way to ignore the children. Irene couldn't help but wonder if her studied indifference was rooted in resentment — or perhaps envy — for the family she and Albert had created.

Irene had no way of knowing if her status as the mother of two tiny children played any role in how her application was evaluated. Of one thing she was certain: There wasn't a single male in her department accused of divided allegiance for having become a father; if anything, having a family was seen as a feather in his cap. But Amelia believed a woman scientist had to choose whether to have a family or to be taken seriously. And perhaps Amelia was not alone. She intimated as much when she said, "This is precisely why people don't want women in labs."

Irene allowed herself to ruminate about losing out on the Columbia job for a couple of weeks before switching her focus to landing one of the other positions she'd applied for. At the time she'd sent off those applications, she remembered viewing them as mere contingencies. Now her future as a clinician-researcher depended on one of those medical schools offering her a job. The wait was nerve-wracking. Finally, she received her one and only offer from the Bronx Veterans' Administration Hospital, one of Mount Sinai Medical School's affiliates. It wasn't what she'd hoped for, but there would be some limited funding for research into the genetic basis of mood disorders. Her dear friend Fredi was now an assistant professor of obstetrics and gynecology at Sinai, though she imagined Fredi was rarely called to the VA for her services. Still, they'd be on the same faculty roster. That was something, at least. Irene made her mind up: Somehow she would make this new position work.

CHAPTER FOURTEEN

I T TOOK BOTH THEIR BRAINS and their brawn for Irene and Albert
to set up the twins' new bedroom. Out with the cribs and in with their
big boy and big girl beds. As they hung pictures and unpacked the
boxes of toys and clothes, they agreed they were lucky to have the money
they needed to smooth the transition to this newest chapter in their lives.
As reluctant as they were to leave their home in Washington Heights, they
hoped this would be the last time they had to uproot themselves and the
children for work. With both of them now earning faculty salaries, it was
within their budget to move to Riverdale, the Bronx, a neighborhood that
wouldn't require either of them to have a long commute. Although it
lacked the rich cultural diversity of the Heights, it did have excellent
daycare options, good public schools, enormous parks, and convenient
shopping.

They weighed the pros and cons of renting versus buying an
apartment. They decided to take the plunge and put in an offer on a four-
bedroom, two-bath unit in a pre-war building. When their offer was
accepted, Albert carried the twins in his arms and danced around the living
room bellowing, "Mommy and Daddy are home owners. Yahoo!" To
which, Ian, the more serious of the two, responded, "You're getting too
excited, Daddy. Calm down!"

The rooms in their new home were large and airy, with windows
offering a view of the Hudson River. It was unusual to find an apartment
so large, but theirs had originally been two one-bedroom apartments
combined by the previous owner. The best part of having so much space

was that it allowed the family to grow and change. For now, one extra bedroom was filled by Tatiana, who continued to help care for the twins when she wasn't in class at Lehman College. She was a tremendous help to both Irene and Albert when things went late at their respective labs. Thinking ahead, they could envision a time when another bedroom might be filled with one of their parents, much as Grandma Bertha had occupied a bedroom in Gladys and Meyer's home. But for now, with Ian and Brin still sharing a room, they had a guest room for visiting relatives and friends.

Another change in their lives was automobile ownership, to which they succumbed when they realized how complicated their lives had become. Albert spent two days a week doing his research at Columbia's Nevis Labs, twenty minutes north in Irvington. The rest of the week he taught on the Morningside Heights campus, which was reachable by mass transit, though driving south on the Henry Hudson Parkway took half the time. For Irene, getting to the VA Hospital from their new home was just a few minutes by car, but a minimum of thirty-five minutes on two city buses, assuming they ran on time. Additionally, the children had to be taken to and picked up from the daycare center, which was a seven-block walk or a two-minute drive. Realizing time was their scarcest resource, they decided to purchase a new, bottle-green Volvo station wagon.

Albert got his driver's license as a teenager. Though he knew it was true of many native New Yorkers, he had trouble understanding how Irene reached the age of thirty-two without having learned how to drive. He thought it was time to remedy that omission. His argument was reasonable. When he was out of town, it would fall on Irene to get the children to daycare, Tatiana to the bus stop, and herself to the hospital. Although she didn't argue with the rationality of Albert's position, Irene wasn't at all sure she wanted to learn to drive. Every time Albert suggested they strap the children into their car seats and go for a lesson, she came up with one reason or another why she didn't have time.

By mid-fall Albert was emphatic: He needed help driving everyone where they needed to be. As confident as he was that his polymath wife would soon be maneuvering the Volvo through the city streets, it was not to be. After three lessons, Irene barely progressed beyond starting the car and signaling to leave her parking space. As a psychiatrist and a neuroscientist, she was not at all surprised. She understood down to the cellular level how anxiety can thwart the acquisition of new skills. Each time she got behind the wheel, she started to perspire and her heart rate increased. When she finally pulled out of the parking space, she drove so tentatively that drivers behind her sat on their horns, making her all the more anxious. Left turns in particular struck terror in her heart. Although she and Albert rarely fought, there were more than a few tense moments when the teacher lost patience with his student.

"You have to give it more gas, Reenie. You're crawling along at a snail's pace. For God's sake woman, you're in New York City! People are in a hurry," Albert cried.

Ian and Brin, strapped in their car seats, listened wide-eyed to their father's unfamiliar tone. A little voice from the back said, "Don't be mad, Daddy. Mommy's driving good."

"I love you very much, Ian," Albert said, "but let's just say you're not yet qualified to make that judgment. Actually, your mother is making us prime candidates for being rear-ended."

"That's exactly my point!" Irene cried out in exasperation. "I have no business being behind the wheel!"

"People with IQs half of yours are behind the wheel. You can do it. Just keep your eye on the road and *concentrate,* Reenie!"

"I *am* concentrating, probably too much. That's why I'm driving so slowly and why I forget to put my signal on when I make turns. You have to believe me. I'm trying to remember all the things I have to do."

"You're doing a good job, Mommy," Ian said.

"I appreciate that and I'm glad you have confidence in me," Irene said as she looked in the rear view mirror at her beautiful boy, his dark, curly hair framing his little face. "Everyone needs a champion."

"I'm a champion, too," Brin chimed in. "Right, Mommy?"

"Oh, yes. You are indeed a champion, Brin," Irene said while she waited at a red light.

"Mommy, when you're all done learning how to make the car go, will you teach me?" Brin asked.

Irene gave Albert a beleaguered look.

"No driving for kids until their feet can reach the pedals...at the very least," Albert said. "Until then, you'll have to rely on your mom and me to chauffeur you around. It's something we're *both* going to be doing for the next dozen or so years."

That night, after putting the twins to bed, it occurred to Irene that some of her anxiety about driving stemmed from her fear of hurting the children. Maybe she'd be less tense if they weren't in the car during her lessons. Then it would be just she and Albert — and the brand new Volvo, of course — that her driving might put in jeopardy. Thereafter, driving instruction took place only when Tatiana was available to watch the children. And though she was still nervous, Irene found herself better able to follow Albert's directions. She even managed to parallel park three times in a row without hitting the curb or tapping the bumper behind her.

Right before the twins turned three, Irene passed her driver's test. It was her second attempt, but she was proud and relieved nonetheless. She was now able to steer a car along the city streets legally, taking account of other cars and drivers, and obeying all applicable traffic rules. She would allow herself to bask in that achievement for a little while, at least. As for attempting the Major Deegan Expressway or the Henry Hudson Parkway, that would have to wait for another day.

§§§

Albert was so overjoyed that his wife had become a licensed driver that he decided to surprise her with a special gift. One Saturday in December, as he was serving pancakes to the family in the shape of Mickey Mouse and Bugs Bunny, breakfast was interrupted by a knock on the door. Albert asked Irene to get it. She opened the door to find two delivery men standing beside a spinet piano festooned with blue and white helium balloons. Albert called out from the kitchen, "If that's what I think it is, congratulations and Happy Chanukah to the newest driver in the family!"

Irene teared up as the men positioned the piano into the perfect spot in their new living room.

"What's a matter, Mommy?" Brin asked. "How come you're crying?"

"Don't you like it?" Ian asked.

"Oh, I *love* it. I've always wanted a piano and could never have one of my own. Daddy was so generous and thoughtful to get me something so special. That's why I'm crying."

Brin got a quizzical look on her face. "Mommy, if you don't stop crying, Daddy's gonna think you don't like it," she said with utter earnestness, "and he's gonna give the piano back to those guys."

Irene wiped her face with her hands. "You're absolutely right, Brinny. I'd better show Daddy how much I appreciate his gift." Then she went to her husband and gave him the kind of kiss she usually saved for after the children were asleep. "Thank you, Albert. I love you more each and every day."

"So you forgive my less than ideal teaching technique during our driving lessons?"

"There is nothing to forgive. You had a difficult student. Thank you for your patience."

Then Irene sat down at the piano and played "Free to Be You and Me" while the twins stood wide-eyed. "Mommy can play my favorite song!" Ian squealed in delight. He grabbed his sister's hand and they danced together around their living room, singing along to the music, "Take my hand, come with me, where the children are free..."

As the delivery men went down the hall, both of them thought the same thing: Nice couple, cute kids, and boy, is that guy ever going to get lucky tonight.

§§§

Irene and Albert shared many things — their commitment to family, a love of the seashore, an adventurous spirit when it came to trying new ethnic restaurants, and a reverence for science. It was science that had brought them together as teenagers and united them through all the twists and turns that followed their reunion on the museum steps. They both approached their work with a sense of urgency. They hungered to unravel the mysteries of the natural world, mysteries that had stumped scientists for generations. It was a pursuit that infused every day with purpose. It also brought them happiness. They enjoyed the egalitarian nature of science, the fact that young scientists such as they could — and often did — challenge the ideas of their elders, venturing forth into a discussion or investigation with renowned researchers on an equal footing. At its best, scientific exploration was a team sport, infused with a sense of collegiality and common purpose.

During their training, both Albert and Irene had been fortunate to have mentors who encouraged them to be bold, to tackle hard problems, to weather the inevitable disappointment of experiments going awry or data making no discernible sense. They also demonstrated what it meant to have the courage to try anew when all appeared to be lost. Although the average man or woman on the street knew little to nothing of the arcane work scientists did — how they could toil for decades trying to answer a single question, often with little acknowledgement, sometimes fending off ridicule for their iconoclastic ideas — Irene and Albert never for a moment doubted the scientific method provided a path to truth. Their support for one another's work was unconditional. They celebrated their victories. When things went poorly in the lab, or a funding request they'd been counting on was denied, they offered one another solace and a reminder that no matter how thorny or illusive the problem, tomorrow was another day.

Albert was in the midst of an exciting time in his study of neutrinos. Although they were technically the detritus of all sorts of reactions, the Big Bang being the most prominent, and the sun's continual fusion being the most constant, Albert found the ubiquitous sub-atomic particles fascinating to study. In the 1950s it was theorized that their three types or "flavors" — electron, muon and tau — change from one flavor to another as they oscillate. Three decades later, physicists such as Albert were working to prove that theory's truth. And while others studied neutrinos for what they could reveal about the origins of the universe, much as archaeologists analyze long-buried objects to understand ancient civilizations, Albert was interested in the neutrinos themselves. His work was getting attention. He'd been asked to collaborate with scientists from the Brookhaven National Laboratory out on Long Island and Fermilab near Chicago. He'd just won a Guggenheim grant to study the "the solar neutrino problem," the discrepancy between the predicted flux of solar neutrinos based on the Sun's luminosity and the flux picked up by neutrino detectors. Although Albert was not one to blow his own horn, Irene knew how pleased and proud he was that his work was being recognized.

Irene, too, had entered a new stage in her career. She enjoyed teaching medical students and residents from Mount Sinai during their Bronx VA rotation in psychiatry. In the negotiations for her start-up package, she'd been promised a small lab in the VA's new research wing, which was due to open the following year. Having a lab of her own would allow her to continue looking for the link between affective disease and genetic biochemical markers. Of course, as a principal investigator (PI), she'd be responsible for finding ongoing funding for her research. Only then would she be able to fully staff her lab with doctoral students and post-doctoral fellows.

After spending two years doing primarily bench research, she was surprised by how eager she was to get back to clinical work. Her patients at the VA, both hospitalized and out-patient, were overwhelmingly male. Many were older, in their fifties and beyond, having served in the Second World War and Korea. Reviewing their histories, Irene noted that many of the older vets had led productive lives after leaving military service, holding down jobs, marrying, raising children. Some of the World War II vets reported that they'd lived with low levels of depression and/or anxiety through much of their adult lives but, as they suffered personal setbacks — the death of a loved one, ill-health, or job loss — life became much harder to manage. Some of these older patients described recurrent flashbacks of combat-related trauma they'd experienced decades before.

One such patient, Norman Baines, made a deep impression on Irene. The fifty-nine year old husband and father of two adult children was seeking treatment for the first time since his service in WWII. Straightaway, his candor won Irene over.

"No offense intended, Dr. Adelson, but I can't believe I'm sitting here in a psychiatrist's office. This is definitely not something I ever thought I'd do, but I just don't know where else to turn."

"Like all medical doctors, my job is to help my patients. What brought you here today?"

"I'd say my number one problem is I can't shake this feeling of guilt for having survived the downing of my B-17. When I tell you how long ago that happened, you'll surely think I'm crazy."

"Traumatic events have a way of sticking with a person, no matter how much time passes. That's not unusual at all."

"Well, forty years ago I was the only one of our crew who made it out alive. I was captured by the Nazis and taken prisoner. Believe me when I say there were times when I was a POW that I wished I'd died with my buddies. I spent days on end in a pitch dark cell at the Luftwaffe Interrogation center. When they were done torturing me for information, they threw me in the *stalag* — you know, the prison camp — to rot. I prayed for liberation, but I was pretty sure I'd never see my family again. It was rough," Norman said, staring at his hands.

"How old were you when you were shot down?"

"Nineteen, younger than my own children are now. Hardly grown, if truth be told."

"Those would be painful experiences at any age, but particularly for someone so young. But I see from your history that until recently, you'd found a way to cope with that sense of guilt. You've led a rich life, both personally and professionally. Not everyone can maintain a marriage for decades or sustain long-term employment. I see you're a math teacher at Bronx High School of Science," Irene said.

"Well, my wife deserves all the credit for the marriage. She's an amazing woman. I really don't deserve her." Norman took a moment to collect himself before he continued. "As for the job, I haven't worked for months. I couldn't concentrate on my teaching or relating to the kids, so I took a personal leave. I *was* a damned good teacher until things got out of hand."

"And when did that start to happen?" Irene asked.

Norman thought for a minute. "I'd say about eight months ago, when my brother died. We were very close. He served in Italy during the war. We married cousins and his house is just down the street from mine. I miss him terribly," he confessed, his voice catching.

"I'm so sorry," Irene said. "Losing a loved one with whom you shared so much is hard."

"Yeah, it's been that, all right. The other thing I find myself stewing over is that I'm coming up on retirement. I'm getting to the point where my pension won't get any bigger even if I teach another year. They call it being "maxxed out." It doesn't make sense to keep working once you get to that point, or at least that's what everyone keeps telling me."

"How do you feel about it?" Irene asked.

"Well, I've loved teaching. I've enjoyed my students. The Bronx Science kids are crackerjacks. They're going to go on to do great things. So no, I guess I wouldn't agree that it would be useless to continue teaching, the pension issue aside. But it's a moot point," he sighed, "since I've become worthless to my students."

"Mr. Baines, prior to losing your brother and confronting the possibility of retirement, did you experience any difficulties related to your wartime service? You've already mentioned your sense of guilt for having survived when your fellow airmen did not. Is that something you've been dealing with since the war?" Irene asked.

"I'd say it's always been lurking in the background, that and some other little hiccups, as my wife likes to call them."

"Like what?" Irene inquired.

"Like I won't get on a plane for love or money, like I avoid elevators, fireworks, and crowds like the plague. I always have lights on in my house at night, even if it's just night lights. I know it sounds foolish, but I hate the dark."

"That doesn't sound foolish at all," Irene said. "In regard to those 'hiccups,' how would you say they've affected your life?"

"I've managed okay over the years. A stiff drink or two helps most times. If I know I have to go someplace that's going to set me off, a scotch before leaving the house seems to help smooth things out."

"Has the scotch been helping you lately?"

"No amount of scotch helps now, and believe me, it's not for lack of trying. Frankly, I think it makes matters worse. I can barely get out of bed most days. I'm embarrassed to tell you that, but I may as well level with you."

"Are you able to enjoy the things you normally like to do?

"I love to read...or I did love to read. I can't focus my attention on a book now. My wife and I used to go dancing a couple of times a month. No way can I make myself do that. I also liked to cook, but my appetite is zilch. I've lost forty pounds since my brother died."

Irene looked at the slim man sitting across from her and noticed his clothes were, in fact, too big for his small frame. "Do you have any other physical complaints, other than loss of appetite?"

It's not just that my appetite's gone. My stomach has been off since my brother got his cancer diagnosis."

"Do you have GI pain?"

"Well, I don't want to get too deep into the gory details, but if I do eat, I end up with terrible gas. My stomach gets bloated and looks like a pregnant woman's. It hurts like hell. Eating just isn't worth it."

"So do you think your weight loss is due to a loss of appetite or your avoidance of food?"

"I'd say it's fifty-fifty."

"I'd like to refer you to one of our GI doctors. Sometimes when a person has mental distress, we don't pay sufficient attention to their physical symptoms. I don't want to ignore anything that's impeding your health. Would that be okay with you?"

"Yeah, that's okay. My wife will be happy, at least. She's been telling me to get checked out by a GI doc for months.'"

§§§

Most of Irene's younger patients had deployed to Vietnam during the United States' thirteen-year-long military incursion. They were much closer to her in age than her WWII or Korean War veterans. A great number of these young vets had experienced a more difficult re-entry into civilian life than the older vets. There were theories as to why. The WWII vets had won a hard-fought battle against fascism and returned home as heroes. Even so, they were not immune to the stress induced by wartime trauma. Up to ten percent suffered from "combat fatigue." Still, many like Norman Baines had found a way to cope. Good economic times, a generous GI Bill allowing them to go to college, and low interest VA loans all helped them create careers, homes, and families.

On the other hand, the Vietnam vets came home to ridicule, thought of as murderers and "baby killers" by the legions of Americans who'd opposed the war. Those who had supported the war viewed America's 1975 televised retreat from Saigon as a symbol of national failure and disgrace. For some vets, the uniform became a symbol of shame. Then too, the economy in the 1970s was shocked by the quadrupling of oil prices. In short order, the country was wracked by recession, high inflation, and unemployment. It was little wonder many Vietnam vets had difficulty re-entering civilian life.

Post-traumatic stress disorder (PTSD) now replaced terms from previous wars — combat stress, war neurosis, shell shock, and combat fatigue — and up to fifteen percent of those who served in Vietnam suffered from it. The intrusive thoughts, flashbacks, nightmares, poor concentration, and irritability vets suffered were all deemed to be symptoms of PTSD, which was now a recognized mental illness. Some of the Vietnam vets Irene treated had associated problems such as alcoholism and drug addiction. For them, holding down a job and maintaining relationships with family, spouses, and children were all beyond their grasp.

One particular vet's story resonated with Irene, maybe because he shared a birthday with Albert. When his mom would allow it, Robert Miller lived with her; when she didn't, he lived on the streets. The last time he tried getting back into his mother's good graces she said she wouldn't take him back unless he went to the VA. That's why he was sitting in Irene's office, keeping up his end of the bargain in order to have a roof over his head. Despite the coercion that led him to seek treatment, Robert seemed to actually warm to Irene's interest in his life. He told his story haltingly, sometimes in a whisper. He'd enlisted in the Marines at nineteen, figuring it was better than being drafted into the Army infantry. When he arrived in Vietnam in the fall of '67, he was one of the half million military personnel serving there. Irene momentarily flashed on how she'd started college just as her patient was being deployed to Southeast Asia.

To the sound of his fingers rat-a-tat-tatting on the desk, Robert described the massive bombardment that hit his Marine garrison at Khe Sanh in the winter of 1968, destroying ninety percent of the base's artillery and mortar rounds. "God damn, those explosions were deafening…and they didn't stop. They just went on and on and on. I thought I'd die listening to those rounds exploding. I still jump out of my skin whenever I hear loud sounds, which is a little bit of a problem here in New York, you know, with the horns blaring and the jack hammers going. They really freak me out," he confessed.

Continuing in a halting voice, he explained how the battle lasted for seventy-seven days. He seemed almost proud to point out it was one of the longest and most gruesome battles of the war. Thousands of North Vietnamese were killed. Among the hundreds of Marines who lost their lives at Khe Sanh were three of Robert's buddies from basic training: Vinson, Radzik, and Poitier. "Seeing them die…that really tore me up. I mean, we'd been through a lot together. We were like brothers, 'one for all and all for one' — you know — that sort of thing. I mean, they would have taken a bullet for me…and me for them. After the V-C killed them I went on a tear. I must have killed at least a dozen gooks at point-blank range. Some looked like kids, but they had bayonets in their hands so, as far as I was concerned, they were fair game. The only trouble is I can't seem to get them out of my head. Their expression when they were hit was always the same, like they were so surprised and then, 'Hell, this is it, I'm gonna die.'"

Robert's parting thought as their session ended was this: "I think I'd feel a hell of a lot better if every time I closed my eyes I didn't see their faces."

§§§

After a few months of treating her VA patients, Irene came to the conclusion that landing in the VA had been *beshert*, Yiddish for destiny. The VA had not been her first choice. It certainly didn't have the prestige or the resources Columbia enjoyed, but she now felt this was the right place for her to do her work. The needs of her patients were so great, the price they'd paid for having worn the uniform so steep, it was both her duty and privilege to seek ways of easing their suffering.

Until coming to the VA, Irene had done her best to bury her anti-war activism in a dark corner of her mind. It was that activism, after all, that had put her in the path of Steve Shapiro. Now, after listening to her patients, she found her thoughts returning to her brief but heartfelt effort to stop the war in Vietnam. The memory that burned brightest was of that dark December morning she and Annie went to the induction center on Whitehall Street. Images of the thousands of chanting protestors, the police barricades and paddy wagons, the hundreds of arrests all came flooding back so vividly that her heart started racing, just as it had back then. What had all that protest accomplished? Not a single boy was saved from being drafted. It occurred to her that some of her patients had likely been processed into the military at that very induction center. She winced at the thought.

Now she had the opportunity to mitigate the damage done by the war by providing relief to her patients. She knew the standard regimen of therapy, support groups, anti-depressant and anti-anxiety medication would help some of her patients some of the time. But there would undoubtedly be others with "refractory" symptoms that didn't respond to any treatment. She needed to get a better understanding of what was driving their illness if she hoped to help them. What was happening in their brains, she wondered, when they re-lived their anguished memories?

Something else that perplexed her was why only some people who experienced the horrors of war were afflicted with PTSD, while others were able to return from combat and move on with their lives. Could there be genetic markers that divided those who could move past the ghastly traumas from those who could not? The burgeoning field of epigenetics recognized that genes can be activated by the environment. Did the experience of going to war increase the likelihood of the expression of genes for mental illness? Immediately, the wheels in her mind started turning, trying to figure out how she might study the hypothesis that there was a genetic predisposition to PTSD.

Despite having no doctoral students, post-doctoral fellows or even lab space to call her own, Irene began designing a project aimed at gathering detailed information regarding the family history of mental illness among her patient population. She knew that having a first-order relative with major depression doubled or perhaps even tripled the risk of developing depression. Should the first-order relative have recurrent major depression, the risk was even greater. A first-order relative with bipolar disease upped the risk for an individual developing the illness to four times that of the general population. Knowing the incidence of mental illness in her patients' family tree would help tease out whether their genetic inheritance had increased their risk of developing PTSD or other mental illnesses.

Her first stop after designing her experiment was the VA's research compliance office, led by the rather dour gentleman responsible for ensuring all research conducted at the hospital met with federal, state, and agency regulations. Thanks to her doctoral and post-doctoral training, Irene made certain her proposal could not be faulted on any of those fronts. Once permission was in hand, she recruited her students to the project. Using the patients' medical histories and clinical interviews, they were to glean important data on whether symptoms of mental distress first arose pre- or post-service, whether the symptoms abated and then returned, and the existence of first-order relatives who themselves experienced depression and/or anxiety once or multiple times. Additionally, she wanted to separate out those who served but did not see combat from those who had. A software program on Irene's spanking new IBM desktop personal computer, which she'd negotiated as part of her start-up package at the VA, would help compile the data her students collected. Her career as an independent medical investigator had begun.

§§§

Irene found it curious that a complaint of gastrointestinal problems often came up in conversation with her patients. When she thought back to her residency at Payne Whitney and while doing the interviews during her post-doctoral work, she remembered that psychiatric patients mentioned ongoing GI problems more than one might expect. She raised that point during her post-doc at Columbia, but others on the team pointed out that it is not unusual for psychiatric patients to have a number of co-morbidities, GI issues being just one. However, what jumped out for Irene were the patients at the VA who associated their mental troubles with "a bad stomach," something akin to having "a bug" that couldn't be shaken. Particularly for the anxious and depressed, GI distress was closely linked to their agitation. Soon she had her students ask two additional questions when they did their patient work-ups: *How often do you have constipation or diarrhea, stomach pain, bloating, or gas? Do you have first-order relatives who have experienced constipation or diarrhea, stomach pain, bloating, and gas?* Although her mentees had a hard time seeing why a psychiatrist should be interested in a psych patient's GI issues — or those of their first-order relatives — Irene wanted to find out if her impressions were borne out by the data. She was well aware a hunch was only as good as the objective evidence that supported it.

When the data started coming in, Irene found her second question yielding little information. The most common response from patients was that they had little to no knowledge of their family members' GI symptoms. However, the first question proved more fruitful: More than half of the vets on the psychiatry service experienced GI problems of one sort or another, some not serious enough to have a track record with the VA's GI specialists, but enough to be a factor in their lives. Others suffered from irritable bowel syndrome, ulcers, or inflammatory bowel disease. A third of the patients who experienced depression complained of chronic constipation. The figures held for her patients who had seen combat and for those who had not, for those who had early onset of a mental illness and those who were diagnosed later in life. As she was putting the final touches on her applications for grants to study the biogenetics of mentally ill vets, she included the possibility of the gut playing a role in their illness. Whether it was causal, coincidental, or an effect of their mental disease was the question she hoped her study would shed light on.

Between seeing her patients, teaching her students, and caring for her family, the only time Irene had to pursue a better understanding of the co-morbidity of GI distress and depression was after she put the children to sleep. Night after night she pored over studies the hospital's medical librarian had found for her. The young woman, a recent graduate of Columbia's library science program, had discovered a plethora of references, some going back to the 19th century. In her reading Irene learned about how, back in the 1830s, an Army physician by the name of William Beaumont treated a patient who'd been shot in the stomach.

Beaumont, who later became known as the "father of gastric physiology," saved Alexis St. Martin's life despite the severity of his injuries. The only problem was the hole in his stomach never healed. Seeing a research opportunity, the doctor hired St. Martin as his handyman, and for the next eight years methodically studied how different foods were digested. Among Beaumont's findings: emotions affect digestion. He concluded the brain is somehow tied to the workings of the gut.

Even before Beaumont's research, an acclaimed and influential London-based doctor, John Abernethy, linked mental disorder to "gastric derangement." He noted the close relationship between the gut and the mind, giving as an example how worrying caused many to lose their appetite. He pointed out that "vitiated digestion" caused restlessness, disordered sleep, and low spirits. He concluded that the nervous system was the link between the gut and the mind. Following in that vein, an article published in 1861 in Scotland noted that "dyspeptic attacks" distressed one Englishman to the point of suicide. "Nothing but family considerations prevented him from blowing out his brains with a pistol..."

The materials the librarian supplied Irene with revealed that in the early twentieth century, some Western physicians, psychologists, and physiologists posited a connection between a patient's emotional state and gastric distress. Soon it was commonly believed that psychological problems could cause ailments such as ulcers. People with ulcers were viewed as restless and prone to anxiety and fear. This view was widespread even into the middle of the twentieth century. It was noted that WWII soldiers at Dunkirk were reported to be suffering from an inexplicably high rate of perforating duodenal ulcers. London's civilians caught in Nazi air raids also reported similar problems. Mental stress was also seen as the causal factor in GI disturbances like ulcerative colitis. The belief in the link between mental and gastric distress was not confined to the West. When asked about the reason for depression by a devotee, a Hindi guru responded in this way: "Worry, hurry, curry."

Irene didn't recall stress being cited as a causal factor in gastric disorders by her medical school professors. She went back to one of her old textbooks to make sure she was remembering correctly. The text cited high levels of hydrochloric acid, heredity, pepsin, tissue antigens, and lifestyle as the leading causes of GI problems. Physiological factors — not emotions — produced the pain and suffering associated with indigestion and more serious GI disturbances, although there was the occasional nod to the idea that stress might cause the stomach to produce excess acid.

Just when Irene was in the thick of her study of the co-morbidity of gastric problems and mental disease, a medical journal arrived in her mailbox that delivered a bombshell. An iconoclastic Australian physician-scientist, Barry Marshall, had long believed that ulcers were caused by a bacterium, a view that was met with universal derision from the gastroenterology community. To prove his theory Marshall downed a brew containing the bacterium *H. Pylori*. In a matter of days he developed a wicked case of vomiting and gastritis. Endoscopy showed massive inflammation in his stomach. A biopsy confirmed his stomach had been colonized by *H. Pylori,* upending the conventional wisdom that no bacteria could survive the stomach's acidic environment. Whether brave or foolhardy, by using himself as a guinea pig, Marshall had shown that colonization by a bacterium — not physiological *or* psychological factors — was the cause of duodenal ulcers. Stress didn't cause ulcers; the pain and suffering associated with ulcers caused victims to be stressed.

One night at 3 AM, as Irene rocked Ian back to sleep after he'd awakened with a bad dream, her mind turned to the causal link between *H Pylori* and dyspepsia. No one had ever imagined that a bacterium could cause stomach ulcers. Could it be that there might also be a microbial cause of mental distress? The gut was filled with legions of bacteria, viruses, and fungi. A recently discovered group of microbial organisms, Archaea, likely inhabited the gut, as well. It was understood that the vagus nerve connected the gut to the brain, providing a communication pathway between the two organ systems. Might it be possible that through that channel, microbial agents could affect the workings of the brain? She thought about the 1910 article the medical librarian had found for her from the *British Journal of Psychiatry,* which discussed treating melancholia with the lactic acid bacillus, the probiotic she gave to Brin after a ten-day course of amoxicillin left her with a bad case of diarrhea. Then there was the article about the 1908 winner of the Nobel Prize for Medicine or Physiology, the microbiologist Ilya Mechnikov, who promoted the use of *Bacillus bulgaricus* found in Bulgarian yogurt as an aid to longevity and a possible therapy for mental illness.

Might there be a scientific basis for the notion that a mood disorder such as depression was caused by the lack of a particular bacterium in the gut, or the presence of another?

As she crawled back into bed and snuggled next to Albert, Irene thought back on something she'd heard during her training at Columbia from the psychiatrist and neuroscientist, Eric Kandel. There was "day science," the rational, pragmatic work on experiments proving or disproving a given hypothesis, and then there was "night science," which allowed a researcher to muse about what was possible. Sometimes night science led a researcher to form a hypothesis out of a mere intuition or hunch. Her query about the possibility of a microbial link between the flora in the GI tract and mental illness surely qualified as night science and, as far as she knew, it was a line of research no one was investigating. She, however, was intrigued.

CHAPTER FIFTEEN

IN HER SECOND YEAR AT THE VA, the promise of lab space was, at last, realized. It was a 350 square-foot room in the back corner of the basement of the new research wing. Other than benches and stools, there was virtually no equipment. For that Irene would have to rely on gathering the hand-me-downs from her more senior colleagues' old labs and the funding she'd won from the NIH to test the hypothesis that genetics played a role in the onset of PTSD. The funding, as modest as it was, nearly didn't happen. Her decision to add a research question about the GI tract's role in the suffering of vets with PTSD almost sank the entire application. One reviewer of her grant proposal was positively venomous in his assessment: "What would make a respectable scientist add a SUICIDAL addendum to an otherwise worthy research proposal?" Irene had no choice but to delete the question about the possible connection between the gut and mental health in order to receive funding for a two-year study on the heritability of mental illness and the onset of PTSD. Hopes of hiring a post-doc or two were dashed. At best, she'd have money for a lab assistant and some equipment.

Though disappointed, she would have accepted the setback more easily had she not seen the lab space given to a couple of other junior researchers. Reading about their grant awards in the VA newsletter piqued her curiosity, so she took herself on an investigatory tour of the new research facility. The one fellow studying cardiovascular disease in veterans had a lab at least four times the size of hers, replete with a wall of windows providing natural light for the well-equipped workspace. The other fellow researching early onset of Alzheimer's in veterans had a lab nearly as large and equally well-equipped. When Albert picked her up from the hospital that night, she was almost too upset to speak.

"Good day?" Albert asked.

"Actually, it was a disturbing day."

"What happened?"

"Well, I decided to take a walking tour of the new research wing. Of course I'd expected the senior researchers to have the most advantageously located and extensively equipped labs and all the junior researchers would have 'accommodations' similar to mine, you know, small, dark, bare bones. But that's not at all the case."

"What do you mean?"

"I mean that two researchers who were brought on board with me have large, lavishly equipped labs, nothing like the empty space I have to scrounge to fill with equipment and materials. You name it. I don't have it and they do.

"I figured I had nothing to lose by being direct, so I asked each fellow how he got such a great research space. Without missing a beat, each told me the space and equipment was part of his start-up package. On top of that, they'd each won generous grants from the VA. I applied to the VA, too, and was turned down. I guess I should thank my lucky stars the NIH came through, even though my contract is paltry by comparison. I can't believe the VA considers the mental illnesses suffered by our veterans less compelling than heart disease or dementia."

"Do you have any clue as to what's going on?" Albert asked.

"I have no idea. I'm at a complete loss."

"You deserve to have money thrown at you, Reenie," Albert said, feeling his blood pressure rise. "Not only are you an innovative, experienced researcher, you're the most economical one I've ever run into. I guarantee you'll use your grant money more wisely than any random sample of highly respected biological scientists."

She looked over and smiled at her husband. "You don't know how reassuring it is to have you in my corner. I can always count on you to make me feel better."

Albert looked over and caught her eye. "I'm not just saying you merit generous funding because you're the love of my life, though you *are* the love of my life. Speaking objectively, you are one damned fine scientist who deserves the resources you need to do your work."

"I have to face facts though, Albert. Being an independent researcher is new terrain for me. Up until now I've worked under the sponsorship of a principal investigator who brought in the grant money. Clearly, I have a lot to learn. Here I thought I'd done such a great job negotiating my start up package because I was promised a lab and a personal computer. But after seeing what the others got, I can see I was actually naïve and inexperienced, and apparently the powers that be took advantage of that. There is so much I want to do, but it'll require funding."

Albert looked over at his wife while he sat at a red light. Seeing the disappointment and self-doubt that lined her face filled him with indignation. If he could, he would find the tightfisted SOBs who funded her grant application and give them a piece of his mind. Obviously, they had no idea what kind of a scientist they were dealing with. He suspected they saw a woman's name on the application, a woman who'd never been funded before, and made all sorts of faulty assumptions about her commitment, her creativity, her work ethic. They may have anticipated a loss in productivity because of pregnancy or child-rearing. If only they knew how Irene drove herself, going back to the hospital or studying after the children were asleep, working on weekends and holidays. The horn that blared from the car behind him interrupted his train of thought.

"You've got a green light, Albert," Irene reminded him.

"Sorry."

They drove the rest of the way to the twins' pre-school in silence. Later that night, after tucking the kids in, Albert kept thinking about the hand Irene had been dealt. No matter which way he looked at it, he kept coming back to the same conclusion. The attitudes he'd witnessed in too many of his colleagues in physics and astronomy must also be at work in the biological sciences. The absolute worst of them saw women — students and colleagues alike — first and foremost as potential sexual partners. And it wasn't just the old-school guys, either. Last week the newly-tenured professor in the office next door told Albert that the best reason to go to a conference was "the chance to get a little action on the side." This was the same guy who rated the female students based on their sex appeal. His evaluation of a new doctoral student doing research on string theory with the department chairman was as follows: Tits, A-, ass, B+, overall hotness, A. Albert cringed when he thought about the guy's wife and little boy. Most of the department viewed him as a rising star for his work on quarks, but as far as Albert was concerned, he was a blight that would undoubtedly hurt the people around him, both at work and at home.

Of course, he also knew plenty of male scientists who mentored their female students without imagining, expecting or requiring sexual favors in return. Many of those would bristle at the mere suggestion that they'd abuse their power to get a woman in bed. They were wonderful teachers and mentors to their students regardless of gender, right up through their post-doctoral training. But something seemed to happen when it came time for their female protégées to take flight. In his own case, his mentors were encouraging, helpful, and supportive, shepherding him from the post-doc level to the faculty level without missing a beat. But he'd observed those same mentors having trouble seeing a young female scientist as a worthy peer standing on an equal footing.

His thoughts involuntarily went to Chien-Shiung Wu, an experimental physicist who worked on the Manhattan Project and the first woman granted tenure in Columbia's physics department. Despite the many accolades and awards she'd won over her long career, Wu bristled at the gender-based bias and injustice she continually encountered. He remembered her sarcastically wondering aloud whether atoms, mathematical symbols, or DNA molecules prefer masculine or feminine researchers. She had reason to be bitter. Her groundbreaking work on cobalt-60 disproved the law of parity in quantum mechanics, but when the Nobel Prize was awarded for that discovery in 1957, it went to two male scientists rather than to Wu. When she retired in 1981 Albert hoped the discrimination she'd faced would soon be a relic of the past, but in his heart of hearts he knew it was not only alive and well, but possibly affecting Irene.

Albert decided to keep his suspicions to himself. One round of grant applications that didn't go as he and Irene had hoped certainly wasn't enough to prove she was being treated less advantageously than her male counterparts. As for the lab space, perhaps Irene was right; she hadn't negotiated as hard or as tough as the other new, male researchers had. He would wait and see how things played out. There was no point in upsetting her. In his heart of hearts, he knew she'd have a tough time accepting the possibility that something as primitive as gender bias afflicted the scientific community. No, he'd keep his own counsel. Perhaps her next grant application would be judged more favorably. More than anything, Albert hoped his fears would turn out to be nothing more than the wild imaginings of a devoted husband.

§§§

When Irene referred Norman Baines to the GI service, she had the opportunity to meet and consult with Dr. Josiah Williams. It turned out to be a fortuitous pairing. Dr. Williams was as bright and curious a physician as Irene had ever met. He'd been at the VA since completing his training at Howard University some twenty-five years earlier. He, like Irene, felt great compassion for, and commitment to, his veteran patients. He, like Irene, found their suffering both poignant and maddening. And…he thought Irene was onto something when she told him her idea about exploring a possible microbial link between gut health and mental health.

"No kidding. That *H. Pylori* experiment in Australia knocked my socks off," Josiah said. "I never would have believed that a bacterium could cause such GI pathology. The old guard still isn't buying it, but I think Marshall is onto something big, really big."

"I know. He's been pummeled by the field for challenging the conventional wisdom on duodenal ulcers," Irene added. "But if he hadn't done the absolutely crazy thing of drinking that broth of *H. Pylori*, we'd all still be in the dark about the probable causation. Sometimes you have to fly in the face of orthodoxy to get to the truth."

"Amen to that. I like how you think, Irene Adelson. I'm accused of unorthodox thinking myself from time to time. I know how it can be a double-edged sword, that is, maybe you're onto something important, but maybe you're just crazier than a loon. The way I see it, without posing these kinds of questions, we end up with nothing but the old canon. I don't know if your idea will lead you down a dead end or open up a new avenue of research, but in my book, it's worth taking a serious look at."

That was music to Irene's ears. "I'm delighted you think so. It occurred to me when I was doing my post-doc that there seemed to be an inordinate number of psych patients with GI complaints. I've got the data to prove a strong co-morbidity among our VA patients. Even my own mother has the co-morbidities of GI distress and major depressive disorder. But I have no money to follow-up on my hunch. In fact, just adding a research question on the topic nearly sank my whole grant application to the NIH. As it is, the funding I got is rather paltry. But I guess I shouldn't complain. At least I've got something to work with."

"Maybe we can work around that, if you'd like a partner, that is. I've got med students and residents. You have med students and residents. We can't take them off our service, but we sure can enlist them to gather data for us when they do their work-ups. Maybe some of them will take an interest in the research and volunteer time in the lab. Call it the poor doctors' version of medical research."

"Really? You'd be willing to work with me on this?"

"Not only willing. Eagerly so."

And with that, a partnership was born.

§§§

Being a tenure-track professor meant Irene not only had to conduct research, she had to get that research published in a respected journal. She was hopeful a publication like the *American Journal of Psychiatry* might eventually publish the results of her study testing the hypothesis of a genetic predisposition to the development of PTSD. She was collaborating with her old colleagues from Dr. Fieve's lab, researchers who, like Irene, had moved on to other institutions. For all of them, the work was slow and frustrating. Although family trees showed clear heritability of mood disorders, the actual genetic link proved elusive. The longer Irene followed this line of investigation, the more she thought it was likely a constellation of genes — rather than a single genetic marker — that predisposed an individual to developing a mood or anxiety disorder, including PTSD.

She knew her own genetic inheritance was merely "a sample of one," making it anecdotal at best. Yet she — and Annie, for that matter — should have been at high risk for developing depression given their mother's recurring episodes. In her own case, the genetic inheritance coupled with the trauma of her sexual assault ought to have led to a debilitating breakdown followed by PTSD. To be sure, the months following the assault were a horrible time, the lowest point in her life, matched perhaps only by her return to work after the twins' birth. Yet somehow she'd found a way to cope, to carry on, and ultimately, to prevail. Why, she wondered? There had to be more at play, something that would act as a countervailing force offering protection from her genetic inheritance and the experience of a brutal and traumatic event.

One Sunday when Irene, Albert, and the little ones drove down to Brooklyn to celebrate Meyer's birthday, Irene had the opportunity to test the waters with Annie about her idea of a microbial link to depression. She and Annie took the kids to Prospect Park so Spence and Albert could concentrate on helping Gladys whip up a birthday feast for ten. Peter, now a tall and lanky nine-year old, reveled in the adoration of his little cousins. Although six-year old Rachel gave him a run for his money, he proudly assumed the role of leader of the pack of Adelson grandchildren. As the youngsters played tag, Irene broached the subject that was, of late, ever-present in her mind.

"Annie, I'd like to fly an idea by you."

"Shoot."

"Well, over my career I've noticed many psychiatric patients suffer from the co-morbidity of GI problems. It occurred to me, particularly after learning that the *H.Pylori* bacterium is likely a causal factor in duodenal ulcers, that perhaps there could be a microbial element to depression."

Annie was skeptical. "Really? If you listened to the patients I work with, you'd know they didn't need a microbe to send them into a tailspin. These folks have experienced terrible trauma and abuse."

"Of course. The same is true for my patients. It's a wonder some of them manage to do as well as they do given the hand they've been dealt. But as a scientist, I want to know why some are ravaged by their experience and others not," Irene explained.

"There are lots of other factors besides microbes, Reenie. Try support systems provided by family and friends, sufficient resources to get psychological or psychiatric help, good nutrition and medical care. All of those things help build resilience in a person who has suffered trauma. I'd look there before turning to microbes," Annie said, rather surprised at her sister's odd twist of inquiry.

"I agree that all of those factors play a role, a big role. But that can't explain all the variance in outcomes. Just think of identical twins raised together who have the same genetics as well as the same medical care, nutrition, and family support, but one develops a major mental illness like depression or schizophrenia while the other doesn't. There is something at work here beyond support systems."

"Well, schizophrenia is out of my wheelhouse. I can only speak to the power of support systems for victims of trauma," Annie said.

"Fine. Let's look only at trauma. Not every soldier who's experienced the horrors of war suffers from depression, anxiety, or PTSD," Irene pointed out.

"True enough, but unless you control for all the factors that we know support a person through trauma, I don't think you can start studying some sort of microbial link to those mental conditions," Annie said.

"That's a fair point, and one I'll do my best to incorporate if I ever get funding to study the connection between the gut and the brain," Irene said. "I'm aware that I might be on a fool's errand, but I am quite heartened to learn that I'm far from the first person to consider this. Even back in the nineteenth century there were doctors who suspected a link between the gut and depression. Though that line of inquiry fell out of favor over time, for me it's like seeing a trail of breadcrumbs off the beaten path of the forest floor. No one seems to notice it because of all the vibrant trees, the diverse wildlife, and the obscure location of the breadcrumbs. Or maybe people notice them but consider them merely incidental or irrelevant. But I can't stop wondering if those breadcrumbs lead somewhere. Maybe they don't. I understand that. But I'd like to try to find out for myself before ruling it out."

"Of course you do. That's who you are, Reenie," Annie said.

"Don't get me wrong. I feel so privileged to work with my patients, to experience the trust they put in me. But always in the back of my mind I'm thinking, 'What's at the root of this suffering? Is there a biological mechanism at play? If I could only uncover it, perhaps I could heal them.' That's what gets me racing off to the hospital every day."

Annie looked at her sister and smiled. "I guess it's fair to say alleviating mental suffering turned out to be the family business."

Irene smiled. "We can thank Mom for that."

"Whoever would have guessed that awful summer of mom's breakdown would change the course of our lives?" Annie asked. "And ultimately, for the better."

"Not I, that's for sure. I never could have imagined anything good coming out of it," Irene admitted.

"Ironic, isn't it?"

"No doubt," Irene replied. "It makes me happy knowing we're both devoted to the same pursuit."

"Me, too, little sister. Me, too."

"So, getting back to those breadcrumbs, you won't think me too crazy if I follow them into the forest?" Irene asked.

Annie put her arm around Reenie. "Let me say this: If a microbial link to depression exists, I wouldn't put it past you to find it. I admit I can't begin to imagine what the mechanism would be to allow a microbe to affect mood. But who am I, a mere psychologist, to tell you not to follow your idea? You're the physician-scientist in the family, so follow your gut. Oh…sorry for the terrible pun."

Irene laughed. "Thank you for your blessing. And I don't think your pun is terrible at all."

"Yeah, it was pretty bad. But that can stay between us. And now, we'd better round up those kids and get them cleaned up for dinner. We have a birthday to celebrate. I can't wait to hear what they'll have to say about the seventy-nine candles on Dad's buttercream mocha chocolate cake. Bet you dollars to donuts those candles will make quite an impression!"

§§§

Irene kept her head down, continuing her research on possible genetic links to the development of PTSD and depression in veterans while quietly investigating a possible connection between mood and the gut. At Josiah Williams's suggestion, she started reading about the enteric nervous system that controls the gastrointestinal tract. A pioneer in the field, Dr. Michael Gershon, was one researcher with whom she had never crossed paths while at Columbia. He was largely responsible for the discovery that ninety percent of the body's serotonin — the monoamine neurotransmitter that modulates cognition, learning, memory, mood, and myriad of physiological processes — was produced in the intestinal tract. He found that although the gut or enteric nervous system could function independently of the central nervous system, the two can and do affect one another via signaling along the vagus nerve. Most interesting for Irene's pursuit was his hypothesis that the vast majority of nerve signals go from the gut up to the brain. Gershon even suggested that this transmission from gut to brain might have implications for brain pathologies including memory disorders, depression, and even epilepsy. Irene could see why Gershon was dubbed the "father of neurogastroenterology," a field about which she knew virtually nothing but aimed to learn more.

Josiah was a good tutor in that regard. He'd been following Gershon's work for years and was intrigued by his observations that neurological diseases such as Parkinson's affected the GI tract long before motor symptoms became apparent. Clearly, Gershon's work lent credence to Irene's interest in the connection between the brain and the gut.

Josiah was also a veritable font of wisdom on the role the gut played in general health. In Irene, the able teacher found a willing pupil and a quick study. He voiced his concern about the damage done to the intestinal flora by antibiotics, that not only killed the bad bacteria in a child's ears or an infected wound, but also negatively affected the gut's beneficial bacterial communities. In his opinion, antibiotics were being wildly overprescribed. He also had concerns about the deterioration of the American diet. Processed foods with little or no fiber were detrimental to the health of the gut and the microbes that thrived on the indigestible fiber that fresh fruits and vegetables provided. He told Irene about a study that had come out just a few years prior that showed the diet fed to infants and young children determined the acquisition of healthful bacteria in the gut. Given the proliferation of fast food and processed foods, he feared for the future health of the children growing up in the United States.

The most fascinating story Josiah shared was that of Dr. Ben Eiseman. In 1958 Eiseman, then chief of surgery at the Denver VA, took a novel approach to treating patients with the potentially fatal gut inflammation caused by the *Clostridium difficile* (*C diff*) bacterium. The four patients had previously been prescribed antibiotics for unrelated ailments, resulting in the obliteration of healthy intestinal bacteria and a life-threatening overgrowth of *C diff*. As a last resort, Eiseman gave his critically ill patients fecal transplants from a donor with a healthy, diverse gut bacterial community. Much to everyone's surprise, in just a few days they went from being on death's door to being well.

The story astonished Irene. Clearly, the microbes in the gut had the power to induce both sickness and health. That, along with the rest of Josiah's tutorial, gave her a lot to think about. If Josiah was right, the widespread use of antibiotics since the 1940s and the changing American diet were having deleterious effects on the gut microbiota. What were the implications for mental and physical health?

She'd given a lot of thought to what Annie had said about support systems mitigating the effects of trauma. If she wanted to truly isolate the effects of the gut's microbes on depression and anxiety, she would have to work with animals in a tightly-controlled environment. Mouse genetic and biological characteristics closely match those of humans, as do symptoms of many human diseases, so she knew they would be a good species to study. Irene decided to use axenic — germ-free — mice as her experimental subjects. Unlike conventional mice, which have billions of microbes inhabiting their gut microbiome, these mice would have virtually no microbial organisms, hence the term, "germ-free."

Irene toyed with many iterations of her experimental design. She thought she could selectively breed her germ-free mice for psychological traits like timidity, anxiety, and sociability. Then, via fecal transplantation, she could introduce the microbiota from conventional mice that had been bred for boldness and sociability; the timid mice would get the microorganisms from the feces of the bold mice, the anxious mice would receive the gut microorganisms of the brave mice, and so on. Of course husbandry protocols and testing regimens would have to be followed strictly, but meticulous methodology was Irene's stock-in-trade. It would be a bold experimental design, and one that would require her to use the latest tools in recombinant DNA to produce genetically modified mice. One thing was certain, it wouldn't come cheap. Somehow, she'd have to convince those who doled out research money to bankroll a project that was, if nothing else, unorthodox.

§§§

Irene was exhausted but excited after submitting her grant proposal to the NIH. Josiah signed on as a co-investigator. She'd done her best to show the promise of the research they hoped to pursue, incorporating Josiah's substantive suggestions and Albert's stylistic ones. She thought the final result was as polished and comprehensive a proposal as she'd seen in her career. Still, she knew it would likely be categorized as "curiosity research," since no definitive treatment or marketable drug would be an immediate end-product. That would put it on a lower rung of priorities for funding from the federal government. Of course, without funding, her research would be dead in the water, as would her prospects for tenure from Mount Sinai. With stakes so high Irene developed contingency plans, marking her calendar with grant application deadlines for the Howard Hughes Medical Institute, the National Science Foundation, and some private philanthropic organizations known for sponsoring medical research. No longer a stranger to disappointment, she dared to hope for good news from the NIH, but planned to be ready if its evaluators failed to recognize the merits of her proposal.

§§§

For the first time in years, Irene and her college friends planned a weekend getaway. Max's wedding had been the last time they'd all been together, but as joyous as that was, they'd had little time without spouses and significant others. In the intervening years phone calls, cards, and letters had enabled them to stay on top of recent events in each other's lives. This retreat would be just for the five of them, together as they'd been before careers, boyfriends, spouses, and children had made their lives so busy.

A dozen years prior, and much to everyone's shock, Meryl had handed in her master's thesis and walked away from Vanderbilt's PhD program in genetics. Once back home in Florida, she did some high school substitute teaching to help pay the bills until she could decide on her next step. Along the way, she reconnected with Billy, a boy she'd dated in high school, who'd returned to Gainesville after earning his law degree. Billy and Meryl shared a love of open-water swimming, a belief in social justice, and the desire to build a family. A year after leaving her doctoral program, they were married, and their two little girls followed in short order. Now, the only hint of Meryl's former passion for genetics was a half-time position in a University of Florida lab.

Of the five friends, she alone deviated from the career path laid out in college. Max completed a doctorate in bee entomology at Duke and landed a faculty job at the University of Connecticut. The only thing separating her from a tenured position now was the university provost's approval of the dean's tenure recommendation. Raisa, an assistant professor at Tufts Medical School, was an up-and-coming researcher in cardiac pathology, newly married to her longtime beau, Theo. Fredi, the only one of the friends still single, had at last found her match in Tom, a political reporter for the *New York Times*. His clever proposal happened during a dinner celebrating Fredi's promotion to associate professor of obstetrics and gynecology. Just before dessert was served, the maître d' brought her a mock-up of the front page of the *Times* with the enormous headline, *"HARDNOSED REPORTER FALLS FOR MT. SINAI DOC. WILL YOU MARRY ME?"* Then Tom fell to his knee and opened the ring box, causing more than a few diners around them to stop their conversations in mid-sentence. The wedding was scheduled for the spring.

The friends chose the very grand and historic Mohonk Mountain Resort in upstate New York for their reunion. It was an extravagance, but they decided to splurge on reservations for the last weekend in September. The resort's gourmet food, spa, bike paths, and hiking trails promised an interlude of indulgence as well as camaraderie. With the exception of Meryl, everyone could drive there within a matter of hours, and Meryl was only too happy to recapture the experience of getting on a plane without having to worry about entertaining her girls or packing a suitcase for Billy. Fredi picked her up at LaGuardia before swinging by the VA to get Irene. Raisa took the train down to Max's and they drove together to the resort. The two cars carrying the college friends arrived at reception just a few minutes apart. The moment they saw one another, they dropped their bags and embraced. It had been fifteen years since they'd left Barnard to follow their dreams, but it seemed like yesterday.

Although the hotel was impressive — reminiscent of a majestic French chateau — Raisa suggested they reserve one of the resort's cottages. She pointed out they could breakfast in the hotel, then return to their cottage before heading out on a hike in the woods or a bike ride on one of the trails. Best of all would be the time after dinner, when they could sit by the fireplace and continue their talk marathon late into the night, being as rowdy as they wanted without disturbing other guests. Raisa's vision of the weekend sounded nothing short of idyllic to them all, and when they pulled up in front of the cottage nestled in the woods, they were not disappointed. They could have been a million miles away from their daily lives, which was, after all, the point.

Over dinner on their first night together they took turns singling out the high point of their life since graduation. Fredi went first, regaling everyone with the story of a woman who'd suddenly begun hemorrhaging after delivering a healthy baby boy. As the woman's blood pressure dropped precipitously, the panicked family, the residents and med students all looked to her to save the woman's life. It was the most daunting and thrilling experience of her career. After the patient was stabilized, she decided to name her newborn son Frederick. Every Christmas since, a card with a photo of her namesake arrives in Fredi's mailbox.

When it was Raisa's turn, she chose the time during grad school that she stumbled on a jam session and sang and scatted to the jazz musicians' improvisations. When she and the sax player —Theo — went out for a drink afterwards, it marked the beginning of the greatest romance of her life. She had never believed she would meet someone who could fill all of her needs so perfectly. She still wondered how she'd gotten so lucky. "But," she added, "it's almost frightening to love someone so much. I mean I was entirely fine before I met him, but now the thought of living without Theo is unimaginable. I know it sounds macabre, but I hope we die together, maybe in an accident when we're very, very old."

"It doesn't sound macabre to me," Irene said. "I admit to hoping for that for Albert and me."

"So I'm not crazy?" Raisa asked.

"My therapist certified me as sane during my residency, and I shared that very hope with her."

"Now I feel bad for not wanting to die simultaneously with Rich," Max laughed. "You two romantics make normal relationships look bad by comparison."

"So if meeting Rich wasn't the highpoint of your post-college life," Meryl teased, "what was?

"For me," Max said, "I'd say it's actually a tie between getting that call from UConn offering me an assistant professorship and the day Rich and I got married. Both have changed my life for the better in ways I couldn't have predicted. How about you, Irene? Something tells me your best moment is somehow tied to Albert."

"Let me preface this by saying that I am passionate about the work I'm doing, and thrilled to be the mother of my twins, but the day Albert and I reunited on the steps of the Museum of Natural History was, without a doubt, the best day since leaving college. It's hard to put into words, but all I can say is that it's Albert who makes life sweet."

"You're making me cry," Fredi laughed, dabbing her eyes with a napkin, "and I'm a pretty tough nut. After...after... that awful time, I thought you and Albert were lost to one another. That seemed like such a terrible shame because you two were so great together."

"You mean after the attack. You can call it what it was," Irene said.

"All right then, the attack," Fredi conceded. "It *was* an awful time. It always made me sad to think that your relationship with Albert was a casualty of that creep's pathology. You have no idea how happy I was when you and Albert found your way back to one another. To me it felt like a sweet vindication, you know, like good besting evil."

"Let me second that," Meryl said. "I always thought you and Albert were a pair. The fact that you reconnected after all those years gave me hope that happy endings are possible."

"When Albert and I met again it was just like this…you know, just like the five of us now. It was as though no time had passed at all," Irene said. "Somehow we were able to get past all the hurt, all the pain. We were very lucky. Now, Albert's my best friend, my confidante, my lover, my partner. You should have seen him when he taught me to drive on the streets of the Bronx. He had the patience of a saint."

Nearly everyone laughed imagining the cautious, analytical Irene learning to drive in the wild and crazy streets of New York, but Meryl hung back. "I have to say, listening to all of you could make a girl feel a little inadequate."

"What are you talkin' about, girlfriend?" Fredi asked.

"Each of you is doing the work you'd dreamed of doing all those years ago, and it hasn't stopped you from building rich, fulfilling personal lives. I guess I never could imagine pulling that off. That's why I dropped out of the doctoral program. I saw how hard the few women in my department worked, how many were single, or childless, or both. As much as I loved genetics, I didn't want to sacrifice having a life for it. It seemed too steep a price to pay. But Irene, you're married, you've got two kids, you're on faculty at a great med school. You've got it all."

"I wouldn't say that," Irene demurred. "There are plenty of things I wish I did better. Many days — maybe most days —I go to bed thinking of all the things I didn't accomplish."

"But you've accomplished so much," Meryl countered.

"That's because Irene is the over-achiever in the group; a definite outlier," Fredi quipped.

"Am I?" Irene asked.

"Yes, you are a statistical outlier," Fredi reiterated. "Just accept the fact that out of a thousand women you'd likely be the only one capable of performing the complicated high wire act that is your life."

"That makes me feel better," Meryl said, "though back in the day I admit I saw all of us being future outliers, you know, the girls who were going to defy the odds and make great contributions to science while having lovely homes and families. When I think about the highlight of my life, I'm actually reluctant to share it with all of you. It's so retro."

"No judgments please, just the facts," Raisa said firmly.

"Okay then, it was becoming a mother. It was the most transformative, miraculous time of my life. Maybe it was my knowledge of genetics that left me in awe. To be the vessel for this embryo which goes on to develop all the organ systems, all the body parts that it will need to survive, to see it born and wonder who it will become, it was almost like a religious experience. I have to admit, Max, that as much as I always respected your religiosity, I never experienced anything like it myself; that is until I saw my daughter emerge from my body. And it happened again when her little sister was born. Those moments were the closest I've been to believing there is a God. Is it possible to see oneself as a feminist and cite childbirth as the defining moment in life?"

"Are you kidding me?" Fredi asked. "As an OB, I can tell you motherhood and feminism are in no way mutually exclusive. I aim to prove that myself as soon as Tom and I make things legal."

"You know what I mean," Meryl said. "My crowning achievements are my kids. That's what my mother would say — and my grandmother, for that matter."

Max sat beaming, her hand massaging her pregnant belly. "I'm with Fredi. Women should have the right to pursue whatever it is that interests them. For me, I'm going to try my best to combine motherhood with my research and teaching. As for your spiritual awakening, Meryl, I think people can come to their belief in God in different ways. The longer I live, the more I study my bees, the more I feel sure that life is not just a random happening in the cosmos. If nothing else, there's an intelligence and meaning inherent in it. I may express my spiritual beliefs through the Church, but there are so many ways to realize the transcendence of everyday life."

"Do you like being pregnant?" Meryl asked. "I'm wondering because I absolutely loved it, though I hear a lot of women complain bitterly."

"You'll hear no complaints from me. There's a miracle unfolding within me. Yes, my ankles are swollen and I threw up my guts for a good eight weeks every day after breakfast, but I've wanted a child since Rich and I got married. I waited all these years out of fear for how it would negatively impact the tenure decision. It's only now that things look secure at work that I took the risk of getting pregnant. I've published nearly twenty papers in peer-reviewed journals, I've gotten a teaching award, done professional service, all of which have me on the cusp of being granted tenure. But I wouldn't have risked it before now."

Raisa had sat quietly through Meryl's description of her love of motherhood and Max's long deferred but much wanted pregnancy. Finally, she spoke. "I admire you for delaying something you've wanted so badly, but you were smart to wait, Max. Tenure is hard enough under the best circumstances. It's been my experience that if you give 'the faculty' — overwhelmingly middle-aged and older men — any excuse to deny tenure to a woman, they'll jump on it. And childbearing and rearing are so removed from their experience. Most of them have wives who take care of all the domestic issues. They can't imagine a woman doing *their* work while being responsible for teacher conferences, doctor visits, and bedtime stories. It was very strategic of you to wait, Max. I'm glad it's working out for you now."

"Me, too," Max replied. "How about you, Raisa? Are you and Theo thinking of starting a family?"

"No. We've decided not to have children."

For the first time since they'd come together, a hush fell over the women.

Finally, Fredi asked, "Never? Not even after the tenure hurdle?"

"No, kids aren't in the cards for us. We both love our work, and we're at it sixty and seventy hours a week, sometimes even more." Raisa put her arm around Irene and said, "With the exception of our favorite outlier here, it seems nearly impossible to be a loving spouse, a first-class scientist, and a good mother all at the same time. Theo and I will likely stick with having pets, probably cats because dogs require too much attention. And the truth is, we're still rather mad for each other. Being together is enough for us."

This was the first time since getting in the car with Fredi and Meryl that Irene felt a tinge of sadness. The thought of living without Brin and Ian brought a physical pain to her heart. No matter how exhausted the dual efforts of nurturing them and giving her all at work left her, those children brought her a kind of joy she'd never known was possible. She was pained to think that Raisa would never have a toddler wrap its arms around her neck and whisper, "You're the best mommy in the world." Her expression must have betrayed her.

"You disapprove, Irene?" Raisa asked.

"It's not for me to approve or disapprove. Whether to become a parent is something only you can decide. You and Theo know what's in your hearts."

"But you think I'm making a mistake," Raisa pressed.

"I only know my own experience. Like Meryl, becoming a mother has changed me in so many ways, for the better, I hope. But I can't lie. It's been hard, sometimes crushingly hard. And without Albert, our parents, our nanny, I could never continue my work. So I understand your reasoning. But some things are not reasonable. And I think wanting a child is in that category. It's beyond reason."

"And you don't find it's hurting your career?" Raisa asked.

Irene thought before she responded and when she did, she found herself stammering. "I…I am frankly… not sure. During my post-doc, the lab manager certainly thought less of me because I had a husband and children. She wasn't the least bit restrained in her disapproval, either. When I lost out on a position at Columbia, I thought that might have played a part in it, but I have absolutely no proof. As for now…now I don't know. I hope not. I certainly haven't gotten the space or the money my male counterparts have received. I can't say if my personal life is to blame, my negotiating skills are faulty, or that my work just isn't worthy."

"Come on, Irene. *Your* work not worthy? I read the paper you authored during your post-doc. Give me a break," Raisa said. "If you were Ira Adelson no one would care if you had kids, but as a woman, believe me, they care. A lot. I've seen it with my own eyes."

"Me, too," Max agreed. "That's why I waited to get pregnant. The prejudice isn't even subtle. It's right out in the open. For years I've heard the snide remarks from some of my male colleagues. Just last week, when an absolutely outstanding researcher missed a meeting, a guy who hasn't done any original work in decades, had the nerve to say, 'She's probably raising her kid's self-esteem at a soccer game.' In truth, she was at home putting the last edits on an article for *Nature*. Too often when a woman is out for any reason, someone will make a crack about how she has her period or a sick kid or is menopausal. Raisa is right. If you don't have space or funding equal to what the male researchers have, I'd say it's a good bet it's not because your work isn't worthy."

Irene was stunned. Was it possible that the brightest minds in science allowed bias to color their views of female colleagues? How could scientists hold fast to prejudicial notions that were rooted in ignorance and irrationality? "I'm finding that hard to believe," Irene protested. "The male researchers at the VA are not evil, nor are they Neanderthals. They see how hard I work, how I'm in my lab at night, on weekends, and even holidays."

"And do you ever bring the twins to work?" Raisa asked.

"Only in a pinch, when Tatiana has an exam and Albert is out of town. I mean it's certainly not something I do regularly," Irene explained.

"And have you seen any other kids around, kids from your male colleagues?" Raisa asked.

"Well, now that you mention it, no, I haven't. But Albert brings Ian and Brin to work sometimes. It's unavoidable. It's not our first choice, but it happens."

"But Albert is a hot property who was fast-tracked for tenure. He can do what you can't. He'll be seen as a 'hands-on' dad pitching in to help his wife, while you'll be seen as someone whose loyalties are divided between home and work," Raisa said.

Irene shook her head, not wanting to believe what she was hearing. "You really think so?"

"Raisa's right," Max said. "It's only because you don't have an illogical, prejudicial bone in your body that you'd never imagine something as insidious as gender bias affecting your prospects at work."

"I know it was a dozen years ago that I left the doctoral program," Meryl said, "but I saw it too. I knew I wanted to get married and have kids, and after witnessing what happened to the few women in the department — the constant slights and harassment, the marginalization, the lack of funding, the denial of tenure and promotion — I ran for the hills."

Irene felt as though the ground had given way beneath her. "Assuming you're correct — and I have no reason to doubt the smartest women I know — there's got to be something wrong with me. Yes, I admit I had my suspicions when I lost out on a job at Columbia. A colleague — another woman, as a matter of fact —told me women with children couldn't be committed scientists. But you're saying this belief is ubiquitous, and that it manifests in plain sight. If that's true, I must be a fool."

"No, not a fool, Max said. "Innocent, ethical, earnest…but never a fool. You judge everyone on the merits of their behavior and their work. But everyone isn't like you, Irene. Most people let stereotypes of all kinds — gender, racial, ethnic, religious — bleed into their thinking and drive their judgments. Just remember this: Before you start blaming yourself for getting less funding or space, put an objective eye on the quality of your peers' work. My guess is, in *any* cohort, your work would rise to the top.

Of all people, certainly you deserve the best opportunities to pursue your research."

"And what if it doesn't happen? What should I do?" Irene asked, her agitation growing. "How would I prove that I didn't win a grant or get a better lab because I'm a woman? I don't want to just accept this."

Raisa was circumspect. "Short of a lawsuit which, in my opinion, is the death knell for any woman's career, you have to be aware of the game that's being played. The rules will favor the men every time. So you have to be smarter, work harder, be more innovative and bolder just to get what they get as a matter of course. That's been true of every woman who has succeeded in a male-dominated profession. The only thing I can say is that if anyone is capable of winning at that game — as unfair as it is — it's you."

CHAPTER SIXTEEN

ALBERT WAS NEARLY AS DEVASTATED as Irene when the NIH rejected her grant proposal. He'd watched her pour her heart and soul into the application, but instead of receiving the hoped for funding to study the gut microbiome's effect on behavior in mice, she got reviewer feedback that ranged from apathy to contempt. Irene felt sick to her stomach every time she reread one particular comment. "This is utter crap. Don't bother to apply again." Albert did his best to neutralize the hateful criticism, pointing out that his grant application to the Guggenheim Foundation had recently been dinged, as well. But in his heart of hearts, he knew that Irene was up against much steeper adversaries: scientific orthodoxy coupled with what he was increasingly convinced was either conscious or unconscious gender bias.

The NIH's rejection was a blow, but Irene decided that if she wanted a career as a research scientist she had no choice but to strengthen her resolve and carry on. She knew she somehow had to develop a thicker skin so that vile, ignorant comments like the one she'd received from that reviewer couldn't get to her, but the immediate challenge was to seek out other funders. With Albert's encouragement and Josiah's help, she reworked the proposal, making the experiment easier and more economical to conduct while keeping the focus on the role played by gut microbes. She would use genetically identical mice, keeping one group germ-free and allowing the other group to develop a normal gut microbiome. Then she would observe how the two groups behaved, handled stress, and acquired new skills.

She applied for grants from the VA, the Howard Hughes Medical Institute, the Wellcome Trust, and the National Institutes of Mental Health. Each time she sent off a grant proposal, she hoped against hope that this one would be the charm, but each and every time she came away empty-handed. With every failure Irene fought mightily not to surrender to self-doubt. Her initial grant from the NIH, modest as it was, would soon run out. The clock was ticking down on her six-year appointment from Mt. Sinai; the all-important tenure decision loomed on the horizon. It was time to face facts.

When she told Josiah she was throwing in the towel and returning to a safer, more "traditional" research topic — the effectiveness of pharmacological agents on PTSD — he protested. "The Irene Adelson I know and respect is no quitter. I must be talking to her doppelganger because she wouldn't be giving up on a study that could very well lead to a breakthrough in the understanding of the gut's role in mental suffering."

His vehemence both surprised and moved her. "Josiah, I see you as a friend as well as a collaborator. You have to agree there's a difference between being a quitter and rationally evaluating the prospects for success. If I were independently wealthy, I'd set up my own lab and do the work we both have so much hope for. But you know how the game is played. No funding, no research... and for me...likely no job. I have to be realistic."

"I'm all for rationality, but I also like taking a chance now and then. It makes life interesting, don't you think?" Josiah said, grinning from ear to ear.

"What kind of chance are you suggesting we take?" Irene asked a bit warily.

"Well, how about one last ditch effort to secure funding?"

"I've applied to all the agencies most likely to offer me money. There's no viable possibility left," she pointed out.

"Ah, but that's where you may be mistaken. You haven't thought about the Barrow Foundation, now have you? Admit it," Josiah said with a twinkle in his eye.

"I've never heard of the Barrow Foundation."

"Well, that may be because they've never funded medical research before, but what they do fund is projects of interest to Eloise and Winston Barrow. It's possible they could consider our study."

"But I'm running out of time. I need to get going on a grant application that might actually lead to funding," Irene said, panic rising in her chest.

"Hold on, girl. I'm not talking months. Let's give the application to the Barrow Foundation a week of our best efforts. We'll send it in and see what comes of it," Josiah suggested. "As we wait to hear back, you can get started on applications to study the effects of pharmacological treatments for PTSD. If we get turned down, no harm, no foul."

Her mind told her it would be a fool's errand, but her heart leapt at the thought of one more chance to pursue the breadcrumb trail that lured her off the beaten path. "Okay, Josiah. One week and no more."

§§§

Winston and Eloise Barrow had grown up working class, but they used their state university educations, intelligence, and business acumen to good advantage, reaping prodigious rewards from their careers in banking and finance. They were an impressive couple, smart, savvy, and elegantly handsome. They had one son, David, who'd inherited their sharp intellect and good looks. As for his outstanding athletic ability, his parents scratched their heads and claimed no credit, since neither had ever played any sport beyond a neighborhood pick-up game. They were delighted and impossibly proud when he was accepted to Princeton, where he excelled as a scholar-athlete and residential college advisor.

Besides athletic ability, another trait the Barrows never suspected to manifest in their son was a vulnerability to major depression. Always a high-spirited, upbeat boy, the good times came to an end for David during his junior year in college. The fall 1984 semester got off to a good start. As an advisor for freshman and sophomores in the Wilson residential college, he connected right away with the students in his charge. But in short order, his heavy course load of pre-med requirements began taking a toll. For the first time, he found himself unable to master course material. He stopped going to soccer practice and doubled down on his studying. Despite weeks of staying up into the wee hours and getting up early to hit the books, he was unable to earn a passing grade in either organic chemistry or genetics. By November, he questioned how he could have ever thought he had the brains to get into medical school. It shattered him to see his dream of becoming a doctor slip away. His normally robust appetite abandoned him. Nights were the worst, when every minute seemed like an hour, and horrible visions invaded his consciousness. Students in adjacent rooms heard his cries throughout the night. Several were concerned enough about the dramatic changes in David to reach out to the faculty fellows at Wilson.

Right before winter break the dean of the residential college called David to his office. His parents were waiting for him. The dean didn't mince words. He told him that after reviewing his GPA for the fall and consulting with his professors, he felt it best for David to take a medical leave from the university for the spring semester. His parting words were encouraging. "I know you, David. I know what you're capable of when you're feeling like yourself, and I'm confident that you'll return to campus when you're well again. Take the time you need. You'll never regret it."

On the drive back to Manhattan, his parents told David what they truly believed: He'd put himself under too much pressure. He felt down and disappointed about the fall term, but it was just a temporary setback. With effective treatment, he would soon be well and back at Princeton. Given all the AP credits he'd racked up in high school, the medical leave would have no effect on his ability to graduate on time with his friends.

The Barrows brought their son to the best psychiatrists in the city. When the doctors recommended inpatient treatment for David's depression, his parents selected Payne Whitney for its outstanding reputation and proximity to their home on the Upper East Side. David participated willingly in all of the treatments, seeking some way — any way — out of his pain. After six weeks in the hospital, David was discharged with prescriptions for doxepin, a tricyclic antidepressant, and lorazepam, an anti-anxiety medication that he was to take before bedtime to help him sleep. He was also scheduled for daily therapy sessions, which he attended regularly. After therapy on a beautiful day in May, David took the subway up to 175th Street, walked to the George Washington Bridge, and jumped off the upper deck into the Hudson River. He was a month shy of his twenty-first birthday.

The Barrow Foundation was established when David was a child, but after his death his parents channeled their grief into their philanthropy. They focused their support on community organizations operating in gritty urban neighborhoods, much like the ones in which they'd been raised. And that is how Josiah learned about the Barrows. His regular Saturday morning volunteer stint at a Boys' Club near his home opened his eyes to their largesse and their personal tragedy. To the best of his knowledge, the Barrows had never funded medical research of any kind. Still, after losing a child to depression, he thought they might consider supporting research aimed at discovering the roots of the terrible disease.

Over one snowy week in February 1988, Irene and Josiah used every scrap of free time to rework Irene's most recent grant proposal, making it less technical and more accessible to the lay reviewers they assumed the Barrow Foundation would rely on. No sooner had they put that in the mail than Irene started developing a proposal to study the efficacy of pharmacological interventions in the treatment of PTSD. But just a few weeks after sending off the application to the Barrow Foundation, she and Josiah received an invitation to make a presentation at the Foundation's offices in Manhattan. Though initially unnerved by the prospect, Irene soon viewed it as an opportunity. As for Josiah, he was over the moon that his wild card idea might be paying off.

The two spent the Saturday before the interview polishing their presentation. Josiah's wife Bernice, a graphic designer, prepared slides outlining their careers to date, their justification for their approach to studying the gut-brain connection, their experimental method, and the possible risks and rewards of following their proposed line of research. The two rehearsed until they felt as prepared as they could be and then did a mock presentation in the Williams' living room. Albert, Bernice, and the Williams' college-age daughters played the role of reviewers. After a series of pointed questions, which Irene and Josiah handled with ease, the reviewers' verdict was unanimous: "You're ready," to which Bernice added, "Now go and knock it out of the ballpark."

§§§

If she lived to be a hundred, Irene was certain she would never forget the day she and Josiah went to the Barrow Foundation offices. It was an uncommonly balmy day in March. The twins had just recovered from chicken pox, the first time they'd managed to get sick precisely at the same time. Since Tatiana had graduated from college and moved to LA for grad school, Gladys and Meyer spent more and more time at Irene and Albert's, an especially great help once the chickenpox struck the household. When the twins returned from their first day back in school, Grandma and Grandpa would be waiting for them, and Irene could concentrate wholly on her presentation. Albert gave her the pep talk of her life before dropping her off at the hospital that morning. "You go in there and just wow those millionaires, Reenie. Strut your plumage. Forget about being modest. Just show them how dedicated, how knowledgeable, how committed you are to this project. I have a good feeling about this, sweetie. I really do."

"I wish I shared your optimism," she replied. "I guess I've been beaten down by all the rejections, though I admit I'm a bit encouraged that they're investing the time to hear our presentation. I don't imagine they'd do that unless they had some interest in the project."

"You bet your life! And just wait until they meet the two of you. What a team you and Josiah make, each with your own area of expertise and experience. And Josiah's such a personable, charming guy, so easy to relate to. You're brilliant and beautiful. You'll see. This may be the break we've been waiting for."

"I hope so, Albert. What would I do without you? Rejection after rejection, you're still my one-man cheering section."

He reached over and kissed her. It was something she would never tire of. "Am I really still beautiful to you...two kids and mountains of lost sleep later?"

"Are you kidding? You're better looking than ever. I think it's all the good sex we have. I've heard it's therapeutic for the skin."

"Perhaps you ought to submit an article regarding your findings to *JAMA Dermatology*," she teased.

"I just may do that," Albert said, reaching over for another kiss.

"Now you'd better get going before the southbound traffic gets too awful. I'll call you after we get back to the hospital," Irene said.

"I'll be waiting. Now, go break a leg!"

§§§

Josiah knew his way around Harlem. He'd lived there when he first came to work at the VA, and met Bernice at the Canaan Baptist Church on West 116th Street. The confidence with which he drove through the jam-packed streets to the Barrow Foundation, his insider knowledge about the best place to park, and his cheerful whistling of Queen's "Don't Stop Me Now" all helped to calm Irene's jittery nerves. As they walked from the car to the Foundation's offices on West 125th Street, they were fully aware of how much was on the line. They were determined to make the most of this opportunity.

Irene and Josiah figured they'd be meeting with the grants administrator and perhaps a few of their usual reviewers, persons who might have little expertise in the area of research they proposed. They'd prepared their presentation with that in mind, making their slides in ordinary English rather than scientific jargon, and with plenty of visuals to help explain their experimental method. Much to their surprise, when they were ushered into the Foundation's conference room, Eloise and Winston Barrow sat at the head of the long teak table. To their left was a middle aged man introduced as their long-time friend, Reginald Noel, whose appearance contrasted markedly with the elegantly attired couple. To the Barrows' right was Dorothy Rice, the no-nonsense grants administrator with whom they'd been conversing on the phone. The room was equipped with a slide projector and a screen, as Josiah had requested. An aide came in and offered everyone coffee or tea. After a moment, it occurred to Irene that for the first time in her life she was the only white person in the room.

Eloise Barrow began the interview. "We welcome you both to the Barrow Foundation. As Ms. Rice has informed you, yours is the first request for funding for medical research we've ever considered. To date, one hundred percent of our grants have gone to community-based organizations that deliver services and offer opportunities to the underserved among us. While it's true we've funded research, that research has always been aimed at evaluating programs developed by those organizations. Because our areas of expertise lie elsewhere, we've invited our friend Dr. Noel, an esteemed medical researcher at the Rockefeller University, to sit in on your presentation. He will be integral to our evaluation of your proposal."

When Eloise Barrow was done she nodded to Irene and Josiah that they might begin. Irene did her best to tamp down the nervousness that began bubbling up the moment she realized the Barrows themselves would be sitting in on their presentation. "Dr. Williams and I want to thank you for this opportunity to explain our project to you," she said. "He will be going first, giving you an overview of our proposed study."

Josiah began with a rundown of their credentials and experience before beginning his tutorial on the importance of the gut to overall health, including his and Irene's shared belief that the gut might play a role in brain functioning and mental health. He explained that the central nervous system — the brain and the spinal cord — evolved from the enteric nervous system — nerve tissue and neurotransmitters belonging to the GI tract. His slides presented images of the vagus nerve, which runs from the brainstem to the lowest part of the intestines and connects the GI tract and the brain. The recent finding that ninety percent of nerve transmissions along the vagus nerve go from the gut up to the brain had clear implications for the gut's influence on brain function.

Then, it was Irene's turn. She began with something she'd left out of the dress rehearsal in the Williams' living room just days before. She didn't need to practice this portion of her presentation; she just spoke from the heart. "I want to thank you again for your interest in our project. Before going into the specifics of our proposal, I'd like to tell you how I came to work in the field of mental health. My wonderful and talented mother has suffered from recurrent major depression throughout her adult life. As is often the case, I believe she had her first episode early in her twenties, though she rarely speaks about that period in her life. When I was nine years old my mother got very sick and was hospitalized for several months in Brooklyn State Hospital, now known as Kingsboro Psychiatric Center. That was a painful time for our family...painful and ultimately pivotal. It was my mother's illness that motivated me to become a physician-scientist who not only treats patients with depression but also researches its possible causes. All of my work, from my doctoral research in neuropharmacology to my current research, is based on the hope of one day understanding and treating the scourge of depression. I know how it can bring people to their knees and rob them of their chance for a good life. For me, this is personal."

"May I interrupt you, Dr. Adelson?" Winston Barrow asked.

"Of course," Irene replied.

"There's no point ignoring the elephant in the room. Since it was so highly publicized at the time, I imagine you know we lost our son to depression."

"Yes, Dr. Williams told me about your son's tragic death. I am so very sorry. It's a terrible loss not only for you and for others who loved him, but for society, as well. When someone of such enormous promise is lost, it's nothing short of calamitous."

Winston Barrow looked down and cleared his throat. "You'll get no argument from me on that point. My wife and I had to learn the hard way — maybe the hardest way possible — about the dimensions of the scourge you talk about. The average person doesn't understand that depression can be a fatal disease. I'm the first to admit I didn't appreciate that when our son became ill. As Eloise made clear, we have never encouraged nor have we entertained a proposal for medical research before now. Your topic, your and Dr. Williams' sterling credentials, as well as your — shall we say unorthodox — approach has caught our attention, which is why we're giving you a forum to air your proposal."

"Understood. And for that we are grateful," Josiah said, bowing his head.

Irene went on to explain how a large proportion of her patients suffered from GI distress as well as depression and anxiety. It was that co-morbidity that led to her collaboration with Josiah, an expert in the workings and pathologies of the GI tract. It also spurred the development of their hypothesis of a link between the gut and mental health.

Again, Winston Barrow interrupted her. "I must say that your interest in what you refer to as the co-morbidity of stomach issues and depression struck a chord both for me and my wife. Our son, who was a fit, athletic young man, had flare-ups of digestive problems through his entire adolescence, right to the day we lost him."

"That's quite common," Irene said. "I've treated too many depressed and anxious patients with GI distress to dismiss it as mere coincidence. Our working hypothesis is that the microorganisms in the gut not only affect the healthy functioning of the digestive tract; they can influence mood. The goal of our study is to test that hypothesis."

Then she handed the presentation back to Josiah. He stressed that ninety percent of the body's supply of the neurotransmitter known to help stabilize mood — serotonin — is produced in the gut. It was his and Irene's working hypothesis that the production of that serotonin was dependent upon a vibrant, diverse community of gut microbes. Josiah singled out three recent developments in human history that undermine microbial diversity: The discovery and use of antibiotics, the war on bacteria in the name of "good hygiene," and the rise in processed foods that deprive microbes of the fiber they require to thrive. "It's like an unholy conspiracy," Josiah said, rubbing his hands together. "All three work to reduce the diversity of the microbes in the gut. That, we believe, has significant implications for the production of serotonin."

Finally, Irene expounded on their experimental method.

"We plan on breeding genetically identical mice. One set of mice will be raised to be germ-free through strict protocols, and the other will have a normal microbiota. After getting baseline readings of their serotonin levels, we'll stress both sets of mice using approved animal care procedures. For example, we'll handle them in a novel environment, increase noise levels, and restrain them, something mice don't generally enjoy. We'll continually assess their heart rate, blood pressure, body temperature, and levels of stress hormones. We'll also give the mice a task to perform, entering and running through an elevated maze. Their reluctance to interact with the maze, as well as the frequency of protective postures such as cowering, trembling, and seeking the protection of a wall will be recorded."

Irene went on to explain that in the second phase of the study, she and Josiah would give the germ-free mice fecal transplants from their non-germ-free, genetically identical relatives. Changes in their stress levels, task performance, and serotonin levels would then be studied.

"In this way, we aim to test three hypotheses," she explained. "First, that germ-free mice react more severely to stress than mice with normal microbiota, second, that introducing a diverse array of microbes to the germ-free mice improves their ability to deal with stress, and third, that gut serotonin levels are directly correlated to microbial diversity.

"This experimental study, the first of its kind anywhere in the world as far as we're aware, will be costly," Irene continued. "Two cohorts of genetically identical mice and the isolators to keep the germ-free mice sterile are pricey. In terms of personnel, we'll require a minimum of one post-doctoral fellow in recombinant DNA to direct things in the lab and head up the selective breeding program. The use of axenic — germ-free — animals as subjects, as well as the requirement for absolute rigor in sterility within the lab, calls for a lab manager with an extraordinary skill set. In addition, we'll require at least one doctoral student in neuroscience and one lab technician to round out the team. I plan on spending a third of my time in the lab; Dr. Williams, twenty percent. We anticipate the study running for three years, at a cost of two hundred thousand dollars a year." Then, as Irene returned to her seat next to Josiah, she said a silent prayer that they'd convinced the audience of their proposal's worth.

Throughout their presentation, Dr. Reginald Noel had quietly taken notes. Now Eloise Barrow gave him the nod to begin his questioning.

"As my dear friend Mr. Barrow has pointed out, yours is a highly unconventional approach to studying mental illness, wouldn't you agree?"

Josiah didn't hesitate. "You bet it is. And it's our belief that the only way we're going to make progress in treating mood disorders like depression is to build on what we know about neurology and psychiatry, and also to think outside the box and consider possibilities that have not yet been investigated. I believe this study may take us down a path that could open new avenues of inquiry. There is no way to know in advance what we'll find; that is, after all, the whole point of the scientific method. But what I do know is the strong linkage between mood disorders and GI disorders is one that deserves to be explored, and I believe we've come up with an experimental design that will teach us far more about that linkage than we know today."

Dr. Noel addressed his next question to Irene. "Dr. Adelson, I see you've received funding from the NIH for work into the genetics of depression. Why are you walking away from so promising a field of inquiry?"

"To be truthful, I have two reasons. First, there are scores of other top-notch researchers working on that question in the US alone, far more if you include researchers around the globe. I've worked with some of the best, and from what I can see, this is a problem that is very complex, and one that is unlikely to produce treatments in the coming decades, perhaps even in my lifetime. I'm an impatient person, Dr. Noel. I've seen what depression has done to my patients, as well as to my own mother. I'm anxious to find something that will lead us to effective treatments sooner rather than later."

"You mentioned two reasons?" Dr. Noel asked.

"Yes, and the second is I just have a hunch that Josiah…excuse me…Dr. Williams and I are onto something. That may not sound very scientific, but from everything I've read on neuro-gastroenterology, everything I've learned in my long and arduous training, and in everything I've seen in working with my patients over the last many years, I believe investigating the link between the gut and the brain will be a fruitful area of research. The inheritability of mental illness is established. But getting from there to treatment will be, in my estimation, a long and circuitous road. If Dr. Williams and I can demonstrate that altering the gut microbial community affects mood and behavior in an animal model, possible treatments for human mood disorders like depression may follow, and far more expeditiously than changing an individual's genetic code."

"That's the big *if*, isn't it," Dr. Noel said with more than a hint of skepticism.

"That's always the case when scientific inquiry ventures past the known signposts," Irene rebutted, a bit more impatiently than she meant to sound.

"True enough. Am I correct to assume the Barrow Foundation is not the first source of funding you've pursued?"

Irene thought a moment about what Albert had said about being bold. "Yes, the project has been turned down by other funders, but as you know, rejection is the name of the game in medical research. I imagine you, too, Dr. Noel have had grant requests rejected," she said, praying she hadn't overstepped.

"I have, indeed," Dr. Noel said, smiling ruefully. "Just the other day, as a matter of fact."

Josiah stepped in. "Most major discoveries are made by people who are viewed with skepticism by the establishment. Newton, Darwin, Einstein, not to mention Dr. Barry Marshall in Australia, who recently discovered the bacterial cause of duodenal ulcers. Dr. Adelson and I are fully aware of how unique our perspective is, but without taking a chance, little is learned."

"Would you be willing to send me a more technical rationale for your study? I have to say, what you've submitted is somewhat lacking in specificity."

"That would be no problem at all," Irene replied. "Dr. Williams and I made this application to the Foundation unaware that someone with your level of expertise would be involved in the review. If Ms. Rice would forward us your contact information, a more technical explanation will be on your desk within a week."

"Or sooner," Josiah said, nodding and smiling to Irene.

"Yes, or sooner," she agreed.

Dr. Noel looked at the Barrows. "I'm all done."

Winston Barrow turned to Dorothy Rice. "Dorothy, have you any questions for Drs. Williams and Adelson?"

"Just one," she replied. "What made you think of the Barrow Foundation in terms of funding? I don't mind telling you I did a double take when I opened the envelope with your application."

Josiah took that question. "I volunteer at a Boys' Club in Yonkers, just a few miles from where my family lives. Most Saturday mornings during the school year I help the kids with science and math homework. Come springtime, I work with them as they prepare for their school's science fair. I probably have interacted with upwards of a hundred children and I've seen what your philanthropy has done for those youngsters. The facility, the materials, the staffing are all comparable to a youth organization you'd find in a predominantly white, upper middle-class community like my own, rather than a poor and working class Hispanic and Black neighborhood. So I know firsthand about the good work of the Barrow Foundation. It did occur to me that applying to you for funding was a long shot, but I figured it was possible you'd consider helping the community in a different — albeit an important — way."

"I'm glad your involvement with the Boys' Club has been so positive," Dorothy Rice said, unable to hide her obvious pleasure. "We've cited that particular Boys' Club as an exemplar to some of our other sponsored organizations."

"And I thank you for that, as well," Eloise Barrow said. "Rigorous program evaluations are important and we require them of all our recipient programs, but hearing your view from the ground level is gratifying." She stood up and extended her hand. "You've given us a lot to think about. I appreciate your candor, as well as your enthusiasm and passion for your project. Dr. Adelson, I hope your mother is doing well now?"

"Yes," Irene said, shaking hands with Eloise Barrow. "She is. We are all so very thankful for that."

"Well, congratulations to her and to your family," Winston Barrow said, as he shook hands with Irene and Josiah. "As Eloise said, you've given us a lot to consider. As you might imagine, people who came up the way we did didn't find success by making bad bets. I can only promise you that we'll engage in serious deliberations before we decide whether or not to place a bet on your research."

§§§

A few weeks later, Irene returned to her office at the end of a day of seeing patients to find a message on her desk. *Eloise Barrow has been trying to reach you all day. Not a medical emergency.* Irene looked at the number and froze. Would Eloise Barrow be calling to say they couldn't fund the project? Worse, would she throw insults at her the way other reviewers had, criticizing her proposal as bizarre and beneath a scientist of her training? What she feared most was that Eloise Barrow might castigate her for playing on her sympathies after the loss of her only child. Irene found herself trembling just at the thought of dialing the number. Instead of making that call, she paged Josiah.

"What's up?" he asked.

"I just got back to my office to find that Mrs. Barrow has been calling me all day. She left her number."

"And?"

"And I'm too nervous to call. Would you mind very much if I came to your office and we did it together?"

"Irene, what's the worst that can happen? She'll explain why she's not giving us six hundred thousand dollars? I think it's more likely that Dorothy Rice would be making that call, or that they'd send their rejection in a form letter," Josiah reasoned.

"But they were so generous of their time and consideration. Maybe they feel we deserve a personal call even though they're turning us down."

"Winston Barrow said he didn't make bad bets, and neither do I. I'll bet you dinner that we're getting the grant. We win and you and Albert take me and Bernice out to a really nice place to celebrate. We lose, I pay, and it may not be so fancy because we'll all be feelin' a little sad and blue. What say you?"

"Josiah, do you really think the answer could be 'yes'?"

"There's only one way to find out, my dear," he pointed out, "and that's to call Eloise Barrow back."

"Do you have time now?" she asked. "I've seen my last patient for today and I can do my paperwork tonight at home. I have some time before I have to pick the kids up from after-school. How's your schedule?"

"When a bucket load of research money is on the line, my schedule can be cleared. So come on over to my office and we'll make that call together, that is, if the bet is on."

"I'm not the type of person who makes bets," Irene demurred.

"Sure you are. Everything's a bet. You made a bet on Albert and that's why you married him. You bet that medical science would be an entertaining enterprise for your life's work. All of us make bets all through our lives. So what say you, Irene?"

"Well, when you put it that way, perhaps I have made some bets. Okay, the bet's on. I'll be in your office in five minutes."

§§§

Irene and Albert took Josiah and Bernice to celebrate at Lutece, a French restaurant in midtown Manhattan famous for being one of the last bastions of grand dining in the city. Since the Barrow Foundation had agreed to fund Irene and Josiah's project for two years rather than the requested three, Josiah volunteered to pay the gratuity. The two couples — separated by a generation, by religion, and by race — shared the triumph of Irene and Josiah's "out of the box" thinking. Following a round of drinks and appetizers for the table, Albert and Bernice ordered the restaurant's famed onion tart. Josiah tried the sautéed *foie gras* with dark chocolate sauce and bitter orange marmalade, while Irene, after great deliberation, settled on the crab *cassolette*. When it came time for dessert, they decided to share chocolate mousse with rum and flambéed crepes, which won accolades from them all. Even the coffee was in a league of its own. Irene couldn't believe a meal could be such a sensual delight.

The night of laughter and good company was bathed in excitement and anticipation for what was to come for Irene and Josiah. At the end of the evening when the waiter presented Albert with the eye-popping check, he was only too happy to take out his wallet, pull out six crisp one hundred dollar bills, and put them in the check holder. As far as he was concerned, it was the most satisfying six hundred dollars he'd ever spent.

CHAPTER SEVENTEEN

B RINGING IN BUCKET LOADS OF MONEY to an institution of higher learning gives a physician-scientist a tremendous leg up in the tenure race. After reviewing the data indicating encouraging results halfway through the second year of Irene and Josiah's two year contract, the Barrow Foundation extended their funding for another two years. That likely weighed heavily in Irene's favor when she came up for tenure review from Mount Sinai. Her new title was Associate Professor of Psychiatry and Neuroscience. That victory, which happened just before her thirty-ninth birthday, was perhaps the sweetest of Irene's career, bringing with it a sense of validation she hadn't even realized she'd been longing for.

Two years into the study she and Josiah had discovered many things. First, they'd found that germ-free mice had much lower levels of serotonin than did their genetically identical cousins with diverse gut microbiota. The axenic mice dealt with stress poorly, taking much longer to return to a state of calm. Once stressed, their performance in the maze was abysmal, in comparison with the mice with a vibrant microbial community. And perhaps most encouragingly, if the germ-free mice were given fecal transplants from the non-germ-free mice, their serotonin levels rose, as did their ability to deal with stress and tackle the maze. The Barrows and Dr. Noel came to the lab periodically to witness the changes in the mice, suiting up every time they visited to maintain the strict lab protocols. Though Winston Barrow joked that the drab basement lab didn't look like it cost six figures a year to run, he was impressed by the obvious pride and enthusiasm of the team, as well as the behavioral changes exhibited by the mice themselves.

After having been turned down by a score of peer-reviewed journals, the Adelson Lab, as it came to be known, finally saw their findings published in the *Journal of Gastrointestinal Motility*, which focused on neuro-gastroenterology, *Biological Psychiatry*, and *Journal of Neuroscience Research*. The entire team was delighted that their work had, at last, seen the light of day. The letters to the editor that followed, however, made it clear that the GI and psychiatric fields were highly skeptical of their results. Some letter writers didn't hold back in heaping ridicule on the paper. Josiah collected his favorites and posted them on the bulletin board next to the desk in his home office:

"This study is nothing but BS."

"Good luck replicating that rodent study in humans."

"Whatever were the funders thinking? What a waste of research money. Such a pity!"

"This is nothing short of bizarre. Perhaps the authors need a fecal transplant to correct their errant thinking."

"I am cancelling my subscription to the Journal of Neuroscience Research. *If this study made it into print, it's clear any well-packaged malarkey will be accepted for publication by this (formerly) reputable journal."*

Irene and Josiah made the rounds of the annual meetings of The American College of Gastroenterology and the American Psychiatric Association and gave lectures at any medical school or research institute who had someone on staff brave or curious enough to invite them. The overwhelming sentiment of their audience was disbelief. The generous listeners said the conclusion that gut microbes could affect mood and behavior was at best premature; the less generous said the conclusion was nothing short of preposterous. They suggested the experimental design was faulty, and when Irene answered every reservation regarding the methodology used, they still walked away unconvinced. The few who accepted the finding that mouse behavior could be altered when new microorganisms were introduced to the intestinal tract were certain it had no implications for the human experience of depression and anxiety. For every curious, interested person who came up to chat with them after their presentation, there were twenty who walked away thinking Irene and Josiah were purveyors of junk science.

The harshest critics turned out to be those schooled in psychoanalysis. They were certain the notion of intestinal microbes holding sway over mood was wholly absurd. Those most open to Irene and Josiah's work turned out to be some GI specialists, who had themselves suspected their organ system's functioning had implications beyond the absorption of nutrients. Some younger neuroscientists who had been Irene's comrades during their training were willing to consider her work as "interesting." Though it was not the enthusiastic endorsement she'd hoped for, Irene took solace in knowing that some thoughtful people considered her findings credible.

Though her work was so often dismissed, Irene's commitment to the study never wavered. On the contrary, she and the rest of her team were energized by what their investigation was uncovering. Josiah, who'd come to medical research in his fifties, found himself staying late and coming into the lab on weekends to monitor the ongoing experiments. And he was not alone. The entire team had the sense they were onto something important. Kathy, the animal technician lovingly dubbed "Queen of the Mice;" Matt, the research tech; and Patty, the lab manager extraordinaire were part-time employees, but they routinely spent more time in the lab than they wrote down on their timesheets. Tineke, the talented post-doctoral fellow working on the project and Lourdes, who bet her doctoral degree on her participation in the study, fairly leapt into the air when their data analysis showed marked improvement in stress response indicators and serotonin levels after the fecal transplantation. The data only confirmed what they'd all observed with their own eyes: formerly timid, anxious mice behaved more calmly and performed difficult tasks with ease once they had the benefit of a diverse microbiome. Perhaps the world was not ready to hear the results of their work, but for these researchers, the findings were nothing short of electrifying.

Now that the lab's research had shown serotonin levels and behavior could be altered by the microorganisms in the gut, Irene wanted to understand what was at play. Was there a specific bacterium that affected serotonin production or was a constellation of bacteria responsible? And by what mechanism did the bacterial colonization and increased serotonin levels change the brain functioning? Even the skeptics could not deny the videos showing markedly altered and improved behavior in the formerly timid, anxiety-ridden mice. But when those skeptics asked how the introduction of microbes into the gut could cause such a change, all she could say was, "At this point we believe it's tied to serotonin levels, but that remains a question for future investigation."

§§§

While tenure, her promotion, the Barrow's generous support, and three published papers ought to have made Irene's stock rise in terms of her standing in her department, the marginalization she'd experienced from the outset of her time at the VA did not abate. Sometimes she felt invisible both in her research and clinical roles. Never once was she asked to collaborate on psychiatric research; rarely was she invited to consult on difficult psychiatric cases. As for those who controlled the distribution of resources, they remained as tight-fisted as ever. Her request for more lab space to accommodate the requirements of her study was turned down multiple times. When she asked to bring Matt, Kathy, and Patty up to full-time status, the request was denied, making hers the least well-staffed lab for comparably funded principal investigators.

After being rebuffed, Irene went to the labs of other recently tenured scientists with a tape measure to document the dimensions of their labs in comparison to her own. Her eyes hadn't lied; they all had significantly more space, and most of them had not brought in the funding she had. She constructed a table indicating each investigator's square footage of lab space per ten thousand dollars of annual grant money. The table showed her male colleagues enjoyed two, three, or even four times the lab space Irene had for the same level of funding. Just looking at the figures in black and white put her disadvantage in stark relief.

With her data in hand, she went to the head of research to discuss the degree to which she was being under-resourced. The chairman was a distinguished-looking man in his late fifties, a physician who'd enjoyed some acclaim and recognition for his research into pulmonary fibrosis. He glanced at the table for a moment and then dismissed Irene's argument out of hand. "I have no need for, nor interest in, seeing your so-called data on space allocation. Forget it, Dr. Adelson. There just isn't any space for me to allocate to you."

"I grant you, there's a finite amount of lab space, but the method by which it's allocated certainly can be discussed. I bring in hundreds of thousands of dollars to this institution every year, an institution which takes twenty-eight percent off the top to cover overhead. There is no logical justification for denying an upgrade to my lab and favoring my less well-funded colleagues."

"Well," the department chair said, getting up to show Irene out of his office, "things are rarely as cut and dried as they may seem. The truth is, it's always preferable for us to count our blessings rather than compare ourselves to others. Now, I've got a meeting. Thanks for coming by, Dr. Adelson. It's always good to see you."

His summary dismissal stunned her. As she walked back to the lab she thought about Meryl's decision to give up her dream of a career in genetics. Now she understood. She remembered Raisa and Max's take on how women in science were treated. In her heart of hearts, she hadn't wanted to accept it, but now she saw that they were clear-eyed reporters of the world as it was. The level playing field she'd wanted to believe existed for scientists of either gender was a fiction. The only conclusion any thinking person could reach was this: Gender discrimination made being a medical researcher — a challenging pursuit under the best conditions — all the harder for women.

Not a day later, Irene was letting off steam about being shortchanged in terms of space and personnel with Dick LaFevre, a senior GI investigator and Josiah's best buddy in the department. The silver-haired researcher looked her in the eye and said, "You know there are a lot of men around here who have never cottoned to the idea of women doing research. They don't think you or any woman is smart enough or temperamentally suited to scientific inquiry."

"You must be joking!"

"No, I'm deadly serious."

"They've said as much to you?" Irene asked.

"Many times. And the tough part from your perspective is that those are the fellas who rule the roost. They'll stick together and champion some guy — no matter how mediocre — over any woman, no matter how exceptional."

"You're confirming my worst fears," Irene said. "But here's the thing. I have no proof, no evidence that I'm being disadvantaged because I'm a woman."

"Irene, I can only tell you what I know to be true. They see women like you — brilliant, innovative, ambitious, highly competent — and instead of celebrating the presence of a great colleague, they see a threat to their manhood. Some of them may not even realize it consciously, I'll give them that much. But regardless, it exacts a toll — a big one — on women in the sciences."

"You're the first person on faculty who has even hinted that resources are meted out based on gender. The unfairness of it is so galling!"

"You want to talk about fairness, find out what other researchers at your level are earning. I'd bet my last dollar that you and the handful of other female researchers here are on the low end of the salary distribution."

"But isn't there some sort of pay scale that we all get placed on?"

"Oh, yes, there's some sort of pay scale, but there's always a range so that those who hold the purse strings have some discretion."

"So now I have something else to get angry about," Irene said, her blood starting to boil.

"Don't get angry, Irene. Get even. I know what I'm telling you is hard to hear and my intention is not to upset you. I think the world of you and Josiah. The way I see it, there is no question the research the two of you are doing is cutting edge. It may ultimately change the whole way we think about the gut, the brain, and the connection between the two. But get on your hiking boots because you've got an uphill climb ahead of you. I'm rooting for you. After all, I've spent my whole career championing the importance of the GI tract in overall health and, as you know, I'm the proud father of five magnificent daughters. All I can say to you is, go get'em girl!"

§§§

Irene's conversation with Dick LaFevre kindled a slow burn of indignation. Based on his conjecture about how salaries were determined, she decided to do a little probing to see if it could be borne out. With the help of one of the psych department's secretaries and an administrative assistant in human resources, Irene discovered she was earning nearly thirty percent less than male associate professors on the faculty. When she confronted her department chair with her finding, he responded without ever once looking up from his paperwork. "You know, Irene, we've got men here who are supporting families. You've got a husband, but these guys *are* the husband. That said, I'll see if there's anything I can do after your annual review."

The review came and went. The seven percent salary bump she got was just a hair better than a cost of living increase, and barely moved the needle on closing the salary gap between her and her male counterparts. How was it, she wondered, that the support they provided their families was viewed as more essential than the support she provided her own?

§§§

Another person might have withered under the weight of the slights and prejudicial treatment, but Raisa's advice rang in her ears. As a woman scientist she had to be smarter, more hardworking and innovative than the men. Being tenacious and believing as she did in the importance of her work helped her put aside her frustration so she could focus on being the best clinician and researcher she could be. It took self-discipline, but that was something she'd had in spades since childhood.

And then, despite the deafening silence from the people with whom she worked every day, there came signs that her efforts were getting some notice from the wider scientific community. Her study of bacteria and serotonin production in the gut received the imprimatur of respectability when her team earned funding from the NIH. After news of that small NIH grant percolated through the research community, the very first male post-doctoral candidates applied to work at the Adelson Lab.

A few months later, Irene presented a paper detailing the results of her study at the annual meeting of the American Psychiatric Association. Afterwards, a researcher from Johns Hopkins and the Howard Hughes Medical Institute (HHMI) asked if she was free to continue discussing her work over dinner. The uninspired cuisine at the hotel's restaurant did nothing to dull the conversation between the physician-scientists. They talked primarily about the findings made by Irene's lab, but from time to time the two working mothers veered off into comparisons of how they managed their professional obligations while meeting the needs of their children, husbands, parents, homes, and in the case of the HHMI researcher, pets. A week later, Irene was floored when she received an invitation to apply for one of HHMI's coveted grants.

"People, not projects," was the motto of the Institute, one of the wealthiest philanthropies in the country. Its aim was clear: Supporting scholars who dared to push the envelope of their disciplines. Each year it chose a small cadre of up-and-coming scientists to pursue their research wherever it led. The investigators received a seven-year appointment, which provided full salary and benefits for them and their research team, as well as a budget that covered the purchase of critical equipment. If the prospect of a no-strings-attached funding for seven years wasn't sufficient, the appointment could be renewed. From the perspective of a researcher, it was nothing short of being plucked by a fairy godmother from the endless grant application treadmill and ensconced in a fully funded, optimally staffed and equipped laboratory; in other words, nirvana.

As honored as Irene was to be asked to apply, she prepared her application with a realistic eye; she now understood that her status as a female scientist might work against her. Her stated research goal was to explore the mechanism by which the vagus nerve communicated changes in the gut to the brain, which she believed led to the altered behavior in her lab's mice. Her hunch was that if the vagus nerve was stimulated in the gut, it could influence the levels of the brain neurotransmitters serotonin, dopamine, norepinephrine, and epinephrine, all of which played enormous roles in mood and anxiety. The hypothesis she aimed to test was whether beneficial gut bacteria led to vagus nerve stimulation, which in turn led to improved neurotransmitter function and, ultimately, enhanced mood.

Irene sent off her application to the HHMI competition as she had sent off so many other applications over her career. Months passed and she gave it little thought. Her lab was momentarily safe, thanks to the continued funding from the Barrow Foundation and the NIH grant. But then, the unexpected happened: She was selected as an HHMI semi-finalist and invited to present her research proposal to its scientific advisory panel at the Institute's new headquarters outside of Washington D.C. It was Albert who suggested they make it a family trip so they could show the kids where they'd met nearly thirty years before.

They got a hotel near the National Zoo. The morning after they checked in, Albert and the twins set off to see the giant pandas just as Irene left to give her presentation. In the cab ride over to Chevy Chase, Irene thought about the talk she'd given so long ago to the judges at the Westinghouse competition. How excited she'd been to present her findings about carrier pigeon navigation! She now understood a lot more about how the world worked, but she was every bit as eager to have the chance to talk about her research. She'd bought a dress just for the occasion, a deep red sheath with a square neckline and bolero jacket, which she thought looked professional while setting off her figure nicely.

When she entered the gleaming HHMI headquarters, she felt ready to speak to a room full of illustrious scientists about her quest to discover the linkage between the gut microbiota and the brain. Her presentation went off without a hitch, and afterwards she had the opportunity to answer the panelists' probing questions. Their curiosity about her work seemed genuine. On the cab ride back to the hotel, she thought if nothing else, some leaders in biomedical research now knew about the work of the Adelson Lab. Plus, the presentation gave her a reason to buy that lovely new dress.

§§§

In the spring of 1993, after returning home with the kids from an open house at the middle school they'd be attending in the fall, Irene got the call she'd never expected to receive. It was the Institute, letting her know she was one of nineteen scientists who'd been selected for the coveted position of HHMI investigator. She nearly dropped the phone when she heard the news. Her appointment would begin just as Ian and Brin entered sixth grade.

Following the public announcement of the newest cadre of HHMI investigators, a science reporter from the *New York Times* called requesting an interview for an article about the Adelson Lab. Back at the hospital, Josiah, the members of her lab, Dick LaFevre, a psychiatric nurse, and department secretary offered their congratulations. She received a memo from the administration that began with a laudatory sentence before focusing entirely on how it would be working out the financial details with the Institute. But not a single clinician or researcher in her department mentioned her appointment as an HHMI investigator, something that sent Albert into a rage over a dinner of Chinese take-out.

"What's the matter with them? Don't they understand what they have in their midst?" he fumed.

"What do they have in their midst?" Ian asked.

"I'm referring to your mother. She's a rock star of research, a brilliant, original thinker. You know that, don't you?"

"No offense, but to me she's just my mom. But if Mom *is* as brilliant as you say she is, they're probably jealous," Ian reasoned.

Brin agreed. "We see that all the time at school. Some of the kids aren't too happy with us when they bomb on a test that we do well on. Ian and I have discussed this at length and have decided it's not our problem, it's theirs. Even Grandpa Meyer agrees. He calls it the green-eyed monster. Envy, that is."

Irene and Albert looked at one another. Out of the mouths of babes...

So Irene returned to work, where many of those on the faculty still wouldn't give her the time of day. But more and more, that unpleasantness took a backseat to the recognition the lab's work was receiving in the wider scientific world. When their paper was accepted by *The Journal of Neuroscience*, Irene and Josiah took the entire team out to lunch at their favorite Greek restaurant. At last, their research was making it into the big leagues.

CHAPTER EIGHTEEN

IRENE'S SUCCESSES AT WORK did nothing to blunt the blow of losing her father.

Since Brin and Ian's birth, Meyer and Gladys had been steadfast helpmates in raising and caring for them. Whenever she and Albert were buried in work or traveling to spread the word about their research, it was Meyer and Gladys who stepped up and helped out. Deep into his eighties, Meyer was still driving up to Riverdale with Gladys, making the journey from Brooklyn after the worst of the morning rush-hour had passed. Irene hoped her parents saw her apartment as their second home. They had a key and a room of their own, a closet for their clothes and two shelves in the bathroom for their toiletries. It made her happy to know they were such a big part of the twins' lives.

Just as Brin and Ian started training in earnest for their *bat* and *bar mitzvahs*, Meyer's health began to fail. A minor stroke landed him in the hospital for a couple of days. It was followed by another one a few months later. By the time he and Gladys were called to say an *Aliyah*[1] over the Torah on the children's big day, Meyer held tight to Gladys's arm as they ascended the stairs to the *bimah*, the synagogue's altar. Without the rabbi's assistance, he would have had trouble getting through the Hebrew blessing he'd recited so often during his long life.

Meyer looked upon his growing frailty with a clear eye. When he thought back on his life — child, young man, soldier, suitor, husband,

---

[1] Blessing

father, provider, grandfather — he was incredulous that nearly nine decades had passed. Such a long life, and yet it seemed to go so quickly, too quickly. He was at peace with the possibility that the end might be near, but he worried about leaving Gladys. Sometimes he would watch as she went about her daily tasks, preparing a meal or making the bed. He'd think about the life they'd created together, the hardships they'd endured and overcome. It struck him that the life they'd had would never have come to pass had he not gone to his cousin's engagement party all those years ago. It was such a little thing, but that chance decision had changed everything.

Until the war began, he'd been trapped in a life not of his choosing. From the time he was fourteen, every day brought the same, soul-numbing routine: A boiled egg and rye toast for breakfast and then downstairs to open up the stationery store, straighten the merchandise, ring up the customers, make small talk with the postman. Things were no better when he locked up at the end of the day and climbed the stairs to the only five rooms he'd ever occupied. Each night, the tedious babble between his siblings and their mother grated on his nerves, but even worse was the sullen silence from his father. He never once offered a kind word or a nod of appreciation for Meyer's efforts to keep the store nicely appointed and the customers happy.

He grimaced remembering how small his world had been. Then the Japanese bombed Pearl Harbor and Uncle Sam plucked him out of his rut and hurled him into the US Army Air Corps. The day he met Gladys, sparks of expectation and hope — not to mention lust — flickered within him for the first time since he was a youth. Perhaps there was a chance for him to know happiness, companionship, and love. He thanked God for putting Gladys in his path and giving him the courage to try for a better life.

One day, as they sat together on the sofa sharing the Sunday paper, Meyer's heart was full. "Sweetheart, I don't say 'thank you' enough. You've given me the most beautiful fifty years a man could ever hope for."

Gladys smiled. She, too, sensed their time together was growing short. Her heart ached when she thought of the day — perhaps not so very far off — when she wouldn't be able to sit quietly with Meyer and enjoy the Sunday paper. But she was determined not to succumb to her fear of losing him. Above all else, she wanted the time they had left to be sweet.

"It has been a good life, hasn't it?" she asked.

"Better than good, I'd say."

"If I could change anything, I wish I hadn't caused you so much *tsouris*[1]," she said. "If only I'd smartened up much, much earlier, I wouldn't have let what other people said make me sick."

"Well, if I could change anything, I would have doubled my salary so you wouldn't have had to struggle so to make ends meet," Meyer confessed.

"But even with our struggles, look at the life we've lived. It wasn't always easy, but somehow we made it through. We always had each other."

"And our wonderful girls…," Meyer added wistfully.

"Oh yes, and how lucky we were with the girls! It's a good thing you convinced me to try for a second baby. Remember when I was afraid I wouldn't be able to manage with another child? Can you imagine life without Reenie?" Gladys asked.

Meyer thought for a moment. "I really can't. And then she grew up and brought Albert into our lives…and then the twins came along," Meyer chuckled. "Aren't those two something?"

"Different as night and day," Gladys said. "Ian's music, I understand. Of course he got that from Reenie. When he plays the cello, my heart melts."

"It takes my breath away. It's amazing to hear those beautiful sounds coming from someone so young," Meyer beamed. "Such feeling, such wonderful technique."

"And what an athlete Brin's turned out to be!" Gladys exulted. "That must come from Albert's side."

"Well, Annie is still quite the dancer, and don't forget Reenie's jogging and karate back when she had the time," Meyer pointed out.

"True," Gladys agreed. "So maybe we can take a little credit."

Meyer laughed. "Especially since all we have to do is cheer Brin on from the sidelines. Thanks to her, I know what lacrosse is."

"I'd never even heard of it," Gladys laughed. "Remember when she brought home that stick and I asked her what it was for? I thought it was something to scoop up fish from the river."

"Don't feel bad. I had no idea what it was either," Meyer admitted.

---

[1] Trouble, distress

"And what about Annie and Spence? Sometimes when I think about the rough start they had — with the dimwits from our families and the damned fools from his — I *kvell*[1] for the life they've created. I still can't believe his parents never relented. All these years have passed and they've never once laid eyes on Peter and Rachel. They have a son who presents cases in front of the US Supreme Court, but all that matters to them is that he married a Jew and became a Jew. That's what small-minded bigotry will do."

"Well, it's their loss."

"What I admire most about Annie and Spence is that they never let the *mishegoss*[2] stop them. They built their careers and their family. What a good job they've done with those beautiful kids," Gladys said. "Peter's a real chip off the old block, devoted to repairing the world, just like his parents. And Rachel…I'm not so sure about Rachel…she may surprise us all and become rich. I've never seen a young girl with such a business sense. What thirteen-year-old starts a day camp for sixty little kids? Somehow she got those other teens at Stuyvesant Town to work for her. The moms loved it, the counselors made a little *gelt*[3], and Rachel ended up putting quite a few hundred dollars into her bank account that summer."

Meyer smiled. "It would be nice to have someone wealthy in the family, just for a change."

They both got quiet for a while as they sat there on the sofa holding hands. "Whoever would have guessed these wonderful youngsters and their parents would make our lives so interesting?" Meyer asked.

"Certainly not me," Gladys said. "If you'd asked me before I met you what my life would be like, I never in my wildest dreams could have imagined anything as good as what it's turned out to be."

"We were never rich," Meyer pointed out.

"But we never starved, either."

Meyer seemed satisfied. "So all things considered, I guess we can say we did pretty well for ourselves."

"All things considered? Yes, we did indeed."

---

[1] Experience pride and satisfaction
[2] Insanity
[3] Money

§§§

Meyer died in his sleep of a massive stroke in the spring after the twins' *B'nai Mitzvah*. He was eighty-eight years old.

After taking in the painful news, Irene and Annie's thoughts immediately went to their mother. Would she be able to withstand so enormous a loss? In fact, what Gladys surrendered to was grief rather than depression. And she was not alone. Everyone who'd been touched by Meyer's gentle spirit mourned his loss. Brin, who always seemed to take things with a grain of salt, sobbed uncontrollably when Albert broke the news that Grandpa Meyer had died. Ian, on the other hand, became very quiet and withdrawn, worrying his father. When Albert shared his concerns with Irene, she acknowledged the depths of her own anguish. Though she'd mourned Grandma Bertha's passing, her sorrow at Meyer's death seemed to know no bounds. Her father was the steady, loving presence she'd depended on during her childhood and beyond. And now he was gone.

§§§

After sitting *shiva*[1], leaving their mother behind in the apartment was wrenching for both Irene and Annie. They had a hard time coming to terms with the fact that, going forward, Gladys would be all alone every day and every night. So a month after Meyer passed, and with a nod from Spence and Albert, the sisters sat down with their mother and broached the subject of having her move in with one of them. They were respectful, making it clear they knew the decision was hers to make, while stressing how much they would enjoy having her become a bigger part of their lives. They pointed out the practical problems of living alone. Who would provide her with company, take her shopping, make sure she was okay? What if she had a medical emergency? She understood what they said as well as what they didn't say — that they were mourning the loss of their father and couldn't bear losing her, too.

Gladys recognized the logic of what her girls were proposing, and she was realistic. At seventy-eight she knew that if she was lucky, her health and abilities would decline gradually rather than precipitously in years to come. Living alone in her eighties held little appeal. And as much as she loved the apartment she'd shared with Meyer for thirty years, being there

---

[1] Week of mourning following a death

without him only deepened her sorrow. As she looked to the future, she wanted to be useful, to have a purpose. She'd be of little help to Annie and Spence; Peter was already off at college and Rachel would be, too, in just a couple of years. But moving in with Albert and Reenie appealed to her. She could be with the twins after school and when their parents were away for work. The room that she and Meyer had stayed in so often would no longer be a home away from home, but home itself.

Clearing out her apartment was difficult. At every turn Gladys found something that brought back memories of better times, when she and Meyer were young, raising their girls, sharing their lives with Bertha. So much meaning attached to such ordinary things. And yet, she had to let them go. She encouraged the children and grandchildren to take anything that had special meaning for them. Annie took her father's shoe shine kit, Irene Grandma Bertha's knitting needles and yarn collection. Albert and Spence equally divided Meyer's unique collection of bowties. Peter wanted the chess set he and Meyer had played on so often. Rachel claimed the china used for so many Sunday dinners. The lamp her grandfather read by was the keepsake Brin requested. Though LPs were old technology, Ian put dibs on his grandparents' classical music collection and their old Victrola. Irene and Albert agreed to move a few of Gladys's favorite pieces of furniture to their apartment. But when all was said and done, the bulk of her worldly goods — a lifetime's collection of old kitchen tools, warm blankets, children's toys, much enjoyed furniture, and favorite books — were surrendered to the Goodwill or the dumpster. It pained Gladys to see the things woven into her everyday life be carted away.

The actual move seemed uneventful enough, but with the loss of so much that had anchored her — her husband, her home, her belongings — Gladys began to feel herself being swept away on a current of gloom. Even the children noticed the change. "What's with Grandma?" Brin asked her father one Sunday morning after Gladys left the breakfast table to go back to her room. "I can't believe she turned down your blueberry pancakes. I've never seen anyone do that before. All my friends rave about your pancakes, Dad."

"Grandma is feeling pretty sad, Brinny," Albert said. "She's been through a lot these last months. We all miss Grandpa. And Grandma's life has changed dramatically. Moving to a new place always takes some getting used to. She may be missing the apartment she shared with Grandpa."

"I miss her apartment, too. I loved going there on Sundays and hanging out all day with Rachel and Peter," Brin said. "That was the best."

"Maybe you should tell Grandma that," Irene offered. "Knowing that you share her feelings might make her feel a little better."

"Feel better? Don't you see?" Ian asked angrily. "I think something's really wrong with Grandma. I've known her my whole life and I've never seen her like this. Mom, you're a doctor. Figure out what's going on and get her the help she needs. And I don't mean sharing some platitude about how we liked playing at her house when we were little."

Brin gave her brother the stink eye, but said nothing.

Irene was brought up short. The clarity with which her children saw the world never failed to astonish her. "Thank you for that, Ian. I think I've been putting my head in the sand, hoping that this was just a passing thing. Dad's right. Moving is hard on everyone, particularly on older people who've enjoyed their homes for so long. But I think you're right. What's going on with Grandma is more than that. Thanks for reminding me to think like a physician, not just as a daughter."

Following that conversation, Irene conferred with Annie and then made an appointment with a psychiatrist she'd trained with at Payne Whitney. When she told her mother that she believed the depression had returned and that it was time to seek help, Gladys was resigned. "I never thought I'd find myself in the grips of the nightmare again, but I can't see how to get through the next moment. I thought I'd licked it. I really did. But it's stronger than I am."

The psychiatrist confirmed the diagnosis: Gladys was in the grips of another episode of major depression. He felt she might respond to a new class of drug, a serotonin-norepinephrine reuptake inhibitor (SNRI), which had just come on the market. In addition, since she'd responded well to ECT during previous episodes, he suggested a series of unilateral ECT treatments, which would likely deliver the quickest relief with less short-term memory loss. Gladys just shrugged her shoulders and said nothing in response. It was Irene who gave the okay to begin the treatments.

This time the ECT would be done on an outpatient basis, meaning someone would have to bring Gladys into the hospital on the morning of each treatment, wait for her to awaken from her mild sedation, and then take her back to Riverdale, where a per diem nurse would care for her until dinner time. Even with the nurse's help, the logistics were a challenge. A calendar was drawn up. Irene, Annie, and Albert would each accompany

Gladys for two treatments and Spence for one. It was easier said than done. All four had to do handstands to rejigger their schedules, but given how ill Gladys had become, they knew they had no choice.

The grandchildren's reaction to their grandmother's treatment plan was unanimous: They were aghast. Peter and Rachel couldn't believe their parents, aunt, and uncle would permit doctors to run an electrical current through their grandmother's brain. "Haven't you seen *One Flew Over the Cuckoo's Nest*?" Peter railed. "That's barbaric. You don't do that to your patients, Mom, so how come you're allowing them to do that to your own mother?"

Rachel piled on. "It's just so cruel. I thought you loved Grandma. She doesn't deserve this."

Annie tried to remain calm in the face of their condemnation. "What Grandma doesn't deserve is to be so sick. Before either of you were born, she suffered episodes of major depression. We learned from those episodes that ECT works well for her. And it's much quicker than medication or therapy in terms of providing relief. Aunt Reenie and I have discussed it and we think this is the most compassionate, effective treatment plan available."

Rachel was indignant. "You call that compassion? I can't believe what I'm hearing. So it's okay with you for Grandma to have to bite down on a stick while they run electricity through her head?"

"You watched a movie that represented how ECT was used long ago. I've seen it employed in the hospital many times and I can attest that it's nothing like that. If you'd like, one or both of you can come with me when I bring Grandma to her treatment. You'll see for yourselves. She'll be asleep. She won't remember the treatment. Then we'll take her home to rest at Aunt Reenie's."

Annie's conversation with Rachel and Peter mirrored the one Irene had with the twins. Brin, especially, was horrified at the prospect of subjecting her grandmother to an electrically-induced seizure. And while Ian showed some mild academic curiosity about how something like that could work to lift depression, he was dismayed to think his grandmother would have to endure the treatment repeatedly. Like Annie, Irene did her best to ease their fears and counter their outrage. But it was only after the seven treatments were completed and Gladys gradually returned to being the grandmother they knew and loved that Peter, Rachel, Brin, and Ian were disabused of the notion that their mothers were heartless monsters.

§§§

The events following Meyer's death took a heavy toll on everyone. As soon as Gladys started to feel better, talk began percolating through the family about splurging on a grand vacation. The decision was made to reprise the holiday at Cape May they'd taken years before. This time they would need a much bigger house. Robert Jaffe, a doctor at the Cleveland Clinic and the married father of three, was ready and willing, as were his wife, kids, and Irma and Bert. Peter, in the throes of his first encounter with love, successfully lobbied to bring along his college girlfriend. All told, there were seventeen people in the seven-bedroom, five-bath rental on the Jersey Shore. It was something of a madhouse, but to Gladys, it was the sweetest return to normalcy she'd ever experienced. Though she still mourned what she'd lost — the husband she'd cherished, the home they'd shared — she gave thanks she'd been given another chance to experience a day free from pain, and the possibility of knowing happiness again.

CHAPTER NINETEEN

THE FINDING THAT GOT Irene and Josiah's work into the pages of *Science Magazine* was that vagus nerve stimulation led to positive changes in mood and behavior in timid and depressed mice. Their study discovered the mechanism by which the vagus nerve senses the metabolites of the microbiome and, through its ascending (afferent) fibers, transfers the information from the gut to the central nervous system. Stimulation of the vagus nerve, either by these metabolites or electricity, which Irene's lab also tested, influences the HPA axis (hypothalamus, pituitary, and adrenal glands), which in turn coordinates the mouse's stress response.

In the discussion portion of their article, they talked about how hyperactivity of the HPA axis was a common finding in patients with the most severe form of depression. It was believed that an HPA in overdrive caused an over secretion of cytokines, which in turn led to a reduction in serotonin levels. They believed that vagus nerve stimulation could be used to tame an HPA axis gone awry, something they cited as the next research frontier into the causes and treatment of depression. If they were correct about the power of vagus nerve stimulation, the implications for psychiatric diseases such as mood disorders and anxiety were nothing short of revolutionary.

§§§

After the *Science* article was published, those who clung to the belief that Irene and Josiah's work was "junk science" found themselves in the minority. By the late 1990s, sequence-based identification of the human microbiome was being undertaken, as were studies that showed the individuality of the adult microbiome, contradicting the long-held belief that all adults had the same array of microorganisms inhabiting their intestinal tract. A trickle of studies were initiated to replicate Irene and Josiah's findings of a correlation between stress levels in mice and changes in their microbiome. It took some getting used to for Irene and Josiah to realize the research community was finally catching up with the work they'd been doing for over a decade.

About the time Irene and Albert were taking turns accompanying the twins on college visits, she received a very cordial call from the co-director of the Center for Neurobiology and Behavior at Columbia's medical school. The two of them met a few years before at a conference, and he'd invited her to lead seminars for faculty, post-doctoral fellows and graduate students a number of times. Irene got along with him from the get-go. Curious and intelligent, he had somehow escaped the occupational hazard of becoming self-important, something Irene had not infrequently noted in men holding esteemed positions in academic medicine. Now this affable, approachable man, head of one of the very best neurobiology groups in the nation, was asking Irene to consider joining the faculty at the rank of full professor.

When Irene put down the phone, she thought back to the time when Columbia had rejected her bid for a faculty job. As much as this offer provided a sweet sense of vindication, her life had grown more complicated in the intervening years. Now she had others to consider. Kathy, Matt, and Patty had worked by her side in the lab for years. It was Josiah who'd given her the courage to pursue her hunch about the link between the gut and the brain. It was thanks to him that they'd approached the Barrow Foundation. Their collaboration was the life force that nurtured the lab's work. And then there was her mother. Irene liked knowing that she could get home to Gladys in minutes if there was an emergency. True, the twins were nearing eighteen and could likely handle a crisis in a pinch. But soon they'd be off to college and her mother would be on her own.

The lab facilities that Columbia was offering were vastly superior to what Irene had managed with for so many years at the VA. She thought about all she could do with the resources available through Columbia, not to mention the colleagues with whom she might collaborate. There were several other HHMI investigators there doing cutting-edge neuroscience research. And it was true that, with the twins off at college, she would have more time to devote to work. But then again, if she moved to Columbia, some of that time would be eaten up by a longer commute. Surely, there was a lot to consider. She'd see what the family thought when she got home from the hospital.

Albert was already there when she walked through the door. Gladys called everyone to the table for dinner just as Irene hung up her coat. One of the things that had helped Gladys recover from her last bout of depression was taking on the planning, shopping, and preparation for the family's weeknight dinners. It was something she was good at, and made her feel useful. On weekends she happily handed over her apron to Albert, but Brin's declaration of vegetarianism caused both family cooks to be on an eternal hunt for non-meat dishes the whole family could enjoy. That night Gladys prepared a bountiful tossed salad, roasted brussel sprouts, and garlic bread. Just as everyone sat down, she brought a bubbling hot baking dish of eggplant parmesan from the oven to the table.

"I hope you all like it. I got the recipe from a woman at the temple. She swears by it," Gladys said. "No meat, Brinny, I promise."

"Thanks, Grandma. I love eggplant."

"Well, bully for you," Ian said. "Is there anything else, Grandma? I don't mean to be rude, but I'm not generally a fan of the purple aubergine."

"Ian, your grandmother worked hard to make this lovely dinner for us," Albert chided. "There's a lot to eat besides the main dish, which I suggest you have the courtesy to try. You may be pleasantly surprised."

But Gladys intervened on Ian's behalf. "Your grandma knows you better than you think. Though your dad's right and you ought to taste the eggplant, there's a hamburger with your name on it in the fridge. You'll just have to throw it in the broiler."

Gladys was delighted that the eggplant dish was a hit. Even Ian managed to admit it was tastier than he'd anticipated, especially when he piled on the parmesan cheese. When the children started clearing the table, Irene decided it was time to share the news that she'd been sitting on through dinner.

"I got a call today from one of the directors of Columbia's Center for Neurobiology and Behavior. He's offered me a job at the rank of full professor and a fully equipped, state-of-the-art lab. I could still see patients, but research would be at least half of the job."

There was stunned silence. After a moment Ian started clapping, and then the whole family joined in. Albert got up and gave Irene a big hug and a kiss. It was clear the family was more excited than she.

"Hallelujah!" Albert exclaimed. "Finally, you can get out of a place that's treated you so shabbily for so long."

Gladys started to tear up. "*Mamelah¹*, such well-deserved recognition. I'm so proud of you. What wonderful news!"

But the twins had different takes on their mother's job offer. "Well," said Brin, "that makes it official, I can now definitely cross Columbia off my list of colleges. It's bad enough that my father's there. But to have BOTH parents at your school, that would be nothing short of ridiculous."

"Honey, unless you did neuroscience research as a Columbia undergrad, you and I would never cross paths," Irene pointed out. "I don't think you need to eliminate such a fine college just because I might be at the medical school which, after all, is miles away from the main campus. You'd be safe from your mother's prying eyes."

"Did I hear correctly? Did you use the conditional *might be*?" Albert asked, somewhat incredulous. "You're not sure if you're going to accept the offer?"

"Well, how *do* you feel about it, Mom?" Ian asked. "We're so busy congratulating you, we never stopped to consider you might not want the job."

"Don't be silly," Albert said dismissively, "How could your mother turn it down?"

"Ian has a point," Irene said. "I have a lot to think about, and the truth is, I just got the call a few hours ago. I've been weighing the pros and cons of staying where I am versus leaving for Columbia. I'm certainly not looking at it as *a fait accompli*," Irene said.

"Let me guess," Ian said. "You like your team and wouldn't want to leave them behind. I can understand that. Your lab rocks. No kidding, every person there is awesome."

---

¹ Term of endearment, particularly for a child

"All true, "Albert agreed, "but you might be able to negotiate a package that would allow them to come with you. That's not uncommon."

"But do you think Josiah would want to pick up and start over at his age?" Irene asked. "Bernice is planning a big bash for his seventieth birthday. And the drive from Bronxville would be longer. I can't imagine leaving him after all these years. He was my first, and remains my only, faculty collaborator. Moving on when something better comes along hardly smacks of loyalty."

"You have to think realistically," Albert said. "Josiah may want to retire in the next few years. And then where would you be? All alone in a place that has shown you so little love."

"What a dreary picture you paint!" Brin objected. "It's not like Mom's been miserable all these years. I mean, she's over at the lab six days a week. Sometimes I think she likes it there more than at home."

Irene felt her face grow hot. "Honey, that's not at all true. It's just that our work involves live subjects that require attention, not to mention time-sensitive data collection."

"Fine," Brin said. "You'd rather be home but you have to go into the lab on the weekends. If that's the case, the fact that you can get there in ten minutes...fifteen if there's traffic, is something to think about."

Gladys listened as everyone voiced a different point of view. But what she wanted most was for Irene to feel free to make a decision that made her happy. "Brinny, you make a good argument, but of course this will be a choice your mom will have to make."

"I know," Brin conceded. "I was just highlighting some of the positive aspects of the VA. Dad has been talking about it as if it's been a real horror show, which I don't think is true, is it Mom?"

"No, not a horror show, but perhaps not as supportive as it could have been to me and Josiah."

"Reenie, what do you want to do?" Gladys asked. "From where I sit, this looks like a wonderful opportunity, but only you can judge whether it's something you feel is right for you. Think it over, and don't be in a rush. Leaving a place you've worked at for so long would be a big step. I am sure of one thing, though. Regardless of what you decide, no one will ever doubt your loyalty to Josiah, least of all him. Maybe the best thing to do is just sit down and talk it over with him. See what he thinks."

§§§

Between their clinical practices and their joint research effort, Josiah and Irene rarely had time to grab a yogurt or sandwich for lunch. When, she wondered, would she be able to have some private time to talk over her dilemma? The Friday after receiving the offer from Columbia, Irene found her moment. Josiah was reviewing the data collected that day, something he did regularly before heading home, and everyone else had left for the weekend.

"Do you have a minute?" she asked tentatively.

"Sure, what's up?" Josiah asked.

"I got a call from Columbia neurobiology a few days ago. They've offered me a job. I said I have to think about it. I thought maybe you and I could think about it together."

"What rank?" he asked.

"Full professor, nicely equipped lab, clinical and research appointments," she replied.

"What's there to think about, Irene?" Josiah asked. "There's no comparison between what they've offered you and the way our employer has divvied up the goodies around here."

"There's no contest if all I consider is resources, but it's more complicated than that. I can't imagine doing this work without you. You're my partner in this crazy adventure we've been on for the last dozen years. We've hatched our research questions together. We've slugged it out through disappointments in funding and experiments gone wrong. We've absorbed all the criticism, been called 'crackpots,' and are finally making some headway in changing the conventional wisdom. As attractive as Columbia is, I don't think I am ready to walk away from our partnership."

Irene saw Josiah's eyes glisten. "I can't tell you how much that means to me," he said, coughing into his hand. "We've certainly had our adventures and misadventures, I'll grant you that. I wouldn't trade any of it for all the tea in China. It's been a great ride."

"That's exactly my point," Irene agreed.

"But you see, Irene, I've had a little something of my own I've been meaning to talk to *you* about. You may not realize it because I'm such an amazing physical specimen, but these grey hairs are a surefire sign that I'm getting to be a geezer. There are going to be so many candles on my next birthday cake, they'll likely set off the smoke detector when I blow them out, that's *if* I still have the lung capacity to do it. Bernice retired last year and she's not been too subtle in hinting that she wants us to spend the rest of our lives traveling, visiting the girls, and playing with our grandkids. Did I tell you Diane is expecting again?"

"You did, the other day. What will that make? Five all together?"

"Yup, that will be her third and Debbie has two. As it is, it's hard for me to get away when Bernice goes to help with the little ones. She's said it many times: I'm tied to my work," Josiah said. "And she's not wrong."

"But you love your work."

"Nobody's chained me to this place. Believe me when I say it will be hard to walk away from all of this. But I think this coming year will be my last working full-time. I may do some emeritus work with the med students, but my seventy-hour workweeks are going to be a thing of the past."

Irene swallowed hard. "Are you really ready to give it up, Josiah?"

"I don't think I'll ever be ready. But if they let me putter around here a few days a week so I can keep those neurons firing and do a little good while I'm at it, that will help me accept the idea of retirement. Unless you die young, everyone gets put out to pasture eventually. I'd rather go while people still think I have something to offer rather than wishing I'd stop taking up space and a salary that could go to someone more productive."

"You're more productive than people half your age, Josiah. Even our post-docs have trouble keeping up with you."

"Well, that's how I want to be remembered around here," he said. "Productive, compassionate, inquisitive."

"You're all of that and so much more," Irene said.

"Yes, like 'old coot' and 'grandfather of five.' Don't get me wrong. Those grandkids tickle my funny bone. They are nothing but pure joy. But I'll miss this, no doubt about it. Who knows? Maybe I'll take up golf," Josiah said.

"Didn't you once tell me you'd rather watch concrete harden than play golf?"

"Busted!" he laughed. "You don't let me get away with a thing. That's what I like about you, Reenie."

Irene got quiet for a moment. "Well...if you're serious about retiring, that will make the decision about Columbia easier."

"I certainly hope so. I wouldn't want to play any role in your turning down something that good. And to tell you the truth, I'd like to be a fly on the wall when the VA higher-ups learn one of the most productive members of our faculty is leaving and taking all her funding with her!"

§§§

Over the years Irene had learned the importance of being a smart negotiator. At the outset of her career, she'd never imagined it would be an essential part of a physician-scientist's skill set, but she'd learned the hard way that she had to bargain hard for the things she needed. She knew she was in a strong position now; Columbia clearly wanted her and she had generous HHMI funding. She hoped her bargaining power would be sufficient to win her demands: First and foremost, bringing along Patty, Matt, and Kathy, her current doctoral students and her post-doctoral fellow. Just as important, she wanted Josiah to be brought in as a project consultant, allowing him access to the labs and providing him a monthly stipend.

The administrator setting up her hiring package seemed like a reasonable woman. When they met for their face-to-face negotiation, Irene made the case for bringing her team to Columbia. Without hesitation, the administrator agreed to offer positions to the three people who'd worked in her lab for so long. She felt sure arrangements could be made for her doctoral students to finish their program at Columbia. Bringing in her post-doctoral fellow would also be possible, but when it came to Josiah, her demeanor changed.

"You want Dr. Williams to be a research consultant to your lab, but from what I can discern from the resume you submitted, he has no research degree," the manager pointed out. "That may have flown back in the day, but we're entering a new millennium, Dr. Adelson. Credentials matter."

"Dr. Williams has been my colleague and my equal from the start of our research on the gut-brain axis. In fact, it's thanks to him that we gained our initial funding. Over the past twelve years his methodology and technique have been beyond reproach. His knowledge of the enteric nervous system has been a gold mine for everyone in the lab, and his commitment to the project is indisputable. Dr. Williams is an essential part of my lab." Irene remained calm but resolute. Then she remembered something Albert had suggested she say. "For me, I'm afraid this could be a deal breaker."

The administrator shifted in her seat. "I'm not authorized to offer Dr. Williams the position you propose. Someone at a higher paygrade than mine would have to okay this. You'll have to excuse me." She got up and left her office. While the manager was gone, Irene went over the contract with a fine-tooth comb, ensuring that all the promised particulars for her lab were there in black and white. When the woman returned, she wore the look of defeat. "The director feels we can make an exception for Dr. Williams, given his long tenure with the project."

Though Irene wanted to get out of her chair and do a happy dance, she managed to offer a response that was measured. "I'm glad to hear that. We can finalize the contract as soon as the amendments regarding my staff, students, and Dr. Williams are included."

When she left that office with the signed contract in her purse, she felt impossibly proud of herself. She used her bargaining power and got the outcome she was aiming for. Irene remembered something her mother had told her when she was a little girl. "Reenie, shy gets you nowhere." Now she could see how right she was.

As soon as Irene got back to the VA, she paged Josiah to meet her in his office. When she broke the news that Columbia would allow him to continue participating in the lab's research as a consultant, he got very quiet. Then he flashed a broad grin and said, "I think that will suit me just fine! But, just to be on the safe side, maybe you should be the one to tell Bernice."

§§§

One outstanding issue remained for Irene. Gladys was now eighty-three, still energetic and entirely "with it," but eighty-three nonetheless. As a physician, Irene was cognizant of what can happen to a person in advanced age. She worried about a medical emergency occurring when no one was at home to help. And then there was the question of loneliness. By the time fall rolled around, Brin would be off to Princeton to study electrical engineering and economics, and Ian to Columbia, where he planned on double majoring in mathematics and cello performance. Irene knew how much her mother would miss them. The whole point of having her come to live with the family was that she not be alone. Come fall, she'd be on her own most of her waking day.

Irene wracked her brain to come up with some way to keep life interesting and safe for her mother. She thought about hiring someone to drive her to appointments, shopping, and even a weekday movie matinee. Irene even considered getting a dog, something the kids had wanted for years, but she could never bring herself to agree to. But in the end, it was Gladys who solved the problem of what to do with her time now that the twins were nearly grown and gone.

She surprised the family one night over dinner. "I have an announcement."

Those were words that no one had ever heard pass Gladys's lips. They all stopped eating and waited.

Gladys dabbed her mouth with a napkin before stating, "I'm going back to work."

Albert wasn't certain he'd heard correctly. "Say what?"

"Don't look so surprised, Albert. I'm going back to work," Gladys repeated. "There's a lot more left in this old lady than you might think. I've been considering what to do with my time once Ian and Brin leave for college. I've been volunteering a few hours a week at the kids' elementary school, and as much as I've loved it, it's just a little entertainment in my week. When I was chatting with the school secretary the other day, she mentioned they're desperate for an attendance clerk. The woman who's done it for the last few years had to leave suddenly because of a family illness. When I told the secretary I did that work for years before I retired and could do the daily attendance with my eyes closed, she got up from her desk and went straight into the principal's office. Apparently the principal checked my records at the Board of Education that very day. Then she called and offered me the job. It's only on a temporary basis, but if I score high enough on the civil service test, she'll make it permanent. I start next week."

"But how will you get there?" Brin asked. "The school must be a mile away."

"It's not that far," Ian contradicted. "Maybe a kilometer at best."

"Whatever it is, I walk there and back on the day I volunteer. Making it into a daily walk will do me good. In bad weather, I'll take a cab. What's money for?" Gladys asked, laughing at her own proposed extravagance.

"Is this a full-time job?" Albert asked, still incredulous.

"Mornings only, and only on school days. Maybe you or Reenie could drop me off when you leave for work, you know, if it's raining or snowing," Gladys suggested.

"I'd be happy to," Albert said, still trying to grasp the daring of his eighty-three year old mother-in-law.

"Mom, let me see if I understand this. You're starting a new job next week after being retired for more than twenty years," Irene stated. "Do I have it right?"

"Don't sound so surprised, Reenie. I still have all my marbles," Gladys pointed out.

"Of course you do, but you've been out of the workforce for so long."

"Attendance is attendance. So now they use a computer. The kids taught your father and me how to use the PC back when they were in grade school. After all, I won't be doing rocket science like Albert," Gladys said, pleased at her own joke. "And they need me."

"Well, I say good for you," Albert said, finally warming to the idea. "If you want to go back to work, that's all I need to know. I hope you enjoy it."

"So it's settled. I'm returning to the labor force. I'll get out, make a little *gelt*[1], meet new people. I'll be home in plenty of time to make dinner, so don't worry about that. I think it's going to work out very nicely."

§§§

The summer of 2000 was a busy time for the family. Albert had just been elected to the National Academy of Sciences, an honor bestowed on only the most highly respected scholars. Both Brin and Ian would soon be leaving for college. While Brin spent countless hours shopping for clothes and items for her dorm room, Ian all but ignored the necessity to pack. It was Gladys who finally got him moving by threatening to pack for him if he didn't do it. She was quick to add that might lead to a surprise or two when he opened his suitcases in his dorm room. It seemed to do the trick.

And then there was Irene's big move to the Center for Neurobiology and Behavior. The lab she'd been given was four times the size of what she and her team managed with at the VA. As she was setting up her bench in the lab, it finally dawned on her: She was a senior scientist now. Not only

---

[1] Money

was her lab exquisitely equipped, her budding negotiating prowess had earned her a new post-doctoral fellow proficient in running DNA analyses of gut bacteria. Though it took until she was nearly fifty, it seemed she had finally arrived.

Irene's thoughts wandered to the painful history of women in science, women who had soldiered on in uncharted territory, doing cutting-edge work despite being denied the jobs, resources, or acclaim due them: Marie Curie, who'd won two Nobel Prizes — one in physics and another in chemistry — and yet was refused entry into the French Academy of Sciences because of her gender; Lise Meitner, the German physicist who discovered radioactive isotopes of radium, thorium, protactinium and uranium with Otto Hahn, but was overlooked by the Nobel Committee when Hahn alone was awarded the Nobel Prize in 1944; Barbara McClintock, the brilliant botanist who worked in obscurity for decades until her discovery of the transposition of genes was finally given the recognition it was due — the 1983 Nobel Prize in Physiology or Medicine.

Irene knew that women of her generation were the beneficiaries of the work of these and other trailblazers. Blatant discrimination in academia was now viewed as insupportable — and illegal — though the bias that lurked within the hearts and minds of those who made hiring and compensation decisions was anyone's guess. Still, Irene and her friends were living proof that progress was being made. Raisa had recently been promoted to full professor at Tufts. Max and her family now lived in Ithaca, New York, where she was a tenured professor of entomology at Cornell. Fredi's career took a turn following the devastating diagnosis of poor ovarian reserve, not uncommon in older women seeking to become mothers. When it became clear she and Tom would never achieve a pregnancy, she changed the focus of her practice to helping others attain what they could not. She completed an intensive fellowship in reproductive medicine and developed a thriving practice. And Meryl, who'd walked away from a career in genetics, was teaching a new generation of students AP biology and chemistry.

Years before, they'd been five young girls, filled with hope and plans for the future. Over time, some dreams were altered or abandoned as life goaded them in new directions, but all things considered, Irene was cheered by what they'd been able to accomplish, both in life and in science.

PART FOUR

2009 - 2039

CHAPTER TWENTY

IRENE WAS ORPHANED at the age of fifty-eight.

After fourteen years of coming home to the aromas of her mother's cooking, one especially lovely spring evening, she found Gladys slumped in her easy chair, book in hand, the classical musical station playing Brahms on the radio. Her body was still warm to the touch when Irene tried in vain to find a pulse. Gladys was ninety-two.

The house was eerily quiet without her. For Irene, life without her mother felt somehow mistaken, as though something on the order of gravity had taken its leave. She hungered for her presence, her advice, her loving reminders to take a breather at the lab long enough to eat the lunch she'd packed. The only consolation Irene had, and it was substantial, was that her mother had lived out her last years peacefully, without a recurrence of the depression that had hounded her throughout her adult life. When she retired for the second time at the age of eighty-eight, she started volunteering for their synagogue, something that fulfilled her enduring need to be useful. The year before she died, she watched a bi-racial man, Barack Hussein Obama, raise his right hand and promise to faithfully execute the Office of President of the United States. It was a day she'd never imagined coming in her lifetime. It made her hopeful for her grandchildren's future.

Losing Gladys made Irene wonder where the years had gone. Her thirties and forties seemed to last forever, with each day filled to the brim with responsibilities, tasks, problems to solve at work and at home. There were so many people to worry about — the children, Albert, her patients, her parents. So much happened on any given day, it was as though time itself stood still. Once the children went off to follow their dreams, the pace of life slowed. And now her mother was gone. Just as Albert had predicted when the twins were infants, it was simply the two of them again. Albert was sixty — which seemed impossible — and she was only a couple of years behind. If Irene ever had doubts they were getting older, all she had to do was look up and see his shock of white curls and remind herself they'd known one another for more than forty years.

With life taking a quiet turn, they took advantage of every chance to see the children. At first that meant traveling to wherever they were attending graduate school or starting a new job: Boston, Seattle, Austin, Atlanta, Minneapolis, Chicago, San Francisco. Albert and Irene would have worried about their children's peripatetic lifestyle, but for their colleagues' stories about their similarly nomadic offspring. As the years passed, each of the twins eventually "landed," finding their life partner and steady employment. They were in their thirties when Irene and Albert concluded with more than a bit of relief that their children had, at last, come into their own.

Ian met his wife Emily during graduate school in Boston. Following a series of one-year teaching stints, they ended up in Ohio after being hired for tenure-track positions at Oberlin College and Conservatory. He taught mathematics and she, cello. They lived on ten acres in an old farmhouse they were perpetually renovating. For the first time in his life, Ian lived close to the Jaffe side of the family, with Irma and Bert residing in a senior living community near the college, and Uncle Robert and his family in a Cleveland suburb just an hour away. Ian and Emily welcomed two sons, Max and Gavin, in quick succession. Both had an uncanny resemblance to their father and to one another. By the time they were four, each of the boys in turn had been diagnosed with ASD, autism spectrum disorder.

Just as her mother's depression had put her on a quest, her grandsons' diagnosis prompted Irene to seek out scientists studying the causes and possible treatments for ASD. She was particularly drawn to the Costa-Mattioli Lab at Baylor University, where researchers had successfully reversed autistic-like behaviors in mice through bacterial-based therapy. They added *Lactobacillus reuteri* — long known to increase oxytocin levels in the brain — to the water of mice who exhibited autistic-like social deficits. Their study showed that if the vagus nerve remained intact, the *L.reuteri* led to higher levels of oxytocin. When the oxytocin bound to receptors in the brain involved with the social reward system, social deficits improved. The lab's findings encouraged Irene on two counts. It replicated her lab's discovery of the role the vagus nerve played in raising oxytocin levels and mood, but more importantly, it pointed the way to a possible treatment for Max and Gavin and all the others living with ASD. Only once did she describe the work of the Costa-Mattioli Lab to Emily and Ian, hoping they might enter the boys in clinical trials when they became available. But she knew that ultimately, the decision would be theirs to make. Such were the limitations of being a grandmother.

Irene's anxiety about the children rose in direct correlation to the length of time between visits. After Albert made that observation, they made sure not to let more than two months go by without spending time with Ian's family. Whenever Irene was with her darling grandboys, their intelligence and uncanny musical ability provided no end of entertainment. Each had perfect pitch, played multiple instruments, and composed original works. Sometimes they would even allow her to improvise with them on the piano. Music gave them unalloyed joy, and they shared it freely. To be sure, no one would mistake them for typical children. Looking someone in the eye caused them profound discomfort, making friends was very hard, and hearing the sound of the air brakes on the school bus was enough to trigger a fit of anxiety, particularly in Gavin. Still, Irene took heart in knowing they had so much in their favor: abundant talent, adoring parents, devoted teachers, and researchers working around the globe to solve the puzzle of ASD.

Unsurprisingly, the course of Brin's life was distinctly different from her brother's. At the age of twenty-seven, she leveraged her Harvard MBA into a job with an eye-popping salary at a tech start-up in Austin. Every couple of years she moved on to a new job with greater responsibilities and even higher compensation. Her longest tenure was at her current job, chief financial officer for a Silicon Valley social media company with annual earnings of over two billion dollars. She and Warren, a government professor at Cal Berkeley, completed nine marathons together before they decided to make permanent their partnership on the road and in life. Brin ran three miles a day until two weeks before their daughter Gabby was born, and did the same three years later when she was pregnant with her second little girl, Meggie. To say it was an active household didn't begin to capture the family's energy. Flying to San Francisco soon became a regular part of Irene and Albert's lives. The fun they had with Brin and her family more than made up for the transcontinental *schlep*.

§§§

Professionally speaking, Irene and Albert had arrived at a very good place. Albert's research on oscillating neutrinos had earned him many honors and even some media coverage. He had an uncanny knack for making the most difficult, arcane concepts in astrophysics understandable to the average man or woman on the street, making him the go-to expert for media outlets. He consulted at CERN, the world's largest particle physics lab on the Franco-Swiss border. As a teacher he'd launched the careers of two generations of graduate students. Now spread all around the globe, they'd gone on to do important research and teach a whole new generation of young people. Like a proud papa, their successes brought Albert a tremendous sense of satisfaction.

Irene, too, was reaping the rewards of her decades of hard work. For nine years, her lab collaborated with the NIH's Human Microbiome Project, a multi-million dollar effort aimed at studying the role of microbes in health and disease. Just as the project was winding down, Josiah hung up his lab coat for the last time and turned his full attention to caring for Bernice, whose Parkinson's had progressed to the point where she couldn't be left alone. Though his presence was sorely missed at the lab, the work continued apace. The lab's discovery of how the metabolites of specific bacteria affected vagus nerve stimulation led labs across the globe to begin studying the effects of bacteria on a whole host of brain disorders, from anxiety to schizophrenia, Parkinson's to Alzheimer's. Researchers the world over invited Irene to their universities to lecture. She received a number of honorary degrees. When she won the Lasker Award for Basic Medical Research, she knew her work had been recognized as transformational.

§§§

Family, research, and patient care were the pillars of her life, but the older Irene got, the more she treasured her friends. In her sixty-plus years of living, she'd accumulated very few: the girls from college; Josiah, Patty, Matt, and Kathy, with whom she'd worked for so many years. Her relationship with Tatiana — a tenured professor at San Francisco State and now "auntie" to Brin's little girls — had evolved over the years from nanny to friend. The web of love and support spun by these relationships brought a strength and cherished sweetness to Irene's life, something the shy, solitary little girl she had been never could have imagined.

Once Irene and her Barnard friends hit their mid-forties, they began an annual rite: the fall weekend getaway. Twenty years later, after staying at many hotels and resorts up and down the East Coast, what they remembered most, what they savored, was the closeness they shared. They laughed, they cried, they shared their inner selves, trusting each other in every way. For each of them, the autumnal reunion was a highlight of their year.

The fall 2017 getaway was set to take place at a guest house on Fire Island, a barrier island off the south shore of Long Island. Just weeks before they were to meet, the #MeToo movement against sexual harassment and assault took off. Wall-to-wall media coverage detailed accusations of abuse by powerful men in nearly every sphere: medicine, the media, government, entertainment, religion, and business. No area of society appeared to be immune. Given the pervasive coverage, it wasn't surprising that sexual misconduct by famous men became a topic of conversation during the Fire Island weekend. At first, the friends focused on the avalanche of stories reported in the media. Things turned personal when Raisa said, "I could tell plenty of stories myself."

That startled Irene. "What kind of stories?"

"Stories about the men I've worked with who see women as sexual prey rather than colleagues or scientists-in-training. The most dangerous have the power to waylay a woman's career."

"I hope you're not speaking from personal experience," Meryl said.

"No one ever messed with me. I'm sure it didn't hurt that the six-foot four, two-hundred-thirty pound Theo came by to have lunch with me almost every day. But I know plenty of other women who've been harassed. Several months ago a young researcher came to me and revealed that her boss was putting the moves on her, offering to trade continued employment and a good recommendation for sex. She's no shrinking violet, so she told him in no uncertain terms 'no thanks,' and then complained to the university. It seems she wasn't the first. Other women on staff — as well as students — had already gone to the college ombudsman or the Office for Equal Opportunity. But you know what? To date, nothing's come of it."

"What? All those complaints and no action taken! That's beyond discouraging," Max cried.

"It's not over yet. Frankly, I'm in awe of this gutsy young woman. She's filed a lawsuit charging the university with permitting an environment of sexual harassment. The problem is, she's paying a heavy price; her research contract hasn't been renewed beyond this year."

Meryl grimaced. "So she'll be out of a job for speaking up?"

"Not surprising, but that's how it looks," Raisa said.

"There probably aren't too many women who haven't run into some variant of the situation you describe," Max said. "There are the 'annoyances' — the inappropriate remarks about our appearance or what we're wearing, the warnings about whom to avoid at the Christmas party. And then there are the treacherous ones, who can rob you of your livelihood…or worse. I don't mind admitting I thank the good Lord that I'm too old now to be viewed as a sexual opportunity."

"I read somewhere that guys think about sex forty times a day," Meryl said. "I asked Billy if that was true and he said it was only a slight exaggeration."

"They can think about it all they want," Fredi said. "It's what they *do* that makes it criminal. Harassing women or threatening to fire them if they don't put out goes over the line. Just try doing your best work when your boss is grabbing your ass. I can tell you, it's not easy."

"That happened to you?" Irene asked.

"During my residency."

"Why didn't you tell me? You shouldn't have had to deal with that alone," Irene said.

"I didn't think you needed to be reminded of that scumbag who assaulted you."

"Who grabbed your ass?" Meryl asked.

"He was my supervising attending physician, and it wasn't just a one-off; he did it multiple times. I wasn't the only one, either. He was a serial ass-grabber. But when that guy retired you would have thought he was God's right hand man — a real Albert Schweitzer — rather than an old lecher preying on his underlings."

"Something like that *may* be going on in my department now. I mean I've only heard rumors," Irene offered a bit tentatively. "The neuroscientist at the center of it all does absolutely outstanding research, but a doctoral student from my lab told me he's in violation of the University's policy on sexual relationships. Personally, I've seen no evidence of it whatsoever. In fact, he's been perfectly pleasant, really a wonderful colleague."

"Maybe he's heard you were a black belt in karate back in the day," Fredi joked.

Raisa saw nothing funny about it. "Maybe it's like Max says; he likes them younger. Or maybe he only preys on the powerless."

"Apparently, there's a push for an investigation," Irene continued. "It's all very hush-hush. Frankly, it's hard for me to reconcile my image of this extraordinarily gifted scientist with the accusations I'm hearing. I mean he's our age, in his sixties."

"Look at Bill Cosby, 'America's Dad,' and someone who played the part of the upstanding, principled guy to a tee. He's been indicted for drugging and raping women — and he's *eighty*, for God's sakes!" Raisa fumed. "And Reenie, you of all people know that the public face of a man tells you little about his dark side."

"But a scientist of his caliber…someone who does such excellent work…I keep thinking…hoping, really, that the accusations are unfounded," Irene stammered. "I don't want to believe something so sleazy can exist within a person who's done so much good in our field."

"You have a pure heart, Reenie," Raisa said, "maybe the purest I've ever encountered. It's always amazed me that despite suffering at the hands of that evil man when you were so young, you always see the best in everyone. He didn't destroy that, and thank heavens. It's one of your finest qualities."

"Sometimes I worry I'm terribly naïve."

"You can call it naiveté if you want," Raisa replied, "but I see it as your own unique mixture of candor and unbridled optimism."

"I'll second that," Meryl agreed. "As for your esteemed colleague, time will tell whether great contributions to neuroscience and lechery can co-exist in the same individual."

§§§

The #MeToo movement proved to be a daily challenge for Irene. Intellectually she knew what had happened to her fifty years before was not rare, but every time she heard another woman tell how a man in a position of power or authority had abused her, her own pain from so long ago awakened from its decades-long slumber. As heads of movie studios, television and radio hosts, actors, comedians, maestros, business leaders, congressmen, top chefs, and federal judges were accused of sexual harassment and violence in quick succession, she felt sick to think of the ubiquity of the abuse and the incalculable pain it caused.

One morning in the winter of 2018, Irene's discomfort rocketed to a new level. The day began as usual. Albert brought their coffee and oatmeal to the table, and then passed her the first section of the *New York Times*. There on the front page was an investigative report on the many women — some just teenagers — who'd come forward to accuse the CEO of the Orion Group of sexual assault. The talent agency represented many a bright star in the entertainment firmament, and the CEO was described as the scion of the agency's founder. Known as a shrewd dealmaker for the actors, writers, and directors he represented, he was one of the most powerful talent-brokers in show business. The article also mentioned that before his success as an agent, he'd achieved some notoriety as a leader of Columbia's Students for a Democratic Society, SDS, during the university's student revolt of 1968. That's when Irene went back to the first paragraph to find the CEO's name. When she read it, her heart seemed to go still in her chest.

Irene hadn't thought about Steven Shapiro in years. Right after the assault, she couldn't stop thinking about the man who'd beaten her and thrust his penis into her mouth. As time passed and she reconstructed her life, she would sometimes wonder about his fate. More than once she'd wished him dead, but that always left her feeling worse, as though matching his evil — even just in intent — sullied her. Around the time she reunited with Albert she decided that perhaps Shapiro's brutality had been fueled by alcohol, youth, and misplaced anger about the war. It was a narrative she stuck with for the next forty years. Never once did she imagine that he'd gone on to assault scores — perhaps hundreds — of other women and girls. After reading the article describing his victimization of women as "routine," she went into the bathroom and threw up.

§§§

Albert sensed how difficult it was for Irene to process the steady stream of revelations unleashed by #MeToo movement, but every time he asked if she was finding it all too much, she waved him away. "Don't worry, Albert. I'm fine," she'd said more than once. But then came the morning when he found her sitting on the rim of the bathtub, tears streaming down her face, the smell of vomit impossible to miss.

"What is it, Reenie? Are you sick?"

"That story on page one...that's him...the man who attacked me."

It took a moment for Albert to grasp her meaning. Then he ran into the kitchen and grabbed the paper. His heart pounded like a cudgel in his chest as he read the lengthy article detailing the accusations against the celebrated agent. The accompanying picture showed a tall, distinguished-looking man, arm in arm with his wife at the Tony Awards the previous June. He looked dapper and agreeable. This was the monster that had attacked Reenie, the creature that had caused their years-long estrangement?

Throughout their marriage, they'd weathered deaths of loved ones and professional disappointments, overstretched schedules and exhaustion, the ASD diagnosis Ian's boys had received, but never had Albert seen Reenie look as fragile as she did when she came out of the bathroom and sat across from him at the kitchen table. He forced himself to quiet the anger roiling within him as he took her hand. They sat quietly like that for a while before Albert finally said, "I'm so sorry. Reenie. Our life together is a total and complete repudiation of his attempt to debase you. I think the best thing we can do is go on living our lives. We'll finish our breakfast. I'll heat up the oatmeal and pour some fresh coffee. You'll go to the hospital and see your patients. I'll give my lecture on Leon Lederman's work on quarks and leptons. We'll carry on, just as we have for all these years. And if there's a god in heaven, that bastard will finally get what's coming to him."

"But he hurt so many others. It's my fault. I should have gone to the police. They could have stopped him. But I just couldn't do it. I couldn't face it," she cried. "Raisa suggested it, but I refused. I was so ashamed. I could hardly bear to be in my own skin. I couldn't imagine telling anyone about what he'd done to me."

"Not even me."

"No, not even you."

Although Albert had never pressed Irene, he'd hoped she would one day trust him enough to share the details of what she'd endured, but she never did. And over their many years together, neither his hope nor her reticence budged. It was one of the very few things about which they were neither open nor direct.

"No one would ever blame you for not putting yourself through another ordeal at the police station," Albert said. "Annie's work shows that even today, most women make the same decision you did then."

Irene got up and started pacing the kitchen floor. "Yes, that's precisely the problem," she said, shaking her finger in the air. "The wall of silence allows predators like him to victimize women over and over and over again. I was part of the problem! But I aim to change that."

Albert's antennae went up. "What do you mean?"

"I don't know exactly. I just know that I want to stop Steven Shapiro from hurting anyone ever again."

§§§

At noon that day Raisa called. "Did you see the paper?" she asked.

"I did."

"About time, wouldn't you say?"

"As I see it, it's fifty years late," Irene responded.

"Look, I'm here for you. This has to be dredging up horrific memories, but Fredi, Max, and Meryl and I — we're your posse. Remember that, Reenie. I've been on the phone with them for most of the morning and I'm calling to tell you that we have your back."

"Just like when it happened; I don't know what I would have done then without all of you."

"We're still here. Speaking for myself, you can call me anytime, and I mean anytime. Three AM is fine. Remember that, Reenie. Nights can be the worst."

"Thank you, Raisa. I don't know what I did to deserve all of you," Irene said

"You're just your singular self. And we love you for it. So, remember, we're with you on this…all the way."

§§§

Somehow Irene got through her day. She worked in the lab, met with patients, and led a seminar for medical students. Albert was right. There was something comforting about just living their normal lives. She was headed back to her office when Annie called.

"Reenie, have you seen the *Times* today?"

Irene felt the knot in her stomach tighten. She got to her office and closed the door. "Yes, this morning."

"So you know."

"Yes."

"I'm so sorry. I didn't see the paper until just now. I wish I'd known earlier. I rushed out of the house this morning to pick up Spence from JFK. He took a red-eye from San Diego. How are you holding up?"

"I vomited after reading the article. I had no idea he'd kept on doing it. How could I not have suspected? After all the work you've done, all the research on serial abusers?"

"The truth is I don't give a damn about Steve Shapiro now. He can rot in hell, for all I care. I am worried about you, Reenie. Should I be?"

"I feel so guilty for not pressing charges when I could have. Maybe if I had, I could have stopped him. I keep thinking about all the other women he hurt."

"This is not your fault. None of it is. Not the attack, not how you dealt with the aftermath. The truth is you did magnificently. You reclaimed your life, which I can tell you is the best revenge against a perp like Shapiro."

"Now I want to help put him in prison. Will you help me do that, Annie?" Irene asked.

Her sister's determination surprised Annie. "Are you kidding me? It will be a privilege."

§§§

As part of the senior leadership team of the ACLU, Spence occasionally rubbed shoulders with the New York City District Attorney, Cyrus Vance, Jr. He admired a lot of his work, including his initiative on alternatives to prison for the mentally ill, However, it gave him pause when Vance decided not to charge the former managing director of the International Monetary Fund in a case of an alleged sexual assault of a hotel maid. Some other incidents made Spence question whether Vance was interested in entering the minefield of sex crimes committed by influential men. But the #MeToo movement had caused a seismic shift in the cultural landscape. Perhaps it might spur the DA to tackle the issue with more vigor.

After Annie told him of Irene's desire to help build the case against Shapiro, Spence reached out to a friend in the DA's office. What his contact told him was encouraging. Apparently the sex crimes unit had a thick file on Shapiro and was chomping at the bit to indict him on multiple charges. This time Vance had given them the green light. When Spence probed a bit further, the contact said his office would likely be "very interested" in talking with a woman who'd been assaulted by Shapiro when he was a young man. Though the statute of limitations for that crime had passed long ago, her information could be helpful in establishing a signature pattern of abuse. It was the strategy the Philadelphia prosecutors planned on using in the upcoming Cosby trial, and one Vance's office might consider for the case against Shapiro.

§§§

The night before Irene was to meet the assistant DA leading the charge against Steven Shapiro, Irene finally told Albert — in excruciating detail — what he'd done to her. The intensity with which she shared her memories shocked him. It was as though it had happened earlier that day rather than fifty years before. The sheer brutality of the assault brought him to tears.

Irene could count on one hand the times she'd seen Albert cry. "I'm sorry I upset you, Albert, but if I'm going to tell a perfect stranger about what he did, I had to tell you."

"That he hurt you that way...," Albert said, his fists clenched. "I'd like to beat him to a pulp."

"What did you say the other day? The life I've lived, our lives together, trump his attempt to degrade me. That's what's giving me the courage to do what I have to do now. I've been loved by you. We created a good life together. As Annie says, that's the best revenge."

"I'd better not get near that animal," Albert said, wiping his face with the back of his hand. "I'm not kidding, Reenie. I don't know what I'd do."

"Better than violence, we'll go to the authorities and I'll tell my story. I guess the fact that I have corroboration — Spence, Annie, Raisa, and Fredi were all there and went to the ER with me — lends legitimacy to what I have to say. Then we'll let the wheels of justice turn. With luck, he'll never be able to hurt another woman again."

§§§

Irene walked into Assistant DA Andrea Capalongo's downtown Manhattan office with Albert, Annie, and Spence by her side. The meeting turned out to be nothing like she'd imagined it would be. Whenever she thought about it afterwards, the word that came to mind was compassion. As Irene related the details of Shapiro's attack, the assistant DA was kind and sensitive, a soothing balm for Irene's agitation. Something that actually shocked her, though, was that Annie still had copies of the photographs Raisa had taken after the attack. Time stood still when she looked at her sixteen-year old self, her beaten face, the stitches under her blackened eye, her vacant look. After glancing at it, Albert had to look away and excuse himself.

Capalongo asked for contact information for Raisa and Fredi, as well as the date of the visit to Harlem Hospital's ER, which Irene supplied. She also requested the photos, which could possibly be used as evidence in the case against Shapiro. The assistant DA thanked them all for coming forward. While she made it clear there was no way she could charge Shapiro with the attack on Irene, what they shared was extremely helpful. She would get back in touch with Irene as the investigation progressed.

§§§

Months passed and Irene heard nothing from the assistant DA. Irene feared that a man of Shapiro's wealth and power had somehow slipped beyond the reach of justice. Then one evening when she and Albert were cleaning up from dinner, Andrea Capalongo phoned to ask Irene if she would be able to come to her office in the next day or two. She had news on the case that she wanted to share.

Again Albert, Annie, and Spence accompanied her. For some reason, she was even more nervous than she'd been the first time, and their presence helped stiffen her spine as they sat in silence in the waiting room. Then Capalongo came out of her office and invited them all to join her in the conference room. The moment they entered they could see this was no ordinary meeting. Capalongo introduced six attorneys from the prosecution team. They were male and female, young and not so young, all sitting on folding chairs on the periphery of the room. "Come in, please. I know it's a bit of a crowd, but I want everyone to be on the same page," Capalongo said, pointing to the vacant upholstered chairs reserved for Irene, Albert, Annie, and Spence.

When the door closed, Irene heard what she'd been hoping for. "We are going forward with the prosecution of Steven Shapiro," Capalongo said. "The grand jury sent up an indictment yesterday. The police are actually arresting him as we speak. Shapiro will be charged with first and third degree rape for one victim and first degree criminal sex act for forcible sexual acts on another victim, two counts of predatory sexual assault and one count of criminal assault, for a total of five charges."

As Capalongo rattled off the charges, Irene felt as though a weight she'd been burdened with had been lifted from her shoulders, a weight she hadn't even been aware she'd been carrying. "That's the best news I've heard in ages," she said. "Thank you for taking all the women who came forward...women like me...thank you so much for taking us seriously."

"We take everything you've told us very seriously. We've done a thorough investigation of the accusations made by the women who came to us. We can't use them all. Some have no corroboration; some of the women have complicated histories which might weaken their accusation against Shapiro. But we have several women who have provided solid evidence of their assault, women like you who sought medical care and/or who told other people about the attack right after it occurred.

"It appears Shapiro has had a life-long pattern of committing violence and abuse against women, particularly very young women. His MO has remained the same. He'd get a woman who was diminished by alcohol in a room, lock the door, and violently assault her. Although he raped many, he seemed to actually prefer forcing his victim to perform oral sex. Most of his victims were aspiring actresses who knew Shapiro had the power to ruin their careers. Not only didn't they come forward and press charges after he attacked them, they continued being pleasant and cooperative in the aftermath of the attack — lest he doom their future in the entertainment industry."

Spence was impressed. "Excellent. It sounds like you're building a strong case."

"We don't bring a case unless we think we can win a conviction. With Shapiro, we feel confident we can make our case to the jury," Capalongo said. "Of course, a big part of the case will be witness testimony, not only of the women whose assaults are the basis for the charges, but also women who can establish a pattern of behavior by Shapiro. That's where you come in, Dr. Adelson."

"Me?"

"Yes. We'd like you to testify. Of all the women who've come forward, your assault is, as far as we can tell, the first. There may have been others before you, but if there are, we haven't been able to uncover them. However, your assault demonstrates that Shapiro's criminal behavior started, at minimum, fifty years ago."

"I've spent my entire career working in the field of sexual assault," Annie said, "and men who commit serial sexual violence often start young. Your expert witnesses can testify to that with the highest degree of confidence."

"We're on it, Dr. Adelson. We're already lining up our expert testimony," Capalongo said.

"And you said you want *me* to testify?" Irene asked.

"Yes, we think you'd be an excellent witness. You're highly respected and would have credibility with the jury. Fifty years ago you were young and innocent — and a bit inebriated — apparently his favorite kind of victim," Capalongo said.

"I want to help, more than you can imagine. I just never thought I would have to testify. Albert and I will have to talk it over. I've never told our children. They know nothing about this. Nor do my colleagues, my patients, my students. There's a lot to consider. I'll need some time to think it over."

§§§

In all of their married life, Irene and Albert had had remarkably few disagreements. There was the tense time after the children were born and when Irene was learning to drive, but mostly they were remarkably compatible. They never veered from their original path of aiming to make one another happy, an easy task given how much their wants and needs, habits and values were in sync. But on the highly-charged issue of whether Irene should testify in Shapiro's trial, they did not see eye to eye.

Albert couched his stance in concern for their children's welfare, as well as their own. "Why," he asked, "do we need to dredge up this terrible time? You heard Spence and that assistant DA. They have a strong case against him. They don't need you. It will upset Brin and Ian's lives — not to mention our lives — for nothing."

Irene couldn't believe her ears. "You think it would be for nothing that I would testify in open court about the worst time in my life?"

"You know what I mean. It sounds as though he'll be convicted with or without you."

"You can't see into the future, Albert. No one can."

"I only mean to say that there seems to be a mountain of evidence against that twisted bastard."

"I don't imagine the prosecutors would want me on the stand unless they thought it would strengthen their case. And honestly, I welcome the opportunity to confront the person who assaulted me."

Albert was dumbstruck. "All of your life you've avoided confrontation. It's not your way, Reenie. Are you sure you want to come face to face with the man who beat you and molested you? Really?"

"Don't you see? I have to make up for not trying to stop him when I might have. I didn't have the nerve to do it when I was a sixteen-year old girl, but as God is my witness, if it takes everything I've got, I'm going to do it now."

"But what about Brin and Ian?" Albert asked. "And the little ones? They won't understand that their grandmother is in the newspaper for doing something brave and just. Kids will tell them terrible things about what happened to you. Am I the only one who's frightened by that? And my parents! I just thought of that. We'll have to tell them. They're in their late nineties, Reenie. Do you really want to put them through this?"

She couldn't believe that Albert, her perennial champion, was arguing against her decision to come forward. "I refuse to be ashamed and I won't be frightened any longer. I'm angry, Albert, very, very angry! He had no right to do that to me...to force himself on me, to beat me. No right at all! As for Brin and Ian, I'll tell them. They're strong, wonderful adults and I have no doubt they'll be all right."

"And the grandchildren? You think they'll be all right, too?" Albert asked bitterly.

"It will be up to their parents to tell them. As for your parents, I think they're stronger than you think, your mother especially. Yes, we'll have to go to them and explain it all, but I believe they'll handle it, perhaps even with grace."

"You said you're angry. Anger rarely improves a person's judgment. Perhaps that explains why you're so sanguine about my aged parents' reaction to the news that their daughter-in-law was viciously attacked when she was no more than a child. Perhaps that's why you fail to imagine what it will be like going to work with everyone knowing what happened to you. People may look at you differently. If you were less angry and more thoughtful, you'd realize that."

That stopped Irene in her tracks. "Oh. Now I see, Albert. All of this embarrasses you. That's it, isn't it?"

"Well, it's not something I would choose to discuss with my colleagues."

Irene nodded. "You're ashamed to have a wife who's been sexually assaulted."

"No! But I don't see why we have to tell the world what happened."

"Because this whole sordid affair humiliates you. Humiliation, shame, self-loathing...I was awash in them all when I was sixteen. I can tell you firsthand that none of those feelings inspire courage. Just the opposite."

Albert sat down at the table and put his head in his hands. Neither spoke for a long time. Finally, he said, "It's more than that, Reenie. More than the humiliation, though I grant you, there's that."

"What else, Albert?"

"You know I've adored you since I first laid eyes on you. Back when those elevator doors opened in that hotel in DC, I knew I was looking at the most perfect girl I'd ever seen. I wasn't wrong. You were, you *are*, my perfect girl. All these years have passed and nothing has changed. I still love you, long for you, lust for you. The truth is, the fact that that creep laid his filthy hands on you, put his penis in you, that his semen entered your body...it brings me to a very dark place. I thought I wanted to know what happened that night, but now that I do, I can't stop thinking about it. I just want it all to go away..."

"And if I testify, you think it will never go away."

"That's right. And instead of all the wonderful things you are, you'll be known as Steven Shapiro's first victim. I'm afraid we'll be haunted by this for the rest of our lives. Am I so wrong to fear that?"

"There's no right or wrong when it comes to being afraid."

"And you're not frightened?" Albert asked.

"I've decided not to give into my fear. I have this chance to do the right thing and I'm going to take it. I'm going to testify, Albert. Believe me when I say I will understand if you aren't in the courtroom."

"You'll understand, but you'll be disappointed."

"I can't lie. I'd like you with me. For your own sake, though, I hope you can find a way to defeat your fears."

§§§

Irene decided to tell Ian and Brin about the assault in a letter, and then follow-up with a visit to each. She hoped that when she was with them, she could answer their questions, as well as listen and learn about the way they would choose to tell their children. One night after dinner, she shared her plan with Albert. He went to his desk and pulled out a piece of yellowed paper from the bottom of the lowest drawer.

"Here," he said. "You may want to use this for your letter."

"What is it?" Irene asked.

"It's the letter you wrote me after you broke up with me that summer."

Irene unfolded the brittle, yellowed paper. She put on her reading glasses and focused on the second paragraph. It surprised her how constant her handwriting had remained over five decades. *It was during the week of demonstrations on campus that a Columbia anti-war activist brutalized and sexually assaulted me... and I was unable to stop him. I will likely bear scars on my body for the rest of my life, reminders of what he did to me. After all, scars are the way the body heals when wounded. I can only hope there'll be some way for my spirit to be repaired, as well."*

"I didn't know you'd kept it, Albert. All these years, you've had that letter?" Irene looked at her husband, his face lined and shoulders stooped. She was filled in equal measure with concern and love.

"They'll probably want that for evidence now," Albert said with resignation.

It was the first time she thought that Albert looked old. She went over and wrapped her arms around him. "Andrea Capalongo doesn't need this for the case. This is evidence for us, proof that even when we were apart, the love that began when we were children lived on. It lives now, stronger than ever. It's what sustains me, Albert. You're everything to me. You know that, don't you?"

"And you to me. You always were...even when, for all those years, you wouldn't have anything to do with me."

"Not wouldn't. Couldn't. It wasn't a choice. You know that, don't you?"

He nodded.

"I need to do this now, to stand up and testify against the man who hurt me, hurt *us*, hurt all those other girls and women. I know this has wounded you. There were two victims that night. I can see that more clearly now than ever. But we're not his victims anymore. Remember that, Albert. His day of reckoning is coming."

CHAPTER TWENTY-ONE

IT TURNED OUT THERE WAS PLENTY of time. Though indicted and charged with numerous sex crimes, it was more than a year before the case of *People v. Steven Shapiro* would go to trial. In the weeks following Shapiro's release on three million dollars bail, his fall from grace was swift. He was ousted from the firm his father had founded. Seemingly in the blink of an eye, the man who had played a god in the careers of a multitude of actors, writers, and directors of the stage and screen became a pariah in the entertainment industry. His personal life offered little succor. His fourth wife, some thirty years his junior, filed for divorce, took their little girl, and moved to New Zealand. An adult son from his second marriage stood by him, but his children from marriages one and three held a news conference to renounce him. Two daughters went so far as to change their surnames to their mother's maiden name.

As Shapiro was shunned, Irene found herself enveloped in love and support by her college friends. The four grey-haired women of a certain age shared a fierce desire to protect and defend the comrade who'd been violated so long ago. Each of them made a promise to be in the courtroom when Irene gave her testimony. In a late night phone call Meryl vowed, "Come hell or high water, my butt is going to be there. I may even bring my girls to show what it means to have the guts to look evil right in the eye. I am so proud of you, Irene, I could bust."

Still, there were nights when Irene had trouble sleeping. She'd lay awake wondering if, like a wounded animal, Shapiro had become more dangerous. The possibility unnerved her so much she called Assistant DA

Andrea Capalongo to ask whether she might be at risk. That's when she learned that Shapiro was required to wear an ankle bracelet, allowing the police to monitor his movements 24/7. Still, her concerns lingered. She'd been a regular at the gym since the children flew the nest, but now she intensified her workouts. And, though it had been years since her last karate class, she began resurrecting some defensive moves in the living room after Albert turned in for the night.

Albert had been right about people looking at her differently once they learned she'd been assaulted by Steven Shapiro. Rather than thinking less of her though, the people she worked closest with at the lab were awestruck that the quiet, cerebral Dr. Adelson had decided to come forward and testify against the fallen entertainment powerhouse. When she called Josiah to let him know she might gain some notoriety — and not for her work, but for being a victim of sexual violence — his response was steeped in the kindness so characteristic of her old friend. "I always thought you were in a league of your own, Reenie, but little did I know what you'd had to overcome."

As was his way, Ian got very quiet when Irene sat down to talk with him and his wife about what had happened so many years before. It was Emily who took the lead, thanking Irene for giving them ample opportunity to prepare their boys. "When the time comes, I'm just going to tell them that when Grandma was young, a mean guy hurt her. Now the police have finally found him and he is going to be put on trial. I think that should be enough."

"Yes," Irene agreed. "Just so they know, so they hear it first from you. And you'll answer any questions they have?"

"Yes, Mom," Ian said. "Whatever comes up, we'll deal with it."

"I feel so relieved. I'm sure you'll do beautifully with the boys," Irene said. But no sooner were the words out of her mouth than Ian jumped out of his seat and started pacing the room.

"What is it, Ian?" she asked. "What's wrong?"

"I just don't understand why you waited so long to tell us. It was part of you, I'm guessing a big part, and you kept it from me and Brin. All those years growing up, we had no idea."

"What good would that have done?" Irene asked. "I was your mother, the person you expected to make everything right. Telling you and your sister that someone had done something so heinous to me would have upset you. It might have even made you fearful, which I never wanted. I wanted you to embrace the world, as you both have."

"You wanted to shield us."

"Of course I did. Don't you want to protect Max and Gavin?" Irene asked. "You love them more than life itself and you know that no matter what you do, they'll still be hurt when they go out into the world. But as their father, you certainly don't want to add to that pain."

"No," Ian admitted. "Still, I wish I'd known. Maybe I could have done something to help," he added a bit shyly.

"Don't you see? You already have. You, your sister, and your father brought joy to my life. Thanks to the three of you, the pain that man inflicted on me receded to a point where I rarely thought about it. My family was my tonic. Never forget that, Ian. Never."

Initially, Brin reacted to the revelation of the assault with a mixture of horror and fury. But when Irene sat down with her to explain why she'd chosen to come forward and testify, her high-flying, tech CEO daughter revealed a tender side Irene rarely got to see. "You know I never thought I could live up to you," Brin confessed. "In my mind, you were the quintessential woman, a paragon. An incredible doctor and scientist, a devoted daughter, a kind mother. I don't remember you ever yelling at us. What mother never yells at her kids? I certainly lose it with the girls from time to time, but you never did. You were always so patient. Little did I know what had been inflicted on you, the healing that had to take place for you to be the person you were. I'm so sorry Mom."

"For what can you possibly be sorry?" Irene asked, genuinely puzzled.

"For being such a pain in the ass as a kid."

"Sweetheart, don't ever think you were a pain to me. I loved your strong and feisty spirit, which I have to say you made quite evident from the start," Irene said. "You're so different from me, wonderfully so. You talk about paragons…you're a paragon of ingenuity and drive. I couldn't be more proud of you.

"I'll tell you what I told your brother. You, he, Dad…you're the source of so much that's right in my life. It was you that let me bury that horrible period under so many happy times. More than that, you helped me expunge the agony of the attack from my life. I can't believe I'm actually saying that, but it's true. And it's thanks to you, Brinny. You and your brother, and your father. You made my world right again."

"Well, if that's true, I'm glad. But you can bet your bottom dollar I am going with you to that courthouse. No way anyone is going to mess with my mother when she finally gets to testify against that sick SOB."

§§§

The month before the trial was set to begin, the DA's office had Irene come in to prepare for testifying. They had affidavits from Spence, Annie, Fredi, and Raisa attesting to their firsthand knowledge of the attack, and Fredi's affidavit regarding the care she and others provided Irene in the days following the assault. They also had photocopies of records retrieved from the bowels of Harlem Hospital's Medical Records Department which proved that Irene had come to their emergency room on the night of April 27, 1968 for treatment of a black eye, lacerations to her face requiring suturing, and a bite mark on her breast. The photos Annie provided showed injuries consistent with the hospital's medical records.

Andrea Capalongo looked Irene in the eye and said, "In preparation for testifying, I always tell witnesses the following: First and foremost, tell the truth. Only answer the question that you're asked. Don't speculate. Your demeanor should be professional. Your job is to relate the facts to the jury."

Then Capalongo and her team walked through the outline of the questions the prosecution would ask Irene when she was on the stand. "Let me be clear. The questions may sound a little different from what you're hearing now. I won't be reading them," Capalongo said. "And if I pose a question that seems unclear to you, just ask for clarification. The same goes for when the defense questions you under cross-examination."

Capalongo's assistant asked Irene whether she would be able to ID Steven Shapiro now that fifty years had left their mark and he wore six thousand dollar suits rather than torn jeans and flannel shirts. On that, Irene was shaky. His pictures bore little resemblance to the hippie activist of 1968. His face now was clean shaven, his hair silver and stylishly cut. The only thing that was the same was his build — at least six-foot three, broad-shouldered, thick-necked. The rest was so very different Irene saw no resemblance to the man she remembered. It was decided the prosecution would not ask her if she could identify the person in the courtroom who'd attacked her. Instead, they came up with a photo of Shapiro from his SDS days. It would be from the picture that Irene would ID the perpetrator of her assault.

§§§

Stories about the trial were everywhere in the media. Although most people had never heard of Shapiro before his arrest, his association with so many of the major players of the entertainment world, as well as the famous and not-quite-so-famous actresses who leveled accusations against him, made it a big story. Albert was right. Whatever Irene said at trial would be splashed across platforms as diverse as the *New York Times* and *Hollywood Reporter* to Twitter and Facebook. As the time approached for her to testify, Irene felt her fears gaining a foothold. Ordinarily when something troubled her, she would turn to Albert, as he did to her, but not this time. He'd warned her that testifying could upend their lives. And now that the time was near, she worried he was correct.

Two days before she was scheduled to appear in court, she found herself thrashing around in bed for hours, her mind producing one horrific scenario after another. When she got up to use the bathroom she remembered what Raisa had once said about calling...anytime. Other than to let family and friends know that her mother had died, she'd never in her life called anyone past nine at night. But Raisa's offer seemed the only safe port in the storm of worry. Irene put on her robe and quietly went into the kitchen so as not to awaken Albert. Raisa's phone rang several times and Irene was about to hang up when she heard a groggy voice ask, "Is that you, Reenie?"

"Yes, it is. You said I could call anytime. I'm sorry I woke you."

"No worries. Just give me a sec to collect my wits... Okay. Tell me what's going on."

"It's just that I'm having a devil of a time sleeping. I've been fairly brave until now, but with my day in court coming up, I find myself beset by all sorts of fears. Perhaps some are irrational, but others are not without foundation."

"Like what?" Raisa asked. "Tell me one."

"What if his attorneys say it was consensual, like that physician in the ER that night? Am I remembering correctly or did he say something about my liking it rough?"

"Your memory is correct. I wanted to punch that jerk in the face."

"I have to say, his suturing was excellent, but he didn't put anything in the medical record about a sexual assault. He probably didn't think there *was* a sexual assault. What if the defense says I wanted Shapiro to do those horrible things to me?"

"First, you were sixteen, too young to give consent to any kind of sexual activity. Second, you were beaten. In a move to defend yourself, you scratched your assailant's face. His face was blood-stained after the attack. I made sure to include that in my affidavit."

"Yes, now I remember one of the young lawyers reminding me to mention that in my testimony," Irene said.

"Next fear?" Raisa asked.

"Well, Albert warned me that by testifying, our lives will be forever changed, that people will look at me as the victim of an assault rather than all the things I've done since. I don't know if I'm ready for that," Irene confessed. "The people close to me have been so supportive, but I had no idea this would become a national news story. Albert sensed it. He cautioned me, but I was so bound and determined to stand up for what's right, I minimized its effect on me, on my family."

"I love Albert, but I disagree with him on this," Raisa said. "It won't define you, but it will certainly demonstrate what a tough cookie you are — tough and triumphant, a woman who, in the wake of a horrific attack, built a remarkable career and a great family."

"You really think so?"

"I do. And remember, the posse will be on your doorstep tomorrow afternoon. Make a reservation at your favorite restaurant. We're going to have a wonderful evening."

"Brin will have arrived by then."

"All the better. I can't wait to see the magnate of Silicon Valley. What a daughter you raised!"

"I'm glad I called. I so value your perspective. Thank you."

"As we said back in the day, 'In Solidarity, Sister.'"

"I'd forgotten that."

"As far as I'm concerned, that's the most prized and enduring remnant of our anti-war activism. Now go back to bed and get some sleep."

"I will. Thanks again, Raisa. Talking with you is just what I needed."

When Irene got off the phone, she turned around and saw Albert standing at the door to the kitchen. "How long have you been there?"

"Long enough for me to hear you tell Raisa what's frightening you. You know you could have told me. I never meant to push you away, Reenie."

"You were right, though. This is more...more than I'd expected," Irene admitted.

"Let's just say we were both right. All the hoopla will have an effect on us, that's a given. The way the press is covering it, you'd have to live under a rock not to know about the trial. But after thinking about almost nothing else for the last few weeks, I've come around to your point of view. By testifying, you'll strengthen the case against that horrible man. Sometimes things come along that test us. I think about those righteous Gentiles in WWII who risked everything to help the Jews. I've come to the conclusion that this is one of the times we have to act selflessly for a greater good. Yes, there may very well be a cost to us, but it's the right thing to do. Can you forgive me for surrendering to my fear?" He closed the space between them and embraced her.

It felt wonderful to rest her head on his shoulder. "I can't believe how safe I feel in your arms. How lucky we were to find one another. And to think, we were just children. What were the chances?"

"Found, then lost, then found again. Doubly lucky, I'd say."

"Yes," Irene agreed.

"Now, let's go back to bed. We'll have a lot to do in the morning to get ready for all our company."

§§§

Irene was to be the first witness to take the stand against Steven Shapiro. The night before, her friends helped her decide on what to wear: a tailored black and white dress, fitted to the waist with a slight flair to the skirt. Over the years, Irene's figure had changed little. She was still a size six, though an inch or so shorter than her original height of five foot eight. She wore her silver grey hair in a bun. Fredi insisted that she wear red earrings to match her thin red belt. When Irene protested, saying it was too festive, Fredi's reply was, "Well, after you're done today, we're celebrating, so the earrings will be perfect."

Irene still wasn't sure. "The DA said I should look and act professional. Won't they make me look like a hussy?"

Brin exploded in laughter. "I haven't heard that word since I showed Grandpa Meyer one of Madonna's music videos. I think it's fair to say that no one would confuse you with a hussy, Mom." That exchange broke whatever tension was in the air, setting the tone for an evening filled with good stories about old times. Everyone's favorite was Brin's remembrance of a night when she was sixteen and snuck out of the apartment at 2 AM to meet her boyfriend. Albert got up, saw Brin was gone, and gave chase. Imagining the esteemed Professor Jaffe pursuing his errant daughter and her ne'er-do-well boyfriend in his PJs and slippers left everyone roaring. It was the ideal balm for Irene's jumpy nerves.

§§§

When they arrived at the courthouse the next morning, Annie, Spence, and Rachel, now a highly-respected attorney in her own right, were already seated in the second row behind the prosecution. The back rows were filled with reporters, their note-taking tools at the ready. Irene and her entourage sat directly behind Andrea Capalongo and the lawyer assisting her. Try as she might, Irene could not stop herself from staring at the two women Shapiro had hired as defense attorneys. How, she wondered, could they defend a predator like Shapiro? Had they no daughters? No sisters? No solidarity with their fellow women?

Just as Irene was mulling over the morality of defending the guilty, Steven Shapiro entered the courtroom and took the seat between his two attorneys. He still cut an enormous figure, and despite his tailored attire, it was clear how powerfully built he remained. What startled Irene was how normal he looked. No one would guess that a predator lurked beneath that beautifully tailored cashmere suit. A young man sitting behind the defense table tapped him on the shoulder, leading Shapiro to get up and embrace him. Irene figured it must be his son. She was so busy watching them, it took her a moment to realize that Albert was squeezing her hand. When she looked down her fingers were grey. She turned to Albert and saw his jaw clenched and his gaze fixed on Shapiro.

"It's going to be all right," Irene whispered in his ear. "He can't hurt us anymore."

§§§

Even before she took the stand, Irene decided she would try to look at Albert whenever she could. She knew it would give her courage, and she hoped it would help him get through what lay ahead. After the bailiff swore her in, she inhaled deeply and steeled herself to right the wrong of her decades-long silence.

The moment Andrea Capalongo began her direct questioning, it was clear she was an attorney who knew how to take command of a courtroom. First she introduced Irene to the jury, asked her about her accomplishments in medical research, the awards she'd won, her family. And then she said, "Now I'd like to take you back to April of 1968. Could you tell the jury how old you were at that time?"

"I was sixteen years old."

"And where were you living?"

"I lived in a dorm on the campus of Barnard College. I was a freshman."

"Only sixteen and finishing your first year of college?" Capalongo asked.

"Yes. I skipped a couple of grades as a child and entered college shortly before turning sixteen."

"And can you recall the events on campus in April of 1968?"

"It was a tumultuous time. Martin Luther King, Jr. was assassinated on April 4th. It was the height of the Vietnam War, and many of the students were vehemently against it. It became known that the university had ties to contractors for the war machine. In protest, Students for a Democratic Society — SDS — occupied the president's office in Low Library. The occupation grew to include other campus buildings, as well. The students went on strike. Classes were called off. As I said, it was a tumultuous time."

"Did you play any part in the occupation of any buildings?" Capalongo asked.

"I'd demonstrated against the war. I supported SDS's position on the war, which was that the US ought to withdraw American troops," Irene explained. "But I did not personally occupy any of the buildings."

"How did you meet the defendant, Steven Shapiro?"

"I never formally met him. I'd heard him speak at SDS meetings, but I was never introduced to him."

"Can you tell the jury about the night of April 27th 1968?"

Irene locked eyes with Raisa for a moment. "My friends and I worked together during the demonstration to support those occupying the buildings. We made food for them and picket signs to carry on issues we cared deeply about, mostly ending the war. That night two of my friends, my sister, and the man who is now my brother-in-law, went with me to Steven Shapiro's apartment for what was supposed to be a strategy session for the next day's activities."

"And what strategy was decided upon?" Capalongo asked.

"Actually, I don't remember any strategizing taking place. When we got to the apartment the lights were dimmed and music was playing loudly on the stereo. People were smoking marijuana and hashish and drinking sangria."

"Did you see Steven Shapiro?"

"There were a lot of people there, maybe twenty-five or thirty, but I don't remember seeing Steven Shapiro when I entered."

"You said that it was his apartment, is that correct?"

"Yes, it was, and I was told he was fine with supporters of the protest using the apartment as a communal place to make the food and picket signs, to hold meetings. But over my several visits to the apartment that week, I never saw Steven Shapiro there."

"So you went to the apartment for a strategy meeting and you realized the meeting was not about to take place. What did you do then?"

"Well, everyone involved in the protest was exhausted. Some people were in chairs asleep. Others were happy just to sit around and relax," Irene said.

"Did you sit around and relax, too?"

"Yes."

"And did you smoke marijuana and hashish while you were there?"

"No."

"How about sangria?"

"I had never tasted it. Someone, I can't remember who, suggested I try it. It tasted so fruity, I really liked it. I had two cups."

"Was that usual for your alcohol intake?"

"No. Until that night I'd never tasted any alcohol besides the wine at my family's Passover Seder. That was my first time."

"What effect did the sangria have on you?"

"I remember feeling my cognition being altered, and my coordination being reduced. But it was a pleasant feeling. After a while, I needed to use the bathroom."

"Did you use the bathroom in the apartment?"

"I did."

"What happened after you used the bathroom, Dr. Adelson?" Capalongo asked.

Irene's gaze was locked on Albert. She nodded her head, and then momentarily closed her eyes. "I shut the light off in the bathroom. I was going to tell my friends that I was ready to go home. We were routinely warned at Barnard not to walk near campus alone at night, advice I always tried to heed, so I was hoping they'd be ready to leave. The hallway was dark. Just as I was walking back to the living room, someone pulled me into a room and shut the door very quickly."

"Did you know who it was?"

"Only that it was a big man. It was dark. I couldn't see his face. I recognized his voice from somewhere, but I couldn't place it."

"What happened then?"

"He started putting his hands all over my breasts."

"What did you do then?"

"I told him to stop."

"Did he stop?"

"No."

"Then what happened?"

"He had me pinned against the door and I was trying to get out from his clutches. Then he locked the door. That really frightened me and I panicked. But just then he had a coughing fit, and his grip loosened. I turned around quickly to open the door. I got it unlocked, but before I could open it wide enough to get out, he slammed the door shut and locked it again."

"Can you tell the jury what happened next?"

Irene cleared her throat. "He pulled me by the hair, snapping my head back so fast I thought my neck must have broken. Then he dragged me by my hair to a bed and...he got on top of me."

"What did you do then?"

"I started to scream for help."

"And what did your assailant do?"

"He covered my mouth and nose so I couldn't scream," Irene said. "I could hardly breathe. I was afraid I might suffocate."

"What did you do then?"

"I took my nails and I...I dug them into his face."

"How did your assailant respond?"

"He yelled out in pain and then screamed at me. 'You want to play rough, I'll show you rough.' That's when he punched me in the face. That phrase about seeing stars? His punch made me see stars. Then he ripped my blouse and tore my bra."

"I imagine it would take a lot of force to rip your clothing, particularly your bra. Did your assailant use a lot of force to rip your garments?" Capalongo asked.

"Yes. For weeks I had bruises over my shoulders from where the straps had been pulled."

"And then, after ripping off your clothing, what did your assailant do?"

"He bit me."

"Can you tell the jury where your assailant bit you, Dr. Adelson?"

In a whisper Irene replied, "On the nipple of my right breast."

"I know this is difficult, but could you repeat that a little louder for the jury, Dr. Adelson?"

"My assailant bit me on the nipple of my right breast."

"And what did you say or do then?"

Irene swallowed hard. "I was crying in pain. I begged him to stop."

"How did your assailant respond to you begging him to stop?"

"He said, 'You're ruining the mood, bitch. Shut the fuck up!'"

"And then what happened?"

"He slapped me across the face very hard."

"Can you tell the jury what happened after he slapped you across the face?"

"He forced me to perform oral sex."

"Do you remember what you were thinking as he did this?"

"I thought I was going to die."

"At this point in your life, had you ever had sexual relations or experienced oral sex?"

"No."

"Do you remember if your assailant ejaculated into you?"

Irene nodded.

"I'm sorry. We need you to respond verbally for the court record. Did your assailant ejaculate into you?"

"Yes."

"And then what happened?"

"I vomited."

"We're nearly done, Dr. Adelson. What happened next?"

"He got very angry that I'd vomited on the bed. He shoved me to the floor and then told me to get out of there or he'd make me lap it up."

"Again, for the record, lap what up, Dr. Adelson?"

"Lap up my vomit."

Then for some reason, Capalongo turned her attention to the bench. "Judge, I'd like to call a short recess so the witness can compose herself."

"We'll take ten minutes," the silver-haired judge said, striking his gavel.

Irene was confused. As she described the assault, there seemed to be a hush over the courtroom, with one exception. Someone had been crying. Then she felt her face. It was wet. She looked down on her dress and saw it, too, was wet from her tears. It was she who'd been crying, and she was crying still. As she stepped down from the witness stand and walked toward her family and friends, she could see she hadn't been the only one who'd been brought to tears.

§§§

After the short recess, Irene returned to the stand. She felt the worst must be over. She'd recounted the terrible things Shapiro had done to her.

The rest would be less painful. Before resuming her questioning, Andrea Capalongo looked at Irene as if to say, "You're doing great." It gave her the lift she needed to continue telling the jury — and the world — what Shapiro had done.

"Dr. Adelson, before the recess you recounted for the jury the physical and sexual assault you suffered on the night of April 27th, 1968. We left off when your assailant told you to get out of the room or he would make you lap up your own vomit. Is that an accurate characterization of your testimony?"

"Yes."

"And did you leave the room?"

"I pulled my clothing together as best as I could and I left. I thought if I could just find my sister Annie, she would make everything all right." Irene looked over at Annie and saw her stifle a cry.

"Did you find your sister?"

"I found her and Spence, her then boyfriend. He took charge of the situation."

"In what way did he take charge of the situation?"

"He brought me to the kitchen where there was more light. He looked at me and asked who'd done this. I guess he could see my clothes were ripped, I was bleeding. I imagine I must have smelled of vomit."

"What did you tell him?"

"I told him I didn't know."

"What happened next?"

"Steven Shapiro came into the kitchen. He said he wanted some ice. That's when I recognized the voice I'd heard during the assault. It was the guy who'd spoken at some SDS meetings I'd attended. His face was bleeding from where I'd dug my nails into his cheeks. Then I knew it was Steven Shapiro who'd attacked me."

"Objection," Shauna White, lead defense attorney said. "The witness is speculating on the identity of her assailant. She said herself she never saw her assailant's face. She's expecting the jury to believe an inebriated girl who'd just been assaulted was capable of making an identification by hearing his voice. The truth is it could have been anyone. That apartment was full of stoned, drunk college kids and she herself had been drinking."

"Your Honor, the defense isn't objecting, she's offering testimony," Capalongo said.

"Objection overruled. Next time, keep your objections short and to the point, Ms. White," the judge ordered. "The jury is directed to disregard Ms. White's musings."

"Thank you, Your Honor. Now, just to be clear, Dr. Adelson, did you notice anyone else with blood running down their face in the kitchen?"

"No. Just Steven Shapiro."

"And you just testified that when you heard Steven Shapiro speak in the kitchen, you finally recognized the voice of the assailant. Is that correct?"

"Yes."

"How certain were you at that moment?"

"Entirely certain."

"I am going to show you a picture now. Can you identify this individual?" Capalongo asked.

Irene looked at the photograph. "Yes. It's a picture of Steven Shapiro."

"Can you read the caption from this photograph that appeared in the April 26th 1968 edition of the *New York Post*?"

"Yes. It says, 'Columbia student and SDS leader Steve Shapiro speaks to demonstrators outside Low Library.'"

Then Capalongo's assistant displayed the picture of Steven Shapiro on a large screen for the jury to see. Irene could hear a few snickers from people in the courtroom who must have found amusing the contrast between the old photo and Shapiro's current appearance.

"Now, let's go back to you and Spence in the kitchen when Steven Shapiro walked in. What, if anything, did Spence do then?"

"He started yelling at Shapiro, condemning him for what he'd done."

"And then what happened," Capalongo asked.

"He punched Shapiro in the face and in the torso. Shapiro fell to the floor."

"Your honor, I have affidavits confirming Dr. Adelson's retelling of these events from Spencer Adelson, Dr. Frederica Garcia, and Dr. Raisa Sokolov, who were in attendance in the kitchen," Capalongo said as she handed the affidavits to the court clerk to enter into evidence.

"And then what happened after Mr. Shapiro fell to the floor?"

"My friend Raisa told everyone to stand back, that I needed medical attention."

"And did they?"

"Yes, there was quite a crowd by this point. They moved aside."

"And did your friend seek out medical attention for you?"

"Raisa, Spence, Fredi, and my sister took me to the hospital, where the cuts to my face were sutured and the bite irrigated and disinfected."

"You Honor, I'd like to enter into evidence the records from Harlem Hospital verifying Dr. Adelson's treatment at the emergency department." She handed copies of the medical record to the court clerk. "I also have photographs of the witness that were taken after the attack by Dr. Adelson's friend, Raisa Sokolov. I'm entering those into evidence, as well," Capalongo said. Then a photo of Irene's face appeared on the screen in the courtroom. Irene could hear several people gasp.

"Now, please tell the jury what happened in the days that followed the attack."

Irene had thought the worst was over, but recalling the days in the aftermath of the assault was gut-wrenching. She testified how she had wished she'd died, because she didn't know how she could continue to live with such shame. She began to weep again as she recounted the way her sister and friends stayed with her for days, never leaving her side. She was unable to eat. Her caretakers insisted that she drink water, tea, or broth. Whenever she dozed off, she awoke in terror.

Then Andrea Capalongo asked her, "Were there any other ramifications of the attack after those first days?"

"I knew I couldn't go home. The semester had ended early because of the demonstrations, but if I went home, my parents would see the bruises, the stitches. I couldn't, I just couldn't do that. My sister had to keep calling them and telling them I was fine, because I couldn't even bring myself to speak to them. You have to understand, they were wonderful people, gentle people. They were so proud that they'd sent their daughters off to college. If they knew I'd been assaulted, it would have destroyed them."

"So what did you do if you couldn't go home?"

"The campus was in upheaval after the demonstrations. Lots of students who had planned on staying for summer school were summoned home by their parents. An opening occurred for a resident advisor position in my dorm. I took it, which gave me a room to live in. I got a job as a typist in the library, so I had money for necessities."

"And when did you go home to see your parents?"

"I waited until after the stitches were out and the bruises were gone. I told my family that I'd walked into a tree while reading a book to explain the scar under my eye. I was quite the bookworm so they believed me."

"What other changes to your life happened after the attack?"

Irene took a deep breath and muffled a little cry. "I couldn't bear to be touched by a man."

"Any man?"

"That's right. Any man."

"What effect did that have?"

"My boyfriend was coming to New York for the summer after he finished his freshman year at college. The plan was for him to work in the city so we could spend time together on evenings and weekends. But after the assault, I couldn't stand the thought of him coming near me. I felt so dirty, so defiled. I believed in my heart that he deserved better than that, so I broke things off with him."

"How long did you feel that way after the attack, that you were dirty and defiled?

"Through college, at the very least."

"And not wanting to be touched by a man, how long did that last?"

"Years. Many years."

"Did you have any relationships with men after the attack?"

"No. Not for years."

"None?"

"That's right."

"Was there something else the attack provoked?"

"Many things, almost too many to mention. I never drank alcohol again, even to this day. I decided never again to diminish my ability to defend myself in the event something went wrong. I decided I needed to gain physical strength so I could fend off another attacker. I started running, eventually doing several miles each day. And I began studying karate."

"And how long did you study karate?"

"I studied and practiced karate until my work and my family responsibilities made it difficult to get to the studio, I'd say about fourteen years."

"And what level did you attain in karate?"

"I earned my black belt."

"Now you mentioned you had no romantic relationships with men, that you couldn't bear being touched by men after the assault. At some point did that change for you?"

"By a stroke of good luck, my old boyfriend came back into my life. But now we weren't sixteen and eighteen. I was nearly finished with medical school. He was doing his post-doctoral fellowship in physics and astronomy at Columbia. Over the nine years we were apart, I'd learned to conquer many of my fears. For example, when I started my MD/PhD program, I became anxious whenever I was the only woman present. At that time, in my field, being the only woman in the room was more common than not. I had to work hard to overcome that fear. I believe knowing I could defend myself ultimately gave me the confidence I needed to do that."

"And did you and your former boyfriend begin a new relationship?"

"Yes, we did."

"And what role did the assault play in that?

Irene looked at Albert. He nodded and she began. "I realized when we got back together how the damage done to me also affected my boyfriend. We'd been young and very much in love. And then I just couldn't go on. I sent him away, but I was too ashamed to explain why. It hurt him badly, traumatized him, really. I understood the dimensions of that trauma only when we started seeing one another again."

"And what was the outcome of that relationship?"

"We'll be celebrating our forty-first wedding anniversary in June."

"And can you tell the jury why you decided at this point in your life, after creating a family and doing important scientific work, to come to court today to tell what happened to you so many years ago?"

"I was too afraid and too ashamed to go to the police when I was sixteen. I found my courage after reading about the accusations made by so many other young girls and women against Steven Shapiro."

"What was it about those accusations that gave you courage?"

"For all those years I'd thought I'd been the only one, that he'd only hurt me."

"Objection. Speculation."

The judge was not sympathetic. "I'll allow it."

"Go ahead, Dr. Adelson," Capalongo said. "You can continue telling the jury how you were affected by news accounts of other women stepping forward to accuse Steven Shapiro."

"Reading the accounts of all those women and girls in the paper overwhelmed me with guilt. Had I done the right thing…the brave thing…back in 1968, had I gone to the police, perhaps I could have saved all those other women from suffering the way I suffered."

Shauna White was up on her feet in a flash. "Motion to strike from the record, judge. The witness's speculation is purely that, and prejudicial, as well. In this country, a defendant is presumed innocent until proven guilty beyond a reasonable doubt."

"The jury is instructed to disregard Dr. Adelson's last comment regarding her motivation for testifying," the judge said. "It will be stricken from the record."

Andrea Capalongo knew that stricken from the record or not, the jury would remember why Irene Adelson had upended her life to enter the fray of this very public trial. She turned her attention to her witness. "I know this can't have been easy for you Dr. Adelson," she said. "The People of the State of New York thank you for testifying under oath about the assault you suffered, as well as its aftermath. I have no further questions."

§§§

Shauna White began her cross-examination with questions that nearly disarmed Irene.

"Were you a student at Barnard in April of 1968?"

"Yes."

"And do I have it right, you began college before your sixteenth birthday?

"Yes, that's correct."

"You must have been quite a good student."

"I enjoyed learning. I still do."

"And when did you become a member of SDS?"

"I don't remember any official membership procedure, but I did start attending meetings towards the end of the fall term, I'd say November or December of 1967."

"Were those meetings very common?"

"To the best of my recollection, general meetings happened every few weeks.

"You testified that on the night of April 27th you witnessed a lot of the SDS — let's call them members — at an apartment using marijuana and hashish. Is that correct?"

"Yes."

"Was it common for the people you were protesting with to use marijuana, hashish, and I think you mentioned sangria?"

"I wouldn't say it was common. To my recollection, the demonstrations were all business."

"So you didn't see people smoking marijuana while they were protesting outside the library?"

"Not that I recall," Irene replied.

Shauna White had a photograph of the protestors outside the library put up on the screen. It showed young men with long hair, beards, and torn jeans. If one looked very carefully, the passing of a joint — a marijuana cigarette — could be seen.

"Dr. Adelson, can you tell the jury what you see?"

"It looks like a photo of some protestors on Columbia's campus."

"And can you tell the jury what you see the protestors doing in the lower right hand corner?"

"I can't be certain," Irene replied, trying not to fall into a trap.

Shauna White magnified that portion of the photo. "Now that the photo is enlarged, what do you see the students doing, Dr. Adelson?"

"It appears they're passing a cigarette of some sort."

"Please read for the jury the caption from this photo that appeared in the April 28th edition of *New York Daily News*." White handed Irene a copy of the newspaper photo.

"It says, 'Columbia protestors smoke dope outside Low Library.'"

"Thank you. Now, returning to the night of April 27th, were marijuana and hashish being widely used?"

"Yes, they were."

"And you previously testified that you did not partake of either marijuana or hashish that night. Is that correct?"

"Yes."

"But you did have two cups of sangria, which gave you a buzz. Is that correct?"

"Could you define 'buzz'?" Irene asked. She thought she heard laughter coming from the spectators in the courtroom.

"You felt inebriated. Is that correct?"

"I don't think it rose to that level, but I did feel...different."

"Just so you know, Dr. Adelson, I believe that different feeling is what's commonly known as a 'buzz.'"

Capalongo objected. "Your Honor, where is this going?"

"Ms. White, ask your question," the judge directed.

"Certainly," White replied. "Now, Dr. Adelson, fifty years have passed since that turbulent time. In all those years, isn't it true that you never once approached the authorities to accuse my client of any crime?"

"Yes, but as I..."

"Please answer the question, Dr. Adelson. Yes or no, is it correct that in *fifty* years, you never once sought redress for the attack you allege?"

"I explained why. I was too..."

"Judge, please direct the witness to answer the question."

"Dr. Adelson, you are directed to answer the question," the judge ordered.

"Much to my shame, the answer is no," Irene said, now visibly upset.

"So that's no, in fifty years you never thought to come forward with any accusation against my client. You were inebriated that night, the room where you were assaulted was dark, and fifty years have passed, and now you're certain it's my client who assaulted you. Is that right?"

"Some things cannot be forgotten. I'm entirely certain."

"And do you remember, for example, what the weather was like on April 27th?"

"No."

"How about what the number one song was in April 1968?"

"I don't recall."

"Who was the New York City mayor in 1968?"

"I'd have to think about it."

"Your honor, I have no further questions," Shauna White said, hopeful she had induced sufficient doubt in the jury's mind about the reliability of Irene's testimony.

"Redirect, Your Honor," Andrea Capalongo said.

"Go ahead," the judge nodded.

"Dr. Adelson, you're a neuroscientist as well as a psychiatrist, is that right?"

"Yes."

"Can you explain for the jury how traumatic memories are stored differently in the brain from things such as the weather or who the mayor of New York was fifty years ago?"

"Certainly. Memories formed under emotional duress, such as a sexual assault or combat, are fixed in the mind in a way that memories of routine things are not. When we're under threat, we experience a surge of the stress hormone norepinephrine, a relative of adrenaline. Memories are made stronger when the hippocampus — the part of the brain responsible for memory — receives signaling from the amygdala, the small structure in the brain that perceives threat. It's that stress hormone and the connection between the hippocampus and the amygdala that cements the memory of a traumatic experience. That's why war veterans often suffer from PTSD for decades. Harrowing memories persist. So, unlike remembering who the mayor was — by the way, I think it was John V. Lindsay — a woman who was sexually assaulted is unlikely to ever forget that assault. She will remember every aspect of the experience, what she was wearing, how her attacker smelled, what was said, what was done to her."

"By the way, how did your attacker smell?"

"He had terrible body odor and his breath was acrid."

"Thank you Dr. Adelson. Oh, and by the way, you're correct. The mayor of New York in 1968 was, in fact, John Lindsay. I have no further questions for the witness, Your Honor."

"Ms. White, do have any further questions for Dr. Adelson?" the judge asked.

"No, Your Honor," White replied, looking down at her notes.

"You may step down from the witness stand," the judge directed Irene.

Afterwards Andrea Capalongo and Spence told her she'd been such a convincing and sympathetic witness, it would have only harmed the defense's case if White had beaten up on her. White had done what she could to raise doubts about the reliability of Irene's memory, but neither Spence nor the ADA thought White had made a dent in the credibility of her testimony.

§§§

After a three-week trial and the testimony of a dozen women who described the beating and sexual assault they suffered at the hands of Steven Shapiro, the seven men and five women of the jury took two days to find him guilty of five felony sex crimes: two counts of predatory sexual assault, criminal sexual assault in the first degree, rape in the first degree, and rape in the third degree. His conviction on the charge of rape in the third degree for his attacks on two aspiring actresses — one sixteen and the other one seventeen years old — was especially significant to Irene. Their testimony was poignant and distressing; he'd done to them almost precisely what he'd done to her all those years before.

In regard to sentencing, Andrea Capalongo asked for the maximum, life in prison. In her pre-sentencing letter to the judge, she wrote, "Mr. Shapiro is a sociopath who has used his power in the entertainment industry to prey on young women whose futures he held in his hands. These women weren't even people to him. They were just there to satisfy his twisted, violent urges. He's a man without remorse, without a shred of empathy, as was demonstrated by the testimony of the women he assaulted."

In contrast, Shauna White asked the judge for a sentence of five years. "This is my client's first conviction. He has been a generous philanthropist to charities in this city for over three decades. He's led a thriving business, employed scores of people, and has been a contributing member of society. All that should be considered as sentencing options for my client are weighed."

At the sentencing hearing, victims were allowed to speak of the impact the assault had made on their lives. One of the women, who'd been only sixteen at the time of her assault, said, "Steven Shapiro treated me like I wasn't even human. He stole my sense of self-worth, of self-confidence. He made me fearful. I trusted no one, not even myself. I was not yet an adult, but in the aftermath of his attack on me, I felt my life was over. I contemplated ways to commit suicide.

"But, thanks to a lot of therapy, supportive family and friends, I've chosen to live. However, to this day, I can't sleep without having a light on. Even then, I sleep fitfully, plagued by nightmares. I used to be so independent; I came to New York alone at sixteen. Now I can't even think of going out alone for a walk in the evening. I've become timid. He changed who I was and who I might have become. Of all the things Steven Shapiro stole from me, that's the worst. He should pay a steep price for that. It's time for him to be held to account."

The other victims made similar heartfelt impact statements. When it came time for the judge to hand down his sentence, it was clear he had heard them.

"While Mr. Shapiro has no criminal record," the judge began, "several witnesses offered testimony at trial regarding sexual assaults beyond those for which the jury found him guilty. This may be his first conviction, but clearly, these are not his first offenses. The evidence before me of other incidents of sexual assaults over the last fifty years is a valid consideration for sentencing. Mr. Shapiro, you are a vicious sexual predator who perpetrated perversion and sexual violence against women. I sentence you to life in prison."

Andrea Capalongo had asked Irene if she wanted to be in the courtroom on the day of sentencing. She'd declined, feeling she'd done what she'd set out to do, but when she read the judge's words in the *Times*, she wept for joy. Her testimony had, in fact, swayed him. She'd gotten up on the witness stand and bared her soul, reliving the worst moments of her life. It had been worth it.

CHAPTER TWENTY-TWO

IRENE'S LIFE TOOK A DECIDED TURN for the better after Steven Shapiro was sent to a maximum security prison to live out the rest of his natural life. She felt liberated, no longer burdened by the secret she'd carried for most of her life, nor weighed down by the guilt she felt when she learned of her fellow victims. It changed things between her and Albert, too. Finally sharing the pain that had been inflicted on them by the assault brought a new level of intimacy and tenderness. Irene sensed her children had taken a new measure of their mother in the aftermath of the trial. With the exception of their teenaged years, they'd never been insolent children, but now they were almost deferential. Even her mother-in-law, Irma, seemed to see Irene in a different light. Phoning her after Shapiro's sentencing, she declared Irene "a shining example" for women everywhere. "I couldn't be prouder of you, Reenie. I am so glad I lived to see that man get what he deserved!"

Albert had been right. For a while, her new identity as a survivor of sexual assault competed with her reputation as a cutting-edge scientist and physician. She fielded requests from women's groups of all stripes who wanted her as keynote speaker for their annual meeting. Though what she wanted most was to return to her lab and her patients, which both suffered from some inattention in the run-up to the trial, she felt obliged to accept several invitations. As time passed, she limited herself to one or two speaking engagements a year. Occasionally, she and Annie would be invited to speak at the same event. To those requests, Irene always said, "Yes."

With the exception of the Covid-19 pandemic in spring 2020, during which time all medical personnel in New York City pivoted from their specialties to treat its victims, Irene continued her investigation of how microorganisms in the gut affect the brain's functioning. Over the decades, the conventional wisdom had done a one-eighty, now viewing her work as trailblazing rather than harebrained. The funding she'd struggled to secure for so long was now plentiful. Her lab attracted the brightest, most creative doctoral students and post-doctoral fellows from around the world — male and female alike. Through it all, her original team from the small basement lab at the VA — Kathy, Matt, and Patty — continued on the project, now well-compensated and highly respected members of the Adelson Lab.

Over the years, some of the lab's discoveries offered clues into the origins of not only depression and anxiety, but also brain disorders such as Parkinson's and Alzheimer's. The research team was optimistic that through their study of the genomes and traits of gut bacteria, it was on track to learn how these devastating neurological conditions could be treated, and perhaps even prevented. Despite being a septuagenarian, Irene remained energetic and excited about her lab's work. And to her surprise and delight, her much younger colleagues seemed to enjoy working alongside her. As long as that remained the case, the "R word" — retirement — was never a consideration.

§§§

The professional accolades and recognition that came Irene's way late in her career were sweet, but they didn't lessen the heartache of losing so many of the people she loved. When the Covid-19 pandemic struck in early 2020, no one on earth had immunity to the novel corona virus. It soon became clear the pathogen was particularly lethal to the elderly. Irene lost Josiah to the virus very early on in the pandemic. He'd moved to Seattle to be near his daughter Debbie after Bernice's passing. When he fell ill, he diagnosed himself with a case of the flu, but soon his breathing became so labored that his grandson made a panicked 911 call requesting an ambulance. The small community hospital treating Josiah was caught entirely off guard. The lab results confirmed his Covid diagnosis the day after he died.

Both of Albert's parents, too, succumbed during the pandemic's initial surge. His brother Robert, a cardiologist at the Cleveland Clinic, had them admitted to the hospital, but even the Herculean efforts of his colleagues in infectious disease and pulmonary medicine fell short. Irma and Burt, both ninety-nine, died in isolation within two days of one another, separated from their children, their grandchildren, and each other. Heightening the family's pain was the mandatory social distancing that made it impossible to gather for a traditional funeral. Only Robert and Ian were in attendance when Irma and Burt's coffins were lowered into the ground, a heart-wrenching end to their rich, long lives.

Millions died before labs throughout the world developed effective vaccines and anti-viral treatments to neutralize the threat posed by the SARS-CoV-2 virus. After being ravaged by the pandemic for years, nations slowly regained their footing, but few of their citizens were left untouched by the plague. Most looked at the world anew, now acutely aware that their lives could be upended — or snuffed out — at any moment.

For Irene, the lesson of life's fragility seemed to repeat with heart-wrenching frequency. Soon after SARS-CoV-2 vaccines became widely available, she and her "posse" lost Meryl to inflammatory breast cancer, a rare and fast-moving variant of the disease. Just two years later, Max was felled by a ruptured brain aneurysm while out in the field observing her beloved bees. The day before Fredi died, she'd called to say she was taking the plunge and retiring at the end of the year. "Fifty years of practicing medicine is enough. Tom is going to hang it up, too. We can't wait to see what comes next. Who knows? Maybe we'll take up skydiving." The next day she stepped off the curb in front of the hospital and was hit by a taxi cab. She died instantly.

Losing so many of the people they loved was a wake-up call for Irene and Albert: Time was shorter than they'd imagined, and if there was something they'd dreamt of doing someday, now was the time. Albert began taking sailing lessons, something he wanted to do since he was a boy. That spurred Irene to dig out her oboe from the back of her closet and begin practicing again. After a few months, she joined an ensemble of faculty, students, and staff — the Columbia University Medical Center Symphony. Much to the family's surprise, Irene and Albert bought a second home, a Victorian cottage on City Island, a tiny spit of land — a half mile wide and a mile and a half long — which still left them in the Bronx, though it felt a world away. In short order, Albert became the faculty advisor to Columbia's sailing team, based on the island. Soon he was accompanying them to regattas and hosting team parties at the cottage. At last, he'd realized his dream of living by the shore.

As their fiftieth wedding anniversary approached, Irene thought about what she'd told her friends so many years before, how she hoped she and Albert could pass together. When his parents died within days of one another, Irene's only consolation was that neither was left to carry on alone. Every time she thought of leaving Albert behind, or of his leaving her, she got a lump in her throat. She shared her fear with Albert once, but was met with a vigorous protest. "Don't be silly, Reenie. We're healthy, we're fit. Our parents lived into old, old age. If anyone can live to one hundred, it's going to be us."

It was one of the few times that Albert was wrong. Shortly after his big eightieth birthday celebration, a time when he was surrounded by family and scores of friends and colleagues he'd amassed over his long career, he started to feel unwell. His appetite fell off and he developed a pain in his belly that wouldn't go away. Irene wanted him to go to the doctor, but as a man who'd rarely taken a sick day, he resisted. She put her foot down when Albert began losing prodigious amounts of weight. "We're going to the doctor whether you like it or not, Albert. We have to get this checked out." The moment the doctor laid eyes on his old acquaintance, he was worried. Tests confirmed his worst fear: Albert was suffering from pancreatic cancer, stage IV. The errant cells had spread to his liver and lungs.

Ever the optimist, Albert decided to go headlong into the most aggressive treatments available. Since the cancer had metastasized, he was beyond the point where surgery would help, but he agreed to undergo radiation and chemotherapy. Sick as he was, Albert investigated clinical trials that were ongoing. He qualified for one that allowed him to continue the traditional therapy while targeting the specific genetic markers of his original tumor. All of the treatments added to his misery. Early on he'd lost his mass of white curls to the shower drain. He couldn't tolerate food. Everything tasted like poison and his mouth was filled with sores. Then the cancer blocked the liver's bile duct and made Albert jaundiced, requiring a stent to hold it open. Opioids were introduced to dull his excruciating pain. After a while, the opioids that provided a measure of relief clouded his thinking more than he was willing to accept. That's when Albert's doctors injected alcohol into his abdomen to stop the nerves from sending pain signals to his brain.

Through it all, Irene supported and comforted him. As a physician, she knew his hope of recovery was only tenuously rooted in science, but he was emphatic in his decision not to give up or give in. He had to stay and fight, if for no other reason than to help researchers developing treatments for the disease that had hobbled him. As much as Irene despaired when she saw him suffering, he was still with her. She hoped beyond hope that he would defy the odds and prove her and all the data wrong, that he would live to see not only his next birthday, but many more. She willed herself to bury her fear of losing him under a mountain of doctor appointments, chemotherapy infusions, and radiation treatments. Albert insisted she continue to go to her lab, if only to check on how the staff, students, and post-doctoral fellows were doing without her steady hand at the helm. She did as he said, but for the first time since her study of Joe's carrier pigeons, scientific inquiry seemed entirely beside the point.

§§§

Albert's bold approach to confronting his diagnosis likely prolonged his life for a few months, but ultimately the cancer had its way with him. After fourteen months of being ravaged by the disease and the treatments aimed at stopping it in its tracks, he finally agreed to hospice care. His last weeks were spent at the cottage, with visits from friends and colleagues, including a number of current and former members of the Columbia sailing team. Brin and Ian tag-teamed, each spending several days with him. One night while Irene stole a bit of time for a nap, Albert died. Ian was by his bedside.

She had always imagined Albert slipping away in her arms, and was devastated that he'd taken his last breath without her being there. Irene berated herself for giving in to her exhaustion precisely when Albert needed her most. The sense that she'd failed him rivaled the agony of accepting that he was truly gone. Had it not been for Ian, she never would have stopped crying. Her darling boy, now a greying middle-aged man himself, buttressed her as she tried to get through that first day. She watched as Ian communicated with the synagogue, the mortuary, the cemetery and arranged for the hospital bed they'd rented to be picked up. He made phone call after phone call to let everyone important in his father's life know that the end had finally come. Without the ballast Ian provided, she had no idea how she could sail through the storm of losing the only man she had ever loved.

§§§

The temple's sanctuary was standing room only on the day of Albert's funeral. Former students, colleagues, old college friends, and even Albert's sailing instructor all spoke to his wit, his generosity of spirit, his extraordinary mind. Peter spoke glowingly of his love for his favorite and only uncle. Robert described the trials of growing up with a big brother who was perfect. "Al didn't even beat me up more than a handful of times, and truth be told, I more than deserved it the few times he did. Only after having kids of my own, and refereeing their disputes, do I understand how ridiculous and amazing that was."

Then it was time for the twins to speak about their father, something they'd decided to do together. As they ascended the steps to the altar, Irene wondered when they'd had the time — and how they had the *gvure,* the strength — to create a tribute to Albert. Her brain felt as though it was shrouded in cotton. She could barely get out more than a monosyllabic reply to a question. But there were her children addressing the hundreds of mourners, speaking lovingly and lucidly about their relationship with their father.

Their deep connection with Albert was evident. But what resonated most with Irene was when they spoke of Albert's love of family. "There's no doubt that our father was an extraordinary scientist," Ian said, "but for Brin and me, the thing that stands out, that guides us in our daily lives, that is a lodestar for us when we're confused or conflicted, is Albert Jaffe the man: son, brother, husband, father, and grandfather."

"Our dad set the bar high when it came to the relationships he valued," Brin said. "First among all the many relationships he cherished was his family. And we sensed that intuitively even when we were very little. Our parents' time with us was sometimes short due to their demanding work, but every moment they were in our presence, we knew we were the center of their universe. That universe also included loving and caring for our grandparents — all four — and nurturing our connections with our aunts, uncles, and cousins."

"Our father taught us myriad life lessons, but what was probably the most important was how to be a loving partner." Ian stopped and cleared his throat. "I've heard that some kids actually feel jealous when they have parents who are deeply in love. Not Brin. Not me. Knowing our father was crazy about our mother — and she him — provided stable ground beneath our feet and the foundation on which we built our lives."

"But I must admit that when it came our turn to find our own life partners, that made things hard," Brin said with a little smile. "How do you match a love story for the ages? It took a while, but we're happy to report that, as our Grandma Gladys used to say, we each found 'the cover to our pot.' My father — our father — knew how to love deeply, freely, generously. He taught us what *could* be, and thanks to the example he set, we have found enormous pleasure and happiness in creating families of our own."

Ian needed a moment before he could continue. Blinking back tears, he said," Now we have to say goodbye to our dad. We know life will not be as it was when he was in this world. There will always be something missing. I will miss his terrible jokes, and his fantastic pineapple fried rice — for those of you who never got a chance to experience it, I'm sorry…it was out of this world. I will miss the loving looks he gave to our mother, the wonderful games he made up for our children, the preposterous, hilarious stories he told them."

"But we know we can't be greedy," Brin said, wiping her eyes with the back of her hand. "We had our dad for forty-nine years. He shaped and enriched our lives, fed us, taught us, but most importantly, bathed us in a love that soaked deep into our skins. We know how lucky we are."

§§§

The family sat *shiva*[1] at the apartment in Riverdale. After all the sympathetic friends and family left their casseroles and baked goods, and Ian, Brin, Robert and their families returned to their own homes, Irene experienced the emptiness she'd heard her deeply depressed patients recount so many times over her career. She felt as though she were two people; a witness to the disintegration of a person's world, as well as the person enduring that unfathomable loss. The witness understood what was happening to the sufferer; even understood what interventions had to occur to rescue the poor woman from sinking into the abyss. Yet the descent into the netherworld relentlessly continued.

Ian and Brin called every day, often inviting her to come and stay with them and their families. Summer was approaching and the children would

---

[1] Week of mourning following a death

be around more. But the idea of enjoying the children without Albert was, to Irene's mind, akin to running a race after having lost a leg. As for going to the cottage on City Island, the place where she and Albert had known some of the happiest times of their lives, it was out of the question. Nowhere would she feel Albert's absence more than at the cottage. But in truth, no place felt right without him.

Out of habit more than anything, Irene went to work. She'd stopped seeing patients some years before, allowing her to focus entirely on her research. Before Albert's illness, she'd approached every day as though it were a chance to discover something new. Her enthusiasm was infectious. Most of the members of the lab were young enough to be her grandchildren, but they felt lucky to be in her midst and eager to learn from her. When Albert got sick, the lab was set adrift without her guidance. Slowly, the members of the team found themselves turning to Esther Woo, the most senior post-doc, to lead the way.

Esther had been with Irene since her days as a new doctoral student, but assuming the weight of the responsibility Irene wore so easily nearly overwhelmed her. She had to dig deep, reminding herself that the lab was on the cusp of changing the landscape of treatment for mood disorders; the work had to continue. Her academic career and the careers of the sixteen full-time members of the team depended on it. As she stepped up her game, she found herself growing into a role she had assumed was years away, that of principal investigator (PI). On her watch the lab got another grant from the NIH, and two well-received papers published, one in *Science,* and the other in *Nature Neuroscience.*

Everyone on the team took special pride in what they'd accomplished in Irene's absence. They worked so hard at least in part for her, to let her step away and take care of her husband without having to worry about the lab. Their loyalty to her was unwavering, largely due to her honesty, transparency, and concern for protégés. It was a common refrain among the team that Irene had been "born without an ego." She regularly corrected anyone new who called her Dr. Adelson. "Please," she would always say, "it's Irene." Those who'd worked for less self-effacing PIs were floored when Irene would go out of her way to make sure a new lab tech was adjusting to her job. She expected everyone to perform at a high level, but she did her best to ensure they had the support needed to succeed.

As much as they'd looked forward to her return after Albert's passing, the Irene who came into the lab promptly at eight each morning bore little semblance to the dynamic, insightful, concerned PI they had known and loved. At first everyone was patient, respectful of Irene's loss. But after a month, people began to talk among themselves. Perhaps Albert's illness and death had taken too great a toll on her. After all, Irene would be eighty on her next birthday. For the first time, she appeared elderly. Perhaps the time had finally come for her to move aside and let someone younger take the reins.

Patty, herself no youngster, had managed the Adelson Lab from its inception. She'd heard the whispers, but she refused to accept that Irene was past her prime. Most of the team was too young to know what it meant to grieve. It was understandable that Irene was listless, perhaps even depressed, but she was not a has-been. Yet, as the weeks dragged on without any change in Irene's affect and behavior, even Patty began to worry. She thought back to the young PI who, forty years before, had apologized for having only a part-time position to offer her. The woman who'd hired her then had become not only a trusted colleague, but a friend. It was time for a serious heart to heart.

Irene, who'd been merely going through the motions at the lab, had nothing more pressing to do when Patty asked if she had time to talk. Patty made sure to close the door behind her when she went into Irene's office. She took a deep breath and then said what she'd come to say. "Irene, you and I have known each other a long time. I think we're coming up on forty-two years. We've been through a lot together. I hope you don't mind if I speak frankly."

Irene looked mildly interested. "Not at all. What's on your mind?"

"This isn't easy for me, but I'm doing it out of my respect and affection for you. You need to get help. Albert died over two months ago. No one expects you to pick up and carry on as though nothing happened. Something earth-shattering happened; I know that all too well. I lost a partner, too. When they lowered Marguerite's coffin into the ground, I wanted to jump in after her."

"I remember it like it was yesterday. It was such a painful time…"

"You're damned straight it was, but I didn't deal with all that pain on my own. The hospice we used had grief counselors. One of them saved my life. That's not hyperbole. She saved my life. *You* need to talk to someone, too. As a psychiatrist, you know what I'm saying is right. Please Irene. Everyone in the lab loves you. We want you back. You need to reach out for help."

Irene's demeanor was muted. "Of course, you're right. I've actually diagnosed myself as a likely case of morbid grief; I think they call it complicated grief disorder now. I understand my functioning is significantly impaired. The trouble is I don't care."

"But you also know not caring is likely part of the condition," Patty said.

"You're right," Irene agreed. "It is."

"Do you think Albert would want you to let go of everything you've loved and nurtured, everything you've worked so hard for? You know the answer. For him, if not for yourself, please Irene, reach out and get the help you need. You likely have many more years to live."

"That's the problem."

"Goddamn it. It is not a problem!" Patty said, with an urgency that startled Irene. "You have so much to offer and so much that you can still learn, enjoy, participate in. It's a sin to not seize the opportunity life presents you with. I don't want to get all religious on you, but it is. You're alive. Even at your age, you still have astonishing gifts. By God, I'm not going to let you waste them."

§§§

Patty was nothing if not a woman of her word. She'd known Irene for so long the Adelson-Jaffe family viewed her as an honorary member. When Brin heard her voice on the phone, her first thought was something terrible had happened to her mother: a car accident, a fall, a stroke or heart attack. It was none of those, but what Patty had to tell her was at least as dire: Her mother was deeply depressed, her grief extraordinary.

"I remember my mother being so sad after our grandmother died, but she got through it eventually," Brin said.

"This isn't that. I knew your grandma. And I know how hard your mother took her loss. This is different, Brin. Your dad and mom were like a matched set. She's lost without him. I mean really lost. I don't think she knows how to carry on."

"I know she seemed very subdued after Dad died. She's still not herself when we talk on the phone. I had hoped that it was just with me and Ian that she felt free enough to show how her grief was affecting her, but you're saying she's so subdued, almost lifeless, *all* the time?" Brin asked.

"That's exactly what I'm saying."

"What do you think I ought to do?"

"I think you and/or your brother have to come to New York and lay eyes on your mom. I feel she needs to be evaluated by a psychiatric or psychological professional — the sooner, the better. I'm not an expert, but that's my opinion," Patty said.

"The timing couldn't be worse. My company's IPO is coming up."

"Excuse my boldness, Brin, but this won't wait for your initial public offering to be in the rearview mirror. Your mother needs help, and she needs it now."

§§§

Brin turned to Ian, and together they turned to their aunt for advice. Now eighty-two and retired from her practice, Annie filled her days volunteering at a women's shelter, reading, knitting, and enjoying her seven grandchildren. Spence was still working at the ACLU, though late in his career he pivoted from protecting women's rights to defending the rights of immigrants. They felt blessed to enjoy good health, particularly with so many of their friends afflicted by the diseases of old age. That they were still able to go dancing every Thursday night was icing on the cake.

Brin's call had confirmed Annie's worst fears about her sister's reaction to Albert's death. The sorrow and numbness didn't seem to be easing. Rather than moving forward in the process of accepting and recovering from her loss, Irene seemed frozen in grief. She needed help and Annie knew it was up to the people who loved her to make sure she got it. She organized a conference call with Spence, Brin, and Ian to plan an intervention. While on the call, they each had the feeling they were hatching a conspiracy. They knew Irene wouldn't welcome what they were going to tell her, but they prayed she would ultimately forgive them. Brin and Ian would come to New York to visit. Annie and Spence would come over for brunch. It would be then that they'd attempt the intervention.

Irene may have been mired in her sorrow, but she was still aware of what was going on around her. When both children just happened to be free to visit, she knew they were worried. After they arrived at her doorstep she tried her best to put on a good face, but her best didn't hide how depleted she was of all the things that made her the person and the mother they loved. When Ian suggested Annie and Spence come over, Irene became so flustered she could hardly speak.

"I don't know...I don't have what I need...Maybe not. I'll see them another time," Irene sputtered.

"Don't give it another thought, Mom," Ian said after looking at the sparsely filled shelves in the fridge and the cupboards. "Leave it to me. I'll go shopping. I'll do all the cooking. You can just relax and enjoy your company."

The phrase, "enjoy your company" seemed so foreign to Irene that she couldn't begin to imagine how that might feel. But neither could she fight Ian. When Sunday morning came, he produced a beautiful spread his father would have been so proud of: a broccoli and mushroom quiche, hash-brown potatoes, fruit salad, and of course, pancakes. Annie and Spence, their backs still ramrod straight, and their steps quick, were thrilled to see Ian and Brin again, but they immediately saw that Irene was in trouble. Her weight had dropped, her face was drawn. She barely cracked a smile when they came through the door.

Over brunch the conversation among Brin, Ian, Spence, and Annie was spirited and wide-ranging. Irene sat and listened, often looking at her hands. She had the bearing of someone who couldn't wait to get out of the terrible spot she was in. As Brin got up to clear the table, it was Annie who started the conversation they had come to have.

"Reenie, you've barely said a word. How are you feeling?"

"I'm all right. It's nice of you all to come. I figure you're here to check on me. How am I doing?"

"Mom, we love you. Of course we want to check on you," Brin called out from the kitchen.

"We're all trying to process losing Dad," Ian added. "It's no small thing. Everyone understands that."

"Yes, but you're worried it's more than that, aren't you?" Irene asked.

"Do you think it's more than that?" Spence asked.

"Yes. Probably so," Irene said without emotion.

"Reenie, please," Annie begged. "You know as well as I do that there are ways of helping people through so terrible a loss. You don't have to suffer. We don't want you to suffer."

"I wouldn't say I'm suffering. I just feel entirely empty. It's not so unpleasant. Many of my patients suffered worse. Mom suffered much worse."

Brin came back to the table and sat down. "You may not care about living like this, but I care," she said. "I've already lost my father, and now, I can't find my mother. My mother never succumbed to the terrible things she faced. My mother did pioneering work despite a scientific establishment that thought less of her because she was a woman. And we all know how my mother rallied after a violent assault. That's the mother I know. That's the mother I love and need. This," she said pointing to Irene, "is not my mother. I want my mother back. Please, Mom."

When Brin noticed the tears coursing down her mother's cheeks, she feared she'd gone too far. In a moment, she was in tears, too. "I'm so sorry, Mom," she said, patting Irene's hand. "You know me; I get carried away."

"It's one of the things I've always loved about you," Irene said. "You know what you need and what you want, and you make it happen. Even as a little girl. Actually, as I think back, even as a baby."

"I need you, Mom. You can't disappear on me, on us," Brin pleaded. "We all need you."

"Brin's right," Ian said. "If not for yourself, do it for us. You need to get help. Annie can find someone who can get you out of the place you're in. We'll all do whatever we can to support you through this. But please, Mom, my boys, Brin's girls, Warren, Emily, all of us...we need you back."

§§§

It was the plea to her sense of duty, of being a good mother and a loving grandmother that forced Irene's hand. She followed Annie's lead and went to a therapist, a lovely young woman who reminded her of Annie early in her career. She said a course of cognitive behavioral therapy (CBT) would be helpful in developing coping strategies to deal with her loss. She suggested they start with two fifty-minute sessions a week. Irene told the therapist she was only doing this for her children, to which the therapist responded, "An excellent motivation to begin the process."

The sessions reminded her of her days as a psychiatry resident, when she entered therapy as part of her training. She found those sessions helpful, and to her utter surprise, this new round of therapy was, as well. The analyst helped her see how her assessment that life was over without Albert was not accurate. Her life was very much still there, just waiting for her to resume the activities she'd enjoyed. True, much of her life was shared with Albert, but some things were hers alone. The therapist suggested Irene start with those. Her work and her music came to mind. As much as Albert appreciated both, he played no role in either. Irene agreed to take up her music again, and rejoin the ensemble at Columbia if they would have her. She would also do her best to reawaken her interest in the lab.

It was not an overnight success. Irene had to force herself to do both. She started with playing the piano at home and found it brought her some comfort. She picked up the oboe and played Vivaldi's *Concerto for Violin and Oboe in B Flat Major*, the piece she learned and loved back in high school. She was a bit rusty, but in time her fingers remembered the sequences they'd learned so many years before. She marveled at the mystery of human memory, and had to admit there was still some life inside her that was just waiting to be tapped. After weeks of playing at home, she approached the concertmaster of the Columbia Medical Symphony and asked if there might be a place for her again. The concertmaster gave her an enormous hug and said, "Irene, we've been waiting for you to come back."

She took things slowly at work. First, she called Esther into her office and thanked her for everything she'd done in her absence. Her work had been stunning, her leadership of the lab beyond reproach. Irene shared her diagnosis of complicated grief, but said she was working hard to heal through cognitive behavioral therapy. She added the data on CBT was quite promising, so she expected she'd soon be bringing her best self back to the lab. But, rather than ask Esther to move aside as her vigor returned, Irene proposed something else entirely.

"As you are well aware, I'm nearing eighty. It's about time I make plans for my eventual successor. I can think of no one better to fill that role than you. Give it some thought. If this is something that appeals to you, I'll start my campaign to have us formally share leadership of the lab. I imagine the administration has some residual good will towards me, given how our lab's discoveries have enhanced the reputation of the university, not to mention the generous grants we've won of late, so I'm hopeful my proposal will be acceptable to the powers that be."

Esther didn't hesitate. "First, let me say I am so glad you're feeling a bit better. We've all missed your guidance, no one more than I. And second, nothing would make me happier than to continue working with you. I'd be honored to be your partner going forward. So, yes, feel free to do what you can to make that come to pass. Whether or not the university is receptive to your plan, I am so appreciative of everything you've taught me. I've become the researcher I am thanks to your teaching and mentorship…and friendship, I might add."

"It's been a two-way street, you know. I've gotten great satisfaction watching you grow into the woman and the scientist you are," Irene said.

Esther was quiet for a moment. "Irene, I think I need to be completely honest with you."

"I expect no less."

"It's very early, but it seems I've become pregnant. It wasn't exactly planned, but Mike and I had been talking about taking the plunge," Esther said. "I'm not getting any younger, but this might not be the ideal time for you to be making the case for my appointment to the faculty."

Irene didn't miss a beat. "First, let me say this is the best news I've heard since I lost Albert. Second, there's never an 'ideal' moment to become a parent, but I hope you and Mike will find it to be one of the sweetest experiences of your lives. I can't begin to imagine life without my children, especially now. Finally, I insist on you taking all of the childcare leave coming to you. I haven't kept track, but last I checked the university offered at least four months. It's something you'll never regret. As my grandmother told me so many years ago, 'You'll be the only mother that baby will ever have.' And I promise you, the work will be waiting for you when you're ready to come back."

§§§

People in the lab began to notice changes in Irene. She seemed more interested in the ongoing experiments and more fully present than she'd been in a long time. Irene noted some changes herself. She'd started to sleep better, feeling rested when she awoke in the morning. She ate not because she knew she needed to, but because she was actually hungry. She didn't need to be persuaded when Patty suggested she try an elixir of *Coprococcus* and *Dialister*, two bacteria the lab had been investigating for the last couple of years. Irene did seem to feel sharper and more energetic after a two week course of Patty's microbial tonic. And when the FDA approved the lab's application for a clinical trial testing the efficacy of the bacteria as a psycho-biotic in depressed patients, Irene could hardly believe her own response to the news: She was overjoyed. She hadn't known happiness like that since before Albert fell ill.

As Irene continued taking baby steps toward creating a life on her own, she knew the true test would be going back to the cottage, the place where Albert had realized his dream of living by the water. Nearly a year after his death, Irene got up the courage to ask Annie and Spence to go with her to City Island. She had no idea in what shape they would find the house. As Annie pulled into the driveway, Irene couldn't believe her eyes. The cottage was just as she and Ian had left it, with its white shutters looking sharp and crisp against the robin's egg blue clapboards, the striped curtains framing the windows. Her first thought was how happy Albert would be to know she'd returned to his favorite spot on earth. She had considered selling the cottage, but being there again revived so much of what she'd shared with Albert. Right then and there she decided it would be her weekend home for as long as she could make her way to that spit of land on the western edge of Long Island Sound.

§§§

As the first step in her campaign for a seamless leadership transition for the lab, Irene went straight to the top, the Executive Director of the Institute. She made the case that Esther Woo would be the ideal candidate, pointing out that it was she who had brought in the latest round of NIH funding and guided the team's research so brilliantly during Albert's illness. Irene was frank. "I don't plan on going anywhere in the immediate future, but I am a realist; no one lives forever. It would be advantageous for both the Institute and for me if the Adelson Lab began a slow transition to its new principal investigator. I can think of no one better than Esther Woo to be my partner and, ultimately, my successor. Of course, I understand the decision is not wholly mine, but I intend to do everything in my power to ensure the continued viability of my lab." Then, just as Irene was about to open the door to leave, she added, "One more thing: Esther is expecting her first child. I've assured her that her pregnancy will have no bearing whatsoever on how the Institute and the University will evaluate her suitability for appointment to the faculty."

Some months later, when the new faculty hires were announced, Esther was among them. Her new title was Assistant Professor of Neuroscience and Co-director of the Adelson Lab. Thinking back to the start of her own career, Irene shook her head at her naiveté. She'd had no idea how the game was played, no negotiating skills, no clue that being a woman was seen as a "handicapping condition" by the men who meted out resources.

Over her career she'd amassed a fair degree of power and the savvy to know how to use it. Now Esther was positioned to continue the lab's work into the future, and in just a matter of weeks, she'd be a mother, too.

CHAPTER TWENTY THREE

WHEN SHE WAS EIGHTY-SIX, Irene decided to sell the Riverdale apartment that had been her home since the twins were toddlers. It had once housed an entire family, including Tatiana, and later her mother, but now she was the sole occupant. It struck her that she was literally taking up too much real estate. Since the lab had relocated to the Zuckerman Institute for the Mind, Brain, and Behavior near the Morningside Heights campus, the apartment was no longer an advantageous location for work. Every day required a rather long and expensive cab ride there and back. She started thinking about where and how she'd like to live. Thinking back to her post-doc days, she had fond memories of stepping outside her building and walking to Dr. Fieve's lab. She decided to look for an apartment within an easy walk to the Institute.

Irene was very much taken with the young family who put in an offer on the Riverdale apartment. They had a little girl and were expecting a second. She liked the idea that the rooms her children had grown up in would again be filled with new life. After accepting their offer, she turned her attention to looking for a new place to call home. A real estate broker helped her find a two-bedroom apartment a short walk from the lab. It was on Riverside Drive, with a spectacular view of the Hudson. The rooms in the pre-WWII building were large, but the apartment's total square footage was considerably less than her Riverdale home. Paring down fifty years of accumulation was not for the faint of heart, and she did occasionally fall victim to a wave of nostalgia, but once the moving van delivered her belongings to her new, freshly painted apartment, she felt positively giddy with a sense of liberation.

On their first visit to Irene's new home, Spence and Annie were taken with the breathtaking views of the river. The apartment itself was lovely, high above the tree line with afternoon light streaming through the windows, and it was located in a real neighborhood, with stores and restaurants an easy walk away. If that weren't enough, the green space of Riverside Park was just across the street. It got them thinking. They were nearing ninety, and Peter and Rachel had been urging them to downsize and move closer to one of them. Now that they were both fully retired they were free to move to the suburbs, but the prospect of forsaking the city held little appeal. When Irene mentioned an apartment becoming available two floors above hers, they took a look and signed a lease on the spot.

Every one of their middle-aged children laughed when Spence dubbed their new living arrangement, "The Adelson Home for the Aged." But, in fact, having all the elders living under one roof reduced the worries of Peter and Rachel, and Brin and Ian. Now, there would always be someone around when one of their parents needed help. And it made family visits so much easier; a visit to one apartment invariably became a visit to both. Peter or Rachel, who were just a drive away, made sure to drop by once a week. Since three of Irene's grandchildren were in school in the city — Gavin and Max at Juilliard, and Gabby at N.Y.U. — their parents, too, were frequent visitors.

Sometimes when Ian and Emily or Brin and Warren were in town, the family — including an ever-changing assortment from Annie and Spence's large brood —would caravan out to the cottage for a weekend by the water. Every bed and sofa would be filled, with the overflow in sleeping bags on the living room floor. Peter's son and his wife even pitched a tent in the backyard when their baby was too young to sleep through the night. "Bourgeois camping," they called it, with hot showers, a washer/dryer and delicious homemade meals just steps away. They must have enjoyed it, because they continued "bourgeois camping" even when the baby managed to sleep the night through. What fun those weekends were for all the generations. Whenever they congregated, someone would always offer a toast: "To Albert, the genius who brought us to this great escape on Long Island Sound!" Their tribute, paid so many years after her dear Albert's death, thrilled Irene each and every time.

§§§

After Esther Woo was appointed to the faculty, the former mentor and protégée became colleagues and partners. They were intentional as they carved out their roles in the leadership of the lab, playing on the strengths of each. And, over the years, their relationship evolved. By the time Irene moved to Riverside Drive, Esther had been granted tenure and had herself become a Howard Hughes investigator in the newly renamed Adelson-Woo Lab. Though directing the nature and methodology of the lab's research remained their joint concern, it was clear that Esther was now leading the charge in their study of microbial treatments for psychiatric disease. Irene felt that was as it should be. Esther had the dynamism, the insight, and the ambition to make the rounds at all the conferences and get their work out to publication. First thing each morning, she and Esther met to discuss the status of their ongoing experiments. Irene played the role of the wise woman to her younger, brilliant, driven colleague, and Esther relied on Irene's razor-sharp mind, her encyclopedic knowledge, and her judgment in matters as diverse as university politics and toilet training her younger child. It was a relationship treasured by them both.

§§§

Sometimes when she was alone, particularly when she was at the cottage, Irene would reflect on her losses: the people who were gone, the physical vigor and stamina that were now in short supply. What had once seemed enduring parts of life had, one by one, taken their leave. First among them, of course, was Albert. His death nearly felled her, but after a struggle, she'd found a way to live on her own. It took courage to accept the slow but relentless decline of her physical vitality. Sometimes when she caught a glimpse of her naked body in the mirror, she was forced to conclude that she'd become an antique. And then there were the losses of friends and colleagues. Each death shrank her world, bit by bit. Raisa was the sole surviving member of her "posse," but her descent into dementia meant the confidante Irene had loved and relied on was no more. Every time she thought about her brilliant, gutsy friend living out her days in a memory care unit of a Cambridge nursing home, Irene shook her head in disbelief.

Every loss required her to create a new equilibrium. Some losses were easier to recover from than others, but all required time and patience, two things she had more of now. All things considered, she felt she was meeting the challenges presented by advanced age. Luckily, there was still a lot happening on the positive side of the ledger. Having Annie and Spence just upstairs brought great comfort. With three of her four now adult grandchildren living in the city, she had so much more opportunity to spend time with them, something that helped fill the void created by those who were gone.

Both of Ian's boys studied at Julliard, Max, the viola, and Gavin, the piano. She attended every one of their recitals, each one filling her with enormous pride. She fretted far less about their autism now. Of course, people who met them likely noticed they were different, but she felt sure their musical gifts and utter absence of guile could win over even the crankiest curmudgeon. It didn't hurt that they both cut a fine figure. Their parents had taught them impeccable manners and daily grooming techniques, so they were appealing on many levels. Max and Gavin also faithfully took a daily dose of microbes calibrated specifically for each of them to increase their sociability. Irene was confident her beautiful grandsons would find their way in the world.

Brin's eldest, Gabby, was following in her grandmother's footsteps and training to become a physician, something that tickled Irene. Finally, she had someone in the family with whom she could talk shop. Now in the midst of her clinical rotations at NYU, Gabby was getting her first taste of what doctoring was all about. Irene loved hearing her recount stories from "the trenches," as Gabby liked to refer to patient care. Every time they were together, Irene marveled at how she was a chip off her mother's block: smart, creative, and determined.

Meg couldn't have been more different from her big sister. As a little one, the delightful imp had charmed everyone with her mischievous escapades, but during her sophomore year at UC Berkeley, that playful child fell victim to Major Depressive Disorder. Irene wept when Brin broke the news that Meg had been admitted to an in-patient psych unit. Her first reaction was guilt. Perhaps she'd passed on a genetic predisposition to fall victim to MDD. But then she thought about the discoveries of the Adelson Lab, which had untangled the mechanism of depression and brought forth better, more effective treatments. With all her heart, she hoped her life's work would help rescue her beloved grandchild from depression's clutches.

Much like Winston and Eloise Barrow had done for their son some fifty years before, Brin and Warren sought out the very best doctors for their child. The psychiatrists in San Francisco used a four-pronged approach: microbial — *lactobacillis rhamnosus* proved particularly efficacious; electrical stimulation of the vagus nerve; a new class of anti-depressant medication; and cognitive behavioral therapy. Meg responded quickly to the combination of therapies, only one of which existed when David Barrow was stricken with MDD. She was now back in school, and from all objective evidence, managing her work and her life with equanimity. Set to graduate in June, she was looking forward to pursuing a career in humanitarian relief.

Reflecting on her long life, Irene knew she had much to be grateful for. She'd known the best of parental love and shared fifty-two years of marriage with a man she adored. Her children had grown into *menschen*: people of integrity, honor, and accomplishment. They were solicitous of her, calling and texting several times a week; they even invited her to join them on their exotic vacations to faraway places. Traveling just for fun and adventure was something she and Albert had rarely done. In hindsight, she wondered if perhaps they had worked too hard.

Though thankful for every day, at eighty-eight she was also at peace with the knowledge that any number of maladies could cut her down later that day or the following week. Her only fear was that she, like Raisa, might lose her mind. There seemed something so terribly unfair about exiting life without one's wits. But, she took comfort in knowing her mother and grandmother had lived the lives they'd wanted until the end. Perhaps she would be lucky on that count, too.

§§§

When Irene was awakened by the phone that dark Monday morning in October, she heard a heavy rain pelting the bedroom windows. The red digits of the clock next to her bed read 5:15. Through the fog of sleep she began imagining the possible calamities that would cause someone to call her at that hour: Something terrible had befallen one of the children, a disaster had ruined the experiment in the lab, Annie or Spence had experienced a medical emergency. Perhaps one of them had died. She tried to rally her faculties to face whatever dreadful thing had occurred. Bracing herself, she answered the phone.

"Hello," she said, the blood pulsing in her ears.

"Good morning. This is the Secretary of the Nobel Committee in Stockholm calling for Dr. Irene Adelson."

She couldn't imagine what kind of small-minded trickster would play a prank on an old woman at this hour. Though it was the season for announcing a new round of Nobel laureates, Irene was sure the time had long passed when the Nobel nominating committee might have considered her work. There were many other, younger scientists who'd made path-breaking findings since she and Josiah had discovered the mechanism by which the gut microbiome influenced mood and behavior. Irene made no effort to mask her impatience. "I'm sorry, but I don't find this at all amusing."

"I assure you, Dr. Adelson, I am entirely serious. For your discovery of the critical role of the gut-brain axis in neurological functioning, the Nobel Committee has chosen you for this year's Prize in Physiology or Medicine. The award would have been shared with your colleague, Dr. Josiah Williams, and also Dr. Michael Gershon, but as you know, the Nobel is not awarded posthumously. You, therefore, will be the sole recipient of the 2039 Prize."

The man had a clipped Swedish accent. He knew of Josiah's work as well as Dr. Gershon's, which had led them to investigate the gut's role in psychiatric illness. She had, in fact, just recently returned from a biology symposium in Stockholm run by Sweden's famed Karolinska Institute. It was an august and select gathering, which brought together the world's leading biological researchers. Could it be possible that the man on the other end of the phone was telling the truth?

"Dr. Adelson, are you there?"

"Oh, yes. It's just that I'm having a difficult time accepting the veracity of what you just said."

"I assure you, your reaction is not at all unusual, but what I've told you is entirely true. You are, in fact, this year's winner of the Nobel Prize for Physiology or Medicine. May I be the first to offer you hearty congratulations?"

"Why yes...I guess so...of course," Irene stammered.

"Many details will follow in the coming days. Someone from the Royal Swedish Academy will get back to you with specifics about the events leading up to the awards ceremony, the ceremony itself, and the banquet. But right now, I need to ask you a favor. The press will be notified at 6 AM, Eastern time in the US. Will you please keep this a secret until then? Can I can count on that?"

"Yes, of course. Then, after six, I can tell my children?" Irene asked, trying to shake the feeling that she was in the middle of a dream that would end at morning's first light.

"Certainly, Dr. Adelson. You may tell whomever you like after 6 AM. Again, I offer you my heartiest congratulations."

Irene hung up and lay back down in a state of shock. Oh, what she would give if Albert were there to share this moment! Back when the twins were small and she'd come home dog-tired and discouraged after a bad day in the lab, his standing joke was that it would all be worth it when she won the Nobel Prize. She tried to picture what he would say now that his quip had become reality. Just thinking about it made her a bit weepy.

Of one thing she was certain: Albert wouldn't want her lying in bed teary-eyed, so she got up, made the coffee, and laid out her clothes. She moved so quickly, it was as though the years had fallen away. "It must be the epinephrine," she thought, as she glided through her morning routine. In no time, she was out of the shower and buttoning her last button. She dried her shoulder-length silver hair and pulled it back into a ponytail at the nape of her neck. As she did every morning, she applied moisturizer to her face, only this morning she didn't lament the creases and wrinkles. She put on her favorite earrings, the ones Albert had given her for her seventy-fifth birthday. Glancing at the clock in the bathroom, she saw twelve minutes still remained before she could share her news. She sat down in an armchair with a view of Riverside Drive below, her phone in hand, wishing time would pass faster. Finally, when she heard the grandfather clock strike six times, she called Ian.

As soon as he answered, she knew she hadn't wakened him. "Oh, I can't believe this, Mom. It's just astounding and wonderful and thrilling and a host of other adjectives I can't think of at the moment. I am so happy for you!" he exulted. "Have you called Brin yet?"

"Well, it's awfully early out on the West Coast. I was thinking I'd wait a while."

"Sure. That makes sense. She is going to be over the moon when she hears this."

"You think so?" Irene asked.

"No doubt about it."

"It is pretty exciting, isn't it?" Irene asked.

"You bet it is. Congratulations, Mom. Love you."

"Love you, too, son."

After she hung up, Irene reconsidered calling Brin. She so wanted to share her good news with her. But the more she weighed the pros and cons, she felt sure her initial instinct was correct; an incoming call at three fifteen in the morning would be too frightening. Instead, she called Spence, knowing that by this point in the morning, he'd likely be doing his calisthenics in the living room. His reaction was simple, "Well done, Reenie! I'll wake Annie and we'll be right down. Get the coffee on!" The moment Irene hung up, the phone rang. It was Esther. "Oh, Irene, I just heard the news on NPR! Holy cow, this is fantastic!! I am so excited for you! Well-deserved my friend, well-deserved. And about time, I'd say!"

When Annie and Spence arrived in their robes and pajamas, they suggested she call Brin even though it was only half past three in California. "You'd better do it, Reenie, or someone else will," Spence pointed out. So, Irene made the call. When Brin answered, Irene blurted out, "I'm fine, I don't want you to think I fell or had a stroke. It's just that I got a call from Sweden about an hour ago."

"Sweden? You got a call from Sweden? What? You're calling me in the middle of the night to tell me someone called you from Sweden? Oh…wait…Mom, isn't it the time they start announcing the Nobels? Was it *that* kind of call from Sweden?" Brin asked, collecting her wits.

"Indeed it was, my darling girl. Your old mother has won the Nobel Prize for Medicine! I can't believe it myself."

"Oh my goodness! Oh my goodness! Warren, wake up. My mother just won the Nobel Prize for Medicine!"

And such was the rest of the morning. There were calls every few minutes from acquaintances and colleagues wanting to extend their good wishes. Neighbors she'd never said more than "hello" to as they waited for the elevator rang her bell and offered congratulations. Emails and text messages poured in. Columbia's president called to say there would be a news conference later that day. Her attendance would be greatly appreciated. Irene called Gavin, Max, and Gabby to ask if they would be free to accompany her. Without missing a beat, each one in succession agreed to save the afternoon for her.

When Irene entered the lab later that morning, she got a standing ovation. Patty, who'd long since retired, was there, as were many of her former students who'd had their start under her aegis and now had active research careers of their own. It was a euphoric moment, a moment she wished could last forever. It would burn brightly in her memory for whatever time she had left on earth.

§§§

Irene envisioned herself wearing something special to the Nobel Awards Ceremony and Banquet, both white tie events. Given all the other activities planned, some other new and stylish clothes would likely be needed. She decided if ever there were a time to splurge, this was it. But with the city's luxury department stores having gone the way of the dinosaur, she was at a loss as to where to go on a high-end shopping spree.

It was her niece Rachel — a partner in a white shoe law firm and an elegant dresser — who provided the answer. On the Saturday before Halloween, Rachel picked up Irene and Annie and drove them to an upscale boutique in Scarsdale. Once Irene mentioned what the outfits were for, the owner herself attended to Irene's needs, showing her gowns, dresses, and suits in size six. Irene found so many to her liking that she bought several, running up a bill in the five figures. Her uncharacteristic extravagance incited a pang of guilt, but the fact that alterations were included helped Irene quiet her conscience. Two weeks later, after the seamstress had done her magic, Rachel, Irene, and Annie returned. When Irene tried on her new wardrobe, the verdict was unanimous.

"Smashing," Annie said. "You look absolutely marvelous!"

"Mom's right," Rachel agreed. "You look fantastic, Aunt Reenie."

And Irene could not disagree. It took her eighty-eight years, but she finally understood the full meaning of the proverb, "Clothes make the man," or in this case, the Nobel laureate.

§§§

That year the United States had five other Nobel winners: two in physics, one in economics, and two in chemistry. The Swedish ambassador in Washington hosted a dinner in their honor at the end of November, giving the laureates an opportunity to get to know one another before leaving for Nobel Week in Stockholm. While in Washington, they also accepted an invitation to the White House. As the laureates entered the Oval Office, they posed for pictures with the forty-eighth President of the United States, Gretchen Whitmer. Irene was an ardent fan, not only because of what Whitmer had accomplished during her two terms — most particularly providing universal health coverage for all Americans — but also because she was the first president to acknowledge having been the victim of sexual assault. Like Irene, Whitmer had been a freshman in college when she was attacked. As they were introduced, the two women embraced. The next day the *Washington Post* carried the picture on its front page with the headline: *President Whitmer and Nobel Winner — Triumphant Survivors of Early Sexual Assault.*

§§§

The Nobel Award ceremony takes place on December tenth each year, the anniversary of the death of Alfred Nobel, a businessman and inventor who amassed a fortune from his patent for dynamite and the sales of a wide array of armaments produced by his factories. Eight years before Alfred's death, his brother Ludvig died while visiting France. A French newspaper mistakenly published the obituary it had prepared for Alfred, condemning him for inventing such dreadfully efficient weapons of war. It was entitled "Le marchand de la mort est mort," or "The Merchant of Death is Dead." Reading it proved to be a life-changing experience for Alfred. The childless Nobel sat down and, in flowing cursive, wrote instructions for the disposition of his large estate, directing his executors to use his riches to fund annual "prizes to those who…have conferred the greatest benefit to mankind."

Nobel's largesse allowed for the recognition of the greatest achievements in science, literature, economics, and peace-making. Now, one hundred and forty-four years after the prizes were established, Irene was about to take her place in the pantheon of Nobel laureates, beside the likes of Albert Einstein, Marie Curie, Francis Crick, Carol Greider, Barry Marshall, and her fellow Erasmus Hall High School alumni, Barbara McClintock and Eric Kandel. The mere thought of it humbled her.

§§§

It was impossible to choose between Brin and Ian to accompany her to all the events of Nobel Week, so she invited them both. Early in December, they flew first class to Stockholm, where they were met at the airport by the Secretary of the Nobel Committee. Nils, their limousine driver for Nobel Week, took them from the airport to the luxurious Grand Hotel, where the Royal Swedish Academy had reserved a beautifully appointed suite for their stay. It was uncanny how their every possible need had been anticipated and provided for. Brin, who'd climbed to the top rung of the corporate ladder, may have experienced such indulgence in her travels, but for Irene and Ian, academics both, the royal treatment left them with mouths agape.

In the days leading up to the award ceremony, they attended dinners, meetings with dignitaries, and press conferences. Irene was so glad she'd bought more rather than fewer outfits at that lovely clothing boutique. Five days after they arrived, the rest of the family flew in from the States: Gabby, Emily and the boys, Spence and Annie, Rachel, Peter, Robert and their families. Warren, Meggie, and Tatiana Kramarov flew in together from San Francisco. Every laureate was permitted to have up to forty guests, which allowed Irene to invite several valued colleagues, as well. Among them were many alumni of the Adelson Lab, including Lourdes Guzman, who was the lab's very first doctoral student, now an esteemed professor of neuroscience in her own right. Esther Woo and her husband left their two little ones with his parents and arrived in Stockholm ready to help Irene celebrate. And of course, in honor of her long and rich partnership with Josiah, his beloved daughters, Diane and Debbie, were Irene's esteemed guests.

As was its custom, on the Saturday before the awards dinner, the Jewish Community of Stockholm invited the Jewish laureates to the Great Synagogue of Stockholm. Irene, the other Jewish winners, as well as their significant entourages, gathered in the historic temple. The laureates received the rabbi's blessing and the gift of a glass replica of the synagogue. It was an emotional moment for Irene as she thought about how proud her parents would be. Precisely one hundred years after the Nazis had begun their all-too-effective campaign to wipe out European Jewry, she was accepting the rabbi's blessing in the majestic synagogue from a community of Swedish Jews thousands strong.

The laureates had one free evening, which Irene used to host a dinner for her guests. She was surrounded that night by so many of the people whom she loved and admired. She also thought of those who were absent: Grandma Bertha, her parents, Irma and Burt, her dear college friends. Though she should have been missing Albert most of all, she felt he was somehow with her that night. It was uncanny, really. Though he'd been gone for nine years, she could close her eyes and feel his presence. At one point, when she turned around she expected to see him standing there with his familiar smile and adoring gaze. Just this one time, she allowed herself the indulgence of believing he was.

§§§

The next day Irene was slated to give her Nobel lecture before an audience of guests, faculty, and students at the Karolinska Institute. She'd worked tirelessly on the talk in the weeks leading up to it. There was so much to say. She penned it at home and asked Esther and Annie to critique it. Irene wanted to be sure it was on point for an audience of world-renowned scientists as well as lay people. Each of her chosen reviewers made astute suggestions. She incorporated many into her talk. When the day of the speech came, she felt preternaturally calm. Irene knew her work as she knew the contours of her face, the wrinkles on her hands, the smiles of her children and grandchildren. And now, she had the opportunity to share the findings she and her team had made, as well as the questions that still remained to be answered.

Irene's guests filled the seats in the front rows of the hall, a friendly audience, to be sure. Dr. Ingrid Karlsson, a medical researcher from the Nobel nominating committee, gave a kind and generous introduction. She spoke about Irene's education and training, including the arrival of her twins during her psychiatry residency. Some of the more notable of the honors and awards she'd received in the last decades were cited. Dr. Karlsson also pointed out that, like so many iconoclastic thinkers who came before her, Irene and her work had initially been scorned. "But despite the ridicule from her many critics, she persevered with a dogged determination. I am pleased to say that today it is Dr. Adelson who can enjoy the last laugh."

Irene felt that introduction set just the right tone to begin her lecture. "Thank you Dr. Karlsson for your very kind sentiments, and thanks, too, to Mr. President, members of the Selection Committee and the Nobel Assembly. It is indeed an honor to have the opportunity to address so august a gathering. I dedicate this lecture to Dr. Josiah Williams, my longtime co-investigator. His knowledge of the intricacies of the human gut, his boundless curiosity, and good cheer made him the perfect partner as we began wading hip-deep into the unknown territory of what today is familiarly known as the gut-brain axis. His daughters Debbie and Diane are here with us today. For them in particular, I express my debt to their brilliant, kind, and wonderful father. I couldn't have had a better collaborator and friend.

"Being a working scientist has been one of my greatest joys. I also spent many decades treating people with psychiatric illnesses. I witnessed the pain caused by disorders such as major depression and bi-polar disease. In the 1980s, I began working with war veterans suffering from PTSD, anxiety, and depression. I thought it odd that so many had the co-morbidity of digestive disorders. That's what led me to Dr. Williams, an attending gastroenterologist at the Veterans' Administration hospital where I practiced. When I consulted with him about my patients suffering from both mental and gastric distress, he thought it no coincidence. He and I both suspected the two maladies were somehow linked. How, of course, was the question. Where to begin the search for an answer kept us busy for the better part of a year.

"As the GI expert he was, Dr. Williams led me to the work of scientists on whose shoulders our own research would later stand: Ilya Mechnikov, the 1908 Nobel laureate in Physiology or Medicine, who postulated the centrality of the gut's microbes to human health, Arthur Kendall, who argued that diet determined the microbial diversity in an individual's gut, Theodor Roseburg, who touted the benefits of microbes in his 1962 book, *Microorganisms Indigenous to Man*.

"Dr. Williams also introduced me to the work of Dr. Michael Gershon, the researcher who founded the field of neuro-gastroenterology. Thanks to Dr. Gershon we knew that ninety percent of the body's supply of the neurotransmitter serotonin is produced in the gut. He also demonstrated that most messaging between the brain and the gut is afferent, that is to say, the communication originates in the gut and travels via the vagus nerve to the brain. Those important findings gave us our starting point. Dr. Williams and I decided to study whether messages sent from the gut could affect brain functioning and behavior, and if so, how.

"We studied germ-free mice with behavioral traits similar to anxiety and depression in humans. You may be asking yourselves how one knows if a mouse is depressed. After spending so much of my life studying mice, I can tell you it's quite obvious if you know what to look for. For example, a depressed mouse that's held by the tail will simply hang there, rather than struggle in an attempt to get away. When given the opportunity to explore, the depressed and anxious mouse just cowers. If given a task, like finding a way out of a maze, the depressed mouse demonstrates few, if any, problem solving strategies. Back in the late 1980s, our lab took those depressed germ-free mice and gave them fecal transplants from genetically identical mice with gut microbiomes teeming with bacteria, viruses, and fungi. Much to our surprise, our data showed that after the fecal transplant our formerly germ-free mice dealt better with stress, explored more, and were significantly better at problem-solving than they'd previously been. That's when Dr. Williams and the rest of our small team knew we were onto something. Our next challenge was figuring out what mechanism was at play.

"We decided to focus our investigation on how the vagus nerve, the informational highway between the gut and the brain, transmits signals that can ultimately affect mood and behavior. We had a hunch that it was the metabolites of the gut's microbiome that affected the vagus nerve, which then transferred the information to the parts of the brain that affected the mouse's stress response. We focused on the HPA axis, the hypothalamus, pituitary, and adrenal glands. We knew from human studies that the HPA axis tends to be overactive in depressed patients. Could it be that somehow messages from the vagus nerve were able to tame an HPA axis in overdrive? We set out to find the answer to that question."

Irene then described the neuroscience of what happens inside the brain during stress, how elevated pro-inflammatory cytokines activate the HPA axis through the secretion of corticotropin-releasing factor from the hypothalamus, which in turn stimulates the pituitary to secrete adrenocorticotropic hormone (ACTH). The end result is elevated cortisol, which is released by the adrenal glands. Irene went on to explain the discovery that had won her the Nobel Prize: how particular metabolites from microbes in the gut communicate to the brain via the vagus nerve, calming the brain's stress response. She worried a bit about losing the non-scientist members of the audience — everyone but Gabby in her own family, for example — but she made sure to have a number of illustrations in order to help the lay people grasp at least the rudiments of her discovery. Then she returned to an area that she hoped everyone might be better able to appreciate.

"Just as we were studying the mechanism within the brain affected by transmissions from the vagus nerve, the ability to examine the microbes of the human gut at the genomic level was expanding exponentially. Our lab brought in doctoral students and post-doctoral fellows whose interests and expertise lay precisely in that area. Some of them are here in the audience today, and their contributions to our work cannot be overemphasized. The

Human Microbiome Project, in which we participated, was critically important in providing us with the genetic profiles of the myriad of microbes that can inhabit the gut. That opened up a new world to us and to labs around the world.

"In short order we started questioning whether it was possible for an individual's microbiome not only to affect his or her stress response, but also to impact the development of neurodegenerative diseases such as Parkinson's and Alzheimer's. We know for certain that the gut microbiomes of Parkinson's and Alzheimer's patients differ from those who are not so afflicted, so our question is not so preposterous as it may seem at first glance. This line of research has kept labs like mine busy for the last two decades.

"Over the years my lab, now led in partnership with my esteemed colleague, Dr. Esther Woo, isolated particular microbes that affect the brain's functioning in specific ways. For example, we found that *Bifidobacterium breve* increases brain derived neurotrophic factor, which encourages the growth of neurons. *Lactobacillus acidophilus* helps relieve stress by reducing the production of cortisol.

"More recently, many of our controlled experiments have evolved from rodents to humans. One example involves *Coprococcus* and *Dialister*. In mice studies we'd found when those microbes were present, the microbiome could synthesize a breakdown product of dopamine known as 3,4 dihydroxyphenylacetic acid. We took that finding and then turned to human subjects. We discovered that after introducing these microbes into the microbiomes of depressed individuals, they reported an improved quality of life. In another study, we found that *Lactobacillus helveticus* and *Bifidobacterium longum* reduce anxiety and depression in patients enrolled in our clinical trials.

"Now, fifty-one years into this journey, we know so much more than when Dr. Williams and I started. We know that depressed patients have different microbiota than those who suffer from schizophrenia, and both of those differ from those with autism. We know that the microbiome can produce or stimulate the production of neurotransmitters and neuroactive compounds such as serotonin, GABA, and dopamine. We know many of the microbial-derived molecules that interact with the central nervous system via the vagus nerve and that lead to changes in behavior and mental wellness. Most importantly, our lab's findings have allowed us to develop treatments for mood disorders through the use of psycho-biotics, live microbial organisms that treat the painful afflictions of anxiety and depression. To know that our work has lessened the mental anguish of so many has brought me great joy. But the journey is far from over.

"The avenue of research that now offers so much promise is the investigation of the gut's role in the immune response that goes awry in such diseases as multiple sclerosis, Type 1 diabetes, irritable bowel disease, and lupus. These and other autoimmune diseases have reached crisis proportions in many of the world's richest societies. People who suffer from these very different diseases all have one thing in common: increased and maladaptive low-grade chronic inflammation.

"We know that the immune system is developed in the first three years of life, and it's during that period that the body gets to know 'self' from 'not self,' learning to attack only when an 'invader' is present. Research coming out of our lab, as well as the labs of scientists across the globe, have shown that it's the child's gut microbes that provide the trigger for the development and maturation of its immune system. If the child is lucky and is nursed as a baby and provided with enough fiber in a diverse diet, he or she will likely be in good stead in this regard. The mechanism is rather elegant. Fiber fermented in the gut by microbial action produces short-chain fatty acids which themselves have an anti-inflammatory action. Short-chain fatty acids also promote the production of immunoglobulin and immunosuppressive cytokines. Microbes play a critical role in building the child's immune system and maintaining it in a healthy state. Perhaps one day, in the not too distant future, it may be possible to use microbes to treat — or better yet, prevent — the autoimmune diseases that afflict so many millions of people in the industrialized world.

"My goal as a physician-scientist has always been to do translational research, to merge basic science with clinical medicine in order to improve the health and the lives of patients. I get tremendous satisfaction knowing that patients today routinely get the diversity of their gut microbiome checked, just as they get their cholesterol and blood sugar levels tested at their annual doctor visit. We have known for many years that changes in the gut microbiota precede symptoms in a number of diseases. Now, by analyzing an individual's microbiome for deficiencies or overgrowths, we have taken an important first step towards the goal of manipulating the microbiome to stop the disease process in its tracks. And for any part my work has played in that, I feel very grateful, indeed."

§§§

Irene awoke on the day of the award ceremony feeling wearier than when she'd gone to bed. She'd enjoyed every one of the events of Nobel Week. Giving her Nobel lecture was the experience of a lifetime, but now she was spent, utterly exhausted. When Brin came to help her get dressed, Irene could hardly move. Brin fussed over her as though she were a sick child, feeling for a fever, taking her pulse. When she found nothing amiss, she proposed calling a doctor to the suite, but Irene demurred. "I think I'm just tired. Everything is catching up with me. You have to remember, you're fifty-eight, I'm eighty-eight. You can absorb all this excitement more easily than I, Brinny. My reserves are not what they used to be."

"You may be right, Mom, but just to be safe, I'm summoning a doctor."

Minutes later a physician arrived at Irene's door with a crew of emergency medical technicians equipped with a defibrillator, oxygen, and a stretcher. Irene was mortified. And when she saw the worried faces of Annie and Spence peering into her room, she began regretting having mentioned anything to Brin.

"Doctor, I am so sorry you have all come up here for nothing," Irene explained. "I am certain there is nothing fundamentally wrong with me. I'm just tired out from all the wonderful events of Nobel Week. I am not sick, I assure you."

"With all due respect, Dr. Adelson," the young physician said in impeccable English, "I'll be the judge of that." Then she and the EMTs went to work. They took her vital signs and drew blood. The doctor gave Irene a thorough exam, listening to her heart and lungs, checking her reflexes, eye tracking, and ability to touch her nose with her eyes closed. The medical team had a handheld machine that could analyze the blood draw, delivering real time chemistry test results on sixteen metrics in a matter of minutes. All they had to do was apply a few drops of blood to a cartridge, insert the cartridge into the machine. In a few minutes, the results would appear on the screen. Irene was impressed.

While they awaited the verdict from the analyzer, Irene engaged the doctor in conversation. Apparently, there was a full medical team at the ready during Nobel Week, an "insurance policy," the doctor said to make sure the laureates remained well throughout. She felt lucky to be selected for the elite group. So far she'd had nothing more dramatic to do than irrigate and stitch up a small cut in the foot of one laureate's wife. As they were chatting, the analyzer signaled the results of Irene's tests were ready. As the doctor reviewed them on the screen, Irene did her best to look over her shoulder, but to no avail.

"Well, Dr. Adelson, according to your blood work and your physical exam, you appear to be a paragon of good health. Excellent numbers on your metabolic panel. Your oxygen saturation is ninety-eight, excellent. Your blood pressure is a bit low, which might account for your feeling a bit tired. But, I know you have a big day ahead of you. I'd say, have a cup of strong coffee and a good meal sometime before you leave for the Award Ceremony. And keep the dancing to a minimum at tonight's Nobel Banquet. As my grandmother always tells me, "Elsa, it's no good to overdo!"

"Your grandmother sounds like a wise woman. I give you my word that I will eat and drink well and in moderation, and keep my physical exertion under control," Irene said, patting the doctor's arm. "Thank you for doing such a thorough work-up. I'm sure you've assuaged my daughter's fears."

§§§

As Irene took one last look in the mirror before leaving for the awards ceremony, she admired the wizardry of the seamstress who had done such a fine job altering the long-sleeved, ultramarine gown with the Queen Anne neckline. It fit her like a glove. The sheath was elegant, but still allowed her to move freely. Best of all were the shoes Rachel found for her — just a small heel, comfortable with plenty of support, and remarkably fashionable. A hairdresser had come up to the suite to do her hair. Irene usually pulled it back in a barrette, but the stylist instead created an elegant upsweep. Brin had insisted on applying her makeup, something Irene had given up doing after Albert died. She'd become used to looking at herself *au naturel*, but Brin said this was no time to look like an earth mother. "All eyes will be on you, Mom. Your features just need a little definition to stand out." Brin's expertise amazed her. She had no idea there were so many steps involved in looking as lovely as Brin did every day: Concealer, foundation, blush, eyebrow pencil, eye shadow, eyeliner, mascara, lipstick. As Brin worked, Irene kept saying, "Just a little, Brinny, remember I'm eighty-eight!" To which, Brin replied, "Don't worry, Mom, I promise no one is going to mistake you for a hussy." They both got a laugh out of that.

Once they arrived at the Stockholm Concert Hall, Irene had to say goodbye to her family, as she was escorted with the other laureates to a waiting area behind the stage. Each of the men — and they still dominated in sheer numbers — was dressed in a black dress coat with tails, a white waistcoat, and the eponymous white bow tie. The female laureates all looked lovely. The woman who was sharing the prize in physics was from India. Irene thought her multi-colored, beautifully embroidered sari was absolutely stunning. Irene was the eldest of the group by at least a decade. Everyone was quite solicitous of her, as though they were at the ready in case she keeled over. Thanks to the advice of that lovely, young physician earlier in the day, she'd had a strong cup of coffee about ninety minutes before leaving for the ceremony. Between the caffeine and the adrenaline pumping through her system, she actually felt quite sprightly.

Apparently the Queen of Sweden and her family had taken their seats on stage, and the signal came for the laureates to make their entrance. The Royal Stockholm Philharmonic Orchestra, seated above the stage, played Mozart while they filed in, two by two, until they had all arrived at their appointed place. Irene was seated between the chemistry laureate from Japan and the literature laureate, a writer from South Africa. They each had a program on their seats to help them keep track of the proceedings. The Chair of the Board of the Nobel Foundation opened the ceremony extolling the contributions made by science and literature, how the former seeks the truth through the scientific method, research, and data analysis, while the latter depicts the truth of the human condition through artistic expression. She closed by saying, "One without the other would leave us with either an ignorant or a lifeless world."

Before the awards were celebrated, each laureate's achievement was introduced in a way that made comprehensible their often esoteric work. When the time came for the award in Physiology or Medicine to be given to Irene, she was introduced in this way: "Depression has been a malady that has beleaguered humankind since before the beginning of written history. It is a condition that robs the individual of joy, hope, the ability to know happiness. Winston Churchill referred to his periods of intense and prolonged depression as his 'black dog.' William Styron, the American writer, deemed it 'despair beyond despair,' an anguish that sometimes leads the sufferer to conclude that it can no longer be borne. Dr. Irene Adelson has spent her entire career studying the neurobiology underlying depression. For decades, she has spearheaded the search for effective treatment to relieve the suffering of her patients. Her work was initially met with derision, then curiosity, and finally acclaim. For her discovery of the role of the human microbiome in the etiology and treatment of depression, she is the winner of the award in Physiology or Medicine. Dr. Adelson, congratulations. Please stand and receive your Nobel Prize from the hand of the Queen."

And that's precisely what Irene did. The moment she had never imagined happening had arrived.

§§§

The majestic awards ceremony was immediately followed by the Nobel Banquet at the Stockholm City Hall. In the center of the enormous venue was a table set for eighty to accommodate the royal family, the prime minister and other government dignitaries, and the laureates and their spouses or, in Irene's case, her son. On both sides of that enormous table were twenty-six rectangular tables set perpendicularly, at which were seated the laureates' guests, representatives from government, industry, and the major universities. In total more than sixteen hundred were in attendance. The dinner that was served was sumptuous, reminding Irene of the night she and Albert, Josiah and Bernice went to that wonderful French restaurant in Manhattan to celebrate their first grant.

Dancing was to follow the splendid dinner. But before the dancing could begin, each laureate — or a representative in the case of multiple laureates for one award — was summoned to the podium to address the gathering. Irene had studied what previous laureates had said over the years. Some were lighthearted in their comments, others more serious. Irene decided to highlight her feelings about being singled out for such recognition.

Trumpets blared and flags unfurled as she gingerly walked up the steps to the podium. She unfolded the paper on which she'd penned her short address and began. "Your Majesty, your Royal Highnesses, your Excellencies, laureates, ladies, and gentlemen. I am here before you this evening humbled by the great honor I've been given. No one can arrive at this summit of recognition by dint of their own efforts alone. At my advanced age, I have had the time to consider what it was that allowed me to climb the heights of scientific discovery. Of course, I worked hard; that goes without saying. But scientific discovery in this day and age is a team sport. And, I would submit, that all great achievement is due to factors and forces that influence the person who achieves great things.

"Tonight, I want to express my gratitude to the many people who, each in their own way, contributed mightily to the human being, the physician, and the scientist I am. First and foremost is the person with whom I would share this award, were he alive today, Dr. Josiah Williams. Dr. Williams and I formed our partnership in 1987. Together, we withstood the slings and arrows of our colleagues, the repeated rejection of our grant applications, and meager resources with which we labored early in our research. Had it not been for Dr. Williams, I am certain I would not be standing here addressing you tonight. It was he who suggested we apply for funding to a foundation that did wonderful work in underserved neighborhoods in the New York City area. We were the recipients of the Barrow Foundation's very first grant for medical research. It was the largesse and vision of Eloise and Winston Barrow that got our work off the ground, making possible the research that eventually yielded paradigm-changing discoveries.

"Tonight in this lovely City Hall sit many of the colleagues with whom I have worked. Some began as students and fellows and are now established scientists in their own right. Three of the people in the audience were in 'on the ground floor,' as we say in the States. Patty Cappione, Matthew Prince, and Katherine Ayers spent the whole of their careers devoted to our research on the brain-gut axis. First employees, then colleagues, and ultimately friends, to them, I say 'thank you' for being so integral a part of our great adventure.

"Finally, my work was supported by my family. For my late husband Albert Jaffe, the noted physicist, and my children, Brin and Ian, there was little separation between work and our daily lives. The children began coming to our labs as tots. They missed more of their mother's time than I would have liked, but as we know, experiments tend to have a life of their own. My children have been here with me in Stockholm for the entirety of Nobel Week. They seem to have forgiven me my dual allegiances, to home and to science, and for that, I am very grateful.

"I acknowledge the contributions of all those I've discussed, as well as my gifted teachers in the public schools of New York City. Thanks to their efforts, a shy little girl from a working-class family gained admission to world-class institutions of higher learning. Most importantly, to my parents, modest, gentle, loving people who encouraged their children to be their best selves.

"To quote the naturalist John Muir, 'When we try to pick anything out by itself, we find it hitched to everything else in the universe.' Tonight I have been 'picked out,' but in fact, I am who I am because of all of the people with whom I've been lucky enough to work, live, learn, and love. It is because of the fertile ground they provided that I had the possibility of growing into the physician and scientist who has been recognized tonight. I am in their debt."

§§§

After the last laureate made his address, the orchestra struck up the music. It was time for the dance she and Ian had practiced so diligently in their suite over the last many days. They listened carefully to each song. Some were too fast, others were not in three-quarter time. It was Strauss's *Danube Waltz* that got them to their feet. As they walked to the dance floor Irene thought she would have to remember to thank Rachel for finding the wonderful shoes which helped make this most special night such a pleasure. When Ian took her firmly in his arms and guided her across the floor, she was euphoric. One-two-three, one-two-three, they glided to the beautiful melody composed nearly two hundred years before. Oh, she thought, if Albert could see us now...

ACKNOWLEDGEMENTS

I had a lot to learn in order to weave the tale of a girl who sets her sights on a career in science. My first task was to understand what could drive a person to toil for years, often in obscurity, to find the answer to a difficult question. Scientists, I discovered, are not only inordinately curious, they are unafraid of questioning orthodoxy. The Harvard biologist E. O. Wilson sums up what drives a scientist this way: "passion, commitment to a subject, excitement over adventure, an entrepreneurial spirit." The ideal scientist, he adds, "thinks like a poet and works like a bookkeeper." Those seeking fame and fortune need not apply; the training is long and arduous, the work demanding, and the rewards often intrinsic to the puzzle being solved. It's thanks to these inquisitive, plucky, determined people that we have vaccines against dreaded pathogens, rockets capable of traveling to interstellar space, and a greater understanding of the wonders of our planet. And that is just a small sliver of what they have wrought.

I was fortunate to have highly accomplished scientists offer me guidance as *Lucky Girl* began to take shape. Chemist, professor, writer, and Nobel laureate Roald Hoffmann was kind enough to share his experience of being a finalist in the 1955 Westinghouse Science Talent Search. His memories of the week he spent in Washington, D.C. helped me imagine what Irene Adelson's first time away from home would have been like, awash in the excitement of being in the nation's capital, thrilled by getting to know so many talented peers. Dr. Rita Calvo, founding director of the Cornell Institute for Biology Teachers and retired senior lecturer in biology and genetics, described the many obstacles faced by women in the sciences in the second half of the twentieth century. Adrienne Shapiro, a physician-scientist, specialist in infectious diseases, and professor at the University of Washington, explained in wonderful detail the career trajectory of a newly-minted MD/PhD like Irene. My thanks to them all.

Recreating the experience of a Barnard student during the tumultuous 1960s was made possible by then Associate Director of the Archives, Shannon O'Neill. Ms. O'Neill, who has since become Curator of the Tamiment-Wagner Collections at NYU, helped me negotiate Barnard's online archives, truly a treasure trove of information. Jennifer Ulrich, an archivist at Columbia University's health sciences library, helped me research the nascent Medical Science Training Program, as well as the neurological and psychiatric research being undertaken at Columbia in the 1970s.

Thanks go, too, to the following for their expertise: Cellist Elisa Evett, for guiding me to Vivaldi's *Concerto for Violin and Oboe in B Flat Major* for Irene's oboe solo; Sam and Jonah Gelberg, for helping me better understand the study of karate; medical researcher and former lab manager Patty Cogswell, for her tutorial in the staffing and funding of university labs; NASA scientist, Dr. Ryan DeRosa, for his help in writing about Albert's career in astrophysics; and litigator Grant Gelberg, for explaining how a prosecutor prepares a witness to testify at trial.

If any errors remain despite this expert help, the responsibility is entirely mine.

It is with tremendous gratitude that I recognize the efforts of the early readers who helped improve this manuscript. Cynthia Frankel, a clinical psychologist, offered astute advice on Irene's work with patients, as well as on the arc of the story. Melanie Novello, an eagle eye if ever there was, detected false notes wherever they occurred and brought them to my attention. Louis Novello's guidance on how to weave Irene's research into her life story was a great help. Joan Cappione, couched her critique in the kindness and honesty that marks everything she undertakes.

My thanks to my wonderful copy editor, Eileen Bach, who offered me a tutorial in the importance of the gerund, as well countless, excellent suggestions to improve the manuscript. Nicholas LaVita was a superb collaborator as he worked toward the final iteration of the cover design. And to my husband, Charles Wilson, who did such a fine job designing the interior of the book, my thanks.

A word about the Bronx Veterans' Administration Hospital: The gender discrimination encountered by Irene at the Bronx VA is fictional. In fact, in 1950 the Bronx VA equipped a radioisotope laboratory for the medical physicist, Dr. Rosalyn Yalow. Yalow spent nearly twenty years at the VA as a medical researcher, developing radioimmunoassay of peptide hormones, a discovery that resulted in her becoming the second woman to ever win the Nobel Prize in Physiology or Medicine.

While Irene is an imagined scientist, nearly all of the research into the gut-brain axis described in *Lucky Girl* has actually been done in labs in the US and abroad since the early 2000s. As a lay person, it was with awe that I learned of the linkage between the microbial communities living within us and conditions as disparate as depression, Parkinson's, autism, and multiple sclerosis. Scientists across the globe are now investigating how specific microbes and their metabolites are connected to these and other pathologies. I would like to acknowledge the work of the researchers who made the findings attributed to Irene and Josiah in *Lucky Girl*.

In 2004 Nobuyuki Sudo at Kyushu University in Japan discovered that fecal transplantation in germ-free mice affects their behavior. Sudo's lab demonstrated that germ-free mice are highly sensitive to stress and produce twice the amount of stress hormones pumped out by mice with normal gut microbiomes. Sudo's breakthrough study is credited with spurring myriad investigations into the neurobiology and behavior of germ-free mice.

Professors John Cryan and Timothy Dinan of the University College Cork in Ireland have created an epicenter of gut-brain research. Their work has uncovered a strong correlation between the gut microbiome's metabolites and how the brain responds to GABA, a naturally occurring amino acid that functions as a neurotransmitter. Jane Foster, of McMaster University in Canada, has demonstrated that adding probiotic species corrects the stress response in germ-free mice by affecting the HPA response (hypothalamus, pituitary, adrenal), just as Irene describes in her Nobel lecture. While most studies on the gut-brain axis have been conducted on mice, Jeroen Raes, of Catholic University of Leuven in Belgium, has found that butyrate-producing gut bacteria such as *Coprococcus* and *Dialister* are consistently associated with higher quality of life indicators in humans.

The power of the vagus nerve to transmit information from the gut to the brain is a focus of much current research. Sigrid Breit of the University of Bern, has shown the vagus nerve to be a modulator of the brain-gut axis in psychiatric disorders. Bruno Bonaz, of the University of Grenoble, studies the vagus nerve at the interface of the microbiota-gut-brain axis. Elaine Hsiao and the Hsiao Lab at UCLA have demonstrated stimulation of the vagus nerve by particular microbes reduces depression in mice.

The Costa-Mattioli Lab at Baylor University, which Irene looks to for help for her grandsons, is responsible for the discovery that specific bacteria can reduce the social deficits of mice who exhibit behavior similar to autism spectrum disorder (ASD). The Mazmanian Lab at Cal Tech has done groundbreaking research on the efficacy of fecal transplantation as a treatment option for children living with severe autism.

To these scientists, and the countless others who are investigating how the trillions of microbes within us affect our mood, behavior, and overall health, I give my thanks. Learning about their work allowed me to breathe life into Irene's quest to solve the mystery of major depression. Although the hypothesis that intestinal bacteria can influence mental health has spurred major research pursuits here and abroad, it remains a controversial topic in microbiome research. Only time will tell if a Nobel Prize will one day be awarded for discovering how to employ the gut microbiome to relieve the anguish of those who experience the "despair beyond despair" of major depression.

Denise Gelberg
Ithaca, New York
April 2021

Made in United States
Orlando, FL
28 January 2022

14155078R00232